IN HARMONY

by Helena Newbury

Cover image photo: Casara / istockphoto
Rear cover photo: Robin Mackenzie / BigStock

ISBN: 1492764280

ISBN-13: 978-1492764281

DEDICATION

To my mother, for all her support.

CHAPTER 1

THE ANSWER IS NO, OKAY? I saw the question in the eyes of the people I passed as I struggled down the icy street to Fenbrook, case strapped to my back and a determined expression on my face. They looked at the long neck of the case rising up over my head like I was carrying a brontosaurus in a backpack, the wide base whacking against my calves, the sheer weight of it hunching me over, and they frowned and muttered to themselves, *"Didn't she ever consider the flute?"*

No, I didn't. When I was six, my father took me to see the New York Philharmonic Orchestra. I was forced into a scratchy purple dress and made to sit absolutely motionless (*"No Gummi Bears, Karen—the packet might rattle"*), fuming at my father while I dreamed of how much better the orchestra would look if they were all dressed like my Barbies. Then the music started and my little jaw dropped, two hours gone in two minutes. At the end, I raised my pudgy hand and pointed to the cellist, her long limbs wrapped around the massive instrument, its varnished wood and smooth curves somehow a part of her. "I want to play *that!*"

I wasn't to know I'd stop growing at 5'4".

But I loved my cello more than anything else in the world and I had a stubborn streak a mile wide, so I strapped the damn thing to my back and I've been carrying it now for fifteen years. Boston was easier, because you could park a car—there's an old joke that the most important accessory for your cello is a Volvo, and no sane cellist is without one. In New York, though, it's subways and sidewalks and endless waiting at side streets for the "Walk" sign (I don't jaywalk, even if there are tumbleweeds blowing past).

I'd forgotten my gloves and the biting wind meant I was steadily losing the feeling in my fingers. I passed a coffee shop and longed for a warming Americano, but even trying to lift a cup to my mouth would have killed what little balance I had, sending me tottering sideways until I fell flat on my back like a turtle, legs kicking in the air.

Ahead of me, Fenbrook's cheery, red-brick exterior, so different from my first college back in Boston. That had been all polished wood floors and silent tension—

My stomach tightened as I thought of Boston. The ever-present fear that I was going to be hauled back there, the knowledge that my life in New York was enjoyed at the end of a tightly-held leash. I could pretend it wasn't there, but I knew my father could give it a sharp jerk at any time.

Or, if I messed up, he wouldn't even need to jerk it. I'd have no choice but to go scuttling back on my own.

I climbed carefully up the ice-covered steps and hauled open the doors. Warm air scented with linoleum polish hit me in the face, a physical accompaniment to the wall of sound.

The din of Fenbrook had taken some getting used to. The first day, the confident chatter of the actors on the first floor had almost pushed me back onto the street. I'd been used to musicians—we let the playing do the talking. And I'd been starting a semester late, so even the other freshmen had a head start on making friends. But—slowly—I'd come to love the place. Having people around me who weren't obsessed with tuning and bowing technique was *good* for me, even if my father couldn't see it. I fit in there—as much as I'd ever fitted in anywhere.

I took a step forward into the warmth and the cello case straps dug viciously into my shoulders. I staggered backwards, almost falling. While I'd been reminiscing, the heavy door had closed on me, trapping the cello case outside in the cold. I tried to turn around, but the case just banged around outside and the shoulder straps held me tight. I tried to back up, but I was off balance and didn't have the leverage to push the heavy door open. I was trapped.

Worse, as I banged and rattled, all the actors—who were standing around gossiping about who'd got which part and who was sleeping with whom—started to turn and look. Understand, these were *actors*: every woman had cheekbones you could slice ham on, every man a chisel-jawed, muscled hunk. It looked—as the first floor always did—as if a movie was being filmed there. The only interloper on their scene of genetic perfection was me, wedged in the door like a kicking, grunting beetle stuck in a spider's web, only with more frizzy hair. I felt myself flushing beetroot as twenty pairs of heart-breakingly beautiful eyes focused on me.

People think that actors must be cruel—they are effectively the cool kids, after all, so it follows that they'd bully the geeks—the musicians. But they don't look down on us so much as wrinkle their perfect foreheads and wonder why we can't just be calm and confident and outgoing like them—as if it was that easy. I got a few pitying expressions and two of them walked over to help.

At that moment, someone opened the door from the outside and I went stumbling backwards—right off the edge of the top step. Dragged down by the cello's weight, I fell with a surprisingly loud scream, my head heading for the sidewalk—

I snapped to a halt, the cello case pressing hard into my back. I was lying in mid air, face up, feet skittering at the top step. Almost all of my weight was held by one shoulder strap, stretched out in front of me and anchored by....

I followed the strap with my eyes. A fist, grabbing the nylon. A strong wrist, skin almost as pale as mine. A cracked leather jacket. I got all the way to the shoulder and his tight, powerful frame before it clicked.

Oh no.....

I looked up into his face. Blue-gray eyes, like a lazy summer's day that's darkening into a storm. Hair cut short and messy, glossy black against his pale skin. And the lips—those soft, full lips that had been the downfall of so many Fenbrook girls in downtown rock clubs or at drug-fueled parties. Even now, they were twisting into a smirk.

Connor Locke.

"I seem to have you helpless," he told me, and his broad Belfast accent made it sound at once both innocent and absolutely filthy. The actors who'd been coming to help reached the doorway and stopped there, smiling.

"Would you like me to lay you down on your back?" he asked, at least partially for their benefit. "Or should I pull you up against me?"

I closed my eyes, feeling myself flushing even more than before. When I opened them, he was still holding me up. It felt like he could have held me there all day, if he'd wanted to.

"Up," I said quietly, and he hauled me slowly upwards. As promised, he didn't step out of the way, so that when I had my footing again on the top step I was right up against him, our faces inches apart. He was wearing some scent that made me think of big, cold skies and icy rocks.

He raised his eyebrows at me mockingly and we just stood there for a moment, close as lovers, while I gasped with the aftershock of fear, my face burning with embarrassment. I couldn't meet his eyes, so I stared fixedly at the blood red t-shirt he wore. Black serpents, twisting over the broad curves of his chest.

"Thank you." The words a hot rush between gritted teeth. Then I pulled the door wide and stumbled inside before I could get caught again. His chuckles followed me up the stairs.

***

At Fenbrook academy, dancers, actors and musicians are all mixed together. Natasha, a dancer I know, is fond of the college analogy. The dancers are the jocks, the actors are the cool kids and the musicians are the geeks.

I prefer my Lord of the Rings analogy. The dancers are clearly the elves. Up on the third floor with its huge windows and natural light, they jump and glide like otherworldly beings, all sensual and untouchable.

Down on the first floor, close to the action of the city, the actors are obviously the humans. Hot-blooded.

Unpredictable. They command the attention of everyone else—deep down, we all want to be movie stars.

And the musicians? Crammed between the other two in a floor that's a rabbit warren of twisting corridors and tiny practice rooms, we're the dwarves. We just want to be left alone with our craft.

Connor was the exception. He was a human living amongst the dwarves, causing chaos.

Fenbrook had only been taking non-classical music students for about five years and—like me—Connor was in his senior year, though he was a few years older. The idea was still scandalous when he started; I can almost hear the music faculty discussing it in shocked tones. *"Amplified* music, you say? An *electric* guitar? At *Fenbrook?!"*

His talent wasn't in doubt—pretty much everything *else* was, but not that. I hadn't really heard him play, because the handful of non-classical musicians didn't really mix with the rest of us, but supposedly he was the next Hendrix. They'd given him an audition and a return plane ticket from Belfast to New York just on the strength of his CD, and once they heard him play it was apparently a no-brainer. Where I'd had to sweat and practice for months just to land an audition for my Boston college, then do it all again for Fenbrook, he'd just dropped a CD in the mail, strummed a few bars and he was in.

What made it especially galling was that, now that he was here, he treated the place as little more than a convenient supply of impressionable dancers and actresses to hook up with. He'd show up for lectures late or not at all. Once, I was pretty sure he was still drunk from the night before. There were rumblings about him being kicked out but, from what I could see, he was still behaving exactly as he had in his freshman year. For

Connor, Fenbrook was one big party.
For me, it felt like life and death.

***

I'd booked a practice room for some solo work. As the door shut behind me, I closed my eyes and let the blessed relief of being alone wash over me. People made me nervous—strangers, doubly so and men, triple.

Fenbrook practice rooms are literally that—room enough to practice in and nothing more. The cello case almost grazed the walls as I turned around, un-slung it and cracked open the battered chrysalis to reveal the gleaming beauty of the instrument inside.

I settled the cello between my legs and leaned the neck down onto my shoulder. Immediately, just from the touch of the wood, I felt better.

It should have been easy enough to concentrate on the music. I was practicing my parts of the *Brahms Double Concerto,* and that was enough to focus anyone's mind. But within seconds of my bow hitting the strings, my attention started to wander. I was downstairs again, dangling in space, completely reliant on Connor. That was the worst part of it—that he'd had to save me. I hated owing anything to anyone.

Concentrate. I stopped, took a breath and continued. Big, slow notes that vibrated through my body. My wrists needed to be smooth as butter to get the changing angles right, but they felt rigid and taut. I'd tensed up.

I knew I'd be reliving that moment at the door for weeks. Everything embarrassing I'd ever done was stuck in my mind on endless loop. Sometimes people would tell me that I needed to "let things go." *How?*

I missed a note and had to stop again. Squeezing

my eyes shut for a second, I shook out my wrists and restarted. I was getting close to the fast part....

I didn't see what his groupies saw in him. I mean, yes, he was good looking in a dark, dangerous sort of a way, but it wasn't as if he was bulging with muscles. He was more lean and wiry, like a panther. Was it just the rock star thing, even if the closest he'd got to stardom was playing in local bars?

The notes were flying now, my breath coming in quick little gasps. Playing fast is a bit like skiing downhill on the very edge of control. It can be heady and brilliant when it goes well. This wasn't going well, so it was just terrifying.

He'd smelled good. Sort of clean and outdoorsy, like the air after a storm. That was new to me, the idea that a guy would have a particular scent. I didn't get up close with many men. Okay, *any* men. I knew my fantasies were now going to have to include an extra element.

Not fantasies of *him,* obviously. But whatever nameless, faceless guy I thought of late at night, as my hand slipped between my thighs, I'd now give him a scent. Not even *that* scent, necessarily.

The bow lanced off at an angle, shrieking in protest. I stared at the ceiling for a moment, letting my hair fall down my back. What was wrong with me? I'd nearly fallen—that was all. I hadn't even been hurt. Why couldn't I get it out of my mind?

Because I'm trying to distract myself from the real problem, I decided.

It was my senior year, and my final year recital was looming on the horizon—ten weeks, three days and counting. I'd have to perform the Brahms, together with my duet partner Dan on violin, for a panel comprising three Fenbrook judges. That in itself was scary, but it was a good piece, I had a great partner and I was certain we'd get a good grade. That wasn't the problem.

Also on the panel would be two talent scouts. One I didn't care about—some guy from a record label who was really there for the non-classical musicians. But the other would be from the New York Philharmonic. Impressing him was my one shot at scoring a trial and maybe, just maybe, saving a dream that was close to slipping out of my grasp forever.

My dream, or my father's dream. Sometimes it was difficult to tell.

My phone buzzed to tell me to meet Natasha for coffee and I stared at the clock disbelievingly. My practice hour was up, and I'd barely scratched the surface of the music. *Great.*

***

There are two places that are so much a part of Fenbrook, they might as well be on the official map. One is Flicker, a movie-themed bar just down the street. The other is Harper's, a café and deli that's practically next door. If Harper's ever closed down, about eighty percent of Fenbrook students would die of starvation.

Both places rely heavily on students for their staff and it's not unusual to look around and find that literally everyone in the room, on both sides of the counter, is an actor, a dancer or a musician.

When I walked in that day, the barista was a guy who I'd seen in a poster for some off-Broadway satire about the financial crash and the woman wiping down the tables was an oboe player I sometimes had classes with. And sitting all by herself at a table in the center of the café was Natasha, a junior year dancer.

I was a senior, but almost all my friends at

Fenbrook were juniors for three very good reasons. Firstly, my father made me start high school a year early. My friends were in the year below, but that meant they were my age: twenty-one.

Secondly, being juniors meant they weren't stressed out by final year recitals or performances. That was annoying, sometimes—it meant they all wanted to go out drinking while I wanted to work (to be fair, that had been the case even in my freshman year). But the advantage was that we didn't talk about work the whole time as I would have done with other seniors. Being with them was an escape. Except for Dan, my recital partner, none of them were musicians for the same reason.

Thirdly, I'd started Fenbrook a semester late. The other freshman students had already formed tight-knit groups by the time I arrived and I was a year younger than all of them. I pretty much hunkered down and didn't speak to anyone for the rest of the year. It was only when the next year's students started that I came out of my shell a little and made some friends.

So that was me. The final year, geeky musician amongst a group of vivacious, beautiful dancers and actresses. The odd one out. The straight man, if you will. I loved them all, and I wouldn't have changed it for the world.

Natasha was asleep, or close to it, slumped down with her head on her hands. I got a triple shot Americano for her, a latte for me and carefully sat down. She didn't move.

I pushed the coffee nearer to her sleeping head. Her hair was almost the same shade of chestnut as mine, only hers was always soft and wavy and sexy when she let it out of her dancer's bun, while mine was a frizzy mess.

The smell of coffee caught her nostrils and they

twitched like a rabbit's.

"...and then we decided to get married, so we're moving to Mexico," I told her.

She sat bolt upright. "WHAT?!"

Despite my worries, I smirked. "Nothing. My life's as boring as always. You can go back to sleep."

She shook her head. "Karen, it's too early in the morning for tricks like that." She sipped her coffee and closed her eyes in bliss. "How's your lullaby?"

I stiffened. "It's not a lullaby. Brahms composed all sorts of things apart from—"

"Okay, okay, how's the *Brahms?*"

"Awful."

"I'm sure that's not true. I know you—you'll be amazing as always."

"Amazing isn't good enough. It needs to be perfect, or I let Dan down. I let everyone down."

"You have months until your recital."

She was right. It was still winter, and I wouldn't face the hell of the recital until spring was taking hold (Fenbrook has a short final year, to give us an extra long summer break before we hit the real world). I had two months and change, but that isn't as long as it sounds when you're trying to get something absolutely right. I knew how fast those weeks would burn away as the date crept closer, and while everyone else was just trying to graduate, I'd be trying to impress the scout for one of the best orchestras in the world.

"You'll be fine. This is what you *do.*" She tried to stifle a yawn and failed.

"Why are you so tired?" I asked.

She looked at me guiltily and I saw her flush.

"Oh," I said delightedly. "How *is* your billionaire?"

"Millionaire."

"Same thing."

The previous summer, Natasha had been propositioned by Darrell, a rich guy who wanted her as his "muse." She'd danced for him at his mansion and they'd wound up in some sort of breakneck romance full of hot sex.

And tears.

One night in my apartment during winter break, aided by Chardonnay and candlelight, she'd told me how she'd been self-harming for years, unknown to everyone but her roommate. She'd been wracked with guilt over something that happened when she was fifteen—something she still didn't feel ready to tell me about. Darrell had found out and it had nearly killed their fledgling relationship. He'd had his own issues, too. They'd wound up helping each other and, eventually, had worked things out. As far as I knew, Natasha hadn't gone back to cutting herself—she certainly *seemed* happy.

"Darrell's okay. Sort of at a loose end. You know he quit his job?"

I nodded. I didn't know the details, but I knew his job had been some sort of soul-sucking, bad karma thing in the defense industry and when it came between them he'd told the company where to go. I tried to imagine what that would be like—to have someone who cared so much for you that they'd give up their whole career: I couldn't.

"He's trying to work out what to do. I think he needs a project—it's been months. Right now, he's just taking me to Fenbrook in the mornings and then sitting around the house. Or he and Neil go on some long blast on their bikes."

Neil was Darrell's friend, a huge, scary-looking biker who—I still couldn't wrap my head around this— had somehow got together with Natasha's flat mate, Clarissa. What the attraction was, I had no idea. She was all Prada and champagne parties and perfectly-styled blonde hair, and he was all muscles and attitude and whispered comments in her ear that made her flush and squirm and...okay, I could sort of see the attraction.

Natasha sipped more coffee. "Anyway, I don't know if it's because he's not working on anything, but he's...."

I waited. "Yes?"

She shrugged, blushing a little. "Insatiable. You know how it is, when they're like that."

I really don't, I thought, a little angrily. I wasn't what you'd call experienced, when it came to men and sex. In fact, you know that thing where you're the exact opposite of experienced? I was that.

Yes, at twenty-one. I know, okay?

Of course, I hadn't shared that with my friends. I'd lied when the subject had come up, and invented a firefighter (no, I don't know *why* a firefighter, I was thinking on my feet) who'd seduced me at eighteen—that seemed believable. Since I'd come to Fenbrook, there'd been various attempts to set me up with someone, none of which had got past the first clumsy kiss.

"Remind me," I said. "It's been a while."

Natasha checked there was no-one listening and leaned forward. "It's not the nights. I mean, you expect the nights. The nights are great. But as soon as we get home...last night he just shoved me up against the wall."

I swallowed. "Really?" I tried to sound only vaguely interested.

"The night before, we didn't even make it home. He turned off the highway and took me into the forest, and then—"

I was leaning forward myself, now. I couldn't help it. "Up against a tree?"

Natasha was suddenly staring fixedly at her coffee.

"Um. There was a log on the ground, actually. He bent me over it."

Something darkly hot swept through me. Was it wrong, that I was *this* interested? What choice did I have, given my total lack of a sex life?

Natasha was lost in the memories now. "And then last night, he gave me this massage, and it went on for hours. It felt incredible—I think it's because he's used to making things, you know? He's so dexterous. And I was on my back—this is, like, two in the morning, now—and suddenly he starts going down on me—"

"Right," I said, my face flushing. "Okay—"

But she was on a roll. "And it went on for hours—I mean, it can't have been hours, but it *felt* like hours, I was just like—"

"Mm-hmm, got it—"

"I mean, I was on the *ceiling*, just floating higher and higher, and then he put his tongue—" She glanced up at me and broke off. "Oh. Sorry. Too much?"

"Not at all," I said lightly. "I'm glad you're happy."

She yawned. "Happy but exhausted," she said apologetically. "Hey, you're coming out tonight, right?"

I considered. Bars were really not my thing, but I knew I needed some breathing space away from the music, even if just for a few hours. Preparing for the recital was a marathon, not a sprint. I had to pace myself, or I'd be risking a repeat of Boston.

Don't think about Boston.

"Sure," I told Natasha.

She grinned. "Maybe you'll meet someone."

"Yeah. Maybe I'll meet a billionaire who wants me to play the cello for him in his batcave."

"It's just a basement, not a—You're as bad as Clarissa!" She drank the rest of her coffee and then frowned. "Wait, what time is it?"

"Twenty after ten."

"*Shit!* Practice started five minutes ago. Miss Kay's going to kill me!"

She ran for the door, long dancer's legs eating up the distance, and I was left alone. A good thing, because thinking about Boston, even just for a second, had started a chain reaction in my head and I knew I wouldn't be able to concentrate on anything else unless I let it run its course. I sat there sipping coffee, outwardly calm, and let the memories surge up inside and consume me.

***

A decision had been made in my life, many years ago now. So long ago that I didn't know exactly when it was made, or even who'd made it: me, or my father. I honestly had trouble remembering a time before it.

The decision was this: *I was going to play with the New York Philharmonic.*

That's a cute dream and a nice ambition when your father's a normal guy. When he's a concert pianist with a string of bestselling albums, things are different.

As I began to show promise, he told the neighbors. I'd sit there, little face a mask of concentration, and play *Bach Cello Suites* and he'd say, *"She's going to play with the New York Phil one day."*

At school, he'd pick me up outside the gates and whisk me off to youth orchestra practice and then to more practice at home. At first I had time for other things, like girl scouts—mainly at the insistence of my mom. Then she left, and one by one the other activities stopped. At twelve, I did my first big solo: *Haydn's Cello Concerto* in front of a hall full of people, throwing up in the bathroom beforehand and then nodding and smiling when my dad asked if everything was okay. The man doing the announcements said I was *Karen Montfort, who's already tipped for the New York Philharmonic,* and I remember feeling both proud and uncomfortable, although I didn't know why, then.

My mom had a new life within a year, with a man she claimed made her feel "free". I didn't understand what she meant, at the time. I thought she was ungrateful; couldn't she see how hard my father worked to give us a home, and me a future? I clung even more tightly to him and he to me, and that seemed to push my mom even farther away.

Thanks to my dad insisting I start high school a year early, I was the odd one out. A year is a long time when all the other girls are getting breasts and periods; spending every night practicing instead of hanging out at the mall didn't do anything for my image, either. When I graduated, I was glad to be out of there and when I got into one of the top music colleges in Boston I was excited beyond belief. *Finally,* I thought, *I'd be around people who understand me.*

People think that if you're good, training side-by-side with the best can only make you better. And that was true, in a way. We were all the best in our high schools and, naturally, we all wanted to be the best in the college. It was just what we were trained to do—we didn't *know* anything else. So every day, you heard the best students playing at a level above and beyond what you were capable of and you tried to match it. And then other kids were trying to match *you*—a leapfrogging race of ability that was always going to end badly. We'd all made the same mistaken assumption: O*nly one of us can be the best, and it's going to be me!* It never clicked that all but one of us had to be wrong.

Most of the other students lived in shared student

accommodation, bitching about the roaches or the walk to campus. I already lived in Boston, so it made no sense for me to move out of my dad's house. I went home every night to a home-cooked meal—I thought I was lucky, at the time.

But while every other student could let off steam with their friends, catching a movie or passing a joint around, I had to go home and tell my father that yes, everything was fine. If I messed up a piece, there was no one to commiserate with me over a sneaky beer—I couldn't tell my father or he'd be disappointed in me. If I started to doubt my ability, or fear that I'd never be as good as the student I'd heard play that day, there was no one to share it with over coffee, no one to reassure me that they felt the same.

I started, for the first time, to understand what my mom had been talking about, but by then it was far too late.

I don't know. Maybe it wouldn't have been any different if I'd lived with the other students. I certainly wasn't the only one to crack under the pressure.

I was the only one they found on the roof, though.

I didn't like public speaking. When most people say that, they mean they get a little nervous when they have to stand up and give a speech to their entire company. But I got that way when I had to socialize with one or two people I didn't know. My eyes locked on the floor, my words had to be squeezed out between lips that were almost sealed together and my voice dropped to barely a murmur. If I had to present to the whole class, I completely locked up. My throat seemed to swell and block and my lungs fought me, refusing to draw air. I'd sit down and shake my head, unable to even start and the teacher would sigh and give me an F. When I went to the music college at Boston, I presumed those days were behind me. I was fine when I was *playing* in public—it was my voice that was the problem.

But despite being very performance-oriented, the course at Boston still required essays—which weren't a problem—and presentations, which were. As the first big one approached, I became more and more scared. When it came to the morning of my turn...well, that's when they found me on the roof.

I wasn't—and I'm pretty sure about this—suicidal. Seriously, the thought never entered my head. But I also couldn't explain what I was doing up there, when they found me. I had no memory of going up there, or of wandering around six floors up. When they tracked the wailing fire alarm to the emergency door I'd opened and raced up to the roof to see what was going on, apparently I was standing quite close to the edge, just...looking.

A difficult couple of weeks followed. Everyone wanted to help. My dad thought I should go into therapy and then return to Boston. I convinced him that I needed a complete change, and to go somewhere that was less of a pressure cooker. When I found Fenbrook Academy in New York, he hated the idea of "distractions" like actors and dancers being around, and wasn't happy about me living alone in New York, either. The thing that convinced him was the connection to the New York Phil.

Fenbrook didn't have the cultural cachet of the college in Boston, but a combination of its location right in the heart of New York and some big name alumni musicians who'd wound up at the New York Phil had led the orchestra to scout there during the final year recitals. It was by no means a sure thing, but if I could pull off a great recital, I had a good shot.

The first few years went well. I liked Fenbrook. I was careful to make friends who were non-musicians, to get away from the pressure I'd felt in Boston, and it worked. I didn't have time to socialize much, but hanging out with Natasha, Clarissa and Jasmine—an actress—reminded me that there was a world outside music. Being away from my dad helped, too, although he phoned more often than was healthy.

Fenbrook, as I'd hoped, was a less pressurized environment, but it was less performance-oriented than Boston. Credit for the course was divided into four quarters—I liked to think of them as slices of cake. Three of the slices were made up of things you did over the years: performances, essays and presentations, each worth 25%. The last slice—the final 25%—was awarded for your final year recital.

Missing a whole semester had shaved a chunk off each of the first three slices. But my performance slice was still thick and solid and coated with frosting—I'd aced every one of them. My essay slice was almost as good. Half of the cake was already in place.

Thanks to my fear of public speaking, though, there was an empty space where the performance slice should have been—a whole 25% was missing from my credits. Everything depended on the recital slice—if I got almost full marks, I'd graduate well. If, on the day, I froze or couldn't perform or something, I'd be left with only half a cake and not graduate at all.

One performance to both get the credits I needed and to impress the New York Phil scout. Four years of hard work, and yet my whole future rested on just ten minutes.

No pressure, then.

The annoying thing was that, for the other musicians on the course, the recital wasn't anything like as scary. By now, they'd amassed almost enough credit to graduate, and a reasonable performance was all they needed to take them the final distance. A few could even scrape through and graduate without it. For me, it was make or break.

I sat there stewing until my phone buzzed to remind me I had advanced theory class in five minutes. I had to have an alarm for everything, or I'd miss a class because I was too busy stressing about missing classes.

Why couldn't I just be normal?

***

Dan, my duet partner, had saved me a seat in the lecture theater. It was the biggest room we musicians got to see, and after all the hours spent in tiny practice rooms we tended to sit there overwhelmed by the sense of space, like battery hens in a football stadium.

Dan was a cheerful, round-faced Canadian and the single most dependable person I knew. I'd chosen him as my duet partner without hesitation—he might not have been the best violinist at Fenbrook, but I knew he'd practice the Brahms until he had it polished, and wouldn't fall to pieces on the day; with my whole future resting on the recital, I needed a guaranteed good performance, not the chance of a great one. He was friendly, generous, thoughtful...exactly what I'd want in a boyfriend, if he didn't have a boyfriend of his own.

Doctor Geisler clapped his hands together, his booming Danish accent filling the room. "Okay! We're starting today by looking at Schenkerian analysis—"

The door opened and Connor walked in. Halfway through the door, he stopped and frowned.

Geisler paused and stared at him. "Are you in this class?" he asked mildly.

Connor looked genuinely confused. "I don't know. *Am* I in this class?"

Everyone laughed—everyone except me. It was

alright for him—he was going to flunk out and he didn't care. Meanwhile, it felt like I was being crushed under the weight of everyone's expectations.

"Why don't you join us anyway?" said Geisler. "Maybe you'll recall whether you're taking this course. And you'll learn something either way." It was always hard to tell whether he was being nice or dryly sarcastic.

Connor nodded and vaulted over the front row of desks so that he could sit down next to a blonde oboist, who giggled even though she probably knew his reputation. Or maybe *because* she knew his reputation.

"Okay," Geisler said again.

I didn't have a lot of time to look down to Connor's row over the next hour, but what I did see amazed me. First, he borrowed paper from the girl sitting next to him—because he hadn't brought any of his own. Then a pen, because of course he hadn't brought that either. I didn't know why he bothered, because he proceeded to take no notes whatsoever, slouching back in his seat and gazing everywhere but at Geisler.

Once, I thought he was looking at me and immediately felt myself flush. He was probably remembering me almost falling down the stairs.

Unbidden, little details swam back to me. That outdoorsy scent, so cool and clean you wanted to fill your lungs with it. The way his jacket had hugged his shoulders, before flowing down to his tight, trim waist.

Oh, stop it! You sound like one of his groupies!

"So, can anyone tell me where the development section of the first movement begins? Karen?"

Oh God! Geisler was calling on me! I knew the answer: Bar 231. Maybe if I got it out quickly, before my body had a chance to react—

"Stand up, so we can hear you better."

No, don't make me stand! He thought he was

being nice, giving me thinking time, but he was just giving the fear time to take hold. I got to my feet, my legs like wet paper. My brain's gears jammed and froze.

"Now, where does Beethoven begin the development section?" Doctor Geisler asked, smiling kindly.

Bar 231. I knew it, I just couldn't get the words out. *What if I'm wrong? What if they laugh?* I could feel my throat closing up, soft flesh locking tight as a nut.

"You did analyze this piece?" asked Doctor Geisler, looking a little annoyed now.

I nodded. *Yes, of course I did! I've even done extra reading!* I knew this stuff! I just couldn't—

"Go on, then," Geisler told me.

I could feel the panic rising inside me, leaving no strength in my legs and drawing all the blood from my face. I knew I was going to either burst into tears or bolt for the door—probably the second one. Then I'd have to lie and apologize and say I'd been ill. I couldn't afford to fail another class!

"Bar 231," said an Irish voice from the front, and everyone laughed.

"I was asking someone else," Geisler told Connor, pointedly. "But yes." And he launched into a long explanation, nodding at me to sit down almost as an afterthought.

I collapsed onto my seat and let my lungs slowly re-inflate. I'd been rescued, by the least likely person I could imagine. I risked a look at Connor, but he wasn't looking at me—probably, he'd just been bored, and saving me hadn't come into it. How had he known the answer, though? From what I'd just seen, he never even took notes!

That's twice in one day he's saved you, a little voice inside me said.

I looked down at Connor. The blonde oboist next to him was grinning and squeezing him around the shoulders in *my hero* sort of a way, with more body contact than was strictly necessary. *That's why he did it. To impress her.*

I focused on Geisler. I couldn't afford any more distractions.

CHAPTER 2

THAT EVENING, as I pushed through the main doors—carefully, this time—and plodded down the steps, I felt like my brain had been stretched out and twisted into a pretzel. Three hours of lectures and then a long afternoon of practice, working at the Brahms until I swore I could hear it playing in my head everywhere I went, had nearly broken me. My eyes were bloodshot and sore from staring at music and my spine was a knotted mass of pain.

I need a billionaire to give me a massage. Maybe Natasha will loan me Darrell.

Footsteps behind me. A clatter of heels and then, with a rush of perfume and a silken swish of long, auburn hair, Jasmine was snuggled up against me, an arm around my shoulders.

I stopped my trudging and looked back at the icy steps in disbelief. I'd had to be careful even in my sneakers; Jasmine had just bounded down them in three-inch heels. How did she *do* that? I could barely even walk in any heel over a couple of inches...which was a shame, because they would have helped my height.

"Can I get changed at your place?" Jasmine asked.

"Changed?" Then I remembered we were going out. I was exhausted. "Actually, I think I just want to go home and pull the covers over my head."

"Nope. Not an option. We need to get you out, before you disappear into a practice room and we lose you forever." She pulled me forward and I started walking.

I really didn't want to go out, but I'm not good at saying "no" to people. Especially Jasmine. Out of all my friends, she's the most like a sister—or how I imagine a sister should be, since I'm an only child. A junior year actress, she looks like she was born for the screen. I don't just mean she's beautiful—she is, but that isn't it. It's that she's eye-catching. When she walks into a room, you can't not look at her—men and women alike. For starters, she has thick red hair almost down to her waist that she either wears in big, pre-Raphaelite curls or in a super-sleek straight curtain down her back. Secondly, she has these huge green eyes that can be innocent and shocked or incredibly filthy, depending on what she's saying. And finally she has the body. She's curvy, and I don't mean that as a euphemism. She has an honest-to-God hourglass figure and she makes the most of it. Guys in particular stop and stare.

I sometimes busked for charity as part of a string quartet in Central Park. One Saturday the previous summer, we were having an okay day with maybe fifty dollars in the hat. Jasmine showed up in a green summer dress that showed quite a bit of cleavage and did nothing more than sit on the grass listening to us. We made three hundred dollars in the next hour, the crowd swelling by the second.

She was the anti-me, beautiful and confident. Maybe that's why we got on so well.

"Fine," I told her. "One drink at Flicker."

A particularly cruel gust of wind lashed at us and I pulled my coat around me. I realized that Jasmine was in a light autumn jacket that stopped at her waist. She wasn't just snuggling up to me to be cute.

"What are you wearing?" I asked. "You'll freeze!"

"Not if we hurry up and get to your place." She towed me along.

I tried to hurry, but no one moves fast with a cello strapped to their back.

"Why can't you just leave it at the academy?" she asked, for what must have been the hundredth time since I'd known her.

I looked at her blankly. "How would I practice at home?"

Jasmine shivered and gave me a very strange look. "Karen, in all seriousness, you need to get out more."

***

When I asked to move to New York so I could attend Fenbrook, my dad argued and grumbled and moaned about how Boston was better and then, when he finally saw that it was the only option, he rented an apartment for me. He didn't wire me the rent money or help me pick out a place, he just dropped off the keys and told me where I'd be living for four years.

I know, I know—poor little rich girl. Don't get me wrong, I'm very grateful for it. But it did demonstrate how our relationship worked.

The place he'd picked was in a nice neighborhood, because he wanted me to be safe. But it was a one bedroom apartment, because he didn't want me to be distracted by anyone, and it was several stops on the subway from any of the areas popular with students, because he wanted me well away from "the party scene" (as if I'd ever go to a party anyway).

It was great, and very generous of him, and not having to pay rent meant that I was one of the few students at Fenbrook who didn't have to work a part-time job (another thing he'd never allow). But the place never felt like *mine*. He'd even furnished it himself, which meant that—just like at home—there was no television (I'd been the only kid at school with a music score on their lunch box instead of Elmo or Batman). In a tiny show of defiance, I was saving up to buy a TV, though I knew I'd have to find somewhere to hide it when he visited.

We trudged in out of the cold and Jasmine gasped as the warm air hit her. "You have your heating come on before you're even home?" she asked in disbelief.

"Isn't that the idea of a timer?"

She sank into the leather couch with a groan of pleasure, long auburn hair trailing languidly over the edge. You could have pointed a camera at the scene and you'd have had a furniture store commercial right there. "Sure. But no one actually *does* it. What if you're late home or you go straight out? You'd have wasted all that money."

"Good point." I didn't like to mention that all the bills went straight to my dad. I had no idea how much the power cost. I had no idea how much the apartment cost, for that matter. He'd given me everything I needed.

And he could take it away just as easily.

Something occurred to me, looking at Jasmine luxuriating on the sofa. "What are you going to change *into?*" I asked. She was in jeans and a sweater—not her usual going-out attire.

"Oh, it's in here." From her purse, she pulled out a wad of black fabric no bigger than my hand, then let it unroll. "Ta da! What do you think?"

"Where's the rest of it?"

"It's stretchy," she told me defensively. "It looks bigger on."

"Uh-huh. Well, I'm going to take a quick shower. Make yourself at home."

In the shower, I turned the temperature up to almost scalding and the force up to the "Massage" setting, hoping that it would help unkink my back. I did that a lot, after a hard day playing. I liked to imagine that it was a big, blond guy with huge biceps massaging me. In my mind, his name was Sven and we sat in his cabin in Sweden looking out at the pine trees while he worked oil into my back.

It occurred to me that that was a lot of detail to get from a shower setting. Maybe I *did* need a boyfriend.

Connor swam up into my mind and I yelped in shock, turning and catching the spray right in my face. When I'd stopped spluttering and the jet was safely hammering away at my stomach, I carefully allowed myself to go back to the thought.

What was *he* doing in my brain? I wasn't interested in Connor—in fact, he was the exact opposite of everything I was interested in. If I was going to date, they'd need to be reliable, and serious, and...*safe*.

Why did my list of requirements for a guy sound like a Volvo commercial?

Connor didn't have any of that going for him. He didn't have anything going for him, except for his looks.

If you're into that sort of look, I told myself quickly. *Which I'm not.*

I realized the shower was turning into an epic, so I cranked off the water, toweled off and padded through to the bedroom to find something to wear. I knew Jasmine wasn't going to let me out of the apartment in my jeans and sweatshirt, but my wardrobe was...limited. I finally found a dark red blouse and a black skirt, and pulled out the one pair of heels I dared to wear. They were only a couple of inches high, so I could walk in them. Just.

I found Jasmine in the kitchen, wearing the dress and making a sandwich. Only that doesn't really describe the scene.

The dress...it looked as if someone had drawn a line across her breasts a millimeter north of her areolae, drawn another line across her thighs a hairs-breadth below the bottom of her ass cheeks, then colored the space in between with a black Sharpie.

The dress, though, paled in comparison to the sandwich. It started off normally, with bread and then ham, and then cheese, and then another slice of bread. But then it seemed to forget to stop, and there was a layer of lettuce and some bacon strips and tomato and then more bread and some cold chicken and pickle and...I watched as Jasmine emptied a bag of chips to form the top layer and crunched a final slice of bread on top. The thing was a foot high.

She turned around as she heard me and beamed, then looked guiltily down at the sandwich. "Um...this is okay, right?"

"Of course!" I sat down at the table and watched as she worked her way through the thing. She ate breathlessly, as if she hadn't had food in a month.

"Jasmine...." I asked slowly, when she was done. "What's wrong?"

"Nothing!" She licked mayo off a finger. "I was just hungry."

I wasn't great at social stuff, but I wasn't stupid either. I gave her a look.

"Okay, I skipped lunch," she told me.

I kept looking at her.

"And breakfast."

I sighed. "I know you're busy with auditions, but you have to make time to eat. I know you think I'm boring, but—" I saw something in her expression. "What?"

She stared at the table.

"Jasmine, do you not have money for food?!" I asked, horrified.

She raised big, guilty eyes to me. "It's not like I spent it on booze and weed," she told me. "I just—I don't make much, and I had three auditions this month, and all of them were way across town and I had to get a cab for one of them because it was nowhere near the subway and none of them panned out so they just soaked up money and my landlord's an asshole and—" She stopped and took a deep breath, and I could see the beginning of tears creeping into her eyes.

"Stop," I told her. I shook my head in dismay. "Idiot."

She sniffed. "For running out of cash?"

"For not telling me." I went to my bedroom and dug for the little tin box in the bottom of my underwear drawer. I didn't actually have that much money—yes, my father paid my rent and bills, but I didn't see any of that money and he didn't let me have a part-time job, so cash was tight. He gave me an allowance to live on—enough for groceries and the occasional item of clothing, if I was careful. I'd been eking out the money each month and squirreling away what I could, and had saved three hundred dollars towards a TV.

I marched back into the kitchen and gave her the wad of notes. "Here." She opened her mouth to argue. "No. You're taking it. And it's a gift, not a loan. I don't want it back." *When do I have time to watch TV, anyway?*

Jasmine looked at the money and then at me. "Thank you," she said at last.

"Thanks for being friends with a weirdo like me." And then we were hugging and I very nearly started crying myself, so I squeezed her quickly and changed the subject. "That dress *doesn't* look bigger on."

Jasmine blinked back her own tears and looked down at herself, then at me. "Well, at least I don't look like I came straight from the office."

I examined my blouse and skirt. "It's *smart,*" I told her.

"You look like a secretary. At least undo a button."

I gave her a mock glare, but undid the top button of my blouse. It wasn't like it made much of a difference anyway, with my chest. Maybe Jasmine had been in line ahead of me, and the boob gods had given her both our shares.

"Great. Let's go." Jasmine started to pull on the same light jacket she'd worn before.

"Wait, seriously? You're planning to go out like that?" The dress left her bare up to her thighs. "You'll freeze!"

She shrugged and indicated my sensible winter coat. "Trendy as your polar explorer special is, I can't afford one."

I had an idea. "Wait here."

I went to my bedroom and rummaged in my wardrobe. Minutes later, I was back with a full-length snow white fur coat.

"What *the fuck?!*" Jasmine asked. "How much money do you *have*, and how many baby seals did you have to club to death to make that?"

"It's not real fur—it's from a thrift store. And it's

not mine! Don't you remember it? It's the one you wore in freshman year for the play about the Russian oligarch. You were the mistress."

Her brow furrowed as she turned the coat over in her hands. "Yeah...Svetlana. *I vant to go to America!* But what's it doing in your closet?"

I shrugged. "Afterwards, the girl doing costumes said they might need it if they ever staged the play again, but she didn't have any room to store it, so...."

"You've been keeping it in your closet for three years just in case?! Karen, you're too...*nice*."

"I own about three outfits. It's not like I need the space."

She pulled on the coat, which reached down to her ankles. On anyone else it would have looked ridiculous but, with her long red hair and the tiny black dress, she just about pulled it off. She hugged me, which was like being cuddled by the Abominable Snowman.

"I don't deserve a friend like you," she told me. "I need to do something nice for you."

"Let me stay in?" I suggested hopefully, my voice muffled by the fur. "I could do some practice...."

She released me and marched me out the door. "Not that."

***

We met Natasha and Clarissa at Flicker. Dan had come along, too, on the proviso that he obey our no-boyfriends rule.

Flicker's known for three things. The first is that, like Harper's, the bar staff is almost entirely made up of Fenbrook students. The second is that the walls have screens showing random movie clips, without the sound. The third is that all the cocktails are named after movies, and they range from the fairly safe to the I-no-longer-remember-my-own-name.

"I'm going to have a Panic Room," Clarissa announced. As usual, she was wearing something incredibly expensive and stunningly tasteful: a deep green top and a diagonally cut skirt. With her blonde hair and perfect make-up, you could have dropped her straight into a Vogue cover shoot.

"Don't," said Natasha, who worked at Flicker a few nights a week and so was an expert. "It's just a Morello cherry floating in gray sludge. Barely a shot. Have a Moulin Rouge or something."

"I'm not having a Moulin Rouge. It comes with pineapple and sparklers and a goddamn plastic elephant. It's..."—Clarissa looked at Jasmine's dress—"tacky."

Jasmine stuck her tongue out at her.

I studied the menu. "I think I'll have a Mamma Mia."

Everyone groaned. "That barely has any alcohol in it!" said Dan. "It's mostly marshmallow fluff. At least have a Pretty Woman!"

I sighed. "Okay, okay—a Pretty Woman. Nat?"

Natasha pursed her lips. "I don't know. Something like The Godfather."

A wave of dead silence expanded out from her. People at the table next to us stopped talking. *No one* had The Godfather.

Nat looked around her, spooked. "Something *like* The Godfather," she repeated. "Not the actual Godfather. Obviously."

We all relaxed.

***

A half hour later, I was sitting with my back to the

room when I heard the door to the street crash open. A blast of cold outdoor air froze my ankles. Three male voices started singing—an old love song from the nineties, with the notes flattened out by alcohol. In their heads, I'm sure they sounded great.

"Shut the door!" yelled someone.

The voices came closer, moving towards the bar. Actually, if you ignored the slurring, one of the voices didn't sound too bad, its Irish lilt making it stand out from the rest. I groaned inwardly as I realized who it was.

Conversation at our table had died when the singing started. It sounded like the same had happened across most of the bar—it was impossible to ignore, since you'd have to yell to talk over it. I could feel the irritation building inside me. We'd come for a quiet drink, and *he* had to burst in and spoil things, not just for us but for everyone in the bar. I *hated* drunk people.

They finished their song, and there was applause. I rolled my eyes. Why were people encouraging them?

I realized that Jasmine was one of the ones clapping. She caught my look. "What? They're not bad."

I kept my voice low. "They're *drunk*."

"So?" Jasmine leaned across to Natasha. "Would," she murmured, looking at someone behind me.

I couldn't resist turning around, even though I knew who it was. Connor Locke was standing at the bar, talking to a busty, blonde-haired girl who was serving. *Probably asking for her phone number.* Connor had two other guys with him, guys I didn't recognize from Fenbrook.

I turned back to the table. "Why?" I asked Jasmine.

"Are you kidding? Look at him!"

I sighed and took another look. He was turned

half away from me, his leather jacket pulled tight around his waist as he twisted, showing off his wide, muscled back. I hadn't really noticed that before. Or—what Jasmine had probably been focusing on—the fact that his jeans were snug over his firm, athletic ass.

There was a mirror on the other side of the bar, and I glanced at it, wondering if I could get a glimpse of his face. Only to find him staring straight back at my reflection.

I whipped back around to the table, hoping he hadn't noticed.

"He's at Fenbrook, right?" Clarissa asked. "Music."

"I barely know him," I said quickly.

"Karen!" Connor's voice behind me. He was suddenly looming over our table. I mentally willed the others to circle the wagons and block him out, but of course they slid their chairs back and turned and smiled. Dan, who'd been sitting next to me, had slipped away— probably chatting to some cute actor—and that had opened up a convenient gap for Connor to slide into.

I slowly lifted my head. He was grinning down at me, his jacket slung over his shoulder, and as he leaned in close his thick bicep was only a foot from my face. I found myself focusing on the tattoo there, to avoid having to look him in the eye. A name, picked out in elaborate lettering. *Ruth.*

I knew that talking to him was a mistake, but I couldn't help myself. "You're drunk," I told him.

"And you're beautiful. But in the morning—No, wait. I got that wrong."

I ignored the jibe and shook my head. "It's only eight o'clock. When did you start: six?"

"Four!" he said, sounding almost offended.

I sighed and shook my head. He'd been out partying all afternoon while I'd been stuck in a practice room. Didn't he have practice to do?

"Rock n' roll," he said, with an extravagant gesture. "That's Connor Locke. Too wild for you?"

"You could use a little taming, Connor Locke," I said without thinking.

He leaned over me. "You going to be the one to tame me?"

I flushed, unable to think of a comeback, and cursed myself for talking to him. Then it got worse.

"Have you recovered from this morning?" he asked.

I blushed, which wasn't the signal I wanted to send at all.

"What happened this morning?" asked Jasmine with forced casualness.

"I had Karen flat on her back," Connor told them.

"That's not...." I trailed off, unsure how to explain, and feeling myself going redder by the second.

"Don't you remember?" asked Connor. "At one point, we were like this." And he squatted down right in front of me, his face about an inch from mine. I didn't have a choice—I had to focus on his eyes, those beautiful, blue-gray jewels. They were....

There was no other word for it. They were *twinkling* at me. I'd have known he was grinning even if the rest of his face was hidden. There was an openness there, an honesty I'd never seen in anyone. Everything for Connor was simple and easy. He didn't have a care in the world.

The opposite of me, I thought bitterly.

I opened my mouth to deliver a witty putdown. My mouth actually formed the first vowel, but I didn't seem to have any breath. I just stared at him for another second, and a wave of heat rushed through me. *I'm too angry,* I reasoned. *He's got me too angry to even speak.*

Connor straightened up. "Nothing? Really?" He clapped a hand to his chest. "She doesn't call, she doesn't send me flowers...."

Natasha, Clarissa and Jasmine all giggled. *The traitors.*

"I'll see you in class," Connor told me. Then he pointed at me theatrically. "Be careful! I might not be there to save you, next time!"

I hadn't thought I could blush any more than I already was, but I felt it happen. Half the bar was looking at us. Then Connor clapped an arm around one of his drinking buddies and they stumbled off across the room.

I could feel the other girls all looking at me, and took a long drink of my Pretty Woman to buy some time.

"I fell over," I said. "He caught me. It was sort of his fault anyway. That's it."

Jasmine glanced at Natasha. "Natasha fell off a stage, once, and *that* worked out."

"He's not—are you *kidding?*" I stared at her. "He's an idiot! He's drunk half the time, he's loud, he's arrogant...."

"He has those eyes," countered Natasha quietly.

"You're taken," Jasmine told her.

"And that voice. I love that accent," said Clarissa.

"You too," said Jasmine.

"He's about to flunk out! He doesn't even bother coming to class most of the time!" I told them.

Jasmine pretended to catch her breath. "Oh no! And I pick my boyfriends by their GPA!"

"He's completely squandered his opportunity! They gave him a scholarship and he's just wasted it on...on...girls and booze!"

Jasmine frowned. "For a guy you hardly know, you seem *very* knowledgeable about him."

I realized the others were all staring at me. *She's*

right. What do I care?

I swallowed. "No, I just—"

Jasmine snapped her fingers. "When we were at your place, you were in the shower for like three years. Were you thinking about him?"

"No!" I almost shouted. *How could she know? How could she possibly know?!*

Jasmine was beaming, delighted. "You were! I was sitting out there waiting for you—well, and making a sandwich—and you were in there flicking the bean—"

"No!"

"—thinking about Connor Locke!"

"No! Really!"

Jasmine collapsed into giggles. "Relax! I know you weren't." She shook her head. "You're so easy to wind up, sometimes."

Everyone laughed, and I let my breath out, smiling nervously. OK, fine. She hadn't guessed. Not that there was anything *to* guess. I mean, I'd been thinking about him in the shower, but not in *that* way.

"How's Neil?" I asked Clarissa, to throw some of the heat off me.

"Great." Only she said it too quickly, and in a not-great way. We all turned towards her. "No, seriously, it's fine. Better than fine. It's just—"

"He wants a threesome?" asked Jasmine.

"He—*WHAT?!*"

"He wants another woman to join you. Or—God, another man? Is it a biker?" Jasmine clutched Natasha's arm. "Is it Darrell?"

"No! Where did you get *threesome* from? No, nothing like that. He's just...Neil."

We waited.

Clarissa stared at her drink. "It's just...when it started, it just sort of...worked. I mean, I don't know why it worked, exactly, but it did. He had this...hold over me."

"And now he doesn't?" asked Natasha quietly.

"Oh, no, God, he *does*," said Clarissa. "That hasn't changed. He just has to say something in my ear and—" She reddened. "That works fine. But I keep wondering if that's all we have. I mean..."—she looked around at us—"...we're very different."

"Opposites attract," I said carefully.

"Yes, but do they *stick?*" Clarissa asked.

***

I'd said I'd only stay for one drink, but it was two before I persuaded Jasmine that I was serious about going. I wanted to put her in a cab back to her place—I figured I could quietly pay the cabbie in advance.

Jasmine, Dan and I left Clarissa and Natasha choosing drinks and braved the freezing wind outside. It was blasting straight down the long street that Flicker was on, numbing our exposed faces, so it was a relief when we turned into an alley. We planned to cut through to a busier street where we'd be more likely to find a cab. Dan was lagging some way behind Jasmine and me because he had his wallet out, trying to figure out if he had enough money left for his cab fare. There wasn't a lot of light in the alley, and he was using his iPhone to count the bills, the screen glow lighting up his face.

"You think they'll be okay?" asked Jasmine.

"Clarissa and Neil?"

"Mmm. It *has* always been about sex, with them."

I thought about it. A relationship based entirely on sex was about as far from my personal experience as it was possible to get. I glanced around while I thought—it was that sort of alley. "I don't know. I—Where's Dan?"

He wasn't behind us. He wasn't *anywhere*. Then I

saw a flicker of light—the glowing screen of his phone, reflecting off the brickwork in a side alley near where I'd last seen him.

Jasmine and I looked at each other, and then Jasmine ran towards the side alley. My eyes nearly bugged out of my head, and I grabbed for her hand but just missed it. I hesitated for a split second and then ran after her.

She stopped at the mouth of the side alley and I managed to grab her arm to stop her going any further. Dan was halfway down, backed up against a wall by a bigger guy who was holding something against his throat. It was only when it caught the light that I realized it was a knife.

"Shit," whispered Jasmine. We both hovered there, unsure of what to do. Scream? Try to help? Would that stop him stabbing Dan, or make him do it?

"Hey!" yelled Jasmine, her voice breaking as she said it. The guy didn't even look round. Dan handed over his phone and wallet and started to take off his watch.

I pulled my own phone out and dialed 911. My brain kept freezing and I had to think about each digit.

Dan almost dropped his watch as he handed it over. The guy grabbed his shirt and ran him towards the opposite wall, pushing him hard when he was halfway across. I winced as I saw Dan bounce off the bricks. It looked like he managed to slow himself a little by putting his arm out, but he still whacked his forehead and folded to the ground.

I screamed his name and ran into the side alley, only to realize the mugger was running straight towards me. I screwed my eyes shut as we passed, waiting to feel the knife slide between my ribs, or feel myself hurled into the brickwork—

But he ran straight past and was gone. I knelt

beside Dan. He had his eyes open but looked groggy, blood trickling from his forehead.

A voice from my phone asked what my emergency was and, in a small, scared voice, I told it.

***

About five minutes later, the police arrived. We had Dan sitting up against the wall—he'd thrown up, but otherwise seemed okay. Jasmine had called Clarissa and Natasha and they'd raced over from Flicker. We were all standing around offering words of support to make up for the fact that we were essentially useless.

Blue and red lights filled the alley and we heard car doors slamming. Two cops strode in: the first was in his fifties, with gray eyebrows fatter than my finger; the other looked no older than us—he could have been one of Fenbrook's actors, in a borrowed police uniform.

"Paramedics are right behind us," the young one said. "Who was here? Who saw it?" He stopped beside Clarissa and Natasha. "Were you here?"

"No," they both said in unison.

"I was here," said Jasmine.

The young cop looked at her and froze for a moment. In itself, that wasn't unusual—Jasmine had that effect on men. But this seemed like something more, like he was *entranced*. At last, he nodded. "Okay. I have a couple of questions, while it's still fresh in your mind."

I figured I should step forward and say that I was a witness too, but as I did I saw the look Jasmine was giving the officer. I recognized that look. And it dawned on me that the cop was quite well built, and good looking, if you went for the clean-cut look. *Oh!* She wanted to give him her statement...and probably her phone number.

As they talked, the paramedics arrived and started shining lights in Dan's eyes and asking him to follow fingers. I half-listened to what the cop was asking Jasmine.

"So you were walking together when it happened?"

"I was sort of leading the way. He was checking his wallet, to see if he had enough money. I think that's why he got jumped," Jasmine told him.

The cop looked at Dan. "And I'm right in thinking he's not your husband or boyfriend?"

I saw Jasmine smirk at that idea. "That's right."

"Okay. So the two of you were just about to, ah...."

Jasmine looked blank.

The cop tried again. "You were—you know—just about to...."

Jasmine frowned, bemused. I realized what was going on in the cop's head, but I was too late to stop him.

The cop sighed. "He was jumped as the two of you were about to complete your business?"

There was total silence for a second.

"*WHAT?!*" asked Jasmine, horrified.

The cop didn't flinch. "It's okay, miss—you're not my concern tonight. Some other night, I might have to run you in, but right now I'm just trying to establish what happened."

Jasmine's outrage made her voice go nearly ultrasonic. "*I AM NOT A HOOKER!* Why would you think—" I saw her look down at her ultra-tiny dress and the long fur coat. "I'm an *actress!*"

"Uh-huh," said the cop.

I finally found my voice. "Um, she actually *is* an actress," I said, stepping forward.

The young cop turned and looked at me—he really was *very* good-looking, I realized. He looked at Natasha and Clarissa. "And I suppose they're actresses, too?"

"Oh no," I told him. "They're ballerinas."

The cop ran his hand over his face, as if this was going to be a very long shift.

The paramedics finished with Dan and walked him past us. "He'll live," they told us. "The cut on his head looks worse than it is. Looks like there's no concussion."

We all took a long breath. *Everything was going to be okay.* I felt almost giggly with relief. Jasmine, meanwhile, looked like she was trying to melt the cop's brain with her glare. I stepped forward to intervene, before she killed him or he arrested her.

Then I saw that the paramedics were helping Dan into the ambulance. "I thought you said he was okay?" I asked.

The paramedic beamed. "He is. Don't worry, his head's fine. I just want someone to look at his arm."

"His arm?" I asked. My giggles evaporated. "What's wrong with his arm?"

CHAPTER 3

JASMINE AND I WENT WITH DAN in the ambulance. Natasha and Clarissa followed in a cab, but they needn't have hurried. An hour after we arrived, we were still sitting in plastic chairs in ER admissions, gradually sobering up under the harsh fluorescent lights while Jasmine told us about colorful fates she'd like to befall the cop.

We all told Dan it was going to be fine. The arm was probably just bruised, or it was a light sprain. But his right elbow swelled and stiffened, and he said he couldn't move it at all.

When the doctors eventually x-rayed it, they told us the detailed version of what we'd already guessed. When he'd slammed into the wall, Dan had put his arm out to stop himself—probably saving him from a concussion. But the impact had shattered his elbow, and broken his ulna.

"How long?" asked Dan, and the doctor couldn't understand why he'd gone so white.

The doctor shrugged. "Eight weeks in a cast. Full mobility: three months?"

Dan just blinked, his mouth open.

"You'll be alright," the doctor said, thinking we didn't understand. "It's only your arm."

I pulled Dan into a hug.

***

By morning, Dan was home and resting in bed, sporting a cast already covered in names and doodles. I promised to stop by with a care package later in the day, then went home to bed.

And found I couldn't sleep, the conversation I'd had with Dan going round and round in my head.

I'd been through the situation with him, and it wasn't quite as bad as it first appeared. He'd pretty much cleared his schedule for the next few months anyway to focus on the recital, so that was the only thing he'd miss. And his grades were high enough that, even though he'd miss the recital completely, he'd still graduate.

Once we'd been through that, though, we had to talk about me.

Since Dan now couldn't play the Brahms with me, I'd have to find something to play solo. Solo pieces weren't normally allowed in the recitals, since part of the aim was to teach you teamwork, but in this case I was sure they'd make an exception. All the work I'd spent on the Brahms so far was wasted. I'd have to find a piece I could play solo and practice it like crazy, hoping I could impress the New York Phil scout on my own.

There was one tiny silver lining. At least with only myself to worry about, I could practice day and night, however long it took. It was going to be a brutal few months, but maybe, if I found the right piece, I could still pull it off.

***

I'd emailed Professor Harman in the early hours to tell him I needed to see him urgently. On my way in to Fenbrook, I stopped off at a Starbucks and picked him up a latte. Not a bribe; a gift. I figured I could use all the help I could get.

I'd never been in his office before. In keeping with his position as the head of music, it was intimidatingly large and the desk was so shiny I felt like I shouldn't put coffee on it, so I stashed the drinks down by my feet instead.

Professor Harman was in his sixties, with a close-cropped white beard and little round glasses. He nodded soberly as I told him about the mugging, and took the time to check that everyone was okay.

Dan, he confirmed, would graduate just fine without his recital. His grades were strong across all his courses and the loss of the recital would only drop his degree one level.

Then the conversation turned to me.

"I know that the deadline for choosing pieces is tomorrow," I told him. "Obviously I'm going to need to change now I'm solo. I was wondering if I could have an extra day or two to decide on the new piece. I want to make sure—"

He was shaking his head.

"You can't let me have an extra day?" I asked.

"I can't let you play solo," he said.

"*What?* But—my partner's injured! That's not my fault!" It was so outrageous, so unexpected, that I didn't have time to be scared.

"Indeed it isn't. But recitals have to be performed

by a group of two or more. Managing your rehearsals, working as a team...that's all part of your training here. If you were allowed to play solo, it would give you an unfair advantage over the others."

I sat there open mouthed for a moment. The fear was starting to kick in now, serpents of panic coiling and twisting in my belly. "Okay...I'll find a duet and ask them to change to a trio," I said desperately. "We can pick a new piece and start rehearsing—" I saw him press his lips together. "What?"

"I can't let you disrupt an existing group. Even if they agreed, if the three of you were to get anything less than top marks, they could complain that they were treated unfairly by having to start over. You'd have to form a duo with someone who hasn't chosen their piece yet."

I went cold. "But we all picked our pieces weeks ago! The deadline's tomorrow!" I stared at him in disbelief. "There isn't anyone who hasn't chosen yet!"

He nodded sadly. "I do believe that's the case, yes."

I couldn't speak for a second, my tongue desert dry. "But...but I have to do the recital," I told him. "Professor Harman, I need to play for the panel—for the New York Phil scout." Then realization hit and my stomach flipped over. "I don't have the credit without my recital. I won't graduate!"

He took off his glasses. "I know. I checked before you came in here. Your performances have been excellent and your essays are fine. It's...unfortunate that you've neglected your presentations so completely."

I couldn't do them! I couldn't stand up in front of everyone and—That's not my fault either!

His words seemed to come from a great distance away. I was falling into such a deep state of panic that I barely heard him.

"You're an exceptional musician, Karen. I'm truly sorry there isn't another way."

I could feel nausea rising inside me; I had to get out of there. "Excuse me," I said as I sprang to my feet and ran for the door. I hit something heavy and warm with my ankle and realized I'd kicked the coffees over, but I couldn't stop.

I left his door banging behind me and ran for the bathroom, pushing past students arriving for class. Crashing into a stall, I fell to my knees and vomited into the toilet bowl.

On the rare occasions I'd been sick, I'd always felt better afterwards. This was different. This wasn't something inside me making me ill, something that could be got rid of. This was everything outside me squeezing inwards, crushing me until I couldn't think, couldn't breathe.

I'm not going to play for the New York Phil. I'm not going to play for anyone. I'm not going to graduate.

My dreams of being a musician were gone, in the space of a few minutes. My whole life had changed.

I sat back against the cold wall of the stall. I wasn't crying. I was too far gone for tears.

Screaming inside my skull was: *How am I going to tell my father?*

***

I stumbled out of the bathroom at some point—I don't really remember. People asked me if I was okay, but I couldn't speak and just sat down on the steps leading up to the next floor. Normally, I'd have been worried about inconveniencing people, but it didn't even occur to me that I was in the way.

People muttered and whispered around me. I was still on the music floor, so most of them were musicians. People I knew, people I'd trained with, but they'd never seen me like that and it was freaking them out.

Somebody fetched Natasha, and I remember her arriving in leotard and pointe shoes and walking me very carefully down the stairs to the main door, one step at a time. I could feel a crowd of musicians watching our retreating backs, waiting until we were out of earshot before they started guessing at what might have happened.

It's difficult to find a private place at Fenbrook— the stairs are like highways and the corridors are never empty. Natasha took me outside, into the freezing air. It wasn't snowing, but it felt like it might start at any moment.

Natasha was speaking, and I picked out the words "panic attack," but as with Professor Harman her words seemed to be coming from a long way away. I didn't feel like I was having a panic attack. I wasn't hyperventilating; I barely seemed to be breathing at all.

Her hands were on my shoulders and she kept telling me to look at her. I *was* looking at her, although she was sort of blurry. I kept thinking how cold she must be, in her leotard, and I wondered why she looked so scared.

And then I don't remember anything at all.

***

I woke to a triangle of faces, one of them with long red hair. I focused, and saw Natasha, Clarissa and Jasmine. I seemed to be lying on my back, looking up at them.

"Hello," I said.

"How do you feel?" asked Natasha. I could see the relief in her eyes, and immediately felt awful for whatever I'd done to scare her.

"Okay. I think." I tried to sit up, and they immediately pushed me back down. I was on some sort of sofa that didn't look like the furniture at Fenbrook. Where was I?

"Are you *you*?" Jasmine asked. "Are you back?"

"Back?"

"You went a bit catatonic for a while," said Clarissa. "You scared the hell out of us."

"Catatonic?"

"Maybe I should slap her," said Jasmine. Clarissa caught her hand.

"I'm not going to graduate," I said suddenly, because I realized they didn't know. I told them what had happened and watched their faces fall. All three of them took turns hugging me, but it didn't make it any better.

When they eventually let me sit up, I saw there were thick black curtains all around us, and I wasn't on a sofa but a chaise-longue. "Where *are* we?" I asked.

"Backstage in the main hall," Jasmine told me. "When you passed out on the steps, we thought we'd better bring you somewhere quiet." She nodded at the chaise-longue. "That's for *Julius Caesar*."

I could tell they all wanted to say something to make it okay, but there was nothing they could offer, no Plan B they could suggest. Flunking students weren't allowed to repeat a year at Fenbrook—competition for places was too fierce. I had no options, other than to start over at a different college—and my father would never allow that. After Boston and Fenbrook, he wouldn't want the humiliation of me trying—and possibly failing—for a third time.

It was all my fault, me and my stupid shyness, sitting there failing presentation after presentation. I'd known I had a problem, but I'd thought I could rely on my playing to make up the lost credit. Now the one weapon in my arsenal was being withheld from me.

I thanked them all, then stood up and pushed my way out through the curtains.

"Are you going to be okay?" asked Clarissa.

"I just need to be alone." I climbed down off the stage and walked through the eerie, empty hall, not looking back.

Outside in the hallway, Vincent—another cellist, who'd once had a thing with Natasha—was standing clutching my cello, having retrieved it for me from Professor Harman's office. He helped me strap it onto my back, and I could tell he wanted to speak...but couldn't find the words.

"What are you going to do?" he asked at last, as I pushed the doors to the street open.

I hesitated on the threshold. "I honestly have no idea," I told him, without turning around. And then I left Fenbrook, possibly for the last time.

CHAPTER 4

STANDING OUTSIDE IN THE STREET with the freezing wind whipping around me, I felt broken inside. Empty, as if something had been ripped violently out of me.

I considered going home, but the empty apartment felt like it didn't belong to me anymore. I'd lived there while I was attending Fenbrook, and that was over.

I wound up going to Harper's. I ordered a coffee and then sat there not drinking it, half-hearing the chatter around me. A mixture of students and civilians, and every one of them had things to do that afternoon: classes to go to, music to learn, boyfriends to see.

I had no life left. My entire existence for almost four years had been about music; it was only when that was taken away that I could see how little else I had. Even my friends were Fenbrook students. How long would we stay in touch when I was back in Boston, working whatever job I could find?

I had...*nothing.*

I pulled my phone out of my bag and it sat in my hand like a lead weight. I tapped the shortcut for my father and then sat staring at his name on the screen, trying to work up the courage to press the Call button.

A girl's voice behind me. "He hasn't even chosen yet. I keep telling him, and he's like,"—she did a fair imitation of an Irish accent—"Ah, I'm not gonna bother. I'm droppin' out anyway."

The words had to rattle around in my head a few times before I could be sure I'd heard correctly. Then I twisted around in my chair.

I recognized the girl from some of my classes. One of the non-classical musicians—a drummer—her hair dyed violently pink, a spiky-ended bar through her nose.

"Are you talking about Connor Locke?" I asked breathlessly.

For a second, she looked like she was going to tell me to mind my own business, but then her expression softened. "Yeah," she said.

"He hasn't chosen his recital piece yet?"

She shrugged. "No. Why would he? He's going to be kicked out any time."

Air filled my lungs. It felt like the first time I'd breathed since Professor Harman's office. I grabbed my cello and ran.

***

When I burst into Professor Harman's office, he was on the phone. I was panting, having run up the stairs lugging the cello.

"Connor...Locke...hasn't...chosen yet," I told him, trying to get my breath.

He blinked. "I'll call you back," he told the person

58

on the other end, and hung up. "Well, yes. I just checked the list—he's the only one who hasn't. We weren't really expecting him to. So?"

"I want to team up with him."

He blinked a few times. "You want to do a duet for cello and *electric guitar?!*"

I took a deep breath. "Yes."

"With *Connor Locke?*"

"Yes."

He shook his head slowly. "Karen, I can't really discuss another student with you, but you must know that Connor's on the verge of being kicked out. It's really just a question of whether he drops out or we give him a push. It's only a matter of time."

"But if I can keep him in?" I said desperately. "If I can keep him in until graduation and if we can do a great duet—I could still graduate...right?"

He took a deep breath and then sighed. I could tell he wanted to say *no*. But strict rules cut both ways.

"Yes," he told me. "In theory, if he doesn't flunk out, and if you score highly enough in the recital...yes, you'll graduate."

"I want to do it," I said.

"Karen, I honestly admire your spirit. I know you didn't take the news well, but...what makes you think you can even convince Connor to do it?"

"I have to try!"

He took a long look at me and then sighed. "I think you're wasting your time. But if you really want to do this, I need both of you in here at 9:00am tomorrow to give me your choice of music."

I nodded and ran.

***

I was halfway down the corridor before I slowed to a walk. My mind was buzzing with excitement. The tiny sliver of light I'd glimpsed in Harper's had widened to a crack. Maybe one big enough for me to squeeze through, if I could tease it open.

There was so much to do. I had to find Connor and get him alone. Sit him down and talk to him.

I slowed more. *Talk to him....* Talk to a guy who drove me crazy every time we met. Who was arrogant and loud and brash and only interested in women if he thought they'd drop their panties for him.

And it wasn't just a one-off conversation. If he agreed to do it, we'd be rehearsing together constantly for months.

If he agreed to do it. This was Connor I was talking about. Connor who showed up for classes when it suited him. Connor who hadn't intended to even submit a choice for the recital, much less rehearse for it.

I stopped in my tracks.

Was I seriously hitching my entire future to the least reliable guy at the academy? He was about to flunk out, and I needed him to be the best.

I leaned back against the wall and then slid down it to the floor.

It came down to a simple question: *Was I prepared to go through hell with Connor to get my life back?*

I knew instantly. It wasn't even a choice. If I gave up now and didn't at least try, I'd regret it for the rest of my life.

I got slowly to my feet and started going through the timetable, trying to remember which classes Connor was in so I could track him down.

An hour later, I was pacing nervously outside the lecture theater. According to the timetable, Connor was inside, in the same music theory class I would have been in had I not been racing to Harman's office when it started. Ironically, the first class I'd missed since I'd started at Fenbrook.

I started rehearsing what I'd say to him. Eager and happy? *"Hi Connor! Can we go somewhere and talk?"* No. Too light. Serious? *"This is something that affects both of us."* No. People who overheard would think I was pregnant. Straight to the point? *"I need you to team up with me for the recital. And rehearse really hard. Oh, and you have to graduate."* That would scare him off.

The doors banged open, almost hitting me in the face, and I stepped back and started searching the crowd for Connor, feeling my breathing getting faster and faster—

He wasn't there.

I recognized the fuchsia-haired girl from Harper's. "Hey! Do you know where Connor is?"

She frowned at me. "What's your interest in him?" She looked me up and down. "You don't look like his type. No offense."

"It's not—I just really need to talk to him."

She shrugged. "I'm pretty sure he's sleeping off a hangover."

I had a flashback to him singing in Flicker. Knowing him, that had been just the start of his night. *Great.*

"Any idea where I could find him? It's really important."

She considered. "He's playing The Final Curtain tonight. I guess you could catch him there, if it's *really* important."

***

61

"The Final Curtain?" asked Jasmine that evening. I'd called the girls together for a crisis meeting at my apartment.

"It's a bar," I said authoritatively. I only knew because I'd Googled it.

"You're going to a bar?" she asked doubtfully.

"*We're* going to a bar," I told her. "I'm not going in by myself."

"I thought you hated this guy?" said Natasha.

"I do! But if it means I graduate...." I looked around at the others. "I'm doing the right thing, aren't I? I mean, I have to take whatever chance I have?"

They all looked uneasy. "What?" I asked.

It looked like no one wanted to speak. Clarissa finally took the plunge. "You're right, it's just...you're very...."

I went cold inside. "Very *what?*"

"Exacting," said Natasha.

"Intense," said Clarissa.

"Occasionally a pain in the ass," said Jasmine, and everyone gasped in shock. "About *music,*" she said quickly.

"I think we just mean...the two of you are so different. It's difficult to imagine you and him working together."

It went very quiet.

"Hey, maybe it'll be good for you," said Jasmine brightly. "You can...you know. Learn from each other."

I nodded politely, but I had no idea what she was talking about. What on earth could I learn from Connor Locke?

***

Apart from Flicker, I didn't go to many bars. OK,

that's an exaggeration. I didn't go to *any* bars.

Now, standing in the bitterly chill air outside The Final Curtain and watching the gum-chewing guy on the door look us up and down, I was starting to feel a long way out of my comfort zone. *This is not what I do!*

Seeing me hesitate, Clarissa and Natasha pressed in on either side of me, and Jasmine skipped up to the doorman and gave him a winning smile. He gave us another cursory glance and then pushed the door wide. The sounds of wailing guitars smacked us in the face, together with a woman's haunting, soaring voice. We were bathed in golden light and the heat of dancing bodies.

I stepped inside.

***

It was bigger than I expected, but packed with so many people that the walls were sweating despite the cold outside. It was a mixture of college kids and blue collar workers, getting drunk on shots and beer and bouncing to the band playing on stage. I looked around in shock—there must have been a few hundred people there. I hadn't realized Connor was playing places that big.

There was enough of a mixture of fashion that Natasha, Clarissa and Jasmine just about blended in. I, in my jeans, boots and sweatshirt, looked decidedly underdressed. And hot. I shrugged off my thick, winter coat, debated, then took off my sweatshirt and hung the whole bundle over a bar stool. That left me in the strappy top I'd been wearing underneath, which showed more skin than I was used to.

"Anyone see the target?" asked Jasmine. She was working her way through the *24* boxed set, in between episodes of *CSI*. Her dream role was a part in a police drama.

I searched the crowd. "No," I said, worried. What if he didn't show up? I looked at my watch—I needed him on board and in Harman's office in less than twelve hours. Could he be in his dressing room? Did they even *have* dressing rooms, in a place like this?

"I'll do a sweep," Jasmine told us. "You three work the bar." And she was gone into the crowd, male heads turning to follow her.

Clarissa sighed and led us off to the bar to get beers. I made the mistake of standing between them and that left me feeling short and graceless. They had confidence and style and legs that went on forever, and I had...what, exactly? Music. And that was in danger of being ripped away from me.

At that moment, the band finished their last track and the room erupted into applause. As they launched into their Facebook, Twitter and buy-our-music plug, I suddenly saw him waiting by the side of the stage.

He was in the same tight jeans he wore at Fenbrook, but he'd stripped down to a black vest. A cherry red electric guitar was slung around his neck, its varnish gleaming.

The band cleared the stage and he stepped on. There was polite applause, and then that Belfast twang I was getting to know came through the PA. "Thank you, thank you. I'm Connor Locke. This is called *Ruth*."

And then, for the first time ever, I heard him play.

When I first learned to drive a car, I was incredibly nervous. I had to think about every movement, run through checklists in my head to make sure I was braking when I should, checking the mirrors when I should. Years later, the movements had become automatic, but they were still precise and controlled.

Turn head left. Look in mirror. Indicate. Pull out. My playing was the same—every movement had to be exactly right.

Connor's playing wasn't like that at all. It was...*lazy*. Not bad-lazy. Relaxed-lazy. Lazy like driving with one hand on the wheel and the other around a girl. *Effortless.*

Something stabbed through me, something totally unexpected. It took me a few seconds to realize that it was jealousy. *That's ridiculous! It's a completely different style of music, on a completely different instrument.*

And yet...did I ever look that relaxed and carefree while playing?

The music surprised me, too. I'd been expecting thrashy guitar solos, but this was slow and almost sad. As he got to the end of the intro, he leaned forward and started to sing.

I was right at the back of the crowd, near the bar. I took a step forward, to see around a tall guy.

Long way from home, plane ticket and a guitar
    Twenty dollars, four leaf clover and the courage of youth
    Met you rum-drunk and said I was a rock star
    You kissed me, made me coffee and said your name was Ruth.

Ruth. The tattoo on his arm said "Ruth." His voice was incredible, his Irish lilt turning the words into little silk-wrapped shots of hard silver that soared and curved and then hit you in the heart.

The music was all deep, rolling chords, smooth as butter, and then his hand suddenly whipped down the strings and the guitar wailed as he launched into the chorus. He had his eyes closed now, which meant I got to look at his face properly without worrying about him looking back at me.

His hair was messy, as usual, like he'd run a hand through it and declared it ready. It looked soft and glossy, like it'd feel amazing against the sensitive sides of your fingers if you stroked through it.

I hadn't noticed before how long his lashes were. They softened what would otherwise be a hard face, with his strong jaw and angular cheekbones. With his eyes closed—just for a second—he looked vulnerable.

I was bad for you, you were bad for me
Twisted love, needed my daily fix of you
Everyone said it but we couldn't see
Held your hand, you cried but you knew it was
true

I realized with a shock that I was at the front of the crowd. How had that happened? I'd only meant to move past one person, to get a better look! I'd just kept pushing through without being aware of it, as if drawn to—

That's stupid, I reasoned. *Of course I wasn't.*

And then Connor opened his eyes and saw me. I looked around in a panic, resisting the urge to run and hide. The top I was wearing suddenly felt flimsy and insubstantial. Every square millimeter of my exposed skin was alive and tingling. And then I met his gaze.

The first thing I saw was surprise. He actually blinked, as if not quite believing it was me. Then, as he continued to sing, he threw me a questioning look. There was none of the swagger and arrogance I'd seen at Fenbrook. This was simple and direct: *What do you want?* But there was a little of that Irish sparkle in his eyes, too. Did he like the fact I was there? No, that was crazy. More likely it amused him.

He held my gaze and I swallowed. I felt like I was inching out over thin ice with nothing but cold blackness below. I wanted to flee back to the safe world I'd always known.

But there was nothing to go back to. He was my only hope.

My head seemed to weigh about a thousand pounds, but I forced myself to inch my chin up and stare levelly back at him. I swore I saw him blink again, as if he wasn't ready for that.

And then a smile touched his lips, and he gave me just the tiniest hint of a nod, as if he approved.

The song ended, and there were cheers and applause and stamping feet. I forgot to clap, and he didn't seem to acknowledge the audience at all for a second, still staring into my eyes.

Then he looked away, and I did too, my face going hot for no reason whatsoever. He smiled and waved to the crowd, back to being the performer again—if he'd ever stopped. More likely, that momentary connection had been my imagination.

I looked up just in time to see him disappear through a doorway behind the stage. A bored-looking guy was sitting in a plastic chair, half-blocking the doorway and watching warily for interlopers. I hurried back to the bar.

"I have to get backstage," I told Natasha.

"Like a groupie?" asked Jasmine. "I can see why. He's even better when he sings."

"I don't *like* him. I just need to get backstage," I told her.

"Like a groupie."

"*Not* like a groupie." I sighed. "Okay, okay, how do

groupies get backstage?"

Jasmine grinned. "Well, traditionally they—"

Clarissa slapped a hand over her mouth. "This is *Karen.*"

"What?" I asked, bemused.

Natasha took me by the hand and pulled me away from the others. "Come on. We'll figure something out." We started wending our way through the crowd towards the stage and then around it to the door.

She headed straight for the doorway, as if she hadn't even noticed the guy in the chair. For a moment, I thought we were going to make it. Then the guy put his arm across to stop her. "Performers only," he told her.

Natasha looked down at him as if he was mad. "I am a performer," she told him. "We're the dancers."

The man shook his head. "It's all bands tonight. No dancers."

Natasha smiled down at him. "We're on at the end. It's a last minute thing." And then, without any apparent effort, she lifted one elegant leg and planted her foot on the wall behind his head, as if she was standing at the barre. Her skirt fell away from her thighs, as if by accident, and I saw the guy's eyes flick to the bare flesh before he could stop himself. "We just need to get limbered up," she told him. "Don't we?"

I realized that was meant for me. "Yes," I managed. "We have to stretch." And I did my loose interpretation of a calf stretch, almost falling over in the process.

The guy in the chair had probably been guarding the door, or ones like it, for a decade. He knew all the tricks and had heard all the lies.

But at that moment, a ballerina's thigh was six inches from his cheek.

"Okay," he told us, nodding. "The room at the

end's free." And he dropped his arm to let us past.

"How did you do that?" I asked in awe when we were out of earshot.

Natasha looked at me pityingly. "We really do need to get you out more, don't we?" She hugged me, then pointed me down the corridor. "Good luck. I'll see you back in the bar." And before I could stop her, she was gone.

Part of me wished she'd stayed. But maybe it was better I meet Connor alone—it was going to be agonizing enough without an audience.

There were only three rooms off the corridor. One was a restroom. One was dark and empty. The last door was firmly closed. I raised my hand to knock, and then stopped.

What on earth was I going to say?

"I think we can help each other," I said out loud, trying it out. Except...could I really help him? He was going to be doing me a big favor, but what could I offer in return?

Maybe I could appeal to his ego. "I thought you were amazing out there," I tried. And then wanted to stab myself, because it sounded so fake. The annoying thing was, he really *had* been good. I just didn't know how to say it.

"Remember how you caught me, when I fell?" I tried. "Well, I kind of need you to—"

"I like the second one," said Connor.

I whipped around. He'd been standing behind me, having come in the same way I had.

"But you're—" I pointed at the closed door.

"I went out there to look for you." He had that look again, curious and amused. "So...what do you need my help with?"

***

He took me into the dressing room, which was fine. Then he closed the door, which wasn't fine at all. As soon as the door closed, everything felt different. Alone with him suddenly became *alone with him*.

My entire life felt like it was teetering on the brink: my future, because without his help I didn't have one; my past, because without his help it had all been a waste.

He pointed me to a stool, its peeling seat patched with tape. As soon as I sat down, he moved over to me and I tensed as he drew close....

Very close, his body inches from mine as he leaned over me. Our faces were almost touching. *Oh my God! Is he going to—*

The rubbery gasp of a refrigerator door opening behind me, and the clink of bottles. And then he was leaning back and offering me a beer.

You idiot, I told myself angrily. I took the bottle without thinking, and sat there shredding the label.

"So," he said, opening his beer. "Here you are in my dressing room." Again, that Irish lilt making everything sound innocent, yet filthy.

There was no delaying it any longer. I took a deep breath. "The recital...you haven't chosen your piece yet."

He shrugged. "Didn't seem much point."

"I need you to do it. With me."

He paused, genuinely thrown by that. "Like a duet?"

"Yes. A duet."

"You know I play *guitar*? Electric guitar. Not violin or piano or...you know. Anything that goes with a cello."

I was surprised, for a second, that he even knew

what instrument I played. Weirdly, a part of me felt flattered. Then I realized that a cello was pretty hard to miss, and I'd been carrying it on my back my whole time at Fenbrook. Of course he'd know that.

"It's sort of an emergency," I said. And I told him about Dan.

When I'd finished, he got up. "But why not just skip it? You're Miss Uber-Geek—no offence. You can't need the grades." And then he peeled off the vest he'd been wearing.

His narrow waist flowed up into a powerful back layered with muscle and broad shoulders that reminded me of an athlete—maybe a boxer. He didn't look like the pretty-boy male model types Jasmine posted on her Facebook page. He looked somehow raw and real, his muscles for use, not show. He was lean rather than huge, everything tight and defined, his stomach hard with muscle.

"It *is* my dressing room," he told me.

I realized my mouth was open. Had I gasped? I had a nasty feeling I had. I tried to focus. "I had some issues with my presentations," I told him. "I need a good recital, or I won't graduate." I stared at his arms. There was another tattoo above the Ruth one, a tangled clump of barbed wire, and I wondered what it meant.

He looked around for something. Hopefully a t-shirt. I was trying to keep my eyes off his upper half, but that left me starting at his crotch. "But the recital's not for months," he said as he searched. "And I'd have to be here to do it...."

He finally found his t-shirt and lifted it, though he didn't put it on. He was waiting for my answer.

I nodded slowly. "You'd have to stay in Fenbrook. And graduate."

He laughed out loud. Not a cruel laugh. A laugh of

disbelief. He pulled on the t-shirt—a band name I didn't recognize stretched across the broad curve of his pecs.

"I could help you," I said desperately. "I could help you get your grades up."

"What makes you think I *want* to stay?"

I just looked at him dumbly. My whole life had been so focused on doing well that the idea of just casually allowing yourself to fail seemed...insane.

"You've been here over three years," I said. "Surely you don't want to waste it?"

He shrugged. "I've had three years living in New York, with enough money to pay my rent and put food in my mouth. I play my guitar and that makes me a little more. That wasn't a waste. Now, working my arse off until I graduate, only to fail anyway—*that* would be a waste."

I nodded slowly. Suddenly, all his partying made sense. I'd seen it as him throwing his degree away, but it wasn't that at all. He'd never had any intention of graduating. His time here *was* the prize, and he'd made the most of it.

I could feel the panic start to knot and twist my insides. He was my only chance!

"If you don't do this," I said in a small voice, "I won't graduate."

Now he'd say "Yes." I was sure of it. However many hearts he'd broken, however many classes he'd missed, he was still human. He wouldn't just let me fall.

But he sighed and looked away. When he looked back at me, I could see real pain in his eyes, as if he wanted the answer to be different. "I'm sorry," he said at last.

I couldn't breathe. This was the one thing I'd never imagined. I'd thought that he might laugh. I'd even considered that he might want money. But never that he might just flat-out refuse. "There must be something I can say," I told him, hearing the panic rising in my voice. "There has to be something I can say that'll—You have to!"

He closed his eyes for a second, as if considering.

And then he pulled the door open.

When I got up off the stool, my legs felt like they weren't strong enough to take me. I walked slowly to the door and, just as I left, put the beer he'd given me down on the table.

"You can keep the beer," he said, sadness in his voice.

"I don't want your *stupid* beer!" I said viciously, tears filling my eyes. And then I was blundering down the corridor, feeling the wetness rolling down my cheeks.

***

I found a door that led out to the street and pushed through it. Natasha and the others were still back in the bar, but I could always call them. I needed to be alone.

Outside, the clouds had finally decided to give up their snow and thick white flakes were blanketing everything. Snow can make anything look beautiful, even an alley filled with overflowing dumpsters.

That was the moment, I thought. That was the moment my entire life to date ended, and some new one began. One spent in Boston. One without music.

Professor Harman had been right—it had been a stupid plan all along. All I'd done was prolong the inevitable for a few hours. I wasn't even angry with Connor, really; I was angry with myself, for believing in miracles.

I stumbled on, the snow crunching underfoot. I

was only wearing the little strappy top and jeans and I knew, in an abstract way, that it was bitterly cold, but somehow it didn't seem to matter. There was a burning pain inside that pushed the cold back, leaking out through my tears to scald my face. The life I'd wasted, ever since I was a kid. All the things I'd given up to practice, practice, practice. All for nothing.

I came to a set of iron railings, and realized I was looking out over water. The bar backed almost onto the river, with just the alley separating them, and the water shone like black glass, reflecting the colored lights of the bars and stores. Further out, away from the glare, it was just a black, gaping maw.

I leaned against the railings and cried, hot wracking sobs that left me breathless. Cried until there were no tears left, but I didn't feel better. I felt like I'd been broken open, my stupidity exposed for everyone to see, and I had no idea what to do next.

"Alright." It came from right beside me and when I jerked around, I saw Connor was standing next to me at the railing.

Numb shock. The tiniest sliver of hope, but I couldn't allow myself to even acknowledge it without being sure. My voice was little more than a croak. "What?"

"Alright." And this time I knew he was serious. I could hear in his voice how deep he'd had to dig, how he was going against every instinct he had.

I wiped my hand across my eyes. I didn't want him to see me crying, even though I knew it was too late. "Why?" I asked.

He gave me a look that made me catch my breath. He looked like he was screaming inside, as if he wanted to do something, but had to hold back.

"It's the right thing to do," he said at last. It didn't feel like the truth, but then why *was* he doing it?

Maybe he felt sorry for me.

Helena Newbury

CHAPTER 5

8.45am.

I was standing outside Professor Harman's office. I'd nearly stopped at Starbucks for coffee, but I'd worried that it might remind him of me knocking the last ones over his carpet. Also, the last thing I needed was more coffee.

I was wired. After I'd said goodbye to Connor, I'd rushed back into the bar and found the others. They were all delighted for me, if a little cautious about the idea of us working together.

"Just remember he's not a musician," Jasmine had said.

"Of course he's a musician! He takes most of the same classes I do!" I'd told her.

"Yeah, he's a musician, but he's not a *Musician* with a capital 'M'. Musicians are sort of...."

"Sort of like you," Natasha said helpfully.

"And he's not," said Jasmine. "He's more like—"

"A dancer?!" I asked, incredulously.

"No, not a dancer. Or an actor. A civilian. A

normal person. Just...bear that in mind."

I hadn't understood, at the time. Now, I was beginning to.

I'd said that we should meet there at 8.45 to be sure of being there at 9:00. And if you agree to meet someone at 8.45, you get there at 8.30, right? Just to be sure.

I'd been there since 8.20. My watch ticked over to 8.46. *Where was he?!*

That morning, I'd printed out a calendar that covered the ten weeks until the recital. I'd blocked out my classes in pink, and the ones we had together in purple. His classes would be blue, as soon as he gave me his timetable. Then we could start blocking out rehearsal time in green.

8.47!

Maybe he was waiting in the wrong place? I should have got his cell phone number. But by the time I'd said goodbye I'd been emotionally exhausted, barely capable of thought.

8.48. I started to pace. What if he'd been in an accident? He could be hurt. *Dying.* And it would be my fault for getting him here hours before he'd normally waltz in. *I couldn't stop, officer. I guess the poor schmuck just wasn't used to the intersection being so busy.*

At 8.55, I ran to the stairwell to see if he was climbing up. Nothing.

Where are you, Connor?

8.59. What if he'd forgotten?!

9.00. *What if he's changed his mind?!*

Footsteps, and I offered up a prayer to whoever would listen to please, please make them be Connor's battered black boots.

The feet rounded the corner, and they were brown

loafers. I looked up.

"Karen," Professor Harman said, slightly wearily. "I see you, but not Mr. Locke. Can I take it you were unsuccessful?"

"No! He's going to do it! It's all agreed, he's just— He's running late! Just give him a few more minutes."

He took off his glasses and rubbed his eyes. "If this is indicative of how you two will work together, I really think it shows that this isn't a good idea."

"Professor Harman, please!"

He shook his head. "I'm sorry, Karen. I gave you a simple deadline and your partner has shown he's incapable of meeting even that. I was wrong to even entertain the idea."

God, no! Not like this! Not just for the sake of a few minutes! "Professor!"

He opened the door to his office. "Sorry, Karen."

We both stopped.

Connor, his feet up on Professor Harman's desk, woke up and yawned. He checked his watch.

"You're late," he told us.

***

Luckily, Professor Harman was too shocked to erupt into full anger and, once Connor had been turfed out of his chair, he settled for irritation. He took out a fountain pen and wrote our names in a book (that's the music department for you—in another twenty years, they'll move to typewriters) and that was it. We were scheduled for the recital.

There was only one problem.

"What are you going to play?" Harman asked.

I'd been giving this some thought. There was absolutely nothing written for cello and electric guitar—

I'd looked—so it would have to be....

"Original composition," I told him.

I could feel Connor's eyes on me. I hadn't shared that little gem with him.

"So, in addition to all the rehearsals, you're going to compose the music as well?" Harman asked.

"Correct," I told him, with no idea how we were going to do it.

He sighed, but wrote it in the book. I could feel the tension in my stomach unwind a single notch. We were in.

Now all we had to do was pull it off.

***

Later that morning, we had our first rehearsal. I knew that, since we hadn't even started composing yet, we couldn't really *rehearse*. I just figured we should get together and play, and exchange ideas. Mostly, I just wanted to get a feel for what it was going to be like to work together.

He let me go into the practice room first, which was surprisingly polite and gentlemanly of him. But it meant that when he squeezed in, I didn't have anywhere to go. And then, when he had to come even further into the room so he could get the door closed behind him, he was pushed right up against me, just like when he'd caught me on the steps what seemed like weeks ago.

We stared at each other, my head level with his chest, my face upturned to him. I was close enough to feel his body heat, and it seemed to radiate from him like a furnace. "Sorry," I said, even though it wasn't my fault.

He closed the door and finally stepped back. Then I had to get my cello out of its case. Backing up with it in my arms, I felt my ass brush against his groin, my hair stroke his stubbled chin. "Sorry," I said again.

And then the strangest sensation, like my hair had lifted just fractionally, and then fallen again. Like something had sucked a few strands of it upwards. *Did he just smell my hair?*

No, don't be stupid. Or if he did, he meant it as a joke. He's playing with you. Just ignore it. I turned and promptly tripped over the cable he'd stretched across the room to power his amp. I caught myself, but his hands were already on my waist, so big they felt like they could almost encircle it.

"I'm fine, thank you," I said, and I said it so quickly it sounded like I was snapping at him. "I mean: thank you. Sorry." I was blushing and trembling like an idiot. What was wrong with me? *I'm just nervous.*

We finally sat down, no more than three feet separating us. He cranked his amp down to almost its lowest setting, so as not to drown me out.

"So," he asked. "How are we going to do this?"

I took a deep breath. "We'll divide the recital into five sections—two minutes per section, so ten minutes total. For each section, one of us will do the melody, the other will do the harmony. I'll lead three, you lead two."

He was grinning. "How about *I* lead three and *you* lead two?"

We'd have to compose the parts we led and then give them to the other person so that they could learn the harmonies. The more I let him lead, the more he had to compose and the more reliant I was on him. "Just trying to save you work," I told him. "I hate to remind you, but we have to get your grades up, too. Let me take more of the composition."

His smile tightened. "I want to do more of the composition."

Because you think you're better? He really was

arrogant...but I couldn't afford to make him angry. "You know what? How about we just make it six sections. Three each. How's that?" *Does that satisfy your ego?*

He smiled sweetly. "Perfect."

"I'm serious about the grades, though. We're going to need to look at how we can—"

"Yeah, yeah. Let's play."

And he was off and strumming and I fell silent. Partially it was the shock of how little importance he seemed to attach to his grades; mostly, it was what was coming out of the amp.

When he'd played in the bar he'd been singing, too. His playing had been great, but it had been just an accompaniment, most of his mind on the words. Now, with nothing to distract him, he could really let loose. It was like a tapestry woven from rich, sweet notes and shot through with threads of crisp magic. I assumed he was playing from memory, because surely no one could be that confident on the fly.

I picked up my bow and tried to follow. At first, it was like trying to coax a huge battleship around a nimble, darting speedboat, and I broke off again and again, my nerves getting worse. But then I saw an opportunity and went for it, and once my harmony was there it added depth to his flighty melody, giving it a whole new feel.

This could work, I thought. *This could actually sound pretty good.*

And then it came apart, him shifting before I was ready and me screeching with my bow. "Sorry," I said instinctively.

"You say that a lot," he told me. "You're one of those people who spend their life apologizing."

"Sor—" I caught myself.

"You shouldn't be sorry. You have nothing to be

sorry for." He was looking at me very intently, and I noticed his eyes again. It was dim in the practice room, the aging bare bulb painting the walls with shadows rather than actually lighting anything up. Those blue-gray chips of ice seemed to almost glow, they were so pale and clear. A little part of me was beginning to see what Jasmine had seen, what the girls who giggled and swooned for him saw.

I looked at his tattoo, and wondered if Ruth had been one of those girls, and what had happened that he'd had to leave her behind. "Is she in Ireland?" I wondered.

Then I realized I'd said it out loud.

He looked down at his arm. "Yes," he said.

"It's none of my business—"

"And yes, it's her in the song. We broke up a few months ago. Before the song; after the tattoo."

I nodded, and didn't know where to look.

"Can I ask you something?" he asked.

"Of course!" Like I had any interesting stories about ex-boyfriends and names tattooed on my body.

"Why's the New York Phil such a big deal?"

I opened my mouth, about to say a lot of things. I had plenty of responses, practiced since I was a kid, about how they were one of the most renowned in the world, about how it would take my career to places otherwise out of reach, about how—

"It's all I've ever wanted," I told him, the words surprising me as much as him.

He was silent for a moment. "*All?*" he said at last.

I nodded. "All."

"Well, we'd better get this right, then," he said. And he grinned, and something inside me that I hadn't realized had been tensed unwound. It was as if his smile made everything okay, reassured me in ways that words never could.

I smiled back, and then thought that I probably looked like an idiot so wiped it quickly off my face. What was going on? Where was the brash, arrogant Connor I'd known—and avoided—for three years?

To cover myself, I pulled out the calendar I'd made and unfolded it. I saw him blink in surprise.

"My lessons are pink. Yours will be blue—obviously."

"Obviously," he said, straight-faced.

"Ones we have together are purple, because—"

"It's pink and blue mixed. I'm not *that* stupid."

I looked across at him, unsure if he was joking. "I didn't mean—"

"Go on."

"Rehearsals are green. And we should mark out some study time for me to help you. Maybe in red."

He went quiet for a second. Then: "Can we keep red for when we fuck?"

I actually jerked as if stung and then stared at him, thinking I'd misheard. "*What?*"

The arrogant Connor I knew was back. He sprawled back in his chair, guitar slung casually down by his side. "Well, it's pretty much inevitable, isn't it?"

I took out a blue pencil and thrust it at him, part of me wanting to bury it in his chest. "Mark out your lessons."

He stared at me and then took it. "The ones I have, or the ones I actually show up for?"

I closed my eyes. "You need to show up for all of them! If they kick you out, you can't do the recital. If you flunk, I flunk!"

He stared at me for a second longer, and then started to fill in squares. "We're like two escaped convicts. Like in the movies, where they were chained together."

Our fates are one, I thought with a groan. Just as I'd been warming to him—only a little, of course—he'd reverted to his true personality. And now I couldn't simply walk away—I was trapped working with him.

I picked up my bow and started work on the rough foundations of the first of my sections. As I played and he filled in squares on the calendar, I swore I felt his eyes on me and let my hair hang down to hide the flush in my cheeks. *He's probably winding up for another joke about sleeping with me,* I thought. But it never came.

***

Two hours of practice went by surprisingly quickly. By the end of it I had some rough ideas and needed to sit down with manuscript paper and a pencil. The next stage would take some time, so we agreed to meet in a week, when I'd composed my first section and he'd composed his.

I'd said I'd do lunch with Jasmine, and she was waiting outside when I came out of the practice room. I shooed her away before Connor came out behind me. The last thing I wanted was for Jasmine to get involved with him—things were complicated enough already.

I couldn't stop her casting a glance back into the room at him, though, as he wound up the cable for his amp. *"Cute,"* she whispered in my ear.

I towed her off down the stairs.

When we were out of earshot, she asked, "So, how *was* Mr. Irish Eyes?"

I shook my head. "Arrogant. An idiot. Well, most of the time."

"Most of the time?"

"All of the time. He fooled me into thinking he might be...you know, *normal* for a minute, but as soon as

I talked about classes he went straight back to jerk."

"I have something that'll cheer you up." I realized Jasmine was even bouncier than usual.

"What?" I asked cautiously, hoping that she hadn't set me up with someone again.

"Darrell and Natasha are throwing a party this weekend. And you can't complain because it's not a weed and beer party, it's *your* sort of party. Champagne and canapés."

"That's not my sort of party, that's Clarissa's sort of party." I wondered if I even *had* a party type.

"Don't quibble. Saturday night. I'll borrow a dress for you from Clarissa." She looked down at her chest. "She's more...your size. And we'll all come round to your apartment in the afternoon to help you." She gasped in sudden delight. "We can give you a makeover!"

"I don't need a—"

"Think of it as my way of paying you back for the money."

That meant I couldn't say "No," and she knew it.

"Fine," I told her. "Anything else?"

"Ask Connor."

I stopped dead by the main doors. "*What?* We're not—"

"Not as a date! God, imagine that. No, Darrell's inviting some of the high society types, and apparently about eighty percent of them are female. It used to be balanced out by the NuclearKillDeathSquad but he's cut the cord with them now. Natasha's worried we'll be short on men." NuclearKillDeathSquad was Jasmine's shorthand for the defense industry executives who used to be Darrell's whole life.

"Why does she want *Connor?* I thought those society women were all twigs in Prada. Are you sure they're going to mix well with—"

"With a super-hot, stubbly, penniless Irish guitarist?" Jasmine sighed. "Sometimes I wonder if you're the same species. Have you never heard of a *bit of rough?*"

I tried to imagine Connor in a room full of women who spent more on clothes than we did on rent. I wasn't actually sure who'd be the hunter and who the hunted. He'd no doubt enjoy it, though, and I did need to keep him sweet....

I hesitated. Something inside me didn't want to be pushing him into a room full of other women.

Stupid. What do I care who he sleeps with?

"Fine. I'll call him." I opened the door and shivered as icy air blasted me. "You go ahead. I have to make a phone call."

Jasmine danced happily off down the street towards Harper's. I pulled out my phone and stared at my father's name in the contacts list. I'd been putting off phoning him since the day before, when I'd almost blown everything by telling him about Dan and the recital. What would have happened, if I hadn't heard the girl talking in Harper's—or hadn't heard her in time? My father would be helping me pack to go back to Boston. My future had been saved by pure chance...and it was still hanging by a thread.

I pressed "Call" and tried to control my breathing.

"Are you okay?" my father asked immediately.

"Fine. I'm sorry I didn't call. There was a last minute hitch with my recital, but it's all fixed now."

"What sort of hitch?"

"Dan broke his arm. But he's fine."

"How did he break his arm? He wasn't drinking, was he?"

My father had a thing about alcohol. And parties. And men.

"He was mugged a few nights ago." I conveniently left out the cocktails at Flicker.

"Shouldn't have been out on the streets at night. You weren't with him, were you?"

My throat closed up. "No. Of course not." Why did everything have to be an accusation? Why did everything always have to be someone's fault? This was why I knew I couldn't fail. The very first words out of his mouth would be "What did you do wrong?"

"Good. Who are you partnering with?"

"His name's Connor. Very talented." That much, at least, was true.

"Another violinist?"

I caught my breath. I didn't want to lie, but if I said, "No, actually he plays the electric guitar in bars and he's probably going to flunk out before the recital," my father would be in New York that afternoon.

"Mm-hmm," I said. If I didn't actually say the word "Yes," it seemed less like lying. *A guitar's kind of like a violin,* I thought desperately.

"Okay. Keep me posted." His voice softened a little. "Are you okay? No...funny episodes?"

By *funny episodes* he meant *freaking out and finding yourself on a rooftop.* He'd never understood my fear of public speaking—I'd tried to explain the terror I felt and he'd just looked at me as if I was mad. In his mind, what happened in Boston had been down to me not managing my time well and not being ready for my presentation. I knew that in a moment, he'd remind me to be prepared and manage things, as if by writing the perfect paper I'd magically be able to present it. This was why I always wrote the assignments, even though I knew I wouldn't be able to stand up in front of everyone and deliver them. It felt like I was disappointing him a little less if I did that.

"No," I told him. "I'm fine."

"Well, you know...just be prepared. Manage things."

I felt like weeping. "I will. Love you."

"Love you too, sweetheart."

CHAPTER 6

SATURDAY MORNING. I'd been putting off calling Connor, partially because I was nervous about calling and partially because I figured that if I left it late enough, he'd make other plans. It was the day of the party—he'd be busy by now, surely?

"Karen," he said when he answered, and it threw me for a second because it sounded good, hearing him say it. *He has an Irish accent, you idiot. Anything sounds good.*

No need to be nervous—I wasn't asking him out on a date. It was just a party. "You're busy tonight, I presume?"

I heard him stretch and fabric move. Then a creak.

"Are you in *bed?!*" I asked, horrified.

"Yeah. So? You sound horrified."

I felt myself flush. "No, not at all. It's your life. Just...surprised."

"What time is it?"

"Eleven."

He yawned. "I should probably get up. Six hours is enough."

I winced. Another creak, and then I heard him walking around. "So...am I busy tonight? No. Completely free. Hold on."

Then I heard, very clearly, the sound of a stream of liquid.

"*Oh my God!* Are you taking a leak, while you're on the phone to me?!"

"I'm running water into the sink, so I can clean a mug." The sound stopped. "You think I'm all class, don't you?" He sounded a little hurt.

"No! Yes! Sorry." I was pacing around my apartment now. "Look, do you want to come to a party tonight?"

I heard the rattle of a cereal carton. "Sure."

"It's not a date," I said suddenly. And then froze. *Why did I say that?!*

"I know," Connor said patiently. "I didn't think it was." He paused. "Unless it is? *Is* it a date?"

I knew he was playing with me now. "No!"

"Are you asking me out on a date, Karen Montfort?"

"*No!*" Why did he have to be so infuriating?

He chuckled, and I gave him the address through gritted teeth.

***

That afternoon, I fought valiantly...but I was surrounded. Surrounded by giggling, over-helpful friends.

I was sitting on a stool in the center of my lounge. Natasha was behind me, cooking my hair inch by inch with ceramic tongs so powerful I knew my hair would crumble to ash if she left them in one place. Jasmine was in front of me, doing my makeup. Clarissa was sitting next to me, cradling my hand as she painted my nails.

I almost would have felt glamorous except that firstly, glamour isn't my thing and secondly, I was in my pink fluffy bunny rabbit dressing gown.

I knew there was something going on. They'd encouraged me to get dressed up and go out before, of course—it's the bane of all single women with attached friends (or "friends who have no problem getting dates" in the case of Jasmine). But this went way beyond anything they'd done before. I would have much rather been left to practice, but saying "No" wasn't my strong suit.

"Did you hear from Connor?" Natasha wanted to know. "I'm worried there'll be too many women."

I grimaced. "Don't worry. He's coming, and he's a walking testosterone factory. Give him five minutes and he'll have one of those society girls in a broom cupboard."

I saw a look pass between Clarissa and Natasha. "What?"

"Nothing," Clarissa told me in a sing-song voice. "Don't move your hand. Let it dry." She wheeled her stool around to my other hand.

Natasha leaned down to my ear. "Last time we had a party at our place, there was some use of the broom cupboard."

I saw Clarissa flush. "You know you called it *our place?*" she asked, to cover herself. "I don't know why you keep renting with me. You could just move into the mansion and have a whole wing to keep your shoes in."

Natasha went quiet. "Not ready yet," she said after a moment. "What about you and Neil?"

"Neil always comes to our apartment, and I'm not

ready to have him move in." She paused. "I still haven't been to his place yet."

There was utter silence.

"You haven't been to his place yet?!" Jasmine almost screeched. "It's been months!"

"That does seem a little...unusual," I offered quietly. "Do you know where he lives, at least?"

"Of course I do!" Clarissa was gripping my hand a little tighter than was really necessary. "It's...in...."

We all waited.

"Boston," she said with a shrug.

"Boston?!" Natasha gaped at her. "The best you can do is the city?!"

"You know Neil—he's a free spirit. When he's at MIT, he's at his place in Boston. When he's in New York, it's our place, or sometimes he crashes with the bikers at the clubhouse. He doesn't attach much importance to it. He says 'A bed's a bed, y'know?'"

"But does he know that *you* think it's important?" I asked. "That you'd like to see where he lives?"

Clarissa went quiet, and then we all went quiet.

"Done!" yelled Natasha, breaking the tension. Jasmine scrabbled to finish my face. "Purse your lips," she told me.

I pursed.

"What's *that?*" she asked, horrified. "You look like Kermit the Frog. Pucker up, like you're going to kiss someone."

I tried to imagine kissing someone—not easy, with no one there and your friends around you. I closed my eyes and imagined Sven, my fantasy masseur. But I'd always focused on his body—I had no idea what his face looked like.

"Purse, damn you!" said Jasmine.

Unbidden, Connor's face swam into my mind and

I felt my mouth change. I assumed my jaw was hanging open at the shock of it.

"Perfect," announced Jasmine, and I felt her go to work with the lipstick.

I tried to push Connor out of my mind, but he refused to move. *It's just because you've been so focused on him,* I told myself. *It doesn't mean anything.*

"Done!" said Jasmine, and stepped back. Relieved, I opened my eyes. Clarissa was blowing frantically on my nails to dry them.

"Can I have a mirror now?" I asked.

"One more thing. Get the dress!" Jasmine was barely restraining herself from clapping her hands together and jumping up and down.

Clarissa went to fetch it, and Jasmine demanded that I close my eyes.

"Oh, come on," I said weakly, but closed them. They stood me up and hands removed my dressing gown. Then they were stepping my feet into the thing and wriggling it up my hips. I was bundled through to my bedroom.

"There," said Jasmine. "Open them."

I opened my eyes.

People sometimes say *I didn't recognize myself,* but it's usually an exaggeration. This wasn't.

I'd never seen myself with perfectly straight hair before. Without all the curls and frizz I looked somehow *sleeker* and more sophisticated. More feminine, in a way. My face was actually on show, instead of being hidden behind a thick curtain.

I had mixed feelings about that. I liked that curtain.

Suddenly, I had cheekbones, a gentle brush of color giving me the elegance I'd never had. Jasmine had worked subtle magic with my eyes to make them look huge. And my lips, normally pressed thin with worry, were plumped up and shining. I don't know if they were *kissable* but they at least looked like lips someone might contemplate kissing.

I was bare all the way down to below my shoulders, the dress having no visible means of support. It was square across the neckline and gave me a hint of cleavage. Glossy fabric the color of fine wine hugged me down to my thighs and managed to make even my modest legs look long.

"It's gorgeous," I said weakly. "Thank you. All of you."

"Wait till you get the heels on," Jasmine told me.

I had a feeling she didn't mean my usual ones. "Oh, no...." I said weakly.

But she was back in minutes with the Heels of Death from my wardrobe. They were stilettos, and I'd worn them only once after being talked into buying them by Jasmine. On that occasion I'd toppled sideways, not six feet from the door of my building, and very nearly gone under a bus—hence the name.

"It's easy," said Jasmine. "They're only four inches. They're basically flats." She showed me the five-inchers she'd be wearing herself.

I would have protested, but Natasha was already strapping one on while Clarissa did the other. They had me walk—well, totter—up and down the lounge.

"Keep your eyes on a point at the end of the room," Clarissa said. "Imagine you're on a catwalk."

"Plant your feet with more confidence," Natasha told me.

"Let your ass sway," said Jasmine. "I don't get it. In the movies, the geeky heroine always gets the hang of it in a few minutes."

"That's a *training montage,* you idiot," I said

between gritted teeth. I went sideways and had to grab for the table, and the shock of it made me finally snap. "This is ridiculous!" I told them. "Why are you even doing all this? I'm not stupid—why the dress and the heels and the makeover? What's going on?"

They all looked at me guiltily.

"It was after you got...upset about the recital," Natasha told me. "We were worried about you. We thought maybe you needed a day off, away from music."

"We thought...I don't know. Maybe if you went to the party and met someone...we just want you to be happy."

They all looked at me hopefully and I felt awful. All they were trying to do was help.

"Let me have another go in the heels," I said tiredly. They all cheered.

"I'll put on *Eye of the Tiger*," said Jasmine.

***

I'd met Darrell quite a few times, when he came to Fenbrook to pick up Natasha. But unlike the others, I'd never actually been to the mansion. As the cab pulled up with a crunch of gravel, they all climbed out without a thought and I was left dumbstruck in the back seat.

Three floors. Too many windows to count. A gravel driveway that was already filling up with sports cars. A water feature big enough to swim in. The front door was open, the men silhouetted by the warm light inside as they came out to meet their women. First Darrell's tall, muscled body, his well-cut suit doing nothing to hide his strong shoulders and forearms. I remembered Natasha telling us how he'd caught her when she'd fallen from the stage, and I could imagine it.

Behind him, looking far less comfortable in his

blazer and jeans, a silhouette that could only be Neil. The blazer, I suspected, was Clarissa's influence. He still wore his hair long and loose, still looked every inch the biker.

Darrell put his arm around Natasha and pulled her close. Neil swept Clarissa right off her feet and into a kiss, and Jasmine and I *awwed* in unison. Whatever problems they were having, the four of them still made insanely cute couples.

I exchanged looks with Jasmine: *And we're on our own.* It wasn't like I minded—I was used to being the single one. But I was glad she was there with me.

Inside, there were waiters with trays of champagne flutes and canapés, a band and many more people than I'd been expecting—at least a hundred. Everyone seemed to be either a leggy blonde in her twenties or a white-haired, rotund man in his fifties—the high society types Darrell knew from charity fundraisers. I could see now why Natasha had wanted Connor to even things out a little—it could have done with Connor and about twenty of his friends. Speaking of which...I looked around, but couldn't see him anywhere. And it wasn't like he wouldn't stand out. *He probably couldn't be bothered,* I thought with relief. Relief and maybe just a tiny hint of disappointment.

"What about him?" said Jasmine's voice in my ear. She gently turned my head to show me who to look at. He was in his early forties, at a guess, with black hair dusted with only a little silver at his temples. Short for a guy—barely taller than me—but in better shape than most of the other guys there, with an ex-athlete's physique. Attractive, in an older man sort of a way.

"What about him?" I asked. Did she mean *what do you think he does?* "I don't know, is he a CEO or something? Something corporate?" I craned my neck round to look at her, and that's when I saw her expression.

She hadn't meant "What about him?" She'd meant "What about *him?*"

"Are you *kidding?!*" I said, as loudly as a whisper would allow. I turned my back to the man. "He's old enough to be my—"

"Don't exaggerate. He's barely over forty. Anyway, I thought you might like that."

"A sugar daddy?!"

"Safe. Responsible. Knows what he wants in life. Tell me that isn't close to your wish list."

That threw me a bit, because it was eerily close to my boyfriend features list. "But he's...."

"Don't think of it as him being old. Think of it as enhancing your youth. Just think how amazing you'll look in ten years' time, at 31, when all his friends' wives are 41 or 51. Of course, they *will* all hate you."

I stared at her. "Please tell me you're not serious."

She smiled, and I saw that she was—or at least as serious as she ever got about anything.

"I am *not* going to talk to him," I told her. Then wondered why she kept glancing over my shoulder and smiling.

No. Surely she wasn't—

"Hi," said a voice behind me. A voice that I just knew went with silver temples.

"*Hi!*" said Jasmine, doing her big-eyed, honored-just-to-speak-to-you look. "I'm Jasmine. This is Karen."

"I am going," I said between gritted teeth, "to kill you." And then, because I was too polite to do anything else, I turned around and smiled at him, just as Jasmine knew I would.

"Kurt Barker-Ross." I got the impression that I was meant to react to that, but I had about as much knowledge of New York high society as Neil did. I settled for nodding politely.

"Karen's a musician," Jasmine told him. Then, before I could stop her, "A cellist."

I saw him do *the thing*. The instinctive reaction all men have when they find out you play the cello. He stared at me, and I knew he was picturing me with my legs spread. I saw a smile touch the corners of his lips and could feel myself bristling.

"Let me get you another one of those," Kurt said, taking my glass.

As he turned to pluck a full one from a waiter's tray, Jasmine whispered in my ear. *"Be nice! Maybe he'll ask you to play in his basement, like Natasha!"*

"That was completely different!" I whispered. But then Kurt was handing me a full glass and, to my horror, Jasmine excused herself and left.

Kurt smiled at me, and I told myself that maybe this wouldn't be so bad. I had no intention of dating him, let alone sleeping with him, but everyone was always telling me I needed to get out more. If I could brace myself and carry on a conversation like a normal human being, even if I didn't particularly like the guy, that was good practice. Right?

"You're lovely, Karen." said Kurt.

That threw me a little. "...right. Okay. Thank you."

"Do I shock you? Not everyone can admit that they like a man who's direct. But deep down, a lot of women like that. Do you, Karen?"

"Um..." I looked around the room for Natasha, or Clarissa. Knowing Jasmine, she'd spirited them away to "Give us some time alone together."

He stepped closer. "I think you do." His voice became very slow and deliberate, emphasizing certain words. "I think...*you want a man*"—and his hand turned to point almost casually at his own chest—"who knows how to give you *what you want.*" It felt like he was trying to hypnotize me. He was staring straight into my eyes without blinking and it wasn't "intense" or "entrancing"—it was just creepy.

"I think you read certain books," he said, "and you wonder if men like me—CEOs—are really like that. If power in the boardroom translates to power in the bedroom. Well let me tell you...*yes it does.*"

"Okay," I said, stepping back. "I think—"

He stepped close again, thrusting his face right up to mine. "Have you ever had a man withhold an orgasm from you, until you were crying and begging to come?"

"Yes," said Connor. "But only when she's been very, very bad."

He stepped between us, a protective wall of muscle and attitude. Kurt had to crane his neck to look him in the eye.

"I'm—" Kurt said.

"Leaving." Connor told him, with exactly the sort of authority Kurt had been trying for.

Kurt suddenly saw something of great interest across the room and went to look at it.

Connor turned to me. "Isn't that three times I've saved you?"

"What makes you think I needed saving?" I said hotly.

"You *wanted* Fifty Shades of Gray...Hair?"

"I don't think what I want need be any concern of yours, Connor."

"I'm serious, you know."

He sounded so sincere that I took him seriously, for a second. "About what?"

"I'd let you come. Unless you were *really* bad."

I stalked away, leaving him smirking. My face was hot, a point between my shoulder blades tingling as I felt his gaze there. In the next room, I ran into Natasha.

"Having a good time?" She was smirking, too. Jasmine must have told her about leaving me with Kurt.

"Spectacular. I have a contract I'm going to need a lawyer to look over, and then I'll be needing some handcuffs and a blindfold."

"*What?!*"

"Where's Jasmine? I need to kill her."

"Outside, flirting with a waiter. Hey, could you do me a favor and see what's keeping Darrell? I sent him down to his workshop to fetch an extra folding table and he's disappeared."

I suspected she was just giving me time to cool off, but maybe that wasn't such a bad idea. I needed a few deep breaths before I saw Jasmine...or Connor.

In the elevator on the way down, my traitorous mind went straight back to Connor. I was glad he'd showed up, even if I'd never admit it to him. But why did he have to be such a jerk? Why all the jokes about sleeping with me?

The doors opened, and the first thing I saw was the polished wooden stage Darrell had installed for Natasha when she'd starting dancing for him. I hadn't appreciated how big it was...or, as I stepped out and looked around, just how big the basement was. I tried to imagine the two of them down here: Natasha jumping and pirouetting up on the stage, Darrell watching her, the two of them gradually falling in love...although from what she'd told me, there hadn't been much *gradual* about it. Was that why they were having problems now, because they'd plunged in so fast?

I looked down the length of the room, seeing what I took to be workbenches and heavy machinery. I had to guess at most of them, because everything was covered in dust sheets. He really had stopped, then, this man who'd been driven to the point of burnout by his work. That was good...right?

I heard a movement, down at the end of the room. Only the tiniest of sounds, but in the utter silence of the basement it was like a scream. I froze, eyes searching for the source.

Darrell was sitting at what must have been his old desk, dust sheets turning the monitors into a white ski slope in front of him. He was leaning right back in the chair, so far that it looked like he might overbalance, and staring at the featureless white in front of him. I'd never seen anyone look so dejected.

I had no idea what to say to him, so I found the folding table and deliberately banged it against the wall as I lifted it. Darrell suddenly came to life, blinking and looking round, then hurrying over to help me.

"Sorry," he told me. "Just got thinking."

I nodded and wondered whether to say anything to Natasha.

***

Upstairs, Jasmine had a glass of champagne and a plate of canapés waiting as a peace offering. "I didn't know he was going to go all creepy dom on you," she told me. "I thought he'd just be all *you beautiful creature* and buying you necklaces."

"No more setting me up," I told her.

"Pinky swear."

I took a canapé. It was impossible to stay angry at Jasmine for long. "Where are Clarissa and Neil?"

Jasmine raised an eyebrow.

"*Here?* At the party?"

"Natasha says they do it every time they come here. This place has, like, sixteen bedrooms or something. They're probably making sure they've christened every one."

Sex in someone else's house. Probably with the door unlocked. Knowing that everyone downstairs had a pretty good idea what you were doing. I just couldn't see myself ever doing that...and, of course, I wouldn't want to. So why did thinking about it send a little crackle of desire sparking straight down between my legs?

"Looks like your Irishman's having a good time," said Jasmine.

"He's not *my*—" And then I broke off as I saw him.

He was talking to a willowy blonde in a white dress, her head thrown back as she laughed at his jokes. We were too far away to hear what they were actually saying, but Jasmine did a voiceover.

"Oh, hi, begorra! I'm the cheeky sexy Irishman! Will you be needin' any help in getting' them panties off, miss? *Oh! Your accent is so cuuute! Let me give you my phone number and you can ravish me on the hood of my Porsche!*"

We watched him step away with a phone number written on a napkin. He stuffed it into his pant pocket and headed for a brunette, her hair elegantly piled up on top of her head.

"Unbelievable," I whispered aloud.

Jasmine shrugged. "That's what he is. He must think he's died and gone to heaven, all these rich girls to work his rough charm on."

"Talking of money...." I said quietly. "How are things?"

"Okay for now, thanks to you. I've been looking around for somewhere cheaper, but that place is pretty much rock bottom. It's New York—what did I expect?" She sighed. "I'm only a little behind at the moment, but when the rent comes due, *that's* going to be a problem."

"Any room to negotiate with your landlord?"

Something flickered across her face. "Yeah," she said distantly. "We've been discussing an arrangement." She gave me a hug. "Don't panic. I'll figure something out."

As we moved apart, something caught my eye. Connor had moved away from the brunette and was stuffing a new napkin into his pocket. Shaking my head, I stalked over to him.

"Really?" I asked. I didn't quite have my hands on my hips, but it felt like that sort of moment. I was angry—and on some level, I realized I was angrier than I should have been.

He looked at me blankly. "Really what?"

"How many napkins do you have stuffed into your pocket?"

He looked down at his pants. "Oh, no. I'm just pleased to see you."

The simply, unashamed crudity of it took my breath away. "You're incorrigible!" I told him, and turned away.

A strong, warm hand grabbed my arm. "Wait: I'm *what?!*" He pulled me back to him. Closer than before, close enough that the rest of the room seemed to fade away.

"Incorrigible," I grated. "It means—"

"I know what it *means*. I just can't believe you said it! Who says *incorrigible?!* You sound like you're in a bodice ripper!"

I felt myself flush. Underneath my bed was a large cardboard carton packed tight with exactly that sort of romance—haughty heroines and square-jawed heroes who said things like "Oh, I like a wildcat." But Connor didn't know that. He *couldn't* know that.

The band started to play and people drifted off the

dance floor—no one wanted to be the first to start dancing. I was too angry to notice.

"It's not my fault your vocabulary only extends to jokes and—and flirting." I told him.

He frowned. "Why do you care who I flirt with?"

I opened and closed my mouth a few times. Why *did* I care? The women who'd given him their numbers were all old enough to know what they were doing. Far more experienced than me, in fact. For all I knew, they were using him just as much as he was using them.

"I don't," I said at last. "I just think going from one to the next like that is...tacky."

"Tacky?"

"Tacky."

He considered for a moment. "Dance with me. That'll stop me chatting up anyone else."

I looked around. The floor had mostly cleared, and we were standing in the center. I felt about a million eyes on me, and I couldn't just walk off thanks to his grip on my arm. "No," I told him. "I don't dance."

He fixed me with a stare, and I felt the strangest sensation ripple down my body. As if, for just that second, nothing else in the world mattered except for me. "*Dance for me, Karen,*" he whispered.

I blinked and drew in my breath. "I—"

He grinned, and the spell was broken. "Do you think that's what it was like for your friend, with her millionaire?"

I narrowed my eyes. For a second there, it had almost felt like—but of course he'd just been kidding around. "You're lacking about thirty million dollars, a mansion and the looks."

He looked at me seriously for a second. "You don't think I'm good looking?"

That threw me. Because I was starting to see that,

yes, if you went for the dark, bad boy look with the wicked smile, if you had a thing for biceps and strong chests and—Anyway, if you went for all that, which I most definitely *did not,* then yes, he was very good looking.

"You're not my type," I told him.

"What is your type?"

"That's—"

"Are we back to Kurt again? Would you like me to bend you over my bed and spank you?"

My jaw dropped open. Unbidden, some very dark images flashed through my mind. "How dare you?" I croaked.

"How dare I?" He was trying not to laugh. "You've gone all Brontë on me again. Are you going to start putting a 'sir' on the end of everything? Do I forget myself? Am I a bounder and a cad?"

I tried to speak, but couldn't find the words. Hot anger was bubbling through my brain. I was drunk with it.

"Why *did* you come over here, Karen? Did you really think those women needed saving from me?"

A little voice inside me was demanding to know that, too. What was it about him chatting up some random women that had me so worked up? "I—"

"Let's dance." Suddenly, his other arm was around my waist.

"What? No, wait—"

He pulled me close and I yelped. Suddenly my body was pressed against his, the heat of his body shocking through my thin dress. I could feel the hard wall of his abs against my stomach and I tried to speak, but I couldn't seem to get any air. I was dimly aware that the band were playing a slow number, and a few couples had drifted back onto the floor around us, but we still seemed to be very much the center of attention.

"I can't dance," I squeaked.

"You're doing fine." We were barely moving, just a few steps in each direction as we turned slowly around. But even that was hazardous in my ridiculous heels, and I staggered and had to hang onto his arm to stay upright. It felt as solid as iron, and I was reminded of how he'd caught me on the steps. He was even stronger than he looked.

Unfortunately, not even he could make me a better dancer. I recovered, but kept tripping over my own feet, my face going red as I felt everyone looking. "Connor—"

And then he pulled me even closer to him and lifted me, my shoes just leaving the floor. He swept me round without apparent effort, and without my stumbling it actually looked good. "Better?" he asked.

I was panting. The whole length of my body seemed to be molded to his. His broad chest was pressed against my breasts, and the touch of him there was making my nipples rise and harden despite me willing them not to. His arm around my waist meant that my groin was mashed to his, and I was uncomfortably aware of the hardness I could feel along the inside of his thigh, and the effect it was having on my body—a dark, twisting heat inside me that I could already feel turning to moisture. *This is Connor, for God's sake! What's the matter with me?*

I looked up at him, helpless. I expected him to be smirking, or outright chuckling at me. I thought he'd make some crude comment, but what I saw in his eyes took my breath away.

He looked just as helpless as me.

The music ended and the arm around my waist eased free—almost reluctantly. I was away across the floor immediately, heading for the safety of the edge. Jasmine was waiting for me, open-mouthed.

"What was *that?*" she asked.

"Nothing. Him being stupid."

I couldn't stop myself looking back over my shoulder at him. He was still standing there, watching me.

"It didn't look like nothing," Jasmine told me. "Do you want to know what it looked like?"

"Not particularly."

"It looked like he wanted to get some Irish inside you."

I winced. "Thanks. Classy."

"I'm serious. I think he likes you!"

I shook my head. "He likes...*them.*" And I pointed to yet another tall blonde who was cuddling up to Connor, running her hand over his back. "He's just messing around with me to annoy me, because he knows I have to work with him."

Jasmine frowned. "You don't...like *him*, do you?"

I rolled my eyes. "God, of course not!"

CHAPTER 7

THAT NIGHT, when the canapés were all gone and the champagne all drunk, when we'd offered our help in cleaning up and been politely refused by Natasha, when we'd half-carried a slightly drunk Jasmine to the cab and taken her home...I thought about Connor.

I was alone in my apartment, still wearing the dress—although I'd slipped off the Heels of Death and was enjoying the blessed relief of bare feet. I was sitting facing the window, playing my cello and looking out at the city lights. I hadn't had much to drink, just enough to make my mind a little dreamy and random. I let my thoughts guide my playing, my body just a conduit.

Connor Locke was long, low notes—the sound of my impending doom. What did I really know about my nemesis? Irish. Bad boy. Arrogant. Drunk, more often than he should be. Magnetic to women—at least, a certain type of women. And yet from what I could see, he never stayed with one for very long.

Except Ruth. What sort of woman had tamed him for long enough—or made him fall hard enough—that he wanted her name permanently etched on his body?

He was enjoying playing with me—I could see that much. He was like a cat with a mouse, knowing that I could never really escape but wanting to draw out the game as long as possible. Exactly how much was he going to make me suffer, over the next three months? Enough that I'd break and call the whole thing off?

It occurred to me that maybe that was what he wanted. If I refused to work with him, he could walk away and all the blame would be on me. Was he just looking for a way out, one that wouldn't make him look like the bad guy?

The weird thing was, I couldn't imagine Connor minding being the bad guy. He seemed like he'd embrace the role. So why, then, was he playing with me? Just because he found it amusing?

I stopped playing, and then started again as I thought about how his body had felt. The movements of my bow got smaller, faster. Notes rippling down over the hard ridges of his abs. Curving and soaring as they arced over the broad swell of his chest. Then hard, strong strokes as the music flowed over the thick muscles of his shoulders, down his back to his—

I broke off abruptly and sat there with the bow resting on the strings. Something had started inside me, a swirling heat that I visualized as deep, deep scarlet, and I wasn't sure how to shut it off.

A part of me wasn't sure I *wanted* to shut it off.

I laid the cello carefully down and started pacing. It wasn't getting turned on that bothered me; it was getting turned on by *him*. *Think about something else.* I stared at my composition notes, but that only made me think of Connor. I slipped out of the dress and hung it up neatly so I could give it back to Clarissa the next day, but that left me in my underwear, and rogue thoughts of Connor's hands on me started to creep in.

This is ridiculous! I do not like him! I told myself. It was just a purely physical reaction, I decided. Like getting goose bumps when you're cold—nothing you can do about it. My body simply didn't know any better, didn't care that he was a loud-mouthed, brash idiot who coasted on his talent. It was only interested in how big his hand had seemed when he gripped my arm. How his chest had felt against my breasts when he pressed me to him, how his hard cock—

I closed my eyes. This was getting out of control.

I'd go to bed. I'd go to bed and sleep, and in the morning I'd be back to normal. I'd go to bed and I would absolutely *not* play with myself.

Minutes later, I was lying there under the covers in just my panties. Normally, I threw on an oversize t-shirt, but that night I didn't bother. Going topless didn't mean I was going to give in to temptation, though. Not at all.

I turned over, unable to get comfortable. It was like an itch, deep inside my body, impossible to ignore. It wasn't completely dark in my bedroom, enough of the city lights making it through the blinds to light up the white covers and the wide, queen-sized bed. A bed that had only ever had one person in it, the entire time I'd been at Fenbrook. The only time it saw any sort of action was when I—

No. Not to memories of him. Not while thinking of his smirk and his twinkling eyes.

I turned over again. Then again. The swirling heat didn't fade, but grew more and more intense until—

I slid one hand down my body and under the thin fabric of my panties. Eyes tight shut, fingertips stroking along my lips, up and down, up and down....

There was too much weight on me. I kicked the comforter off and lay there almost naked. I tried to keep my mind empty, but Connor's face was there immediately and I let out a groan of anger that sounded a lot like lust. *Think of Sven!* I thought desperately. *Strong hands working your back, all slippery with oil....*

But my body didn't want Sven. I felt the ghosts of other hands on my body, on my arm and back. Felt my nipples stiffening at the memory of him.

We all have our preferred positions. Mine is on my back, knees wide, heels digging into the bed. My fingers were slick with my moisture now, stroking up and down my lips, and my thumb was beginning to circle my clit. Ripples of energy were skittering down my body, growing stronger each time. I could feel the orgasm building inside me, but there was something missing, something not right.

It doesn't feel like him, a traitorous little voice told me. *That's what's wrong.*

I pushed the thought away, and let my knees flop wider. I was panting now, my fingers frantic at my opening, feeling the lips swell and spread. My thumb kept circling my clit, so super-sensitive it was almost painful, yet I wanted to stroke it raw. I was desperate, aching for release in a way I'd never known before.

I could feel the orgasm trapped inside me like a tethered balloon. However fast I stroked and rubbed, it refused to rise any higher. I needed something else.

I swung myself off the bed and yanked out the carton of books. They were in neat alphabetical order, double-stacked with the filthier ones on the lower level. But when I pulled out the five bodice-rippers at the end, they revealed my other secret. A black, unmarked box which I opened with shaking fingers. Inside, a translucent pink dildo.

I'd tried a couple. A vibrator was good, in its own way, but I never got over the alien-ness of the buzzing. It felt too mechanical, too unrealistic. And the dildos I'd seen with carefully textured surfaces, with their skin colors ranging from ivory to black, had gone too far in the other direction. Mine, though, was made of some jelly-like material, and the color helped, too. It didn't look *too* real. Yet when you closed your eyes....

I quickly stripped off my panties and lay back on the bed. I teased myself with it a little first, tracing my lips with the head, imagining some faceless man doing the same. But he wouldn't stay faceless. However hard I tried, it was Connor I saw. Connor's thick biceps either side of my head, as he supported his weight above me. Connor's tight ass flexing as he positioned himself to—

I rolled my head back and groaned as I slid the head into me, feeling myself stretch. Just the thought of it, of the man I thought of as an arch-enemy entering me, was enough to send my climax rising and twisting, almost faster than I could control. In my mind he started to thrust, and I stroked the dildo back and forth, my teeth biting my bottom lip as the smooth rubber stretched my walls. My heels grew warm as they rubbed back and forth on the bed, and I imagined gripping his ass with both hands and pulling him in deeper....

I arched my back as it slid into me, gasping as it opened me up. I'd started to sweat, my breath coming in choking gasps. But it wasn't enough. This was Connor, I realized, inserted into my normal Sven fantasy.

He wouldn't take you like this, the little voice in my head said. I ignored it for a moment but when it came back, I allowed the thought to creep in. How *would* Connor Locke take me?

Without even thinking about it, I rolled over onto

my hands and knees, one arm under me to keep the dildo moving. Immediately, it was better, more *real*. I had my eyes tightly closed, but I imagined there was a mirror in front of me, and in the reflection I could see Connor, driving into me from behind.

I let my body slump forward onto my shoulders my head awkwardly turned to the side, so I could rub at my clit with my other hand. I was driving the dildo in deep, now, deeper than I normally would. *He wouldn't care. He wouldn't care that I'm a virgin, he'd drive it in fast and deep and oh God so big—*

I imagined those big hands on my hips, hard fingers digging into my flesh. I arched my back and dragged my breasts along the sheet so that it caressed my nipples, burning sparks leaping from them straight down to my groin. I could feel myself teetering on the edge and as I shoved the dildo in one last time, all the way to its root, I gasped, "C—Conner!"

The orgasm ripped through me, starting at my head and rippling down to my core, then exploding outwards to devour me completely. I could feel my legs twitching, my body clenching and squirming around the rubber length buried in me. I was heaving for breath, rivulets of sweat running down my chest to drip from my aching nipples. When the climax passed, I was a shuddering, weak-kneed mess.

***

I woke naked, the comforter dragged half over me in the night, the dildo nestling against my thigh, warm and intimate from my body heat. I could feel the traces of my shameful arousal on my inner thighs, and there was no denying the pleasant soreness. I really had done all that...while thinking about Connor.

I took a long shower and decided that it had been an aberration. Probably I'd been a little drunk from all the champagne. Anyway, it was out of my system. Things could go back to normal.

Only he seemed determined that nothing would be normal at all.

There was a message on my phone, surprisingly early in the morning for Connor to have been up—I wondered if he'd gone to bed at all. *Call me about rehearsal.*

I was due to meet him the coming Thursday for our next rehearsal. I sighed—did he want to cancel or reschedule?

I dialed him and he answered immediately. "Hi. Sleep well?" he asked.

My face was immediately burning. *There's no way he could know.* "Like a baby."

I heard Connor smile. "I must have tired you out...."

I froze.

"...with all the dancing," he finished.

I breathed again. "It was only one dance. I have more stamina than that." Any other time, I would have chosen my words more carefully, but I hadn't had my coffee yet.

"I'm sure you have *lots* of stamina." How did he do that? How did he manage to make absolutely everything into a teasing, flirting mass of innuendo? When I didn't reply—I was too busy silently seething—he continued. "I thought we'd rehearse at my place on Thursday. More space than a practice room."

I shook my head, then remembered he couldn't see it. "I'd prefer Fenbrook," I said doubtfully.

"Great, that's settled then." And he gave me his address, simply steamrollering my dissent.

When I'd hung up, I tried to see a silver lining. His place was a fair distance across town, so I'd have to get a cab—at least that meant I wouldn't have to lug my cello. But Fenbrook felt familiar and safe. Neutral territory. His place...that was different.

I sighed. I could still see myself in my mind's eye—on my knees, thrusting the dildo inside me.

"It didn't happen," I said, with so much conviction I almost believed it.

CHAPTER 8

THURSDAY MORNING and the gray sky was lightening minute by minute, the clouds swelling with snow. As the cab drove through gradually worsening neighborhoods, I scanned the skies for the first falling flake. But it felt like the weather was waiting for something.

When we eventually pulled up outside an ancient, towering tenement I could feel the cabbie's hesitation. It didn't look like the sort of place a girl with a cello would go.

Connor was waiting outside for me, his leather jacket pulled tight around him against the cold. He took my cello while I got out and then wouldn't give it back.

"I'm fine, thank you," I told him. "I've carried it for years."

"Not up these steps, you haven't."

"Why do you always think you know what's best?"

He ran his hand through his hair. "Why do you always have to fight me?"

We glared at each other.

"Fine," he said, and led the way up the stairs.

I heaved the cello case onto my back and started up after him. After the first flight, I started to see what he'd meant. Whoever had built the steps must have been six foot plus: each step was double the normal height. Climbing them was like hauling yourself up a vertical rock face.

"Okay back there?" he asked sweetly.

"Just fine."

I could hear the smirk in his voice. "Only five more to go."

Five? I hadn't figured on him being on the very top floor. By the third floor, I was panting. By the fourth, my legs were burning and my back and abs were aching from the strain of leaning forward—the only way I could keep from tumbling backwards. When we finally reached the top floor and I saw a blank wall instead of the start of yet another flight, I wanted to kneel down and kiss the floor.

Connor unlocked the door and showed me in. My legs were shaking so much that I didn't even look at the room—my eyes were locked on the bed, where I could safely drop the cello before I collapsed. I staggered over to it, shrugged out of the shoulder straps and let it thump onto the ugly green blanket. Then I sat down heavily next to it and allowed myself to flop onto my back.

I heard Connor close the door. He regarded me for a moment and then said, "I always knew I'd have you flat on your back on my bed, someday."

I groaned and struggled up to sitting, the muscles in my legs still burning. I gave him a glare and then finally focused on the room.

It was surprisingly big, for a bedroom. Then I

realized it wasn't a bedroom at all—it was his entire apartment and it was *tiny*. There was a kitchenette in one corner and what I assumed must be a bathroom behind a flimsy partition wall in the other. You could pretty much cook a meal while sitting on the edge of the bed.

Pizza boxes and more than a few empty beer cans were in a heap in the corner—and I got the impression they'd been scattered across the floor only a few minutes before I arrived. His amp and guitar sat next to an old wooden kitchen chair—it and the bed were the only furniture. It was barely warmer or less draughty than the corridor outside.

Connor saw me looking and shrugged. "Probably not what you're used to," he said with a smirk.

"No, no. My place is...." I tried to think of something to say that wasn't a lie. *Bigger? Cleaner? In an area where you're less likely to get mugged?* "...not so different," I finished weakly. I was cursing myself for not hiding my surprise better. What had I expected? I'd known he was at Fenbrook on a scholarship.

There was a mirror on the wall, a long crack splitting it into two uneven pieces. Wedged into the side of it was a strip of photos from an instant photo booth, all showing the same woman. She had midnight black hair tonged ultra-straight, flowing down over her shoulders like oil. She was smiling as if in victory, as if she'd let her guard down in the privacy of the booth and allowed herself a moment to crow about something, her thin lips pressed even thinner. Anyone else would have tried for at least a few different expressions as the camera flashed, but she'd stayed in the same frozen pose for all of them.

"Ruth. Like in the song," said Connor. He seemed to be watching me very carefully.

I looked away and massaged my aching legs. "Shall we start?"

I sat on the edge of his bed with the cello between my knees. He picked up his guitar and sat across from me on the kitchen chair. We had more space than in the tiny practice room, but it was somehow more intimate. He'd invited me into his home....

He started to play the first of the sections he'd be leading. I stopped him on the first note. "Wait: where's the music?"

He looked at me as if I was mad. "In my head."

I blinked. "It can't be *in your head*. This has to be perfect." I'd spent the week since our last rehearsal composing my first section and practicing the hell out of it.

"And so it will be." He started to play again and it was...beautiful. Sad, but with a thread of hope running through it. On the second pass through, I did my best to follow along with a harmony.

"See? All without music," he told me.

I sighed. "Please write it down for next time." I could feel the stress coiling and building inside me, cold snakes twisting in the pit of my stomach. He had to have all his sections written and be note-perfect on them in just over nine weeks...and the worst part was, I couldn't get angry at him about it. He could walk away at any time and kill my future stone dead.

I pulled out my own first section—clean black lines on snow white paper. He didn't have a music stand, so he made an impromptu one on the bed out of a couple of pizza boxes and propped it there.

As we played my section, I felt the stress begin to gradually ease—this part, at least, was under my control. But then my mind started to wander. I kept looking at his hands and the way they moved over the strings, fingertips sensitive but firm. Imagining them on my nipples. On my clit. *Playing me the way he played me last night.*

That was just your imagination, I reminded myself. *He's not interested in you, except as someone to tease.* And even if he had been, I certainly wasn't interested in him...not beyond the physical, anyway.

I felt myself flushing. I'd never been attracted to someone that way before—not so strongly. Especially not a person I didn't like!

We tried his section again, which meant I had to concentrate like hell to play it from memory. It was hard to focus, though, with Connor glancing up at me, blue-gray eyes under his thick, dark brows. He was cradling his guitar, one hand strumming while the other wrapped around its neck, and I started to imagine it was me in his arms. If I was turned away from him, in exactly the same position, one hand would be on my cheek, his fingers toying with my lips. The other arm would be wrapping around my hips, his hand right on my groin. Maybe sliding under my clothes, his fingers gently opening me—

The bow slid off the strings at a strange angle, shrieking in protest, and I stopped. Connor stopped, too, and looked at me. "Problem?"

I flushed. "No. Not at all. Just new to it." I cast about for an excuse. "This would be easier with it written down."

He grinned. "I don't believe in writing stuff down. I like to let it flow."

That pretty much summed up the differences between us. His life was a disordered, chaotic jumble...and yet somehow he was happy. Mine was perfectly regimented and disciplined...and yet I was stressed out of my mind.

As we tried his section again, I noticed something.

Before, I'd thought that he was uncertain of the piece because there were slight variations each time. But watching how confidently his fingers toyed with the strings, it came to me that it was deliberate. He knew the piece just fine; he was tweaking it because he wanted to. And there was no way he could know it that well unless....

"You've been practicing," I said, astonished.

He kept playing for a few seconds and then stopped, letting the notes fade away before he spoke. "You don't have to sound *that* amazed."

"But you don't practice. I mean, I'm in those practice rooms every day, and I haven't once seen you coming in or going out the whole time I've been at Fenbrook."

"I don't practice *there.*"

"Why?"

He shifted uneasily, but I didn't want to let him off the hook. A suspicion was forming in my mind.

"Why, Connor?"

He sighed and then looked right into my eyes. I could tell that he wanted to lie, to come out with some easy quip or flirty comment. But then his expression softened. "Because everyone can hear you when they walk past."

I looked at him blankly. "But...you're good. I mean, you're *really* good."

He just looked at me.

I almost laughed. "Connor, the whole academy knows how good you are. You know that!"

He kept staring at me, and there was a flicker of something, something I never thought I'd inspire in anyone. Hope.

"Oh my God...." I said slowly. "You really *didn't* know that. Did you?"

He shrugged. This uber-confident, arrogant loudmouth, this guy who got to Fenbrook on a scholarship, who everyone talked about being the next Hendrix...he was just as insecure as the rest of us. He just kept it hidden away on the inside.

And yet he'd revealed it to me.

I moved about a millimeter towards him, and it went through my head that *I'm about to hug him.* Fortunately, I caught myself before I threw my arms around him, and managed to make it look like I was just leaning forward.

"Look," I told him. "Everyone thinks they're no good. Everyone. That's called being a musician. Didn't anyone ever explain that to you?" I could see in his face that they hadn't. I tried to imagine what it would be like, to live with that daily, hammering dread that *maybe I'm just no good,* but to not even know that it was normal.

Those beautiful, blue-gray eyes were fixed on me, and for just a second he looked vulnerable, like he had on stage. Was it possible that the Connor I knew was just a mask?

I waited for him to look away, and he didn't. I could feel my breathing getting faster and faster, and I felt like I was cresting the brow of a hill on a rollercoaster. I had to do something, quick, or something was going to happen.

Part of me wanted it to.

"So you practice right here?" I asked, breaking his gaze and looking around the room. "Don't your neighbors mind?"

He stared at me for a split-second longer and then seemed to shake himself. "Not here," he said, his voice a little strained. I heard him take a deep breath, and when he continued he was back to his usual, cocky self. "I'll show you where."

He unplugged the amp and then took the extension lead it was plugged into and leaned out of the window. I saw him tie it to a piece of string that dangled down from above. Then he picked up his guitar and amp and motioned me to follow him.

I picked up my cello and followed.

At the end of the hall was a door with a ragged hole where its lock used to be. Cold outside air whistled down from the dark stairwell beyond, and I began to see why the place was so draughty. He held the door and nodded for me to go first.

The stairs were dank concrete and just as steep as the ones up to his apartment, but there was only one flight. I'd figured out where we were going, but when I emerged it was still a shock.

New York lay spread out around me. We were six stories up and the tallest building for several blocks so there was nothing to get in the way. I could see for miles in every direction: cabs picking up passengers, a couple arguing in the street, even what looked worryingly like a guy selling drugs on a street corner. It was like being God, even if only of this neighborhood.

He showed me where to sit, on the edge of a rusted air conditioning unit. Then he went over to the edge of the building and hauled on the string, lifting the extension lead so he could plug into it. The amp crackled into life.

I looked at him in amazement. "You sit here and play?"

He shrugged. "It's big and open and...it feels like I can breathe up here, you know? And no one's listening. No one who cares." He played a few notes, and they soared away over the rooftops.

The wind roared overhead and I shivered.

"Cold?" he asked.

I looked up at the clouds. "A little. But more...I don't know...I'm not used to being exposed."

I felt him looking at me, and I realized I'd just given him a great lead-in for yet another jokey comment about sex. But he just said, "Yeah. I know."

More of that tension, the silence swelling and building—

"You must freeze, up here," I said quickly. I actually *was* starting to get cold—my coat was down in his apartment.

I heard him step up behind me, his body sheltering me from the worst of the wind, and I caught my breath. Was he about to wrap his arms around me, like I'd imagined downstairs?

"Here. Put your arms up."

I lifted my arms above my head, and then something soft and warm was pushing down over them, blocking out my view. He must have grabbed it, just as we left his apartment. It was a weirdly comforting feeling, having someone pull a sweatshirt onto you.

When my head popped out and I looked down at it, I saw it was a black Fenbrook one, the sort we'd all been given in freshman year. I wore mine, sometimes, but I had trouble getting my head around the idea of Connor hanging onto his for all that time.

My hair was all bunched up under the sweatshirt and I suddenly felt his hands, warm against my neck as he scooped it up and then let it flop down my back. Little prickles of energy crackled down my spine. I was wearing a bra and a vest top and my own sweatshirt and then his Fenbrook one, yet all I could think about was my naked skin, so close to his palms.

"Thank you." His voice was shockingly close. I could feel the heat of his breath on my neck.

"For what?" My toes were trying to curl up inside

my shoes and my nails were digging into my palms.

I could hear how difficult it was for him to say it. "Letting me know it's okay to be...y'know. Not sure of yourself."

We stayed like that, silently looking out over New York, for a long time.

***

That evening, I sat again in my apartment and tried to compose, but once again I couldn't concentrate. Before, I'd been distracted by thoughts of Connor's body, of his hands on me. Now, I couldn't stop thinking about how he'd opened up to me. I was starting to see his cocky, confident persona in a whole new light.

Did the girls he dated—or maybe *dated* was the wrong word, given the time his relationships seemed to last. The girls he *slept with*—did they ever get to see the real him? Or did he keep up the pretence the whole time, convincing them that he didn't care about anything—not his grades, not his future—nothing except the next party? And if that was the case....

If he'd concealed his insecurities for all these years, was it possible that he was concealing other things, too? Like an ability to actually care about someone, instead of just having a series of one night stands?

I caught myself. This was ridiculous—I was like a schoolgirl with a crush, seeing things that weren't there. Connor had a reputation for a reason. Okay, maybe he wasn't quite as arrogant as he seemed, once you got to know him, but he still wasn't someone it would be smart to get involved with. *Not that I'd want to get involved with him anyway...right?*

My cell phone rang, and the screen showed

Natasha's smiling face. Normally, I'd have begrudged the interruption, but that night I practically snatched up the phone to answer.

"Nat!" I said warmly, unable to stop myself grinning. She was exactly what I needed to take my mind off Connor and the recital.

And then everything twisted around and I closed my eyes in guilt. She was crying.

CHAPTER 9

NATASHA WAS STANDING IN THE DOORWAY of her apartment, waiting for me. She led me straight through the lounge and down the hall to the bathroom.

Scattered on the tiles were several razor blades, some dressings and alcohol wipes and the vintage cigarette case she kept them all in. Her old cutting kit.

I could feel a yawning chasm open up beneath me. I was so ridiculously out of my depth it was untrue. This was a job for Clarissa, with her cool, calm efficiency. Or Jasmine, with her worldliness. But *me?!* I was the geeky one, the inexperienced one. What the hell did I know about this stuff?

Natasha was standing frozen in the doorway, looking like she might throw up at any moment. I had to do *something.*

Get it out of sight, I thought, and started picking everything up and tidying it away. I considered dumping the whole lot in the bin, but I knew it wasn't that simple.

When it was gone, Natasha seemed to relax a little. I led her by the hand into the lounge.

"Start at the beginning," I told her. That seemed like a safe thing to say.

She shook her head in disbelief. "I haven't cut since we got together," she told me. "Months and months. But...."

I forced myself to shut up and wait.

"He hasn't been sleeping. Every night, he has these nightmares. He lies there awake and he thinks I don't know...."

I remembered Darrell at the party, sitting down in the workshop. "Have you talked to him?"

She shook her head.

"Nat, you have to. I mean, I don't know much about relationships, but—"

She shook her head again. "I think—If I try to change things...." She sighed. "It's like—Look, when we got together, that felt like a chance in a million. We were right for each other, and it was magical, and it all *worked* and—Now it feels like it's a house of cards. They all fell into place by sheer fluke, and it's horribly, horribly fragile. If we even breathe wrong, it's all going to collapse."

I bit my lip. "But that means you can't talk about stuff. And you're worried about him...."

She nodded.

"And you're getting more and more stressed about it, and that's why you cut?"

She nodded, tears welling up in her eyes. "Just once," she said in a tiny voice. "It didn't even make me feel better, it made me feel *worse*. But now he'll see it, and he'll worry, and I don't want to worry him again, and—"

She descended into tears and I shushed her and

hugged her close. *What would Clarissa do?* I thought desperately. I'd just have to fill in as best I could. "Look," I said. "I don't know if I'm the best one to give advice, but...."

Natasha looked at me, tears in her eyes, hanging on my every word, and I felt sick with fear. *What if I tell her the wrong thing, and they break up and it's all my fault?*

"First of all, I think you two need to talk. You two are the only ones who can fix things." That was safe enough, right? It was the sort of advice I read in women's magazines, and it was less likely to wreak havoc than if I got directly involved myself.

Natasha shook her head. "But...I don't know what to say. It feels like we need something, like—new ways of coping. And I've got no idea what they should be."

I so desperately wanted to help her, but I was the least knowledgeable person in the world when it came to men. Whatever I told her would be wrong. "Have you thought about the two of you going for therapy?"

She shook her head firmly. "He's not ready, and I know I'm not. He's the only person I've told everything to. I haven't even told Clarissa everything." She looked up at me guiltily. "I haven't even told *you*."

I nodded. "That's fine. I understand." I took a deep breath. My mind was racing with ideas, things I could suggest...and I didn't dare voice a single one of them.

"Just talk to him," I told her at last. "You'll figure it out."

She sniffed and nodded, and the fact she'd accepted my non-advice just made me more uneasy. I felt like I'd stepped back when I should have stepped up.

Natasha took a deep, shuddering breath and wiped her eyes. "I'm okay," she said.

It sounded like she was trying to reassure herself as much as me. Neither of us was convinced.

***

We sat on the couch for a half hour, steering the conversation steadily further and further from dangerous waters. We passed through relationships, then Fenbrook, then Flicker, then our favorite movie-themed drinks, and from there it was an easy jump onto the safe dry land that was movies. We decided to make a night of it, and Natasha started browsing Netflix while I went to order pizza.

Searching around the hallways of Natasha's apartment for cell service, I saw the glow of a laptop screen through the half-open door of Clarissa's room. Ordering online seemed radically more sensible than spelling out the address to a harassed pizza shop worker over a bad connection, and Clarissa wouldn't mind. I ducked into her room and sat down at the desk.

I fired up a browser and Googled for pizza. *Address. Crust. Toppings.* "Nat," I called, "What do you want on the pizza?"

"Umm...." I could tell from the way she drew it out that her brain was buried deep in Netflix. "Give me a minute...."

I sighed and sat there patiently...for about five seconds. I've never been good at waiting. On the other hand, I didn't want to hassle Natasha when she was in such a fragile state.

There was something else running on Clarissa's laptop. A media player, minimized to the taskbar. I clicked on it, curious as to what movie she'd been watching.

It popped up to full screen, and I drew in my

breath as I saw it was porn. A blonde-haired woman lay on her back, her long legs wrapped around the long-haired man who lay atop her. Both were completely naked, their faces turned away from the camera.

I let a little smirk creep over my face. Not that it was all that weird, Clarissa watching porn, but—

Wait.

Clarissa's room was dark, apart from the glowing laptop screen, so I hadn't really taken a good look at it. But the bed in the movie looked very familiar....

I switched on the desk lamp and looked at the bed, just a few feet from me. Same covers. Same wall behind it. I looked at the couple on the screen and bit my lip in shock.

I hit *Play* without thinking and Clarissa's loud gasp exploded around the room. I scrambled for the volume control and muted it.

"What was that?" called Natasha from the lounge.

"I saw the pizza prices!" I shouted back. "Hurry up and decide what you want!"

On screen, Neil was thrusting hard into Clarissa, laying kisses along her cheek and then taking possession of her open, gasping mouth. She was wearing a necklace I'd never seen before, a beautiful silver chain with delicate crystalline shards hanging from it.

This is wrong, I thought. *This is twisted. They're my friends.*

Neil took hold of Clarissa's legs and pushed them back, folding her, knees to her chest. For the first time, I got a good look at his cock. Dear God, he was enormous! I felt the heat rise in my face as I watched it sink into her. God, wouldn't it hurt, being...*spread* like that? In my mind, even though I knew it was wrong, it was *me* lying on the bed, *me* crushed under his weight, *me* whose nipples his mouth was slathering, hard buds shining in the dim light....

I hit the Play button again to pause it and quickly swapped back to the browser. I was almost panting, my eyes wide. I wasn't sure which shocked me more: them making the video, or me watching it.

I need to leave, I thought. *Just leave. Then I won't be tempted to watch any more.*

"Nat!" I called in a strangled voice. "I need to order. What do you want?"

"OK, sorry. Give me two secs."

I stared fixedly at the pizza order. I didn't even *look* at the video controls, so tempting and clickable and—

No one will ever know.

I clicked "Play," and then drew my breath in as I saw that there was another half hour of the video to go. Surely they didn't...God, solidly? For a half hour? I jumped forward—

Neil on his back with Clarissa on top, her breasts bouncing and swaying as she rode him. I clicked forward again—

Clarissa on her knees, her mouth tightly closed around Neil's cock. I stabbed clumsily for the button, feeling drunk, my face hot—

Clarissa bent forward on the bed, just as I'd been in my fantasy after the party, her breasts grazing the covers as Neil thrust into her from behind—

The door opened behind me. I killed the movie window with a split-second to spare.

"Let's go for good old-fashioned pepperoni," Natasha told me. Then, looking at my reddened face, "What?"

"Nothing," I squeaked. Then, because that didn't sound very convincing, "A porn site popped up."

"Oh, Karen." She kissed the top of my head. "Bless

your innocence."

***

A week went by. Connor and I started to rehearse every day, at his place and—with a lot of persuasion—in the practice rooms at Fenbrook. I got used to the rooftop, after the first few times. I'd bring coffee from Starbucks and we'd sit there alternating playing with warming our hands on the cardboard cups. Once you got over the shock, playing outdoors looking over the city was sort of...liberating. We practiced the first two sections—mine and his—until they shone, and we started to sound good. The way Connor would change the odd note here and there each time drove me nuts, and I had to beg and plead with him before he gave me a written score, but I started to get a very tentative feeling that just maybe we could pull it off.

I asked him every time I saw him how his classes were going. We each had a big essay on Stravinsky to complete, and whenever I asked him about it he got sullen and evasive. Eventually, I had to stop badgering him for fear of making him give up completely.

It was four days before I could speak to Clarissa without going beet-red, and it was lucky that I didn't run into Neil during that time. Every time his name was mentioned, I could see his tan body against her paler one, his muscled ass tight as he thrust into her from behind. My guilt of having invaded their privacy by watching it was nothing compared to my guilt over how it had made me feel. It wasn't *them,* as such—I wasn't turned on by Neil, or Clarissa, or even the two of them together. It was the raw, hot nature of it, the realness of it. I couldn't stop thinking about how it would feel to be taken like that.

And that thought brought me back to Connor and the fact that, despite still not being sure if I even liked him, he haunted my every waking thought.

Not just my waking thoughts, either. Midway through the week, I had the dream.

CHAPTER 10

INTERLUDE – KAREN'S DREAM

SHAFTS OF SUMMER SUNLIGHT were lancing down from the windows, catching dust motes that betrayed the servants' laziness. Under my dress, my corset held me tighter than any lover, forcing me to focus on every shallow breath.

As I fanned myself against the heat, there was a commotion at the door. A man in strange, tight blue trousers and a shining black jacket burst in.

"My apologies, Lady Karen," panted my butler, clutching the arm he'd injured in the war. "I couldn't stop him."

"That's perfectly alright, Daniel," I told him, making a mental note to fire him. "I'm sure you did your best. Sir! Explain yourself!"

He walked closer, swaggering in his heavy black boots. Perhaps he was one of the workmen repairing the roof in the east wing. My heart fluttered as I remembered how some of the brutes had attempted to catch glimpses of me undressing through my bedroom window.

He was still coming. "Sir! I must protest!" I said, noting the muddy boot prints he was leaving across the marble. The poor maid would be on her knees for hours.

He didn't stop, and there was a dark gleam in his eyes now. Fourteen generations of good breeding gave me the strength to stand my ground. "Sir! Please!"

He stopped only when he stood so close to me that I could feel the heat radiating from his body. With one finger, he lifted my chin and stared down at me with blazing eyes that sent a strange ripple through my body.

I opened my mouth to say, "Sir!" again, but suddenly his lips were upon me, and to my horror his tongue was demanding entrance to my mouth. My fists beat weakly against his back for a moment, but then I felt myself go limp in his arms. He caught me easily as I swooned, hoisting me up in his arms.

"Will there be anything else, Lady Karen?" my butler asked as the man carried me up the stairs.

I hung there limply, eyes half-closed and arms thrown out over my head. "No..." I managed.

In my room, he threw me on the bed, duck down pillows bouncing onto the floor. He stripped my dress from my helpless body as I writhed, caught between passion and protest, his boots dirtying the sheets. He lay kisses on me as he worked, and by the time he had me twisting and thrashing in just my corset and underthings, I was quite beside myself. "Sir!" I gasped as his lips found my heaving bosom, "I am not that sort of woman! You mistake me for Lady Natasha, or Lady Clarissa, or Jasmine, the town harlot!"

He spoke, at last, and his accent seemed very far from England. "Karen," he growled. "Karen!"

With deft hands, he loosened the laces of my corset and stripped it off, my naked breasts throbbing in the cool air. He feasted on them, his tongue finding my nipples as I gasped and trembled beneath him. He stripped me of my undergarments and I threw one hand over my eyes to shut out the sight of my coming ravishment. But I could not deny the way my traitorous body was reacting to his expert touch, and a second later I lifted my hands to gaze up at him.

He was already naked, and I gasped anew at the sight of him, his manhood like that of a proud stallion. "But Sir!" I told him. "I am a—"

No. I could not bring myself to tell him. He must not know that he was about to plunder my maidenhood. He was no doubt used to far more worldly women.

And then he was running his palms over my pale, trembling thighs and I realized even his hands were filthy, marring my noble body forever. But I didn't care, the spiraling energy that coursed through my body with his every touch robbing me of any sense. His hands slid up to cup my breasts and I groaned, arching my body towards him like some cheap whore.

He was already hard, I saw. Hard and throbbing and ready to rob me of that which I had kept for so long. "Sir!" I begged, "Be gentle!" But a part of me didn't want that, didn't want the delicate touch of a gentleman, and I spread my thighs wantonly for his entry.

He thrust inside me and I threw back my head and groaned. His weight settled between my open legs as he began to move, each inch a tight, silken delight...and I could protest no longer. "Sir!" I gasped, head thrashing on the pillows, "Sir! Take me! Take me!"

"Yes," said Connor.

***

I sat bolt upright with a gasp that sucked in half the air in the room. My darkened bedroom was cool, but my body was damp with sweat, the t-shirt I'd been sleeping in stuck to my heaving bosom—

Heaving breasts, I corrected.

I slid from the bed and found my legs were shaking. When I reached down, my lips were puffy and slick.

I staggered through to the bedroom and turned on the light. The sight of own disbelieving, panting face in the mirror was enough to bring it home to me.

I couldn't deny it any longer. I was firmly in lust with Connor Locke.

CHAPTER 11

HE WASN'T THERE.

I sat in the lecture theater looking at his empty seat, one finger swirling round and round on the touchpad of my laptop. There were a million reasons why he might not have shown up for Geisler's class: he might be off auditioning for some bar gig, he might be sleeping off a hangover, or he might have talked some actress into a torrid liaison and still be in her bed. That last one made my mind begin to wander. Probably they'd been at it all night and they were still dozing, him spooning her from behind, his strong arms wrapped protectively around her—

I pushed the image away. There was another reason why he might have chosen not to show up, and it was the one that worried me most.

Geisler called an end to the lecture and asked us to pick up our essays as we left. I packed away my things at the slowest pace I possibly could, eventually resorting to dropping my pen three times to ensure I was the last one to leave. He handed me my essay as I left, a red A circled in the top corner.

There were no others left on his desk.

***

I called Connor as soon as I got outside and he picked up almost immediately—which only confirmed my suspicions. I didn't mention the essay, just telling him that we needed to meet, *now,* but I knew he'd be able to tell something was up from my tone.

He told me to meet him at his gym, not far from his apartment, and I jumped straight in a cab. This was too important to wait.

***

My father thought gyms were for posers, preferring trail running, so I'd never been a member of one. Clarissa had given me a guest pass to hers, though, and for one morning I'd walked amongst the toned, lean bodies in their Lycra and headphones, in an airy space filled with softly humming treadmills and beautiful, sculpture-like weight machines.

This was not that sort of gym.

The walls were breezeblocks, whitewashed so long ago that they were a crumbling gray, fading to sickly yellow near the ceiling where the cigarette smoke had collected until they finally banned smoking. The boxing ring had been fixed so many times the surface looked more tape than canvas, the ropes fraying and worn. There was a metal bucket beside it and I looked up at the ceiling for the leak. Then I saw someone spit in it.

No one there was without a tattoo, and they weren't the black, tribal bands or Chinese characters you see on men in their teens and twenties. These were faded, blue-green designs stretched over muscles hardened by brawling: names and knives and devils riding motorcycles.

I was the only woman. I'd like to say that every head turned to watch me, that I could feel all the testosterone spike into lust, but this was *me*. I barely warranted a glance, even with the cello case on my back, before they turned back to their punch bags and medicine balls.

Connor was near the back, stripped to the waist and throwing punches at a bag that was as big as me. His muscles shone with sweat, his hair damp with it. He looked wonderful, even through the haze of my anger.

"What?" he asked, and it was like the snapping jaws of a wounded animal.

"You didn't even hand it in, did you?" I asked coldly. "You didn't even bother."

His gloved fist thumped into the bag, the impact of it making me jump. "I did my best."

"How could you do your best when you didn't even *hand it in?!*"

He hammered the bag, two quick punches and then a final, harder one. The bag swayed, its chain creaking. Anger was darkening his face now. "I don't have to answer to you. You knew what I was like when you got into this." He punched the bag again for emphasis, grinding his fist into the yielding softness.

"If you flunk, I flunk," I told him, the words hissing between my teeth. "I could have helped you! If you were having problems with it you could have just asked!"

He glanced at me, then focused on the bag, throwing a quick flurry of punches at it. One of them skated off the side, and as the bag swung back towards him he had to step back, missing his next shot. "It's not that simple."

I pushed between him and the bag. "Then tell me. Tell me what's so hard about writing an essay."

He glared at me. "Get away from the bag, Karen."

I'd disliked him, sometimes, but I'd never been scared of him before. I was then, just for a second. The moment stretched out, building and building until one of us had to give in.

I shook my head at him in disappointment and walked away. Behind me, I heard him slamming punch after vicious punch into the bag, putting all his energy into hitting something he could never beat.

***

I should have got a cab as soon as I left the gym. The streets in Connor's area weren't the worst in New York by any means, but they were a long way from the best. But I was lost in thought, trudging on as the slush soaked through my sneakers and left them as chilled and numb as my brain.

I wanted him. Even angry as I'd been, the sight of his lean body with its strong, broad back had still been enough to send little ribbons of desire twirling right down to my core. But the more I wanted him, the less I understood him. I knew now that, behind the cocky exterior, he was just as insecure as the rest of us. I could sense that he was smart—much smarter than he let on. So why not at least *try* with the essay? I could have understood an F, but to not hand one in at all...why would he do that, except to spite me?

I'd built him up in my mind, turned him into some sort of romantic hero. I had to remember he was still the Connor I'd always known. Loud. Arrogant. A dropout.

And where women were concerned, only after one thing—well, from *other* women, not from me. I still had no idea why he'd even agreed to my plan in the first place, except that he must have pitied me. And the worst part was, however badly it went, I had no choice but to stick with him. He was still my only chance.

I'd almost reached the men before I saw them. One was lounging back against the wall while the other stood at the edge of the sidewalk. There was enough room to get through between them, but it would be uncomfortably close unless one of them chose to move out of the way. A human toll bridge, waiting to extract their fee.

"What's in the case?" one of them said. Despite the chill wind, he was only wearing a thin sweatshirt.

I was tempted to say, "*A flute,*" but even through my anger I knew that would be a bad idea. I put my head down and kept walking.

"I'm talkin' to you," he told me, and suddenly stepped forward, stamping his foot down. It was a test and I failed it, flinching and stopping.

"What's in the *case?*" he said again, his lips parting to show stained teeth, and I felt my anger fizzle and die, icy fear rising in its place.

"I—" I backed up a half step, and they took a full step towards me, closing the gap. "It's—"

A car pulled up beside us, and for a horrible second I thought it was their friends. I had a fleeting vision of being dragged inside and taken God knows where. Then I saw the blue stripe, the lights on the roof.

"Everything okay here?" said the cop, leaning out of the window. He looked strangely familiar: short dark hair and a serious look.

"Just fine, Officer Kowalski," said one of the men, as if they were old friends. "How are you this fine morning?"

"I wasn't talking to you." The cop didn't even look at the man. He was staring straight at me. "Some place we can take you?"

I glanced at the men who'd stopped me and then nodded. Without words, I opened the rear door of the cop car and slid my cello case in, then climbed in after it.

As we pulled away, the driver—an older cop—gave Kowalski a look I didn't quite understand, as if he was patiently mocking him. Then I realized where I'd seen them before. "You were in the alley," I said. "When my friend was mugged."

The older man laughed. "Kowalski here recognized you. Thought you might be out of your depth, so far from home."

"Thank you!" I looked back through the rear window. The two men who'd hassled me had resumed their guard duty, waiting boredly for the next person.

"You were lucky," said Kowalski. "This is out of our way. We were following up on some stolen property—our normal beat's over by Fenbrook."

I nodded. It hit me again how good looking he was: strong jaw, deep blue eyes...clean cut, in a way that fitted well with a police uniform. I could imagine him in the military too, all stern authority. He was almost the opposite of Connor's jokey charm.

It took me a while to notice the silence, as if they were waiting for me to say something. "Anywhere you could drop me is fine," I offered.

Kowalski smiled. "We're heading back towards Fenbrook. We can drop you there."

The silence continued. Were they waiting for more thanks? For an explanation of what I was doing on the wrong side of town?

At last, Kowalski spoke and it hit me that the

silence had been him working up to it. "So, umm...I didn't catch your name that night in the alley?"

"Karen. Montfort."

"Ryan. Kowalski. My friend here's Pete Huxington—'Hux'."

I nodded carefully. This was weird...it didn't feel like he was about to ask me out—not that I had much experience to go on. But his friend Pete looked like he was trying not to laugh.

Ryan drummed his fingers on the dash for a second. "So, um...your friend Jasmine...?"

Oh!

I smiled. "Single. If that's what you're asking."

Pete elbowed his partner, chuckling.

Ryan beamed and rubbed the back of his neck. "Uh...yeah. Yeah, pretty much."

"I'm guessing you already have her phone number...what with her being a witness," I said.

Pete banged the steering wheel. "See? Did I tell ya, or did I tell ya?"

Ryan shifted uncomfortably. "Didn't feel right, using her number like that. And there was...."

"The way you mistook her for a hooker?" I asked helpfully.

"Yeah. That. Was she...annoyed about that?"

I thought back to our time waiting for the doctor at the hospital. *"Seriously?!"* Jasmine had raged. *"A hooker? How dare he? Really, how dare he?! Typical fucking cop!"*

Then I thought back to the party at Natasha's house, and Jasmine setting me up with Fifty Shades of Gray Hair.

"She was fine with it," I told him. "And, in your defense, it *was* a very short dress."

"Well, yeah," Ryan said hopefully. "Yeah, exactly. So, uh...."

"Would you like her number?" I asked sweetly.

CHAPTER 12

I DIDN'T HEAR FROM CONNOR for three days. I picked up the phone to call him at least five times, but always stopped at the last second. If I hassled him, he could walk away from the whole thing. I needed him a lot more than he needed me.

In the meantime, I wrote the second of my three sections. It came slowly at first, but the more of it that spilled out onto the strings, the more there seemed to be to follow. It took me by surprise, because it wasn't like anything I'd written before. It had more force and confidence and there was an underlying pattern of hard, barely controlled anger. Playing it left me feeling shaky, and oddly sad inside.

On the fourth day, he called. I snatched up the phone on the first ring.

"I'm sorry," he said.

I felt a shard of hope the size of a grain of sand, and grabbed it tight. "I shouldn't have blown up at you," I told him. "Can we meet?"

The walk to Fenbrook was eerily quiet, the forecasts of heavy snow keeping most people indoors. I looked up at the clouds overhead, hoping they'd hold off until I got home.

An hour later, we were in a practice room. Flaunting the rules, Connor had brought in a couple of glazed donuts and a coffee each from Dunkin' Donuts. Dunkin' Donuts was my second favorite takeout coffee after Starbucks. It had always made me think of cops sitting in patrol cars, and I made a mental note to ask Ryan, if I ever saw him again, if that myth was actually true.

Connor played the second of his sections, and I could tell immediately that he'd spent most of the last few days preparing it. It was very different to my own piece, much softer and more timid but with a slow rhythm that built and built until it demanded attention. I wasn't sure how the two would sound next to one another, but I was looking forward to finding out.

Watching Connor as he played, I couldn't shake the feeling that I was missing something. He'd obviously spent hours composing the music and then practicing it, probably up on the roof of his apartment block. He'd been big enough to apologize and come and meet me yet, when I tentatively asked if we could talk about his essay work, he just shook his head. It was beyond frustrating. We had more essays due before the recital, and if he didn't hand something in for those, either, I was certain he'd flunk. And then all our work would be for nothing.

An hour in, coffees finished and the donuts reduced to sticky crumbs, we took a bathroom break and—against all laws of men and women—I returned first. Only to knock over his guitar case as I came in, sending it crashing to the floor.

I propped it up again, but something was sticking

out of the lining at the top—a folded piece of paper dislodged by the fall. I went to tuck it back inside, but something about the writing on it made me stop.

The handwriting was normal enough, but the letters made no sense. *You kissed me mad me cofy and said yor nam was Ruth.*

I slowly drew out the paper and unfolded it. I recognized the lyrics from when I'd heard Connor sing them, but this version had been distorted, the words and even the sentences twisted almost beyond sense. Reading it, I could feel him trying to push what he wanted to say through a mind that wouldn't quite comply, his frustration evident in his spiky pen strokes. I suddenly knew why he'd never handed in an essay.

Too late, I felt his presence in the room. When my head jerked up, he was standing there fuming in the doorway. He looked just as disappointed in me as I'd been in him at the gym—before I understood.

Without a word, he grabbed his guitar, case and jacket and stalked from the room. Seconds later I heard his feet pounding down the stairs. I looked at my cello, still propped up beside my chair. By the time I packed it away and got the case on my back, he'd be out on the street.

I left it, and ran after him.

I caught him in the first floor hallway, but when I grabbed his arm he just shook me off and was out of the main door before I could stop him. I wrenched it open to follow...and then staggered back in shock. While we'd been practicing, the clouds had finally let go and a full-on blizzard was in progress, the flakes flying horizontally and smacking into my face so hard they hurt. As I stumbled down the steps, freezing air filling my lungs, I realized my coat was still on the back of my chair upstairs.

I blundered after him, hair streaming behind me in the wind. Snow splattered the front of my sweatshirt, the color disappearing in seconds under a coat of white. "Connor!"

He didn't even slow down. Shoulders hunched, guitar slung across his back, he marched on, away from me, away from Fenbrook. I had a horrible feeling that, if I didn't stop him, he'd never come back.

I forced my legs to go faster, sneakers sliding on the fresh snow. "Connor, *wait!*" A blast of wind shot straight down my throat, making me gasp and turn to try to catch my breath, and he slipped further away.

I gritted my teeth and stepped into the street, where the traffic had mashed the snow down. Pounding alongside the sidewalk, trying to watch for headlights coming at me through the blizzard, I managed to get alongside him and grab his arm. "*STOP!*"

He turned and hauled me bodily out of the street, dumping me back on the sidewalk. "You've got your answer: I'm too fucking stupid to write an essay, that's why I never handed one in. That's why I won't be graduating! So you can take your cello and shove it up your pretty little arse, 'cos I won't even be here for your recital!"

I stood there gaping at him. "*Stupid?!*" I asked, dumbfounded.

He just stood there glaring at me and I realized he didn't know.

"Oh my God," I said, half-aloud. "Oh my God, you thought...Connor, you're *dyslexic!*"

He cocked his head to one side, as if suspecting a trick.

"You're not *stupid!* You just have a problem with words! That's why you're fine with playing and composing and writing scores." I gaped at him. "Has no one ever said this to you before?"

There was the tiniest flicker in his expression, as if he could see a distant light and didn't trust it to be real. He looked away and then back to me. "I thought that was just an excuse. What people say when they're bone idle."

I felt something twist inside me. His assumptions were no worse than mine; I'd taken him for lazy without bothering to find out the real reason. "No," I told him. "No, it's not. It's been holding you back—it's like trying to play without being able to hear properly." I stepped closer. "I can help you!"

He looked at me doubtfully. "You think you can fix it? In the time we have left?"

"We can figure something out. I can help you get through the essays." I was very close to him now. "If you'll let me."

He gave me a long look, and then his hard expression finally melted. "Jesus, put something on before you freeze," he told me, whipping off his jacket and pulling it around my shoulders. His hands were warm, even through the leather.

***

We were back in the practice room minutes later. Save for me shivering, it was as if the whole thing had never happened, and yet I knew nothing would ever be the same again.

"I can't believe they never helped you with it when you were young," I told him quietly. "You should have had a helper in the classroom, assistance during exams...."

He wasn't looking at me, his focus turned inward and to the past. "Not in this school. If you got out with some maths and English, you were doing well. The teachers didn't care as long as you weren't trying to burn the place down. And my parents...well. They didn't have any expectations to shatter."

I studied him as he sat there, hunched over in his chair, his body closed even as he opened up to me. He'd gone so long without talking about the problems he was having, had worn his reputation as a bad boy like a suit of armor to disguise what was really going on. I could see it on his face—humiliation, at finally admitting to someone that there was a problem. And hope—the faintest possibility that maybe it wasn't his fault. That maybe he finally had some control over his future.

I started to worry that I'd promised something I couldn't deliver. Sure, if he'd had help from the start, back in high school, he could have achieved much more. But we had less than two months until the recital and graduation. Could I really turn him around?

"Let's play for a bit," I told him, to try to break the tension, and he nodded eagerly. I played my second part again, so alien to me with its confidence and force, that theme of suppressed rage running underneath.

It must have burned at Connor all those years at Fenbrook to think that he was the interloper, the stupid one amongst the talented kids. I went cold inside as I wondered what he'd thought of *me,* when he'd seen me in class getting 'A's for my essays. It was a lot easier to understand his rage at the gym, now. It had always been there—maybe always would be—that deep river of anger—

I stopped playing.

It's him!

I looked down at the cello, rewinding the music in my head. Hard and forceful, confident and even cocky. Barely-controlled anger underneath. My second section was Connor. I'd written him into the music.

I looked across at Connor and thought of his second section. Just like mine, it had been very different to his normal music. Slow, and almost timid. Oh God...*he'd written me!* Nervous and shy and...there'd been something else. A sort of dark rhythm underneath that had built and built, wanting—*needing*—to be met by a harmony. What could that—

I flushed.

Was that really how he saw me? A librarian with hidden passions? And what did it mean, that we'd unknowingly written each other into our music?

He was staring at me. "What?"

I swallowed, unable to stop the smile that twitched at my lips. "Nothing."

We practiced our second sections again and again, but there were some parts that just wouldn't come together. The cello, with all its somber grace, just wouldn't do what I needed it to do. In a sense, it wasn't *him,* in the same way his guitar wasn't me. And we didn't know each other's instruments well enough to help.

"I have an idea," he told me. And he put his guitar aside and held out his hand. It took me a second to realize that he wanted me to pass him my cello.

Understand, when you play the same physical instrument for years, it becomes part of you. No one played my cello but me. It wasn't the cost—although the cost was hard to forget—it was the handing over of something so personal, so precious.

I bit my lip, turned it on its peg to face away from me and passed it across the short gap that separated us. His fingers brushed mine for a second as he gripped the neck, warm and strong.

He cradled the cello between his knees. "Like this?" he asked.

I swallowed. "More vertical. Lift her a little more."

He looked at me. *"Her?"* That familiar smile played across his lips, and even though he was mocking me I somehow didn't mind at all. I shrugged.

His hand ran up and down the slender neck, skimming over the polished wood until he found its balance. He handled its weight so easily that I was never worried about it sliding out of control—it was heavy for me, almost too big for me, but in his hands it looked almost frail.

Connor turned the cello just a little and ran a palm down its gently curving side. Out over the full swell at the top, then in at the narrow waist. Out again at the lower, flaring curve, following the smooth flank of it.

I found I was barely breathing.

He put his hand out for the bow, and I pressed it into his palm. He looked along it like a knight would a sword, then experimented with the flex of the horsehair. He gripped it—too close to one end. "Like this?"

Without thinking, I reached out and took hold of the bow in the correct position, a hand's width further along. Our thumbs were touching. "There."

He gripped the bow again, his fingers over mine. The warmth of his hand seemed to soak through my fingers and up my arm in a rush, coursing straight to my chest. "Like that?" he asked.

I nodded dumbly.

He started to play, very slowly, with me guiding his movements. The cello let us hear every touch he made, every slow brush of the bow on the taut strings. He was heavy where I'd always been gentle, and I had to pull his hand back to keep him from being too firm. The sensation of hearing the notes and at the same time feeling him making them, of having another person touch the strings even as I guided his touch...it was strange. And beautiful.

"Okay," he said at last. "Do you trust me?"

I slowly slid my fingers from beneath his. They tingled, as if electrically charged. When he began to move the bow, I had to keep the very tips of my fingers brushing the back of his hand, so great was my fear of him damaging something. It wasn't music—it was him exploring the limits, working out how he could coax what he wanted from the instrument. Free of my hesitation or fear, without all the careful grace I'd had drummed into me over the years by my teachers, he was able to make sounds I'd never heard before, things I wouldn't have thought a cello capable of.

He plucked the C string hard, producing a sound similar to a bass guitar. From there, he began to improvise a walking bass line. Then, attacking the strings with the heel of the bow, he managed to make a sound that was uncannily like a guitar distortion effect.

"There," I said. "That." And he nodded.

Then he put the cello aside, and it was my turn.

His guitar felt so completely different to my cello, the soft hiss of the amp a constant reminder that I was connected to something, that every tiny movement was going to result in a roar. It was like moving from a bicycle to a sports car, trying to get used to the monster controlled by your right foot. The first time I plucked and the room reverberated to the sound, I almost dropped it.

"Don't be afraid of it," he told me. "Connect with the sound, not with the strings." And he brought his chair around behind me. "Shuffle forward."

I moved my stool forward, and he sat down behind me, opening his legs and pressing in close, his thighs against my ass. He folded himself around me and I smelled the cool clean scent of him. One hand gently wrapped around mine on the neck, the other idly caressing the back of my hand on the strings before settling over it. Suddenly, everything was very close and still in the room, my heart a rising drumbeat.

"Don't run from it," he told me. "Control it. Get angry."

Normally, I'd never have done that. I'd never have allowed the mask to slip, to let myself show rage as he showed it. But I was already so far out of my comfort zone that it didn't seem that much further to go, to let my sense of outrage and unfairness over the recital, over my whole future being at risk, spill over into my playing. The power of the guitar still made it feel like trying to control a raging, snapping beast, but my anger gave me the strength to wrestle it into submission. I lost myself in the howling and wailing, cathartic in a way that my normal style never could have been. When I stopped, I realized I was exhausted: physically and emotionally. My fingers were sore and shaking, my body cramped from clutching the guitar. My mind felt fried from struggling with the unfamiliar, my soul pleasantly cleansed, at least for a while.

His mouth was almost at my ear. "Slide down an octave like you did at the end."

I hadn't even been aware of doing it—it was just what I'd do on the cello. I did it again, and this time I heard it. The matching partner to what he'd done on the cello, a rush of energy and emotion teased from the strings. "There," he said, and I nodded.

I was suddenly aware of the closeness of his body, his chest pressed hard against my back, his arms wrapping me into him. And against my ass, the press of his cock, hot and hard.

We stayed there for three trembling breaths.

"We should both try some things," I told him. "If we got a couple of acoustic guitars, we could both experiment. Sort of...meet halfway."

I felt him nod, his body not moving an inch. "Good idea."

A second's silence. Long enough for one of us to say something...but neither of us did. After another two beats of my thumping heart, he slowly unwound from me and got up.

CHAPTER 13

A few days later, Clarissa and I had dinner at a classy restaurant downtown, as we did every month. When we first started doing it, I hadn't understood why she'd want me as company rather than Natasha, her roommate, or Jasmine, who could have told her all about her latest one night stand. Then it clicked that it was about money. Clarissa came from by far the wealthiest background of any of us and her parents gave her a generous living allowance. She never made an issue of it and was certainly never superior or snobby about it—and that was kind of the point. When she went out with Natasha and Jasmine, she had to be very careful to pick places they'd be able to afford, so that they didn't feel uncomfortable. She couldn't discuss her shopping trips or bitch about how much her BMW cost to service. She couldn't tell some story from her days at a private school, or talk about the fumble in the bushes she'd had at seventeen with the valet parking attendant at the country club.

With me, it was different. My parents certainly

weren't as wealthy as hers, but our backgrounds were similar enough that she could relax.

Sitting in the back of the cab, watching the city lights draw dancing patterns on the seats, I thought about what had happened in the practice room: the way he'd pressed up against me, the scent of him so close, the rasp of his stubble against my cheek when he'd turned his head to speak....

The feel of his cock, hard against me.

It means nothing, I told myself. I knew enough about guys to know that they'd get hard at the slightest provocation. He'd been hard because he'd been pressed up against a warm body. Nothing to do with *me.*

Unless...it was.

Ridiculous. I'd finally admitted to myself that he turned me on—I was actually wet, by the end of the session—but it would be crazy to think it went both ways. What on earth would he want with me? I wasn't Clarissa, with her easy elegance and razor-sharp dress sense, or Jasmine with her curves and eyes you could drown in, or Natasha with her poise and grace. I was a geek. A geek who couldn't keep a hold of her feelings, at that: I'd started having stickily vivid dreams about a guy I didn't even like—

That made me stop. At first it had been so simple—he'd been a jerk and I'd hated him. Then I'd started to see underneath the mask, and I'd started to warm to him a little. Now, knowing about the dyslexia, I could understand his anger. I felt sorry for him—though I knew he'd never want my pity—and I wanted to help him.

But did I *like* him? He still drove me crazy at least half the time. He was my exact opposite in nearly every way, the chaos to my order. And yet...every time I saw him, I became a little less sure about the things that

In Harmony

made us different and a little more sure about the things that made us the same. We were worlds apart, but sometimes I felt like I was more deeply connected to him than anyone I'd ever met.

I sighed. The one thing that was clear…was that nothing was clear. I didn't know what, exactly, I felt for him, other than the shamefully intense response he drew from my body every time he was close. Maybe some girl time would help me sort my head out.

***

One of you has to arrive first at a restaurant. We'd long since learned that this should be Clarissa, who has no problem whatsoever waiting at the bar and fighting off guys. That night when I arrived, she already had three men clustered around her. She'd been there for five minutes.

"You're a ballerina?" asked a heavy-jawed man in a suit, who looked like he might be a gangster. "That's amazin'. You must be all bendy and shit."

"You sure I can't buy you a drink?" asked another.

The third one smiled. "Hey, can you—"

"Hi!" I said, cutting him off before he could ask if she could put her ankles behind her head. "Shall we go?"

We swept out of the bar to a chorus of disappointed sighs. I wondered what it must be like, to have that constant male attention everywhere you go. I'd never had a single person be that enraptured by me.

I noticed as we sat down that Clarissa had a store bag with her. Not Prada, for once. Some unpronounceable brand that sounded like it might be Scandinavian.

We started reading the menu, and even though the meal was going to make things seriously tight for the rest of the month, it was still great to bathe in luxury for a few hours. The descriptions sounded like the chef had conducted a three month love affair with each and every creature before reluctantly whacking it over the head. *Slices of outdoor-reared organic duck breast, marinated in a dark soy and anise syrup, anointed with oil and seared, then served drizzled with a reduction of fresh blackcurrants.*

"I have to show you this," Clarissa told me when we'd ordered. She took a silver dress from the store bag, the fabric so soft and shining that it seemed to flow over her outstretched arm like liquid.

"That's *amazing,*" I said with feeling. "It's like...future-sexy."

She grinned. "I know! With silver heels. I might do silver lipstick."

It wasn't often that I got into clothes, but I could imagine the outfit perfectly. "You should wear the spiky necklace—that'd be perfect."

She looked bemused. "*Which* necklace?"

"The spiky one. The one with all the little crystals."

She frowned and then all the color drained from her face. "I've only worn that for—"

Too late, I remembered where I'd seen it.

She lurched forward. "*Please* tell me you didn't see it on the internet!" she whispered.

I could feel the heat rushing to my cheeks. "No, I— It was on your laptop," I said in a tiny voice.

I saw the fear turn to anger in her eyes. "*Bathroom! Now!*" she told me viciously, and stalked off towards it leaving me to catch up.

The bathroom, mercifully, was empty. She turned to face me and I actually took a half step back when I saw her expression. "I'm sorry," I said quickly.

"How could you? My *laptop?!* That's my *private*

stuff! No one else was meant to see it!" She took a step towards me and I had to fight the urge to run. The thing about Clarissa is, she's quite tall, and she was in killer heels. And I'm not, and I wasn't. She towered over me, and I suddenly felt the tiled wall behind my back, my cheeks hot with shame and guilt.

"It was an accident! I was just going to Google for pizza, and it was open on your taskbar and I'm sorry!" I said in a rush.

She frowned. "So you only saw, like, a freeze frame?"

Something in my expression must have told her *no.*

"You played it?!"

"I didn't know it was you, at first! I thought it was just porn. Very tasteful porn!"

She'd reddened almost as much as me, now. I could tell she didn't want to ask, but needed to know how bad things were. "But you only saw a second of it, once you realized it was us?"

I've never been good at lying. I looked at the floor.

"*Karen!* How could you?!"

"I don't know! I was waiting for Natasha and I just sort of...watched some."

"All of it?!"

"I sort of skipped through. Only, like...three or four bits." I closed my eyes. "I'm really sorry."

Clarissa wheeled away from me with a groan of frustration and went over to the sinks. She stood clutching the marbled countertop, staring at her own reflection in the mirror.

Very slowly, I edged over to her. "Sorry," I said again.

She didn't respond.

"How can I make it up to you?"

She kept staring straight ahead.

"Please?"

I finally saw her eyes flick to me in the mirror and then she sighed. "You're on standby next time Jasmine calls drunk in a bar at three in the morning needing a pick up."

I nodded frantically. "Absolutely."

"And you have to let me get you into a dress next time you go out—no arguments."

"Deal."

She let out a long sigh. "Okay, *fine*. You're forgiven. At least it means I can talk to you about Neil."

She led the way out of the bathroom. "Wait," I said, hurrying after her. "What's wrong with Neil?"

***

We'd finished our entrées and were on our next glass of wine before she finally told me.

"We don't communicate," she said, turning the wine glass slowly in her hands. "It's like I said before...we have the sex thing, and the sex thing's great. Better than great. I mean, it's hard to get across how good it is." She looked at the table. "Have you ever had sex that's, like...*beyond?* Not just the sex itself but everything—the buildup, the talking about it beforehand....have you ever had sex like that?"

For a second, I wondered whether to tell her I was a virgin. "No."

"It isn't that the relationship's based on sex. That would be okay, because we could go somewhere from it— we could get to know each other and grow it. This is more like...the sex has given us a relationship, with roles and rules and things, and so there's no room for a normal relationship. It's like one of those things you read about with a contract. Masters and slaves."

"You have a *contract?*" I could feel my eyes going wide.

"No! But it's like that. Like we have very defined parts to play and we can't go beyond them, and that keeps us at a distance. It's not that we don't want to communicate, it's that we're not allowed to, in a weird way, because that would spoil what we have. Does that make any sort of sense?"

I sipped some wine and tried to get my head around it. "You mean, like...if you were the secretary and he was your boss, and it was fun *because* of that, it would also limit it because you'd always have to be his secretary? If you married him, or even changed jobs, it might not work?"

She leaned forward. "Yes! Exactly like that!"

I frowned. "So what are *your* roles?"

She flushed.

"Sorry. Don't tell me if—"

"No. No, I need to." She took a deep breath. "Well, he's a biker, obviously. I mean, he's so many things. He's a geek, in a way, and smart as hell—he's at MIT for God's sake. And he's a hippy. But for the sake of the relationship, he's a biker. A tough biker who"—she colored more—"knows what he wants. And I'm meant to be this posh, innocent"—she lowered her voice—"submissive."

I nodded.

"And so part of it is, he's all strong and silent and can just growl at me any time to take my panties off and follow him into a closet. And that's great, but...we can't talk about stuff because the people we're playing wouldn't do that."

I nodded. "And you can't just stop playing the role and be yourself...."

"...because I'm scared of breaking the whole thing. What if this is all we have? What if I push him away?"

I thought for long enough that I finished the rest of my wine. As Clarissa poured me another, I said, "But you can't go on like this forever. Is the sex really good enough that you'd risk the long term, just to enjoy the short term?"

She just looked at me guiltily.

"*Really?* It's *that* good?" I asked.

She shook her head sadly. "You have no idea. Seriously, he makes me feel things I didn't think I could. It's like being high...I actually have to come down again afterwards. It's not like normal sex."

A little stab of jealousy went through me. I knew it was wrong, but...I hadn't even experienced *normal* sex yet.

Clarissa's eyes were distant. "Have you ever just had...I don't know how to describe it...just an automatic reaction to someone? Like you'd feel that way about them, physically, even if you didn't like them?"

I blinked. "Yes."

She barely seemed to hear me. "When I first met him—it was when I took Nat to Darrell's place for the very first time—I thought he was this big, stupid, arrogant *lump* and yet...even then, even when we were yelling at each other, there was this...*thing* going on."

I nodded, leaning in, my heart thumping. "Yes."

"Later, I figured out how smart he was, and I really started to like him, but my point is that even when I thought I hated him, this thing was so strong that...." She sighed. "I'm sorry, I'm probably not making any sense at all."

"You are," I said faintly. "But with you, it was mutual. How did you know it was mutual?"

She shrugged. "I didn't. I thought he hated me. I

thought we were mortal enemies, and I cursed myself for being weak and wanting him even though I hated him."

"So how did you...?"

"Well, the second time we met, we were fighting—again—and then he stepped right up to me and said that someone should teach me a lesson, and—" She flushed and looked down at the table.

"What?"

She shook her head.

"*What?*"

"I can't believe I said it."

"What? What did you say?!"

She took a deep breath. "Bear in mind that it was in the heat of the moment. I said: '*Well, why don't you, then?*'"

The sound of the words hung in the air over the table.

"Oh," I said.

"It just sort of slipped out. And then he kissed me and I kissed him back and he pushed me down onto the table—stuff went everywhere—and...well. At some point, Nat and Darrell walked past the door and saw, but she didn't tell me until later. Though, honestly, Godzilla could have ripped the roof off the house and we probably wouldn't have noticed."

I nodded, deep in thought. If Connor felt that way about me, would I know? I wasn't even completely sure how *I* felt.

"So?" Clarissa asked.

"Hmm?" I was still worlds away, my head back in the practice room.

"So what do you think I should do?"

I thought hard. "What is it you *want* to talk to him about? Specifically?"

"I don't know...anything and everything. Our

futures. Where it's going. What he's going to do after MIT. I'm a planner, Karen—like you. I'm not saying house or babies or anything—not yet. But I like to at least talk about the future. For Neil, even planning a vacation is too big a commitment. Sometimes I wonder if the sex thing is holding back the relationship...or if he's scared of the relationship and he's using the sex thing to fend it off."

I pursed my lips and thought. My gut told me that she wasn't being unreasonable, that maybe Neil just needed some sense slapping into him...but what did I know? I was a virgin, for God's sake, the least qualified person possible to advise on a sexually-charged relationship. Just as when Natasha had asked for my advice, I felt that if I told her the wrong thing and it split them up, she'd never forgive me.

"I'm not sure," I said slowly. "Give it time, maybe?"

"That's just it...I get the feeling we're running out of time." I could see the worry in her eyes. *Tell him,* I thought. *Tell him what you need. Confront him.* But I couldn't say it. I was someone who, at twenty-one, still had all her bills paid by her father. I couldn't even run my own life—I shouldn't be trying to run anyone else's.

It broke my heart to do it, but I leaned across and gave her a hug instead of a solution. "I'm sure you'll figure it out," I told her.

She sighed. "Thanks." She looked at me for a moment and frowned. "Wait: you said *with you.*"

"What?"

"You said *with you it was mutual.* As opposed to with...?"

Help! "No one."

She relented, but the suspicion never quite left her eyes.

In Harmony

CHAPTER 14

I SPENT THE NEXT FEW DAYS trying to work out what I felt. I'd see Connor in lectures, down at the front, and space out watching him, the lecturer's voice turning into a distant drone. I understood, now, why he never took notes. Before, I'd thought he was lazy because he wasn't scribbling everything down or rattling it out on a laptop. Now, I saw him sitting there frantically trying to memorize what he was hearing and I winced in sympathy.

I noticed he was there for every lecture, now. He'd turn around and smile at me and I'd smile back, and every time there'd be this weird flip-flop in my stomach...this *was* just physical, right?

Of course it was. Just physical.

When the lecturer announced the next essay—due in a week's time—I locked eyes with Connor and gave him a solemn nod. I'd figure out a way to help him with it and, together, we'd turn around his grades. He looked skeptical, but gave me a nod in return.

That afternoon, I met up with Connor in one of the dusty passages right at the back of the music department. I indicated an ancient, outsize wooden door. "Behold."

He looked up at it. "What's behind there? The Fenbrook monster?"

"Storeroom. They had to get pianos in and out, back in the day." I unlocked the door and put the key in my pocket, then slowly pushed the huge slab of wood inward.

Inside, pitch blackness. Towering shelves holding files of sheet music and countless instruments. Including, if the department secretary was to be believed, a couple of acoustic guitars we could use to practice on. Hopefully between us we'd be able to come up with some ideas that let the cello and electric guitar meet in the middle.

"There has to be a light switch somewhere," said Connor, and he started feeling around the walls. There was, but when he clicked it, it did nothing.

"I don't think anyone's been in here in a decade," I told him. I pushed the huge door the rest of the way open to let as much light as possible in from the corridor. It was harder than it should have been and, when I looked up, I saw why. There was one of those old fashioned chain-and-weight door closers at the top, trying to pull it closed. Dangling from it was a large cobweb. I shuddered—the whole place was dark, dusty and crawling with God-knows-what. "I'll hold the door. You go and look."

He plunged into the darkness. The room was long and narrow and the light from the door only reached about six feet in. He disappeared, and then reappeared lit only by the light from his phone. Ten feet. Twenty. The light shrank and shrank and I could feel myself getting nervous, even though I was the one standing by the door. "Connor?"

"Still here. Black as *fuck* in here, though. Ah! Guit—No, wait. That's a lute. God, there's all sorts of crap in here." He was completely out of sight now, the light of his phone hidden by his body. "Ah! Got it. Guitars." I heard rummaging and scraping. "There's a crate, but it's stuck. Give me a hand."

I looked uncertainly at the door. "The door will close."

"Wedge it."

I dug around and found a book of sheet music, but it didn't seem right to stuff Beethoven's *Moonlight Sonata* under the door. I dug around some more and found an old scales practice book and figured that would be okay.

Connor's voice echoed from the other end of the room. "Today?"

"Don't rush me!" I wedged the book under the door as hard as I could and triple-checked that it couldn't possibly come loose. Satisfied, I turned towards Connor. "Shine the light! I can't see anything."

He held the phone out towards me and I walked towards the glow, the light from the doorway fading with every step. I couldn't see where I was putting my feet, and the air was dry and horribly still, like a tomb. I kept thinking of that cobweb by the door, and wondering how many more were hanging right above my head, or in front of my face....

Finally, I was next to him, our faces lit by the ghostly white light of the screen. Something in my expression must have given away how nervous I was, because he gave me an encouraging smile. "There. That wasn't so bad, was—"

A long, ugly sound, the sound of paper being rent

apart by brute force. I didn't understand—I actually turned to see who was ripping a book in half. It was only when I saw the door swinging closed that I realized what had happened. The wedge had worked just fine until the thirty year-old volume had simply split in half from the strain. Now the huge door was closing itself, the chain rattling loudly as the iron weight dragged it closed.

Connor reacted faster than I could, sprinting past me to the door. He reached it just as it closed. He'd taken the phone with him, leaving me in pitch blackness, and I tried to contain my panic. *It's not locked. I have the key. He'll open it again in a second. Any second....*

"Um...."

"What?" I asked quickly.

I saw the light—just a faint glow at the far end of the room, moving up and down. "You know how the door opened inward?"

"Yeah?"

"There's no handle on our side."

Cold, twisting fear, rising up inside. *"What?"*

"I'm serious. There was one once, but it's been taken off. Just screw holes. There's nothing to pull on."

I looked around me. I knew that the room was fifty feet or more long. I knew that, narrow as it was, there was still a good six feet of space in front of me. I knew that the ceiling was high overhead. But in the utter blackness, none of these things felt true anymore. I felt as if I was in a coffin with the walls creeping towards me, pressing tighter and tighter.

"Shine the light down here." My voice was ragged with fear.

"What?" He was distracted, still searching for some way to open the door.

"Shine the *light!*" Almost a sob.

Immediately, he shone the light towards me and a

dim, ghostly glow washed over me. The walls were pushed back, breathable air opening up in front of me. I started blundering towards him, hands stretched out in front of me.

"Are you okay?" he asked.

I couldn't see him, but I could hear the worry in his voice. I couldn't answer, though. All that mattered was getting to the light of his phone, getting closer to the hairline crack of light around the door. I was almost panting with fear, the speed at which it had come on only adding to the panic, my throat closing up. Every step brought the threat of a cobweb brushing my face, every shelf my fingers touched felt loaded with creeping, scuttling life—

And then I reached him, and my hands instinctively grabbed at his arms and pulled him close. I panted against his chest.

"Karen? *Karen?!* Are you okay?"

And somehow, my face pressed against the soft cloth of his t-shirt, I was. He was clean and solid and real and, if I closed my eyes, I could forget how dark it was and imagine we were out in the sunlight somewhere. I took a deep breath and then another, feeling my fear ebb away. "...yes," I said slowly. I started to feel stupid. "Sorry. I just panicked."

"It's okay." His voice was more tender than I'd ever heard it—except maybe outside the bar, weeks ago, when he'd agreed to help. *Pitying the poor scared girl.* I could feel my face grow hot, and was almost glad it was so dark.

"Were you kidding, about the door?" I ran my hand over the wood.

"Kidding? No, of course not! There's no handle." Like an idiot, I still felt the need to check for myself, but he was right—there wasn't.

"Okay, let's not panic. We just need to call someone to come push the door from the other side," he said.

I waited. "Okay—so call someone."

"I'm just deciding who to call. Someone reliable...someone who'll come and get us right now...." He was trying to be casual about it, but I could see him scrolling through name after name on his contacts list. "Thing is," he said, "most of my friends are people I meet from bands and stuff. They don't go to Fenbrook and the ones who do...they don't show up every day. Or even most days."

The party animal, the guy who spent his life hanging out with friends...didn't have even one he could absolutely rely on.

"Call Jasmine," I told him. My phone was in my bag outside the door, so I gave him the number. She answered on the third ring.

I'd seen too many movies where the trapped person starts off with something like *"Now listen carefully, I'm—"* and then gets cut off. "I'mshutinthemusicstoreroom," I said, all in one breath.

"What?" asked Jasmine.

"Come rescue me. Please. Second floor, right at the back. Big door. Pitch black in here. Spiders. Help."

"I don't recognize this number," said Jasmine. "Whose phone is this?"

"Connor's. He's in here with me."

There was a pause.

"What are you doing in a storeroom with Connor with the lights off?" asked Jasmine.

"Just come and rescue me! Please!" I hung up. "She's on her way," I told Connor.

And then there was silence. And as I relaxed a little more, the silence grew to be...comfortable.

Even *intimate.*

The phone's screen was lighting up a little of the room in front of me, but Connor was standing just off to the side and I couldn't see him. That meant I couldn't tell exactly how close he was to me...and that started to play all sorts of tricks on my mind.

We're in a dark room together, a little voice said. *If he feels the same way as you....*

Stop it, I told myself fiercely. "Say something," I said out loud.

"What?"

"Anything. Just so I know where you are."

There was a pause. "Thank you," he said.

"For what?"

"Helping me."

"I haven't helped you yet. And you helped me."

That silence again.

"Say something else," I said. "Tell me about the tattoo...tell me about Ruth." As soon as I'd said it, I regretted it. Why did I want to know about her?

"We met in New York, but she's from Ireland. One of those funny things, you know? Come thousands of miles and meet someone from back home."

"Uncanny," I said, feeling sick.

"Lasted six months. Then we split, and she headed back to Ireland."

"Why'd you split?" It was out before I could stop it.

There was a long pause. "We had a falling out." And there was a bitterness in his voice I'd never heard before.

Quick, change the subject. "That's one tattoo. Tell me about the other one."

"That means I was in prison."

The darkness went from being warm and

comfortable to a freezing, yawning void in an instant. "I'm sorry," I said quickly.

"It was a fair cop," he said mildly. "I deserved to be there."

I didn't ask the obvious question, so he went ahead and answered it for me. "Three months, because I was young and the prisons were full. GBH." He sighed. "That doesn't mean anything over here, does it?"

If it did, *I* had no idea what it meant. "No."

"Grievous. Bodily. Harm." He sighed, and I heard him tilt his head back to rest against the wall. When he spoke, it sounded like he was dredging the words up from deep within. "I was the stupid kid everybody made fun of. One guy in particular. And I got used to that. After a while you just accept it, and you accept getting the shit kicked out of you, too. But this one fella, that wasn't enough for him. He caught me with my guitar one day and he smashed it."

I stayed silent, listening.

"It was a piece of crap, if I'm honest. Could never tune it dead right. But it was the *one thing*, you know? The one thing I could do, the one thing in my life that wasn't shitty. And I watched him lift it over his head and bang it down on the curb, until it was in pieces, and I knew I wouldn't be able to afford another one. And...I sort of blanked out. Next thing I knew, I was standing over him and he had a bust jaw and a broken rib."

"Oh." It was a lousy thing to say, but I couldn't think of anything else.

"I was lucky—he healed pretty fast, no lasting damage. I was young, so they wiped my record not long after."

The story was reverberating through my head, the images so different to the Connor I knew. I couldn't imagine him hurting anyone.

You were right about him, a little voice inside me sang happily. *Back at the start, when you avoided him, when you thought he was trouble.*

But he wasn't like that. He'd helped me. He was *kind.* Or was I just hopelessly naïve? I stood there in the darkness and let it all seep into my brain...the prison record, the parties and the booze....

And I didn't care. I only cared about who he was *now.* I was getting to like that Connor; I was getting to like him a lot.

"Do you think we can do it—the recital?" I asked.

"Honest answer?"

"Yes, honest. Of course honest!"

"No."

My jaw dropped open. *"No?!"*

"Not unless you get that stick out of your arse." I didn't need to see him. I could hear the grin in his voice. Relief slammed through me.

"I don't have a—Well, you need to sharpen up a little. Since we're being honest."

"Yes ma'am."

I hesitated. "Do I really come across like that? Uptight?"

"I meant your playing."

"I know. But do I?"

The silence this time was heavy with possibilities.

"Maybe a little bit." The sound of rustling cloth— he was moving. "But nothing that couldn't be fixed."

I swallowed. Was he moving towards me? "Fixed how?"

"I was thinking...." His voice was very close now— right behind me. I tensed, but I didn't turn around. "I was thinking about maybe...."

Something dropped onto my cheek and scurried down my neck and under my top. I screamed at the top of my lungs and started pawing at my clothes, but it was moving, scuttling across my stomach, its legs hooking into my belly button—

I ripped my top over my head and threw it to the ground, backing up against Connor as I slapped at myself. My hand brushed against the crawling thing and swept it off into the darkness—

The door swung wide. "Ta-DAA!" said Jasmine as light flooded the room....

...to reveal me standing in jeans and bra, my back nestled up against Connor's chest. Jasmine's eyes bugged.

My mouth opened and closed a few times, but nothing came out.

***

"There was a spider," I told Connor. We were in the practice room, dusting off the acoustic guitars.

"Okay." He couldn't stop smiling.

"There *was!* What did you *think* was going on? I wouldn't just rip my clothes off and—" *And throw myself into your arms.* Except part of me would, but he wasn't to know that.

"Okay."

"Now Jasmine thinks there's something going on."

"But you're going to tell her there isn't?" Another one of those ambiguous questions he was so fond of.

"Of course!" And then I watched his reaction very carefully. Was it really possible that he liked me? Just before Jasmine had opened the door, it had felt like he was about to kiss me....

But he just gazed back at me, and what I could see in his eyes was the same conflict I'd seen that night outside the bar, when I'd asked him why he'd agreed to help me. *Maybe he's wondering how to let me down gently. Poor geeky girl who has a crush on him...*I looked away and extricated myself as best I could. "She doesn't understand that we're just...friends. I mean, we are friends, right?"

He gave me a slow nod. "Absolutely."

"Okay."

"Okay."

I should have felt better—I finally knew where I stood. *Friends.* I had a friend who I lusted after. A friend I was starting to feel something deeper for. A friend who, apparently, had no interest in me. Was it all my fault? Had I hesitated too long, back when I was denying even being attracted to him? Or had he always felt this way, and everything else was in my head?

Why were men so difficult to read? Why couldn't they come with a neon readout on their forehead showing exactly what they were feeling...and for whom?

"Do you want to go out?" Connor asked.

My train of thought hit the sudden turn and derailed completely.

"What?!" I was just surprised, but it came out as horror.

"As friends. Not as a date. Obviously." He said it quickly, but was he just clarifying...or backpedalling?

"Obviously," I echoed. "Where?"

"Somewhere you haven't been."

"How do you know where I haven't been?"

"I have a pretty good idea of the sorts of places you go."

I folded my arms. "Oh, really? Maybe I'm not as predictable as you think."

He counted off on his fingers. "Harper's and Flicker, because they're basically part of Fenbrook. A few favorite posh restaurants. Classical concerts." He studied me closely. "The New York Public Library and the Museum of Natural History."

My jaw dropped open. *How did he know?!* "Not even close," I said. "I go to...MMA fights! And I go to the parties afterwards! In really seedy bars!"

He leaned in close. *"Really?"*

"No. Not really." I hung my head. "God, I'm so boring!"

"All the more reason to come out with me tonight. Eight o'clock."

"Where?"

"It'll be a surprise."

CHAPTER 15

I N A WAY, not knowing where we were going made it
easier; if I'd had to dress for an upmarket restaurant
or a low-rent bar, I'd have spent hours second-
guessing my clothes. I put on jeans and a hooded top and
declared myself ready. Then I added some lipstick. Then
took it off again because we were just friends. Then put it
on again just *because*.

My phone rang, and I was so distracted that I
didn't even wonder who it might be, just snatched it up
and put it to my ear. "Hello?"

"How's practice?" asked my father.

Guilt rose up like a fist and slammed me in the
gut. "F—Fine," I told him, not very convincingly.

He hesitated for a second. "You *are* practicing,
aren't you, Karen?"

My breath was suddenly trapped in my chest. I
had been, of course. Every spare moment I got...but not
that night. I felt myself cringe. What was I doing? Going
on some mystery not-really-a-date when—

"It's not long until the recital," my father said, stealing my thoughts. "You should be practicing whenever you're not actually in a lecture." He hesitated again. "There's not...there's not a *boy,* is there?"

"No! No, God, of course not! Don't be silly!" I'd been saying the same thing for so many years that it sounded true, even to me. It *was* true. We were just friends, even if I was secretly lusting after him.

"Everything okay with the apartment?" he asked, as he always did.

"Yes." I had my eyes squeezed shut, now. "Everything's fine. Thank you."

"No letters about bills or anything?"

He knew there weren't. That was the point. My chest grew tight because I knew what was coming. "No," I told him. "It's all running fine. Thank you. Thank you for paying for everything."

He managed to sound shocked. "Oh, sweetheart! You don't have to thank me! I know how hard you're working. That's thanks enough."

He would cut me off—that was the unspoken threat. If he found out about Connor, found out I wasn't rehearsing tonight, found out I was lying to him, he'd simply stop paying for the apartment, the bills, and my allowance. And I'd have no choice but to slink back to Boston and live with him.

"I should go and rehearse," I told him in a small voice.

"Don't work *too* late. No good being tired in lectures."

"I love you."

"Love you too, sweetheart."

I hung up and sat down on the bed. What had I been thinking? He was right, I should be rehearsing. I'd call Connor and tell him I couldn't make it. Remind him that he should be rehearsing, too. I scrolled through my contacts list with my thumb, but my eyes were hot and blurry, no matter how viciously I swiped at them with the back of my hand. *Don't cry. Don't cry. It wasn't even a date—it was just two friends going out. You're just upset because you got caught. You knew it was wrong, to try to—*

Have a life.

I sniffed and stared at Connor's name for a long, long time. And then I called a cab.

***

We met on 5th Avenue, which was my first clue. As we headed into Central Park and joined the crowds, I got it. "Ice skating?"

"Ever do it?"

"No." It looked like it might be fun. Then I saw the slashing, gleaming blades cutting into the ice at five thousand miles an hour and stopped.

"Are you *insane?*" I asked.

Connor looked genuinely bemused. "What? It's not going to hurt *that* much if you fall over."

"Fingers!" I waggled mine in front of his face. "We're musicians! What happens if you lose a finger?"

He grinned at me. "You're sweet."

I tried to ignore the warm rush that exploded in my chest. "I'm serious! I'm not risking my hands, and you shouldn't either!"

He patted me on the head.

I should have been infuriated—*Was* infuriated and yet...it was completely different to how he would have done it when I first met him. It didn't feel like he was mocking me, now. It felt like a shared gag. And the touch of his hand in my hair made me go tingly right down my back.

"Do you trust me?" he asked.

I looked at him. "Against my better judgment...yes."

"The blades aren't that sharp. And I borrowed these." He passed me a pair of thickly padded gloves. "Just to be on the safe side."

The warm glow he'd lit inside me grew stronger. He'd known that I'd be paranoid.

He knew me.

I took the gloves, laced on some skates and allowed him to lead me out onto the ice. I was nervous, but how hard could it be, right? I could see little kids out on the ice, and they were managing fine. It was probably easier than it looked.

It wasn't.

Who came up with the idea of taking a human—with two perfectly good, flat feet—and balancing them on two razor-thin pieces of metal on a slippery, hard, freezing cold surface and calling it *fun?* Probably the same person who somehow injected every child under ten with pro-level ice skating skills, allowing them to whiz past me at the speed of sound while I did a Bambi impersonation.

I staggered, my feet scrabbling for purchase and finding none, and fell on my ass for the seventeenth time.

Connor slowed to a stop beside me and offered his hand. "Want to stop?"

"No!" I said defensively as I got up. "I want to—" With absolutely no warning, I fell again, almost doing the splits as my legs shot from under me. "*Stupid* ice," I said under my breath.

When I looked up, he was doubled over with laughter.

"What?" I asked, bemused.

"Do you realize that you *never* swear?" he asked. "I mean, not even once, the entire time I've known you?"

I reddened. "What's so great about cursing?"

"Nothing. It's just...it's adorable."

I flushed in a whole different way.

He was still grinning, his eyes distant as he remembered something. "When you came to the bar that time and you stormed out, you said, '*I don't want your stupid beer.*' That was the moment I knew."

I blinked. "Knew what?"

He went pale for a second. "Knew...that I had to help you." He swallowed and rallied. "You were obviously helpless on your own."

I sighed and let him pull me up. He got me to my feet, but I slid forward and whacked right into him. There were about six layers of clothes between us, but I could still feel the warm wall of his pecs against me, my head cradled in his neck. *Was that him, or me? Did he pull me harder than he had to, or did I slip more than I needed to?*

"Sorry," I said, and I saw his body tense at the heat of my breath on his neck. I drew back a little and looked up at him....

There was a flash, and we both looked round.

A man on skates holding a camera had just taken a picture of us. "Am I okay to use that? It's for the park website—romantic couples, y'know?"

"We're not together," I said quickly. I wanted to get in there before Connor did, because if I heard the same words from his mouth I knew they'd hurt.

"Oh! Sorry." He beamed and skated off. Connor and I looked at each other in mutual embarrassment. I was freezing, bruised, my hands were numb despite the gloves and I was pretty sure my jeans were soaked through, but I wasn't going to quit until he was ready.

"Hot chocolate?" he asked, and I wanted to hug him.

***

We wandered down the street, ostensibly looking for a cab but focused mainly on each other, our fingers gradually thawing in the heat from the cardboard cups. Fairy lights were lighting up the trees above, casting a soft glow over us and it felt magical. Like anything could happen.

"Can I ask you something?" he said.

I could feel his eyes on me, and I tensed up. "Sure."

"Why are you having problems? I mean, you ace all your performances, you get straight As...why do you even need the recital? What's *your* weak spot?"

I hadn't shared my problem with anyone. Other people must have wondered why I always skipped the presentations, but they didn't know *why*. I'd always been too self-conscious about it, but I wanted to tell him. I wanted to tell him everything.

"I can't speak in front of people," I told him. It sounded so pathetic, when I said it out loud.

"You're scared?" he asked.

Yep, I thought guiltily. *You have an actual problem, a learning disability. And I'm basically just afraid.* "Yeah."

He was silent for a moment, and I thought I'd stunned him with how ridiculously minor my problem was. But he was frowning, really concentrating, and it hit me that he was imagining what it was like for me. No one had ever done that for me before.

"That's rough," he said at last, and I could hear he

meant it.

"It's stupid," I said. "I should just get over it."

He put a hand on my shoulder and stopped me. "No, it isn't. You can't function if you're scared." The hand lifted to my cheek, and I drew my breath in.

"What are *you* scared of?" I asked, more to cover what I was feeling than because I expected him to tell me.

"Trying," he said simply. "You can't fail if you don't try."

I looked up into his eyes. Another piece of the puzzle that was Connor Locke fell into place. The party lifestyle was easy. Playing solo in bars was easy. Battling the dyslexia, doing the recital...that was *hard*.

And yet...he was doing it for me.

And then I felt it. Something bigger than thought, heavier than an ocean. It hadn't crept up on me; it had been there, hanging above me, for weeks. I just hadn't acknowledged its presence.

Standing there under the fairy lights, I finally let it slam down into me, and I felt like I was falling and flying at the same time. Oh my God.

"Are you okay?" Connor asked, concerned. "You look...spooked."

A cab drew near and I practically ran under its wheels to get it to stop. "I'm fine!" I yelled over my shoulder. "I'll see you tomorrow." And before he could protest, I was bouncing into the back seat and waving goodbye.

Even before his hand had dropped from its bemused wave, I had my phone out.

"Natasha? It's Karen. I'm in love with Connor Locke!"

A second of bar noise and whispered voices. She must be in Flicker, with the others.

"Duh!" chorused Natasha, Clarissa and Jasmine down the phone.

CHAPTER 16

"What do you mean, '*duh*'?" I asked. "You *knew?!*"

I heard the phone being put down on the table as Natasha put me on speaker. "You *have* been spending a lot of time with him," she said.

"And he is super-hot," said Clarissa.

"And I caught the two of you in the storeroom," said Jasmine. "Are you sure it's love and not just...you know...the understandable desire to wrap your thighs around him?"

I thought back to the sidewalk. My heart was still hammering from it. "Nope. Definitely the real thing."

All three of them *squeed*.

"What do I *do?*" I asked.

"Tell him, obviously." It was Natasha's voice, but I could hear them all making noises of agreement.

"I can't. I don't know if he feels the same. I don't know if he feels *anything*. He might just feel sorry for me."

"Okay," said Jasmine. "What you need is a signed

contract from him saying he promises not to reject you if and when you choose to tell him. Then you can tell him safely."

I hesitated. "Really?"

"No, you idiot, not really! I was making a point! There are no guarantees in this stuff. You just have to go for it."

I bit my lip. "What if he says 'No' and we can't work together after that?"

Jasmine was in full romance-guru mode. "You can't put love on hold for your career!"

"I'm serious! If we don't do the recital together, I don't graduate."

She went quiet for a second and when she spoke again, she'd sobered up. "Hmm."

We all sat there in silence, them in the dark, noisy warmth of Flicker and me in the back seat of a cab, rushing through the streets. Everyone was thinking hard, but no one came up with anything. It was Clarissa who eventually dared to speak. "This is still huge. You're in *love.*"

"I've never been in love before."

There was a shocked silence from the other end, which was when I realized I'd said it out loud.

"Never?" asked Jasmine reverently. "That's so romantic!"

"He better not break your heart," said Clarissa.

"I haven't even told him yet! I *can't* tell him!" I thought for a second. "I'm seeing him tomorrow. He's coming to my apartment to rehearse." Suddenly, the world seemed to be shifting under me. When we'd arranged it, it had been no big deal—just a chance to work on his essay with him. But now....

Now, I either had to risk everything and tell him how I felt...or sit there and pretend not to be in love with him.

**

    Construction work meant the cab had to take a circuitous route to get back to my area, which gave me some thinking time. I'd ended the call (after the girls had drunk toasts to me down the phone) and was sitting in the back of the cab, stewing.

    It was ridiculous—I couldn't hide how I felt, just because of the recital.

    It was ridiculous—I couldn't risk my entire career, just because I was in love with him.

    I went round and round as we drove through block after block and didn't make any progress. What if it was just me? What if he saw me as just a friend?

    "I'm sorry, Karen. I don't feel that way about you. I mean, you're not really my type, you know?"

    I imagined crying in front of him. Or passing out. Or running from the room. I was pretty sure that however badly it went, he'd be able to work with me afterwards, but could I work with him?

    And what if—by some slim chance—it went well? What if he *did* feel the same way, and we ended up...what, exactly? Going out? Boyfriend and girlfriend? I tried to imagine Connor with a steady girlfriend, and couldn't. Imagining him with *me* just seemed ridiculous.

    And if he *did* feel the same way about me...why hadn't he said anything? Why hadn't he asked me out?

    For months, I'd held back the tide, denying how I felt about him...and now that I'd finally admitted it, I couldn't do a damn thing about it.

    I stared out of the window without seeing until finally I saw something that made me jerk back, surprised. A street sign I recognized, despite having never been there in person before. Jasmine's street.

"Wait. Turn in here, please," I told the cabbie.

If I couldn't solve my own problems, maybe I could help my friends.

***

I'd never been to Jasmine's apartment—she'd always preferred to meet at mine, or at Flicker. As I got out of the cab, I could see why.

The neighborhood itself was bad—worse than Connor's, by my estimate. And the building Jasmine rented in was by far the worst on the block, with enough graffiti, chips and cracks for the rest of the street put together. I was sure the rusting fire escape wasn't up to code and two windows were boarded up.

Jasmine had said she wouldn't accept any more money for rent, but I knew she was still tight. I also knew she was safely in Flicker with the others, where she couldn't stop me helping her.

It was a total spur-of-the-moment thing. I figured if I talked to her landlord and offered to quietly pay him something towards the rent, I could give Jasmine some breathing room—and she wouldn't be able to reject it because, by the time she found out about it, it would all be done.

I didn't have much money on me, but the allowance my father sent each month would arrive soon. If I budgeted super-tightly, I could probably spare a hundred bucks or so—and that was better than nothing, right? I could arrange it with the landlord now and then PayPal him or something.

I checked the bell pushes. There was one with Jasmine's surname, so I was in the right place. Jasmine had said that her landlord had taken the whole of the first floor, so I pushed that one.

The man who opened the door was balding, with greasy hair slicked back from his temples. The belly that pushed out his Nicks t-shirt suggested that his sweatpants were for comfort, not exercise. "Yeah?" he asked doubtfully.

"It's about Jasmine—she rents from you?" I said, trying to make my voice as bright and bouncy as hers.

He frowned. "Mm-hmm?"

I shifted my weight from foot to foot. It was freezing, out on the doorstep. "She said that she'd been having some problems paying. I'm her friend."

His expression changed. "You have her rent? She still owes me."

"No, I don't actually have any money...."

He gave me a *you're wasting my time* look.

"But Jasmine said she was talking to you about working out an arrangement."

He looked shocked. "She told you about that?"

"Yes. Maybe I could help with that? Like, each month?"

He blinked a couple of times and looked at me a little closer. Then he opened the door wide. "Come in," he said.

Inside, it was warmer. But if anything the interior was even less well maintained, with water stains and cracked paintwork. A couple of the lights looked like they hadn't worked in years.

"Let's go into Jasmine's apartment," the landlord said, and led the way up the stairs.

As he unlocked the door, I started to get a weird feeling in the pit of my stomach. He was the landlord and Jasmine was behind on her rent—he probably had a perfect right to be there. But it still felt wrong, wandering into her place when she wasn't there. Or was it something else that was bothering me?

It was a small apartment—bigger than Connor's, but still only three rooms: a lounge and kitchen combined, a bedroom beyond that and a door to what I assumed was the bathroom.

Something crunched underfoot. I had a pretty good idea what it was, and I didn't want to lift my shoe to find out if I was right.

The landlord smiled at me...and then walked straight through to the bedroom. "You coming?" he asked. And pulled off his t-shirt.

I stood there gaping.

"What?" he asked, sounding genuinely puzzled. Then a sly smile crept across his face. "Oh. Is she coming too? Were you meaning, like, you and her at the same time?"

"Sorry!" I said, and bolted. I was so shocked that I didn't have time to be scared, or to really process things, until I was two streets away and sitting panting in the back of a cab.

And then I called Jasmine, who was still sitting in Flicker, and told her we had to talk.

CHAPTER 17

"I can't believe you went there without telling me," said Jasmine. It was the next morning and, despite the cold, we were sitting on the swings in a kid's playground down the street from Fenbrook. It was early enough that we were the only ones there, surrounded by yesterday's snowmen.

"I thought I could help. I didn't know that you—"

"I haven't done it yet. We'd just talked about it. I was going to do it last month, but then you saved my ass with the $300."

We sat in silence for a second, swinging slowly back and forth. "Whose idea was it?" I asked.

"Mine," said Jasmine. "I thought...you know, I thought—" She took a deep breath, and I waited while she got her voice under control. "I thought that if I took the lead and set the terms, then I could control things. Better than having him pressuring me when all my stuff was already out on the street."

I closed my eyes. "There must be another way." I

frowned. "Doesn't your brother live in New York?" I vaguely remembered her mentioning it, one night in Flicker. Then my stomach lurched as the rest of the memory swept in—she'd been talking about avoiding him.

Jasmine shook her head. "No. That's a whole world I don't want any part of. He's trouble. He's done time, for God's sake."

"People change," I said, thinking of Connor.

But Jasmine shook her head firmly. We sat there for a moment, legs kicking occasionally to swing us, trying to keep moving so that our feet didn't freeze. Then Jasmine took a deep breath and said, "Now that you know about...the arrangement...I need your help with something else. But you need to promise me something."

"Anything. What?"

She turned and stared at me. "You need to promise me you'll still be my friend after I tell you."

Cold fear clutched at my chest. "Jasmine, of course! What is it?"

She looked towards the horizon. "I've decided to start escorting."

I sat there in dumb shock for a moment. "Jasmine, *no!*"

"You said—"

"I'm not judging! I'm just saying—isn't there another way?"

She shook her head. "I have to pay my rent, but between Fenbrook and auditions I don't have time to work any more hours. Escorting is the only thing that'll cover it, and it'll cover it *well.*" She kept staring straight ahead. "I've really thought about it. I can work in the evenings, which is perfect because it leaves the daytime free for auditions and classes. I figure I'd be good at it—I mean, it's just acting, right? Acting and sex, and I'm good at both."

I bit my lip.

"I need to find an agency and go for an interview." She finally looked over at me. "I really don't want to do it on my own. Could you...come along with me? Moral support?"

I thought of her in a hotel room, crushed beneath some married, forty-something businessman and closed my eyes. No. No way. I couldn't let her do it.

But...I couldn't stop her, either. I could feel the fear rising up inside me. The fear of losing her as a friend, if I stopped her doing what she wanted to do. The fear of being wrong—what if she got thrown out on the street, and had to drop out of Fenbrook, and it was all my fault? Worst of all, the fear that I'd do the wrong thing, make the wrong call, because I didn't know what the hell I was doing. I was a twenty-one year old virgin, for God's sake. I'd barely lived—what chance did I have of talking someone through this huge decision?

So I did the only thing I could do. I folded.

"Of course," I told her.

"And you won't tell Nat, or Clarissa?"

I nodded.

She jumped up and hugged me. "You're the best friend ever!" she told me.

Which was weird, because I felt like the worst.

***

I'd arranged to meet Connor that afternoon at my place, for no better reason than it had a desk we could work at side by side, and I knew he wouldn't want to do it at Fenbrook with everyone watching his struggles. I made sure I was home a half hour early and spent thirty pointless minutes cleaning things that were already clean and tidying things that were already tidy. If I could cook, I would have baked cookies.

A buzz on the entry phone. The exact same noise it made when anyone arrived...so how come it felt different, knowing it was Connor? It was something about inviting him into the same place I spent so much time thinking about him...Connor the reality colliding with Connor the fantasy. Just down the hall was the shower where I'd been unable to get him out of my mind. A little further on, the bedroom where I'd used the dildo on myself, with his face filling my mind. The bed where I'd had *that* dream. How was I going to keep myself together, with all that around me?

I hit the button and, a few moments later, heard his low double knock at the door. As I reached for the handle, my heart was hammering.

What's the matter with me? I've been lusting after him for a month. I'd thought that was bad—sitting in rehearsal after rehearsal thinking about his hands or lips on me. But now I was actually thinking about *him*. Connor was wired deep into my soul, but I had to pretend there was nothing there at all.

I opened the door in what I hoped was a *I'm just your friend* way. "Hi!" *Too loud.*

He was gazing up and down the hallway. "I can't believe this is where you live." Then he took a step inside and saw the size of the place. "*Jesus!*"

"It's not *that* big." I closed the door behind him, feeling incredibly guilty. "I'm tidy. That makes it look bigger than it is."

"Are you kidding? Watch this." He paced out a length. "There. That's the size of my apartment."

He wasn't even all the way across my lounge. I flushed. "My father chose it. He pays the rent. I would have chosen somewhere smaller." *Liar,* I thought.

He cocked his head to one side. "No TV?"

Most people didn't spot that. It takes a certain sort of mind to notice what isn't there. "Yeah. My father sort of...doesn't like television. We never had one when I was a kid, and when he furnished this place—"

"He *furnished* it?"

I hesitated. "Is my life sounding really weird now?"

"A little. Although some things are starting to make sense." He leaned against the wall and regarded me with those blue-gray eyes that saw everything. "If he doesn't like TV, he's either an academic, a hippy or an arty-type. You don't strike me as having been raised by a hippy, so my money's on arty-type."

"Pianist."

"A pianist who makes enough money he can send his daughter to Fenbrook and put her up in *this*." I watched him put it together. "Karen Montfort. *Hugo* Montfort?"

I nodded.

"My music teacher in Belfast used to play his CDs. Shit! Hugo Montfort...."

I pointed to the table. "We should get on with it."

He eyed the table as if it was a pit of snakes, but nodded and sat down. I could see him looking at the towering pile of lecture notes I'd assembled.

"Don't panic," I told him. "We don't need all of it. This is *everything*, right back to when I started, plus some stuff from Dan to cover the first semester."

Connor frowned. "Yeah, you started late. Where were you, that first semester?"

I looked at him. "You remember that? You didn't even know me back then."

He got that look again, just for a second, as if he was battling with himself. "This new girl started and got

203

straight A's," he told me. "Everyone remembers that."

"Apart from my presentations. I was in Boston, first semester. I don't want to talk about it."

He nodded, and I immediately felt guilty. He'd opened up and shared so much of himself with me, and I still couldn't tell him about that day they found me on the roof.

I took a deep breath and told him my plan for helping him with his essay. I couldn't catch him up on every lecture, and I wasn't going to try. For one thing, I was pretty sure that he'd absorbed a good amount of the material from the lectures he'd attended. For another, he only needed a small subset of them to get the knowledge he needed for the essay. We'd go through the question together, then he'd tell me what he understood by it and what he thought he'd need to cover in the answer. I'd catch him up on any lectures he'd missed, using my notes. And then he'd dictate the essay to me, and I'd type it out. It wasn't cheating, really—I was just acting as interpreter between the written notes he needed and his brain, and back again.

We worked side by side for hours, because we found that across the table from each other felt too weird, like I was lecturing him. Side by side had its own drawbacks, though. When he leaned in to look at some music, his head brushed my hair and all the hairs on the back of my neck stood up. When I pointed to something on the essay question, I brushed his hand and we both looked at the offending contact for a second, not saying anything. Every silence felt huge, every look we exchanged loaded with meaning. But still, I couldn't tell him how I felt. What if it was all just me? What if I said something and he just looked at me in amazement? What if he *laughed?*

"I'm making coffee," I said abruptly and fled to the

kitchen. While the machine did its thing, I rested my forehead against the cold refrigerator door and took a long breath. I couldn't tell him. If it went wrong, then what? If we couldn't rehearse together—if he even didn't manage to get his grades up—I was doomed.

I opened my eyes and straightened up. Unless I got some sort of clear signal from him, I had to keep it to *friends*.

"You okay?"

I span around. He was standing in the doorway, watching me.

"Fine." I passed him his coffee. "Let's work."

The essay didn't have to be in until the end of the week, so there was no reason we had to get it done that night. But once we'd started, it felt like we couldn't stop—not only were we worried about losing momentum, but I got the sense that Connor was actually enjoying himself. With the barrier of his dyslexia lifted, he was able to put everything he'd learned at Fenbrook to use—and as I'd suspected, he'd picked up a lot more than people had given him credit for. When you can't easily write stuff down, you get *very* good at listening.

We worked for another two hours straight and broke for coffee. Another two hours put us past the halfway point and we both agreed that stopping would be wrong, so we ordered pizza. A final three hours put grease stains on my lecture notes and a finished essay on my laptop.

And we realized it was one in the morning.

"I'll call a cab," he said.

I knew he couldn't afford it. And I didn't want him walking from the subway station—not in his neighborhood. "You can stay here," I said as casually as I could.

He already had his phone in his hand. "Are you

sure?"

I nodded at the couch. "Jasmine's slept on it before. I'll get you a blanket."

I went to my bedroom to search for a blanket. Friends let friends stay over all the time, right? Even male friends of females. It didn't mean anything.

I found him a blanket and a still-wrapped toothbrush and took them through to the lounge, then stood there looking up at him, the bundle clutched to my chest. "So. Um. Anything else you need?"

He looked at the bundle—the bundle...or my chest? *Of course the bundle.* "No. That'll do me fine. Thanks, Karen."

I nodded and stood there like an idiot. *Tell him! Tell him! He's standing right here in your apartment and he's about to spend the night! There's never been a better time!*

"Goodnight," I said quickly and almost threw the bundle at him, then went to my bedroom without daring to look back.

I thought that once I was safely in my room, that would be it. It wasn't—I had to figure out when to undress. Normally, I'd have stripped off and thrown on an old t-shirt to sleep in before brushing my teeth. But did I want to pad around the place bare-legged and with my panties on show? What if I ran into him? On the other hand, if I stayed dressed right up until I dived under the covers, would that seem weirder?

Possibly I'm overthinking this, I thought.

I started to undress. When I was down to my panties—as naked as I was going to get—I stopped for a second and looked in the mirror. I tried to see myself as a man would see me—as Connor would see me. I knew my breasts were too small, my shoulders too wide. Was it even possible that he could find me attractive, next to all the busty actresses and lithe dancers at Fenbrook?

I imagined his eyes on me. I was sure I'd felt them in the practice room a few times, but what did that mean? Men will look at any woman. Had he kept looking? Did he want to see me? Did he *want* me?

I touched my hand to my cheek, watching myself in the mirror, and trailed it down over my breasts. My nipples were already stiffly pointing, almost too sensitive to brush against. My hand slipped down over my stomach. Lower....

There was a knock at the door. "Karen?"

I whirled to face the door. Adrenaline was suddenly crashing through me, my heart thundering in my chest. My mouth opened and a big, big part of me wanted to call out, "*Come in.*"

"One sec," I said, and pulled on an old, soft t-shirt. I looked down at my bare legs and then dived into bed, pulling the covers over me. I took a second to run my hands through my hair. "Okay."

He cracked the door open and then swung it wider when he saw I was decent. "Hi," he said.

He was shirtless, his chest smooth and magnificent, broad pecs leading my eyes down to hard abs and a narrow waist. I'd had the image burned into my mind ever since his dressing room, but remembering it and seeing it were two different things.

"Hi." The covers were around my waist. I suddenly wondered if he could see that my nipples were hard through the thin t-shirt, but didn't dare glance down to look. Instead, I let my eyes rove down below his waist. He was in black jockey shorts, and his legs were thickly muscled and dusted with curly black hair. I dragged my eyes back up his body and sat there waiting for him to tell me why he was there.

"Sorry to bother you. But,"—he paused, staring

into my eyes, and my chest clenched tight—"...do you have any floss?"

I stared at him, thinking I'd misheard. "Floss?"

"Dental floss."

"I know what it *is*. Yes. There's some in the bathroom cabinet."

He nodded. "I thought so. I just didn't want to go looking in case...you know."

I made a quick mental list of everything in the cabinet. I wasn't on the pill. I wasn't on any medication. Nothing he shouldn't see. "Thanks. It's fine."

"Okay then."

"Okay."

"Goodnight, then."

"Goodnight."

He hesitated for another second on the threshold and then backed out and closed the door behind him. I stared at the white-painted wood for several minutes. Had that been for real, or just an excuse to come in, to see if I was...what? Naked and ready? Had I avoided embarrassment by diving under the covers, or missed some massive opportunity?

I put a pillow over my face and screamed into it as loudly as I dared.

***

An hour later, I was still awake.

It didn't matter that he was two rooms away. He was *there,* right in my apartment, as warm and alive and *real* as he could possibly be.

I imagined going in there and gently shaking him awake. *Connor, I have to tell you something.* But what if I was wrong? He was the man...why wasn't *he* making a move, if he felt the same way?

I thought of how he'd looked at the door, how those smooth slabs of muscled chest would feel under my palms. How solid and unyielding he'd be if I pressed my body to his, all the way from lips to toe. I wanted him, more than I'd ever wanted anything in my life.

I let my hand, under the covers, find the softness between my thighs. Not rubbing, exactly, just...resting there. I imagined it was his hand, or the hard outline of his cock through his pants, and that was all I needed for the heat to start building.

He could be here, right now in this bed. All I have to do is go and talk to him.

I remembered the way he'd nearly kissed me, in the storeroom, and my whole body went weak. I wanted him to take me. I wanted him to—

"Fuck me." My whisper was as quiet as I could make it, barely audible, but it was there. And hearing it, hearing my own mouth form that deliciously hard "k", sent a wave of heat down my body, oily black and dangerously addictive. My hand *was* moving now, thin cotton pressed tight against my moistened lips.

All I have to do is go in there.

It was a game, almost. An edgy fantasy, because it could so easily become real. I rolled over onto my stomach, my hand beneath me. My cheek was pressed against the pillow, eyes on the door. *What if I just went in there, right now, and told him?* My hips were moving in small, firm little arcs, grinding myself against my fingers, faster and faster—

I suddenly tore back the covers and swung my legs out of bed. Three quick steps across the room and I had the door open.

What am I doing?!

The floors were new, solid polished wood. They didn't make a sound as I crept towards the lounge.

All the time lying awake had let my eyes adjust to the darkness. I could see the outline of him stretched out on the couch, the blanket I'd given him down around his waist. His bare chest rose and fell softly in the glow of the streetlights.

I stepped closer.

This is weird. And stupid. And stalkerish.

Closer still. Close enough to touch him, though I didn't dare.

What am I doing here? Am I going to wake him up?!

I stared down at him. It wasn't just the sex, I realized. It wasn't just wanting him. It was what had hit me after the ice skating, what had been building slowly for weeks—maybe even since I first met him, on some level. I was in love with him, and I had to tell him.

There was a voice in my head that sounded a lot like my father. *He's your one shot at the future you've always wanted. You have a chance—a slim chance—to save your career, and you're going to throw that away for...what? A stupid infatuation with a man who's done prison time for hurting people?*

I gazed down at him. I couldn't imagine him hurting anyone. I was only a few feet from him, now, and I squatted down until our faces were at the same height. *I could lean forward right now and wake him with a kiss.*

I waited there, feeling it all boil through me. The lust and the fear and the love.

What if he wakes up? What if he wakes up and sees me like this?

Then my stomach lurched. *What if he's already awake? What if he's lying there faking and he knows I'm watching him?*

I went absolutely still and listened to his

breathing, deep and rhythmic. Was he lying there with every emotion screaming, desperate to scoop me up in his arms and pull me to him?

Or was he completely unaware of my existence?

Very slowly, I stood and walked back to my bed.

***

The next morning, I crept into the shower super-early so I could be sure of being dressed before Connor woke up. I stood there under the spray and told myself over and over that I'd made the right decision. Until I knew how he felt, I had to keep my own feelings hidden. Well, fine. I could do that. I could be the perfect, innocent friend.

It occurred to me that the shower was turning into one of my epics, so I got out, wrapped myself in a towel and opened the bathroom door, only to find Connor standing there. He was maybe a foot from me and, with tousled hair and a little extra stubble, he looked if anything better than the night before. I suddenly realized that my towel wasn't much bigger than Jasmine's hooker dress, only covering me from breasts to thighs.

We stared at each other. "It's all yours," I told him.

He nodded, but he wasn't looking at the bathroom. He was looking at me.

"I'm dripping," I told him.

He just stared at me. And then reluctantly stepped aside to let me past. I walked to my bedroom on trembling legs, feeling his eyes on me the whole way. I shut the door and stood with my back against it, breathing hard.

It's just because he's in your apartment, I told myself. *Once you're rehearsing again, everything will be fine.*

211

***

We had coffee and chatted about Belfast. He had two brothers, one of whom was in prison.

"Now that I know about me," he said, "I'm wondering if he's dyslexic too. He dropped out of school when he was a kid. I was lucky: I had my music." He sipped his coffee and looked at me. "And I have you."

I tried to will my hand to be steady, but the surface of my coffee rippled and shivered.

***

Later, at Fenbrook, we rehearsed again and things weren't back to normal. They weren't even close.

I couldn't take my eyes off him: the way his fingers worked the strings, the frown of concentration as he got to a difficult section, even the way he stretched his back when we took a break, his chest flexing under his t-shirt.

For the third time in a row, I missed my cue and came in late. "*Sugar!*" I said under my breath. "Sorry."

When I looked up, he was quaking with silent laughter. "What?"

He went to speak, but started laughing again. "*Sugar?!*" he said eventually.

I flushed, but it didn't bother me as it would have done a month before. I wasn't intimidated by him anymore. "It's what I say."

"We need to teach you to swear; fortunately, you came to the right place. Give me a good, strong 'Bugger'"

I looked at him. "Bugger," I said tentatively.

"Like you mean it."

"*Bugger!*" It actually felt pretty good.

"Now let's progress to a F'ckin' 'ell."

I took a deep breath. "Fucking hell."

"No, more Irish. There's no 'u' or 'g' or 'h'. And make it more mournful, like you're a kid who's lost his pocket money and can't buy any chips."

"*F'ckin' 'ell!*" I said, louder than I meant to.

The door opened and Professor Harman put his head through the gap. "Everything okay in here?" he asked, in a tone that implied it certainly wasn't. I went white.

"Just...getting into the spirit," Connor told him.

Harman gave him a long look and then closed the door, and we both burst out laughing.

***

When Connor got his essay back, a little over a week later, he bounded up to me to show me the red-circled B.

"That's great—" I started to say, but his hands were already closing around my waist. He lifted me into the air, spinning me around and around as the other students moved back out of the way. When he set me down, both of us were high on the moment, panting, our faces inches apart. We stared at each other and—

He moved back. "Thanks," he said. "For helping me."

I'd been a fraction of a second away from closing my eyes and puckering up, and my face flushed red at the thought of how close I'd come to making a complete fool of myself. "No problem."

We turned and walked away.

CHAPTER 18

IT WAS FOUR WEEKS UNTIL THE RECITAL. Connor had handed in another essay and managed another B. Four of the six sections of our piece were finished, and we were both working away composing the final two. We figured we'd earned a break, so we all went to Flicker.

The snow had melted and the sun was doing its best to warm the frigid air, but it was cool enough that everyone was still in coats when we arrived. Connor, of course, was in his trademark leather jacket. Jasmine had grown attached to the fur monstrosity I'd found for her—she'd named it "Abe" for "Abominable Snowman"—while Clarissa was in an almost floor-length leather coat that probably cost a month's rent. Natasha was sporting some high-tech jacket Darrell had bought her—his looked like it matched—and Neil, of course, looked like Neil, in jeans and a biker jacket.

And me? I was in the same sensible winter coat I'd worn since it first got cold. Some things don't change.

Some do, though. I was going to tell Connor how I felt.

I'd thought about nothing else all week. I wanted to be on familiar ground and I didn't want to be alone when I did it. If it went wrong, I wanted the girls to be on standby with hugs and alcohol. They'd been briefed, of course.

I wanted to make an impact, so when I peeled off my winter coat it revealed a scoop-neck black sweater that—with a lot of help from a push-up bra—managed to give the illusion of curves. I'd spent about an hour on my hair, too, using tongs to coax most of the frizz out of it. It didn't equal Natasha's soft, lustrous locks, but it was a start.

We all sat down and I knew as soon as I looked at Darrell that something was horribly wrong. His skin was almost gray, and his hair didn't look sexily messy—it looked greasy and unkempt. Heavy bags had formed under his eyes, and when he sat down it was with a sad sigh of relief, as if even the walk from the cab had been an effort. That was something else I'd noticed—he'd brought Natasha in a cab, not on his bike.

I tried to catch Natasha's eye, but she was quizzing Connor on which bars he played in.

"So! How are things?" I asked Darrell brightly.

He smiled at me, and underneath the mask of tiredness I could see the old him peeking through. "Okay."

And that was it—just one word. Back when he and Natasha were first together, he'd talked non-stop about bikes and riding and how Natasha inspired him. He'd been hungry for new experiences, full of life. Now, he seemed like a different person.

"What are you working on?" As soon as I said it, I wished I could take it back. I watched Darrell collapse in on himself, his body hunching over the table, his gaze locked on his glass.

"I'm...between things, right now." And he glanced up at me, eyes almost pleading with me not to ask anything more.

A deep unease started to shift and churn inside me. This was *Darrell,* sexy, confident, multi-millionaire *Darrell.* Natasha had spoken of nightmares, and he certainly looked like he wasn't sleeping...but what had changed, that they were now reducing him to *this?*

I understood how losing your job could make someone depressed, but hadn't Darrell essentially worked for himself? Couldn't he just design, or build stuff, or whatever it was he did in that massive workshop? When I was there for the party, it had all been covered in sheets, but that had been weeks ago. Had he not worked since? Had he not worked since he quit his job? A man who had been insanely driven, even obsessive, about his work seemed to have stopped dead, and in my mind that pointed to something being deeply wrong.

When I looked over at Natasha, she was staring back at me, her teeth worrying at her lip. She gave me a slow nod, the internationally recognized women's symbol for *we'll talk later.*

I looked across at Clarissa. She was sitting on Neil's knee, and he was nuzzling her neck. She was smiling, and if it hadn't been for our conversation in the restaurant I would have thought they were happy. Looking closer, though, I could see the worry in her eyes.

"I'll get some more drinks," said Connor, standing up. This was it, the perfect time to get him alone and—

I couldn't do it. I looked desperately at the girls and nodded towards the restroom. "I'm going to—you know," I said as I stood.

"Good idea," said Jasmine, jumping up.

"Me too," said Clarissa, sliding off Neil's lap.

"Yep," said Natasha.

We left Darrell and Neil sitting there in shock, suddenly alone at the table.

In the restroom, Jasmine pinned me to the wall with a pointed finger. "Don't even *think* about backing out."

Natasha beamed. "I've been talking to him. He's nice. Nicer than when we first met him, less...."

"Arrogant," said Clarissa. "And still *edible*. Seriously. *With a spoon.*"

I looked at myself in the mirror. "But...I have no clue if he feels the same way."

"You've been working together for months," said Natasha. "You must have *some* idea."

I thought about all the times it felt like we'd nearly kissed. The feel of him against me, the heavy silences. "I don't know! There are moments, but they don't add up to anything solid."

"Circumstantial evidence," said Jasmine wisely. She was still dreaming of a part in a police drama. "But if you wait to find a warm gun you'll miss your chance. You gotta go with your hunch. What does your gut tell you?"

My stomach was swirling and fluttering with nerves. "I think...I think...*yes.*"

"Then go for it," said Clarissa.

"But if he does like me, why hasn't *he* done something? He's had enough chances!"

Natasha shrugged. "You won't know that until you ask. So get out there!"

"But what if he changes his mind about the recital, or"—I realized I hadn't told them about his dyslexia, and didn't feel I should—"or...or doesn't work as hard and doesn't graduate? If he flunks, I flunk!"

"He's your *friend,* whatever else he is or isn't. Do you really think he'd do that to you?" said Jasmine.

I considered that, then opened my mouth again.

"If the next word out of your mouth is *'But',*" said Clarissa, "I will physically hurt you. *Go!*"

I took a deep breath and nodded. Then marched through to the bar.

Connor was leaning forward over the bar, grinning, and I instinctively smiled myself, even though he wasn't looking at me. I felt my confidence grow. This was the right thing to do.

I walked around the bar towards Connor, and that's when I saw her. She was sitting at the bar right next to him, but she'd been hidden from my view behind a pillar. He had his arm around her waist, and as I watched she leaned in close and whispered something in his ear, and he laughed and pulled her closer.

She had honey-blonde hair and a silver, low-cut top. She had jeans that looked like they were sprayed onto her toned, perfect ass. She'd been with him no more than five minutes, but she was already touching him like I never had, patting him on the back and then letting her hand idly stroke the muscles there. Flirting with him exactly as any woman would, if they weren't an over-analyzing, flat-chested geek.

I changed course and swung around to the far end of the bar, where the girls were waiting for me with open mouths.

"I know her," said Jasmine sadly. "She's in some of my acting classes—her name's Taylor. She's actually a sweet girl." She glanced at me. "I mean, I still want to kill her. Obviously." She looked at Connor and Taylor. "Bitch."

I wasn't angry with Connor. For a man known for his endless stream of girlfriends, it was amazing he'd stayed single this long—he must have finally bounced back from whatever Ruth had done to him. Or, worse, maybe he'd been ready weeks or months ago, and he *had* been interested in me, but I'd delayed so long that he thought nothing would ever happen. It was all my fault. *If I could just rewind time and not go to the restroom....*

My heart was breaking. I'd never understood that expression, never felt anything even remotely like the pain brought on by seeing the two of them laughing and smiling together. Everything good we'd had together was being ripped asunder inside me, never to be made whole again. I didn't want to cry. I just didn't want to feel that way anymore.

The barman came over to me. "What'll it be?"

I looked him straight in the eye. "I'll have The Godfather."

There was a little intake of breath from behind me. "*No one* has The Godfather!" said Jasmine.

The barman and I stared at each other. I nodded firmly.

He reached right down to the bottom shelf, rooted around at the very back and pulled out several large bottles with dusty tops. With a pallbearer's face he poured exact measures of them into a steel bowl, as if a cocktail shaker would be inappropriate. He mixed. He sprinkled in a mystery powder. He mixed again. And then he brought over three glasses, setting them all before me.

The first one was a standard shot glass. "The Godfather," he said, pouring a shot of what looked like black oil into it.

The second was a heavy-bottomed whiskey tumbler. "The Godfather Part II," he intoned reverently, filling it to the brim with the same black ooze.

The third was a standard tall glass. He poured in

the dregs and then added soda water to dilute it. The drink was a muddy brown. "The Godfather Part III," he said sadly. And then he stepped back, as if from a firework.

I looked across at Connor and Taylor. He finally saw me, and gave me a happy wave. In his mind, he'd done nothing wrong.

I drank.

CHAPTER 19

I WOKE UP, and it wasn't like throwing off the peaceful veil of sleep. It was more like sleep didn't like the taste of me and spat me out.

Something was wrong with me. My brain was too big for my skull, and expanding rapidly, the pressure and pain building by the second. When I turned my head to look at the clock, violet lances of agony spiked through my skull.

I was in my own bed, in my clothes—although my shoes were missing. The clock said 10:20am. I felt like I could sleep for another week, so what had woken me up? The pain in my head?

My stomach gave a warning lurch. No. Something worse.

I tried to get up, but all my movements were slowed down, my mind unable to cope with doing anything at normal speed. I had to focus on slowly swinging my legs out of bed and then carefully sitting up, and every millimeter triggered a fresh explosion in my head and gurgles in my stomach. When I tried to stand, my legs felt like rubber so I crawled to the bathroom on hands and knees.

The last thing I remembered was ordering The Godfather. What happened?

I decided I'd think about that later. I had to get to the bathroom before—

I crawled faster, hard wood under my knees and then white tiles and then—

I grabbed the toilet with both hands and vomited longer and harder than I ever had in my life. Long, long after my stomach was empty it continued to convulse— seemingly out of sheer spite. *I will never drink again,* I pleaded. *Never ever ever. Not even when Jasmine gets her big break. I promise. Never! Just please make it stop!*

I chose what I thought was a safe moment, closed the lid and flushed. Then I knelt there begging for it to finish its cycle because I needed to throw up again. *Come on! Come on!*

This went on for a half hour.

Eventually, my body figured out that there was nothing more inside me, but I didn't dare move in case I was wrong. I dozed off like that, still clutching at the bowl, and then woke with a start. I wanted to brush my teeth but, not up to the taste of mint yet, settled for washing my mouth out.

I crawled back to my bed, my throat raw. This time, I noticed the glass of water next to my clock and the Post-It stuck to it in Connor's handwriting: "DRINK THIS. TAKE THESE." There was an arrow and I followed it down to two white pills.

I didn't argue and gulped them down with the water. My stomach grumbled but indicated that, if I lay extremely still, it would play ball.

I begged for sleep to take me back and, eventually, it did.

When I woke up again the pain in my head was still there, but it had shrunk to a level that allowed me to actually think. I started to ask questions like, "What happened last night?" and "What did I say to Connor?" Clearly, he'd been the one who put me to bed. Did that mean we'd spent the evening together, before I'd become incapable of standing?

I closed my eyes as I thought about him and Taylor. Had I had a cat-fight with her? Had I declared my love for Connor and he'd laughed? I wracked my brain, but there was just a black void between drinking The Godfather and waking up. The only thing I could be sure of was that everything hadn't come out well. I clearly hadn't pushed my way between Connor and Taylor, told him how I felt and squealed in delight as he swept me up into his arms, because if that had happened he'd be here with me in my bed. Instead, he was probably across town somewhere in her bed. Probably waking up and having sleepy, languorous morning sex with her—

I felt like I was going to throw up again.

I opened my eyes to try to distract me and saw another note on my door. It was at eye height, so I hadn't noticed it when I'd crawled to the bathroom. It said "GO TO KITCHEN."

I pulled the covers over my head instead and lay there, half asleep and drowning in misery, until my stomach started to do a different sort of rumbling. Around noon, I finally pulled the covers around me like a protective cocoon and trudged to the kitchen.

There was a frying pan on the stove with oil already in it and a note on the handle saying "FRIDGE." There was a box of eggs I didn't remember buying and a pack of some sort of strange, flat bread. When I opened the refrigerator there was a pack of bacon. Connor must have bought all this stuff the night before....

That's when I spotted the final note, on a plate. It said, "EAT = FEEL BETTER" and, crucially, there was a smiley face underneath.

That smiley face gave me hope. If I'd done anything too awful, he wouldn't have done all this for me...right?

The bread-like things turned out to be potato bread, and delicious when fried up with the bacon and eggs. I started to feel like I might one day be human again.

My phone beeped with a Facebook update. *You have been tagged in a photo.* There was another one above it, and another and another. Thirty-seven in all.

I went to the first photo and my fork clattered to the floor.

The photo had been taken in a nightclub, with garish purple lights bathing the scene. A woman with my face but in a tight silver dress was dancing on a table, her arms above her head.

The next photo seemed to have been taken in a Chinese restaurant. The same woman was attempting to hug a worried-looking man in chef's whites.

The next one I recognized as Battery Park, because the Statue of Liberty was in the background. The woman was imitating her in the foreground, wrapped in what looked like a tablecloth and holding aloft a hot dog.

Thirty-seven photos, each with ten or twenty "likes."

I called Jasmine. "This is awful! Someone's Photoshopped my head onto some woman's body!"

"Oh, no," said Jasmine. "That's you."

The world stopped turning, and I spun off into

space.

"How do you feel, this fine morning?" Jasmine asked.

"But that's not me! I don't even own a silver dress!"

"You do now. You insisted on going shopping at an all-night market at midnight. You said you needed a whole new look. You changed back later, when you got cold. Just before the strip club."

"*Strip Club?!*"

"Oh...you haven't gotten to that yet?"

I flicked forward. There I was, back in jeans and sweater, standing between two disgruntled doormen. Signs advertised an all-male strip show.

"They wouldn't let you in," Jasmine told me. "Despite your insistence that you could walk in a straight line. You couldn't, as it turned out."

I almost didn't dare to ask. "Did I say anything to Connor?"

"Not that I know of. He seemed happy enough. Worried about you, actually. He's just a big fluffy bunny rabbit, isn't he, under that hard man exterior?"

"And Taylor?"

"He sent her home about the time you got completely out of control. Then he took you home in a cab."

For the first time that day, I felt a tiny ray of hope.

***

By mid-afternoon, I was feeling slightly better, even if my stomach lurched every time I thought of facing the rest of Fenbrook. I lay on the couch, dozing and drinking peppermint tea, glad that at least it was Saturday and I didn't have to *do* anything.

When the sun went down, I couldn't rouse myself to turn the lights on so the room dimmed to a pleasant gloom. My phone's ringtone shattered the silence. The screen said *Connor.*

I put it to my ear, closing my eyes in the hope that would help me concentrate. "Hi."

"How are you feeling?" He sounded concerned and slightly amused. That was better than angry.

"Not good. Better for breakfast. Thank you. Where did you even manage to buy potato bread at three in the morning?"

He laughed. "I stayed all night, to make sure you were okay. I went to the store this morning, while you were still sleeping it off."

I bit my lip. "I'm sorry if I messed things up with Taylor."

"Taylor? Not much to mess up. We were just larkin' about."

I put my palm to my face and took a few deep breaths to stop myself screaming in frustration.

"Karen?"

Not now. I wasn't going to tell him now, when I was hungover and humiliated and a mess.

"I'm fine," I told him. "Just exhausted. I think I'll sleep some more. You didn't want to rehearse tonight or anything, did you?"

"Nah. A friend from back home's crashing."

When I'd hung up, I lay there and planned it out. Tomorrow morning, first thing, I'd get a cab over to his apartment and tell him. Simple and direct and to his face, and he'd react how he'd react.

I was done playing games; tomorrow, everything would change.

***

The next morning brought snow, the last gasp of winter before it handed over to spring. It wasn't heavy, but it took everyone by surprise and between that and it being early on Sunday morning, cabs were thin on the ground.

That didn't stop me, though. A glacier that split the city in two wouldn't have stopped me.

I pressed the buzzer for Connor's apartment, only to find it didn't work and probably hadn't since he'd moved in. Now I knew why he'd come down to meet me, when we rehearsed there.

Luckily, the main door's lock was as broken as the buzzer. I trudged up the five flights of stairs, glad that at least I wasn't carrying my cello this time, and stood outside his door for a second to get my breath back. There was a chance he wouldn't be there, since I hadn't called first. But who went out before nine on a Sunday morning?

I knocked, and my heart started pounding. I went through it again and again in my head, just as I had backstage at the bar when I'd asked for his help. *I have to tell you something. I have to tell you that—*

A thin-faced woman with ruler-straight hair opened the door. For a second, I tried to tell myself that I'd got the wrong apartment, but I recognized her from her photo.

A friend from back home's crashing.

"Yeah?" said Ruth.

Her accent was just as strong as his and immediately I was imagining them together. She was wearing a vest top and I saw that she had a tattoo, too: A guitar, with a name running down the side. I knew what name it would be.

"Well?" she asked as I stood there frozen. Each word was snapped out with a viciousness that made me

229

flinch, the hiss of a lioness warning me off her mate.

I turned and ran.

***

It was too early for the low-lifes and the dealers to be out on the streets so no one hassled me as I blundered down the street, wiping at my eyes. I didn't want to cry in public.

I held it together even in the back of the cab. I held it until I got home and then I collapsed on my bed and sobbed and sobbed.

CHAPTER 20

I GOT THE FULL STORY from Connor the next day as we prepared to rehearse in a practice room.

"Saturday morning, I get a collect call. She was standing at a payphone at JFK with a handbag—that's all she brought, a handbag—and no money. She had nowhere else to go."

I was staring down at my cello, ostensibly tuning it. "So the two of you are...?"

He sighed. "I don't know yet. It's complicated."

I thought of the lyrics I'd heard. *I was bad for you, you were bad for me.* But I knew he loved her, or had loved her. They'd permanently etched each other's names on their bodies, for God's sake. If I came between them now, even if I stopped them before they'd properly got back together, what did that make me?

"You'll have to write a new verse now," I said as brightly as I could.

He nodded. "Or maybe a whole new song."

We ran through the first two sections, and it was

like moving through the stages of our relationship. In the first pair, the ones we'd written when he barely knew each other, the cello and the guitar were almost fighting. My piece was all me; his piece was all him. For the second pair, we'd written each other, my section angry and confident, his timid but passionate. That left the final pair—one piece each—the final stage in our relationship. And both of us were hitting a brick wall writing it.

We'd been playing around with the acoustic guitars, trying to find ways to make the cello sound like an electric guitar and vice versa. We had some ideas, but I could tell he was as stuck as I was.

"It'll be fine," he told me. "It'll all work out."

I gave him a plastic smile. Nothing was fine, not at all.

***

It was myself I was angry with. Firstly, for not just blurting out how I felt back in Flicker, or later, when I was drunk. Now it was too late—forever. I'd seen the look in Ruth's eyes when she opened the door to me. Whatever she'd told Connor about needing a place to crash, she was in New York to get him back.

There was a part of me that said I should tell him, even with Ruth in the picture. Some romantic notion of fighting for my man, no matter what. But unlike Ruth, I didn't know how he felt about me—what if I poured out my heart and he said "No"? Would Ruth allow him to keep working with a woman who was madly in love with him? More likely she'd pressure him to pull out of the recital and drop out of Fenbrook—after all, that was the path he'd been on when they'd last been together.

There was another reason, though. I didn't know

how to fight. I'd never felt that way about anyone before, let alone had to compete for them. Maybe Jasmine would have had the strength to go up against Ruth, but I knew I didn't.

***

The following night, I was in Flicker with the girls. I'd managed to get Natasha alone for a few minutes while Jasmine and Clarissa fetched more drinks.

"So? How's Darrell doing?" I asked.

Natasha shook her head. "He still doesn't sleep. He lies there awake until four or five in the morning and then finally collapses for a few hours."

"And before all this started—back when you were first together?"

"He'd go down to the workshop and work. That's how he dealt with it."

"And now he doesn't."

"Now he doesn't. Since he quit his job, he hasn't worked at all."

I shook my head. "I don't get it. He's this amazing designer and engineer, right? So why doesn't he just make something new, if work is what he needs to be happy?"

She looked at me, and her eyes were suddenly moist.

"What? Nat, I can't help if I don't know."

She took a deep breath. "It's not that his work made him happy. He was"—she sighed—"Karen, he was making weapons."

I blinked. "*Weapons?!*" I knew he'd worked for the defense industry, but I'd had vague images of aircraft, or radar or something.

She nodded.

"Like...guns?"

"You remember when I started dancing for him, as inspiration? He was working on some big project and I didn't know what it was?"

I nodded.

"It was a missile. A missile that would wipe out half a country. He came up with a way for it to dodge by shifting its weight around as it flew."

I felt sick inside. "Based on...."

"Based on watching me dance, yes. Based on *me.*"

I'd gone numb. I'd always liked Darrell, but now, hearing that.... "What happened when you found out?"

"He told me why he was doing it. He—" Her voice broke and she had to swallow and start again. "He watched his parents die. Killed by extremists in the Middle East. He came home and designed his first weapon out of anger—for revenge—and it should have ended there, he should have grieved and moved on. But the weapons company used him...exploited him. They encouraged him to build more and more, bigger and better, and he did—for years. Until I came along. It was killing his soul, Karen, but it was a focus for all that anger."

I sat there digesting it. It was a horrible story, but in a way I was relieved because it helped me understand why Darrell had done what he did. And I saw how his life had been changed by meeting Natasha. "You found out," I said, "and he quit his job because he loved you."

She nodded. "But he's still angry, inside. And now, it has nowhere to go. It's eating him up from the inside."

"That's why he can't just make something else," I said slowly. "It won't help with the anger because if it's not a weapon, it's not *revenge.*"

Natasha nodded. "So he lies awake at night and sits around all day and it just gives him more time to think about the past. You remember in Harper's, when I told you he'd gone sex mad?"

I nodded.

"I think that was him trying to find a way to cope with it—to take his mind off it. But it didn't work, and now he's just...." She sighed. "I think he's depressed. I mean, actually, clinically depressed."

"And you're not....I mean, the sex thing has...?"

"Put it this way—you know I cut, that night when you came to my apartment? I thought he'd see the scar. I needn't have worried."

"God...you haven't...? Not since...?"

"We haven't had sex in a month."

I sat there and thought for a moment. "What does Clarissa think?" I'd been wondering, ever since that night when Natasha called me over to her apartment, why she hadn't been having these conversations with her roommate.

Natasha hesitated. "She thinks we should split up."

My jaw dropped.

"She likes him. She just...she thinks that we can't be happy together. She thinks he needs the weapons, that maybe that's the *only* sort of work that'll make him happy. Neil's worried about him, too. He always hated Darrell designing weapons, but he hates seeing him depressed." She bit her lip and I saw her eyes well with tears. "But I didn't want us to split up, so I stopped talking about it with her, but now I think maybe she's right, maybe we'd be happier apart and—shit, I don't know!" And she started to cry, big hot tears splashing onto the tabletop.

I bundled her into the restroom. "Look," I said with a firmness I didn't feel. "I'm not like you three. I don't have all your experience, but I know how good you and Darrell are together. There must be a way to fix it."

Natasha lifted her mascara-streaked face from her hands. "*How?!*"

"I don't know. But trust me, okay? I'm going to think of something."

***

Natasha cleaned herself up and we went back to our table where Clarissa and Jasmine were waiting with fresh drinks. Natasha was still red-eyed and I was worried that Clarissa would demand answers, but as we got closer I saw that wasn't going to be a problem. She and Jasmine looked distracted...worried, even, as if they had bad news. As we approached, I realized they were looking at me.

"What?" I asked as I sat down.

They looked at each other, neither wanting to be the one to tell me. Then Clarissa nodded across the bar.

Connor was there, laughing and joking with Ruth. It was impossible to tell if they were *together* or just together, but Ruth seemed to be doing her best to touch him at every possible opportunity.

The world dropped out from under me. He'd brought her *here?!* He hadn't even gone to Flicker much before we started working together, preferring the blue collar bars downtown. In fact, that night he'd wandered in drunk and singing had been the first time I remembered seeing him there. Then I'd brought him along with me the night he'd got together with Taylor...I'd as good as introduced him to it!

"It's not fair," said Jasmine. "You should get custody of Flicker."

"We didn't break up," I told her. "We were never together."

Natasha squeezed my hand. "I'm sorry, Karen. I really wanted the two of you to work out." She caught my eye and I knew we were thinking the same thing: with her and Darrell on the verge of breaking up, Clarissa and Neil having problems and now Connor and me off the cards, it seemed like there was no hope for any of us. Even Jasmine was single—she'd never mentioned Ryan, the cop I'd given her number to, so I assumed he'd never called.

"I'm going to the bar," I told the others, and stood up.

"You still have half a Pretty Woman," Jasmine pointed out.

"I'm not going to get a drink. I just...." I looked across at Connor and Ruth. *I just want to be alone,* I thought, and walked off.

It wasn't quite true. I didn't want to be alone; I was sick of being alone.

At the bar, I found a spot where I couldn't see Connor and Ruth. I knew I was being rude, that I'd have to rejoin the others in a few minutes, but I needed to get my head straight. Maybe we could all move to a different bar; Flicker was clearly cursed.

"You look like you could use a drink," said a voice beside me.

I didn't recognize him from Fenbrook. Tall and lean, with a shock of blond curls. His voice was as refined as his suit. A Harvard man, at a guess—maybe final year, maybe just graduated.

"That didn't work out so well, last time," I told him.

"Come on. One drink."

I stared at him for a second. He wasn't bad looking, in an all-American sort of a way. And there was that ache inside me that Connor had left—the need for closeness cruelly denied. I just wanted to connect with someone.

"I'll have a 101 Dalmations, please." I told him.

He frowned. "But that—"

"Doesn't have any alcohol in, no. But it's what I want."

He shrugged and made a big show of holding up a fifty to attract the barman's attention. A few minutes later I was sucking vanilla milkshake through a straw, the "spots" chocolate buttons stuck to the inside of the glass.

"I'm Anthony," he told me. "And you are?"

He seemed nice, if a bit fond of flashing his money. And he'd bought me a drink and the girls would be happy to see me actually talking to a man and Connor was happy with Ruth and—

"Karen." Saying it made my mind up. I'd been standing at the bar, but now I sat down on a stool and he sat down next to me.

"Actress, dancer or musician?" he asked.

He knew about Flicker, then. Probably what had attracted him to the place, the chance to meet some young starlet or ballerina. He was going to be disappointed. "Musician." And then, anticipating his next question, "Cello."

He smiled, just like Fifty Shades of Gray Hair had at the party. "Oh—"

"Yes. The one where you sit with your legs spread." I'd meant to say it just a little testily, to let him know how I felt about that line. But it didn't quite come out like that. It came out as confident, even flirtatious.

He told me he was at Harvard and about his plans after graduation. I told him about playing with the quartet in Central Park and composing and cramming into tiny practice rooms. It felt good, to talk to someone outside Fenbrook's little world. I glanced over to where the girls were sitting and got an encouraging smile from Natasha. I didn't dare risk looking at Connor. If I saw him and Ruth were kissing, I felt like my heart would shatter.

We kept talking and I only realized how much the bar was filling up when someone squeezed their way between Anthony and me, cutting off the conversation. More people were pressing behind us, leaning over us to talk to the bar staff. When the guy between us moved away with his drinks, Anthony waved me closer. "I can't hear you otherwise," he said.

He had a point. The din was rising around us and with music blaring as well...but what was he suggesting—that I sit and he stand next to me? That we share a seat?

I stood up and moved over to him. He pushed his stool out a little from the bar and patted his lap. *Oh.* I hadn't been planning on *that.* But when I looked round, a woman had already slid onto my vacated stool.

Anthony was smiling at me, which made me feel like an idiot for hesitating. It was no big deal, right?

I sat on his lap, glad I was in my usual jeans instead of a skirt or dress. Even so, I could feel the heat of him through the thin denim.

"That's better," he told me, his mouth right up against my ear. It meant that he didn't have to shout, which was good. But it also felt very intimate, and that I wasn't so sure about.

I told myself I was being stupid, and when we started talking again it seemed okay. He said he was sick of the women at Harvard, and told me how much he liked my hair.

And then someone bumped against his head from behind and apologized, and as if in response he grabbed hold of the bar and pulled the stool closer in. The bar counter had an overhang, so that put my stomach snugly against its edge and our lower bodies under the counter. Out of sight.

He told me I was beautiful and then, completely unasked, kissed me on the neck. His lips were too soft and too wet, and I could feel the cool spit they left behind. I was so focused on that, I didn't notice his hand on my leg, gliding along the outside. And then sliding around to try to push between my thighs.

"No," I said, but he didn't seem to hear. His hand was like a knife-edge, sliding down. "No," I said again, louder, definitely loud enough for him to hear even over the din. I clamped my knees hard together.

He made a shh-ing noise, as if I was being silly. And then I felt his expensive leather loafer against my ankle, hooking my leg outwards, and suddenly my legs were open. His hand was on my crotch, rubbing me there, and no one could see—

"Take your fucking hands off her," said a deep, Belfast voice.

We both turned at the same time to see Connor looming over us. Anthony stopped rubbing, but didn't move his hand.

"We're fine," he told Connor. "We're fine, aren't we?" he asked me, the panic just creeping into his voice.

Connor's eyes were on mine. "No," I whispered.

The stool, Anthony and I were all suddenly sliding back from the bar as Connor yanked on its metal stem, the base making a nasty screeching noise on the floor that killed all conversation around us. Anthony snatched his hand from my crotch, but not in time to stop everyone seeing it.

Connor's hand grabbed mine and he pulled me from Anthony's lap. I recognized the look on his face. I'd seen it before, in the gym. He drew back his arm.

"I'm calling the cops!" the barman yelled, and I thought of Connor's past. And his future.

"Connor!" I grabbed his arm before he could hit Anthony, but he shook me off. "It's okay!"

"No," said Connor. "It's not." And he swung.

It wasn't like you see in the movies, all slow motion and artistic, with someone flying through the air. It was quick and brutal and over in a second, Anthony's head snapping back with a sound that made me want to vomit. He fell backwards off his stool and smacked into a table, flipping it over and scattering drinks, a glittering wave of glass and alcohol sloshing across the floor.

The girls ran over and we all stood there watching as Anthony tried to raise himself up and then slumped back down to the floor. I still had hold of Connor's arm and I clung to it for dear life, but he seemed to be as shocked as I was. Blood was dripping from Anthony's lip onto his clean white shirt and fanning out into a red flower.

"Are you okay?" Connor asked.

I nodded dumbly. Moments later, blue and red flashes filled the windows. A lot of people chose that moment to leave, but the girls and I stayed. I had to see what happened to Connor—help him, if I could. But I had a horrible feeling I already knew how this story would end—a broke, flunking Irishman with a history of violence, attacking a clean-cut Harvard student. Connor was on his way to jail, and I felt hot tears prickle my eyes.

The bar staff pushed everyone except Connor and Anthony back and we had to watch from across the room as two cops arrived and questioned them. Now that he was safe, Anthony looked to be mad.

I ran forward, narrowly avoiding being tackled by the barman. "I saw it," I said to the back of the cop's head. "He was only defending me." I pointed to Anthony. "That man assaulted me!" But I already knew it wouldn't make a difference. Even if they charged Anthony with something, Connor was still in trouble.

And then the cop turned around.

"Karen?" said Officer Ryan Kowalski.

Jasmine dodged past the bar staff and ran up beside me. "It's like she said. That asshole's hands were all over her. Connor just went...a bit Irish."

"Jasmine?" said Ryan.

Clarissa and Natasha ran up, at which point the bar staff pretty much gave up on trying to keep people back. "We saw it too," they said together.

Ryan sighed and rubbed a hand over his face, as if it was going to be another very long shift.

***

It took a half hour for Ryan to reason Anthony out of pressing charges. The turning point was when he asked me if I wanted to press sexual assault charges against him. I did, but I wanted Connor to stay out of jail more. I stared at Anthony until he got the message and relented.

When he'd slunk into a cab and was heading back to Harvard, I ran over to Ryan. "Thank you," I said, and I meant it. "If it had been any other cop...we were really lucky."

He gave me a solemn nod, and then sighed. "It wasn't completely luck. I knew this bar was where you guys hung out. I figured we should be the ones to check it out."

He was gazing across the bar, and I realized he was looking at Jasmine. With a look some would have called longing.

"Why didn't you call her?" I asked, bemused.

He looked at me indulgently and then indicated his uniform. "I remembered what I was," he said. "And what she is. Cop and actress. Different circles, you know? I don't think it's meant to be."

And with that he was gone. I stood looking at the spot where he'd stood, and then looked over my shoulder at Jasmine. Jasmine with her life lived by the skin of her teeth, with her string of cheating boyfriends and ill-advised one night stands. "But you're exactly what she needs," I said sadly.

Raised voices from the other side of the bar. Connor and Ruth were arguing, with her doing most of the talking and him shrugging off her questions. A second later, he stormed past me and out into the street.

I ran after him and found him standing outside taking deep, shuddering breaths to calm himself. He looked up when he saw me. "You okay?"

"Are you?"

"Well, I'm not in jail. Thanks."

"Thank *you*. For—" It hadn't affected me, really, until that moment. Maybe the adrenaline had held it back, or maybe I'd just been too worried about Connor. But now it hit me: the way Anthony had used me for his pleasure, what he might have done with me if he'd got me outside, or into the restroom. I started shaking, and couldn't stop. The worst part was knowing that, save for some good luck, there would have been one less person like Connor around to balance out the Anthonys of the world. *He'd* been the one nearly sent to jail. "Why did you do it?" I asked, close to tears.

"Because you needed me," he said. He was still breathing hard, trying to control his anger.

"But you hit him!" I shouted. "You hit him, after you'd pulled me away from him!"

Helena Newbury

"Because he deserved it," said Connor. He turned away from me.

Hot tears were running down my cheeks. "But you could have gone to jail! Why?!"

He turned to me and I saw it in his eyes—the same internal struggle I'd seen when I'd first asked him to help me.

"Because I love you, you idiot!" he said.

Everything went very quiet.

"What?!"

He started walking towards me. "I've loved you from the first time you asked for my help, when you called it a *stupid* beer. That's why I had to help you, even though I thought I'd mess it up."

"But—but you didn't say anything! You never said anything!"

"Because I knew I didn't deserve you. Because I was a stupid waste of space who couldn't even write a bloody essay, and I knew I'd mess things up for you. I just wanted you to be okay. That would be fine, that was all I needed. Just see you graduate and go off and find some posh guy to marry. But—"

He'd reached me, now. I stood there silently looking up at him, barely daring to breathe.

"But you helped me, and...it started to feel like I was good for something after all. Maybe even good enough to be with you. But I didn't dare mess it up between us...."

"What about Ruth?" I asked, my throat so tight it was almost a whisper.

"She's just a friend. I'm sleeping on the floor."

My world turned upside down. I'd waited so long that it took a second to register that all the pieces had just slotted into place.

Then I reached up and grabbed him around the

244

neck, dragging his face down to mine and we were kissing, my hands on his cheeks as his tongue slipped into my mouth, his warm fingers in my hair. I was afloat on a silver river of pure, heady elation. We kissed hungrily, starved for months.

"You daft mare," he gasped when we finally broke apart. "I thought you didn't even like me!"

I stared up into his eyes. "F'ckin' 'ell," I panted, and then we were kissing again. It went on for long, glorious minutes, the energy soaking down through my body and making my toes dance in delight. When we broke for the second time, he stared very seriously into my eyes.

"We could go to your place," he said, and what he was implying made the swirling rush of energy become a deeper, darker heat that twisted straight down to my groin.

But that raised an issue, one I hadn't even considered until then. One that I needed help with, fast. "Not tonight," I said breathlessly. "Tomorrow. Let's go out tomorrow. Is that okay?"

He nodded, lips twisting into that familiar smile— and *for me!* "Yeah. Tomorrow is great."

I caught movement out of the corner of my eye and looked over to the door of Flicker. The girls were lined up outside, watching us and grinning. Ruth was behind them and though she wasn't smiling, she didn't look mad, either. She seemed to be appraising me and that scared me more, somehow.

Ruth was a problem that could wait, though, if she proved to be a problem at all. I wanted to enjoy the perfect moment and nothing—not even an ex-girlfriend—was going to stand in my way. I pulled Connor close and kissed him again, and this time it was sweet and tender, tasting each other and laying down promises of what was to come.

When we eventually let each other go and he climbed into a cab with Ruth, the girls gathered around me. "So what's the story there?" asked Jasmine.

"His ex, from Ireland." Everyone went quiet. "He's sleeping on the floor. I trust him."

"But do you trust *her?*" asked Clarissa, and I went quiet, too.

Jasmine gave me a hug. "Connor's not stupid. He'll kick her out now you're together. Or he could just move in with you."

I took a deep breath. "Easy, there. We haven't even gone out yet." I leaned in to whisper in Jasmine's ear. "I need your help. My place, tomorrow morning."

CHAPTER 21

I DIDN'T REALLY KNOW what was appropriate. Then I realized that the situation was far too weird for anything to be appropriate, so I just went with breakfast. I made coffee and then hit the local bakery and brought back a huge tray of croissants, pains de raisin and pains de chocolat, Danish pastries and muffins. Then I wound up drinking most of the coffee, because I was nervous. Then I got more nervous because I'd drunk too much coffee.

Jasmine arrived, yawning.

"Sorry," I said. "I know you're normally still in bed at this time."

"I'm normally still *out* at this time. What's up?"

I double-checked that the door was closed and that no one had snuck in. No: we were alone.

I took a deep breath. "How do you have sex?"

Jasmine blinked.

"You know how I told you about how I lost it to a firefighter when I was eighteen?" I said. "Well—"

247

"Yeah, yeah, you made it up."

Now it was my turn to blink. "You didn't believe that story?"

"Karen, none of us believed that story. We didn't want to hurt your feelings."

"Oh." I'd been proud of that story.

"But we thought you were just exaggerating a bit, dropping the age. Everyone does that. You've *never* done it?"

I shook my head.

"Never? Not even, like, *that time doesn't count because...?*"

I shook my head again.

"Wow. And now you're dating Connor Locke and you think tonight's the night?"

I nodded. "I mean, I know it's our first date, but we've been friends for so long...."

"Say no more. Fortunately"—she smiled and picked up a Danish—"you've come to the right person."

"I don't want him to know," I blurted. "I want to seem like I know what I'm doing."

"By the time I'm finished with you, Connor won't know what's hit him. She bit into her Danish and thought for a moment. "Okay. First thing, are you ready?"

"No. That's why I'm talking to you."

"No, are you *ready?* Is everything neat and tidy?"

I looked around the apartment. When I looked back at Jasmine, she had her head in her hands. "*Down below,*" she said.

"*Oh!*" When I'd reassured her that, yes, my grooming was fine, thank you, we moved onto the sex.

"Condoms," she said. "Got some?"

I shook my head.

"Get some. Get plenty. You've been waiting years

for this, and all that tension from being cooped up in practice rooms together...it'll be like a dam's burst. Now: sex."

I picked up a pen.

"Really? You're going to take notes?"

I put down the pen.

"Okay. Wear your heels."

"The Heels of Death?"

"Of course the Heels of Death. Keep them on in the bedroom. Guys love that."

"How do I get my jeans off over heels?"

"You're wearing *jeans?*"

I frowned. "I hadn't thought about what to wear."

"You hadn't *thought about what to wear?!*"

"I'm not really prepared for this, am I?" I said sadly.

She sighed. "Right. *Dress or skirt.* Show off those legs. Top half off, or take the dress off. Underwear and heels. Underwear off, heels and stockings stay on."

"Stockings?"

"Do you want to do this the Jasmine way, or the wrong way?"

"The right—The Jasmine way. But are you sure this isn't a bit...much?"

"You're right. It's a common male complaint: I wish my girlfriend was less sexy."

I nodded. "Got it. Stockings. Suspender belt?"

"Whoah there. Let's not move onto the advanced course just yet, rookie. Hold ups will do you just fine. Otherwise I'll have to teach you how to get panties off while leaving the belt on."

"Uh?"

"See? OK, now when you get to the bed—or wherever—you probably want to start off by going down on him. Then—"

I raised my hand.

"Karen, you don't have to put your hand up. What? Oh, God, *really?* You've never gone down on a guy?"

I gave her a look. "I'm glad I picked you to help me, Jasmine. Thanks for not making me feel stupid."

"Sorry. It's just...*really?* Okay, okay, fine. Here." She put her finger out in front of me.

"What do you want me to do with that?"

"Put it in your mouth."

"*What?!*"

"It'll help. Go on."

I looked at it doubtfully. "Have you washed your hands?"

"Just suck on my damn finger already!"

I opened my mouth. "This is deeply weird," I told her, and closed my lips around her finger.

"Okay, now suck. Jesus, not like that! You're not a power vacuum. It's got to be a firm, wet suck. And watch your teeth. No teeth, ever. Well, not unless he likes it." She pushed her finger a little farther into my mouth. "Use your tongue. Right, but...no, not like that. Swirl it around and down the sides, and over the top."

I did my best.

Jasmine pursed her lips. "Hmm...no. Ow! Teeth! Oh, look, just give me your finger."

A little hesitantly, I held my finger out to her. Immediately, her lips engulfed it, her mouth hot and wet. Her tongue slathered up and down its length and then played with the very tip. Her soft lips caressed the bottom knuckle while her cheeks sucked at the rest. I actually felt a wave of heat ripple through me. "MMFF!" I said, Jasmine's finger still in my mouth.

"Mmm*mmm!*" said Jasmine triumphantly, clearly meaning *like that*. I tried to replicate what she was doing and, eventually, she nodded and withdrew her finger. I pulled mine from her mouth with a wet slurp. It was tingling, and I stared at it.

"Wow," I said, genuinely amazed.

"Yeah," said Jasmine, leaning back smugly in her chair. "That's what they all say."

We broke to eat and I wolfed down a pain de chocolat.

"I need a favor from you, too, when we're done," Jasmine told me. She looked nervous, all of a sudden.

"Anything. You know that."

She nodded and ate another Danish. "Okay," she said when she'd licked the crumbs from her fingers. "Moving on. You probably want to start off in missionary. Please God tell me you know what missionary is?"

I flushed. "I'm not *completely* sheltered."

"Okay. So what you *don't* do is lie back and think of England. Get your hips going, like this."

"Like I'm hula hooping?"

"Smaller circles. Like—Look, lie down on your back."

I got down on the floor on my back and opened my legs, and Jasmine prepared to climb between them. We stopped and looked at each other.

"*Or*...we could just look at some porn," she said.

"Yes, let's do that," I said quickly.

We fired up my laptop. Jasmine gave me a USB stick.

"What's this?"

"All my porn. I had to cancel my internet service when things got tight, so I downloaded my favorites."

"But why did you bring it? I didn't tell you what I needed help with."

She looked suddenly antsy. "There's something

else on there...I'll show you afterwards. Go on, open it up."

I clicked on the icon for the USB stick. Inside was a smorgasbord of porn, neatly sorted into directories and sub-directories. It was easily the most organized thing I'd ever seen Jasmine create.

"Jasmine, there must be, like, a thousand files here."

"Two thousand." She sighed. "I only had time to grab the best stuff." She pointed me at a particular movie and we started watching. A blonde-haired woman was writhing on a bed beneath a shaven-headed, muscled stud.

"Okay," I said. "Feeling weird now."

"Focus. Observe the pelvic swirling. Observe also the way he pins her legs back in a minute...*there.*"

"*Ow!*"

"Yeah, you need to be stretchy for that. Natasha? No problem. And apparently Neil's into folding up Clarissa like a pretzel. We all need to take up ballet."

She closed the movie. "Now after that—if he hasn't come yet—I'd go for cowgirl."

I blanched a little. "Isn't it a little early to be getting into roleplaying and stuff? And I don't think they even *have* cowboys in Ireland."

"Jesus, how sheltered *are* you? It's you riding him, face to face. Haven't you ever watched any porn?"

I flushed, thinking of Neil and Clarissa's video. "Now and again."

"OK, so ride him: he gets to play with your boobs and you can rub yourself at the same time if you need to. Oh! Tweak your nipples. They love that."

"Right. Heels stay on, no teeth, hula hooping, cowgirl, tweak my nipples. Got it." I actually felt pretty good. Some of it might be a little over the top, but at least

I wouldn't be going in cold.

She clinked her coffee mug against mine. "And now for my favor."

I was still grinning. "Go for it."

"I want you to help me choose an escort agency."

The smile died on my face.

She bit her lip. "Come on, you *promised....*"

"I know, I know. I'll do it, I just...Jasmine, are you *sure?* Is this really the only way?"

She shrugged. "It's either this or pimp myself to my landlord. If I'm going to do it, I might as well get paid top dollar, right?" I could hear the tension under her bravado.

"And there's really no chance," I asked gently, "that you could move in with your brother?"

She sighed. "Karen...." She picked up a pain au raisin and started picking the raisins out. "I spent a long time trying to get away from my family. They're a...*curse.* You touch one of them, even for a second, and you pay for it for years. I am *not* going to wreck my life here by reconnecting with them."

I nodded. "Okay. Sorry."

She had a shortlist of agencies saved on her USB stick, and we went through them one by one. "I like this one," she said, showing me a garish site with pictures of escorts posing in lingerie. "I'm pretty sure I could hold my own against those girls."

I shook my head. "You like that because you can see the competition, because they've got photos. Do you really want a photo of *you* up there, with your face showing? What if somebody you know sees it? What if your acting coach at Fenbrook sees it?"

Jasmine shuddered. "Yeah, good point. Next."

We went through about ten sites, and my screen gradually filled up with pop-ups. *I'm going to have to disinfect my laptop when we're done,* I thought sadly.

"This is nice," I said. It was a tasteful site with moody black and white pictures of the escorts. A breast here, a stockinged thigh there. Faces were never shown.

"It's very...tasteful," Jasmine said doubtfully. "Do you think I'm tasteful?"

"Absolutely! God, Jasmine, look at yourself! You're gorgeous and eloquent and confident and men would love to...." *To pay money to have you spread your legs for them,* I finished silently.

Jasmine beamed. "You really think so?"

Sometimes she really confused me. She was so confident, but just occasionally I got a hint of a scared, insecure girl underneath. "Yes," I said firmly. "I really think so."

There was a number to call if you wanted to apply. Jasmine typed it into her cell phone and then stared at it.

"Wait," she said. "Got any booze?"

I looked at the clock. "It's ten in the morning."

She gave me a look. "I'm about to sell my body. It's kind of a big deal."

I dug out a bottle of chardonnay and poured her a large glass, which she drained. Then she hit "Call."

"They're probably not open," she said hopefully. "Not at ten in the—Oh, hi! Um. I'm calling to apply?" I listened as she gave her height, weight and measurements, her hair color, eye color and age.

And then the questions turned to sex. I could only hear Jasmine's end of the call, but they seemed to be asking what she was prepared to do. "Yep. Yep. No problem. Oh yes. Oh! No. Um, I haven't before, but I would. No. Nope. No!"

Her eyes went wide at the last one, and I wondered what on earth they'd asked that would have shocked even her. She went quiet for a while as she listened to the person at the other end and then said, "Okay, that's fine. Okay. Thanks. Bye."

She hung up. "I have to go for an interview on the fifteenth. If that goes okay, I could be getting bookings the next day."

We looked at the clock: it was five past ten. Going from actress to prostitute had taken a little under five minutes.

"That was scary easy," said Jasmine. "Will you come with me, to the interview?"

My stomach flipped over at the thought. "Of course," I told her, and we hugged.

"You realize I want a full report on what happens tonight?" said Jasmine as she retrieved her USB stick and prepared to leave. "You're my protégé now. Don't let me down." And then she drew me close. "And don't let the bastard break your heart."

***

When she'd gone, I stood there for a moment enjoying the spring sunshine soaking through the room. I was nervous about the date with Connor, but I was *happy,* and it was the first time in months I'd felt that things were going to be okay. We still had a struggle on our hands with the recital and Connor's grades, but as long as nothing went wrong, we could pull it off.

I'd been so focused on just graduating that I'd deliberately put all thoughts of the New York Phil out of my mind. But as I basked in the sunlight, I dared to hope. I had no idea how the scout would react to a duet as weird as ours, but if we aced it there was always a chance. Maybe, just maybe, I could get my dream back.

My phone rang and I didn't recognize the number. "Hello?"

Syrupy-sweet words given a kick by the heavy Irish accent. "*Karen!* I'm not interrupting your practice, am I? Connor told me how hard you two are working."

Ruth?!

"No, it's...fine." I could feel my toes curling in response to the woman.

"When can you meet for coffee? I want us to be friends."

My brain shorted out. She wanted us to be friends?! "Er...great. Noon?"

"Perfect." She almost purred as she said it. "Let's do Harper's. Okay?" She made it sound like she was in a hurry, so I couldn't think about it for long.

"Sure," I said, and she hung up.

I had to run through the conversation in my head a few times before I realized that she hadn't given me any choices at all, apart from choosing the time. But hey, this was a good thing, right? I'd assumed exes were always evil and to be avoided, but Connor considered her a friend and his friends should be my friends. Maybe that's just how it worked—everyone was just mature and sensible and friendly about exes. It wasn't like I had much experience to go on.

I had to scramble to get ready because I needed to go shopping before I met Ruth. She'd managed to throw out my entire day, turning what should have been a fun trip into a mad dash.

When I hit the stores, I spent most of the time searching for the perfect dress. I eventually found something I thought would work—a black jersey number that came down to just above my knees and had a neckline that was just the right side of my comfort zone. I grabbed some hold ups and a bra and panties set, bought some new makeup and then found a drugstore.

I stood at the condom display comparing differen'

sizes, thicknesses, textures and colors for so long that someone actually came over and asked if I needed help—at which point I grabbed four different boxes, paid and ran.

**

When I got to Harper's, Ruth had already made herself at home. She was sitting there sipping a black coffee and browsing through a Fenbrook newsletter. For some reason, it made me angry; I didn't want her in Harper's, or around Fenbrook, or anywhere near Connor and me. It felt like she was going to pollute our beautiful, clean future with his past.

I took a deep breath and told myself not to be childish.

As I approached, Ruth stood up and pulled me into a hug and cheek kiss, as if I was an old friend she hadn't seen in months. She was taller than me, and seemed to be made entirely of bone and muscle, intimidatingly stylish in a white blouse and black leather jeans. She looked—my stomach flipped over—she looked like the sort of girlfriend Connor should have.

"I'm so glad we can be friends," Ruth told me, as if we already were. "Tell me all about Connor and you."

It was like being quizzed by an evil stepmother. She was the same age as me, from what I could tell, and yet somehow managed to make me feel like a child. I told her about the recital, and Dan, and how Connor had helped me. I told her about working together, and how we'd fallen in love.

When I'd finished, she nodded. "I understand, luv. When you're working together all hours, it's easy to start having feelings for each other."

That threw me. She made it sound like it had

happened by accident, like it was all a mistake, and it wasn't. Was it?

Ruth leaned in as if about to share a secret and I leaned in, too. "I was a bit surprised, to tell you the truth," she said. "You don't *seem* like his type."

"What's his type?" I asked quickly, before I could stop myself.

She blinked at me. "Less...studious. More...worldly."

More *you,* I thought viciously.

Ruth tilted her head to one side. "Oh, luv. I haven't upset you, have I?" She stood up to leave, and then leaned down again and kissed the top of my head in a way that made me squirm. As she turned to go, the point of her shoe knocked over my bags. Lacy lingerie and four boxes of condoms spilled out across the floor.

"Oh," she said as I scrambled to pick everything up. "Tonight's the night, is it?"

I went beetroot red, unable to speak. I was just about to grab the padded, push-up bra I'd bought when her toe pinned it to the floor. "Wise move," she said, as if offering friendly advice. "Try not to worry about it though, luv. Some blokes go for small ones."

There was some tittering from the tables around us. I kept my eyes firmly on the floor.

"This has been fun," said Ruth. "Facebook me." And she was gone.

CHAPTER 22

I should have been in the practice room, waiting for Connor and warming up with something easy, but instead I was standing outside and staring at the wall.

I'd chosen a poster to stare at, just so that I didn't look weird, but I wasn't even aware of what it said. My mind was back in Harper's, going over and over what Ruth had said. There had to be some truth in it. He *was* used to more experienced women—had to be, given that pretty much anyone qualified as *more experienced* next to me. What if I was lousy in bed? What if I made a total fool of myself?

Warm lips kissed me just behind my ear and I leaped a clear foot into the air. I landed and found Connor standing behind me, grinning. I punched him on the shoulder.

Part of me was nervous—aside from the things Ruth had said, it was the first time I'd seen him since he'd said he loved me. I had some crazy, instinctive worry that maybe it had all been a dream, or a horrible mistake.

But he took my hand and drew me in close, and then he was leaning down to kiss me, warm and slow, my lips flowering open under his as his hands slid through my hair. For a second, I was worried that someone would see us kissing...then I switched to hoping they would. *Screw Ruth,* I decided.

Connor turned me back around to face the wall, grabbing me around the waist and nuzzling my neck.

"What are we reading?" he asked, looking at the poster over my shoulder.

For the first time, I focused on it. Most of the posters around Fenbrook were lurid colors, to try to catch your attention. This one was white, the sign of officialdom. I read it and sighed. *"The Fenbrook Improvisation Challenge. A Timed Composition for Extra Credit.* Even *I'm* not hardcore enough to enter that."

"Hardcore?" he asked.

"Shut up. You know what I mean. You have to be *seriously* good."

"What's so hard about improvising? I can improvise."

I craned over my shoulder and looked pityingly at him. "No, you *fail to write stuff down* and have to wing it from memory. That's just sloppy—"

"It's rock n' roll, is what it is."

"Which reminds me, you need to write down all of your sections *properly. Neatly.* Not on the back of a pizza box."

"Yes ma'am." And it sounded so good, with his accent, that I would have forgiven him anything.

"Anyway," I told him, "the improv challenge is horrible. They play you a melody and then you have to compose around it, and then perform it. Live on stage, in front of everyone, and you only get one shot."

"How many days do you get to compose?"

"You get thirty minutes."

He went quiet. "Okay, that *is* pretty hardcore."

I turned to face him. "Surely you remember all this? They do it every year, just after the recitals."

He thought about it. "I missed last year's. Hangover."

"What about the year before?"

"Also hungover."

"Connor, have you ever actually been to a recital, your entire time at Fenbrook?"

"Yes!" Then he looked down at his feet. "No."

I just stared at him.

"It didn't seem very important, alright? I was never going to do my final recital—I always thought I'd flunk out long before this. And I didn't see any point in going along the first three years, just to watch that year's seniors do theirs."

It suddenly made sense. The insecurity he'd opened up to me about in his apartment—what could be scarier than hearing student after student perform, if you doubted your own ability?

"Come on," I told him. "Let's rehearse."

But as soon as we were inside with the door closed, it was difficult not to think that *we're alone together*. We caught each other staring: me at his arms as he took his jacket off, him at my bare stomach as I shrugged off my cello case and my sweatshirt rose.

"We have to work," I said seriously.

He just looked at me with those big, blue-gray eyes and I nearly threw myself into his arms right then.

"*Don't,*" I said, half warning and half joking.

He stared for a second longer and then relented.

"We're going out tonight though, yeah?"

I nodded "Oh yes." *Tonight's the night,* I heard Jasmine say, and a little thrill went through me. Then I heard Ruth saying the same words and winced, annoyed at having it tarnished.

Our recital piece was made up of six sections—three composed by him, three by me—and so far we'd written four of them. With just over a month to go, we still each had one section left to write. I'd started to try to mix the sounds of my cello and his electric guitar together, but I couldn't get it to mesh. It felt like the sections were tracking our relationship: the first pair had been very different, very *us,* before we knew each other; for the second pair he'd written my personality into the music and I'd written his; somehow, I knew the third pair would be us coming together.

Since the first rehearsal, the tiny practice room had been thick with tension, both when I thought I hated him but wanted him, and when I knew I loved him but didn't know how he felt. Now, though...now it was different again. Before, I'd gazed at his arms and imagined them wrapped around me, or seen the way his jeans pulled tight around his thighs and dreamed of running my hand over the warm fabric. Now, I sat there *knowing* that, that night, we'd be together. We'd...fuck.

I thought back to my dream of him, of me as innocent virgin, corsets and heaving bosoms and pleas for gentleness as he ravished me. I thought of Jasmine and riding him cowgirl and hula-hooping. Was that any more realistic than my fantasy? Could I really pull off *seductress?*

"You okay?" asked Connor.

"Fine. Why?"

"You haven't played a note in about five minutes." He was grinning, as if he somehow knew exactly what was going through my mind.

I flushed and stared at my music, trying to get the thought of him fucking me out of my head. At that exact second, my phone rang. The screen burned accusingly with my father's name.

"Do you need to get that?" asked Connor.

I thought about how I'd have to lie to him, telling him how everything was going just fine with Connor, "the violinist." The irony was that it *was* going well. The piece was really coming together. If only my father would trust me....

"No," I told Connor. "I'll call them back." I turned my phone off. I'd call him back the next day and apologize, but I wasn't letting anything—not even my father—spoil our first day together.

***

I'd been so focused on what was going to happen after the date that I hadn't thought about where Connor was going to take me. When he announced dinner and a movie, I got this big, silly grin on my face. It was about the most traditional, couple-y thing we could have done, and it felt perfect.

We had dinner in a French place tucked away in a backstreet, where the tables were so small we could talk in whispers without even leaning into each other. We spent at least half the meal eating one-handed because we were holding hands across the table, and when the waitress said how cute we were it didn't feel cheesy or silly at all. It felt fantastic.

"After we graduate—" he began.

I gave a little intake of breath.

"Oh come on—you think I'm going to jinx it?"

"Yes," I said seriously.

"Okay...*if* we graduate...the New York Phil, huh?"

It felt like there was just enough of a chance that I could dare to talk about it. I let the glow of excitement build inside me. "Yes. Playing concerts, touring the world...." I grinned. "They play in Europe. I've always wanted to see Europe."

And then I caught myself. I'd been imagining it for years...and never in that time had anyone else ever been in the picture.

"I mean...you know. If you think that would work with...us," I said.

He frowned in confusion and then stared at me. "Karen...Jesus, you don't have to ask my permission!" He sighed and traced my cheek with a finger. "You've spent so long doing what everybody else wants. It's okay to do what *you* want. I'd never stop you following your dreams. You do what you need to do, and we'll figure out *us.*"

It was like a rush of pure oxygen after being cooped up in a tiny box my whole life. I wanted to throw my arms around him and kiss him right there in the restaurant...and then I went ahead and did exactly that, just to show I understood.

***

The movie was a romantic comedy, fun and simple and immediately forgettable. I was surprised that he'd pick something so tame and...*normal,* but cuddling up beside him, his arm around my shoulders, I didn't care what we watched. I kept looking across at him, his face lit by the screen's glow, and thinking *he's mine.*

It was only in the bar he took me to, afterwards, that it started to make sense. It was perfect—not too dressy and not too casual. In my dress and the smarter-than-usual jeans he'd worn, we could have been an advertising poster for the place.

"You've never been here before, have you?" I asked as he brought the drinks over. "Or the restaurant. And you don't normally go to the movies, do you?"

He gave me a long look and then hung his head and said, "Clarissa. They were all her suggestions. I had no fucking idea where to take you."

I burst out laughing. "What do you *normally* do on dates?"

He held out his hands helplessly. "I don't *go* on dates. You know what I'm like." He looked abashed. "What I *was* like."

I narrowed my eyes, smirking. "You play some rock club, and there's some young thing at the front, all innocent and big eyes, and you play a solo she thinks is just for her. And then you get her back to your dressing room, ravish her on the counter and both of you get drunk on cheap beer."

"Did you really just say *ravish?*"

My face went hot, but I was grinning. "Don't try to change the subject! Is that accurate?"

He looked everywhere but my face. "...yeah. Pretty much. That's how I met Ruth."

I nodded quickly—I didn't want to talk about her. "And tonight? That was...?"

"That was me trying to give you the perfect date. How did I do?"

I smiled. "Perfect. But next time, if you want to take me to some place with...you know, a mosh pit and beer all over the floor...that'd be fine too."

"I think it's just possible that this is going to work out."

He finished his drink, and I realized I'd finished mine. We sat there looking at the empty glasses, neither of us wanting to be the one to say it.

At last, he said, "Would you like...."

"...to go to my apartment?" I finished.

He stared into my eyes. "Like you wouldn't believe."

***

We were kissing before we even got in the door, turning around and around as we moved down the hall as if we were dancing, our lips never separating for an instant. It was as if we'd been starved of each other all the months we'd worked together, straining at chains that had finally been released.

We fell onto the couch, the same one I'd watched him sleep on what felt like years ago. I was on top, kissing down his neck as his hands roamed over my back, smoothing the jersey dress over my body. His large hands cupped my ass and I drew in a long breath, my whole body trembling at his touch. One of his knees parted mine, rough denim against smooth nylon, and then we were scissored together, kissing long and deep as his hands rubbed my thighs, the edges of his hands nudging my dress higher and higher. When it reached my stocking tops and his hands touched bare flesh, he froze and lifted me—easily—so he could look down at my legs, then grinned with delight at what he saw. I had a little warm rush of pride. *Score one to Jasmine.*

He rolled us over, and then I was looking up at him, running my hand over the stubble on his cheek, stroking through his soft, feathery hair. His hands skimmed up my hips, my stomach...I groaned as he lightly squeezed my breasts. Pleasure arced between them, joining and flowing straight down between my legs, and I squirmed beneath him. My hair was fanned out around me like a halo and he smoothed it against the cushions with his fingertips.

"You're perfect," he whispered. "I knew it when I saw you on the steps."

"I was lucky," I told him. "Lucky you saved me."

He gave me one of those smiles. "Not that lucky. I knew what was going to happen when I opened that door."

My eyes went wide, more delighted than angry. "It was *deliberate?!*"

"To tell you the truth," he said, "I was hoping you'd be a little more grateful."

I thumped him on the arm and he chuckled, and then I was twisting us back around so that he was on the bottom, and unfastening his jeans. My breath was coming fast now, my fingers clumsy at the belt buckle. He raised himself up on his elbows as I pulled his jeans down, lifting his tight ass so I could free them. I could see the bulge of his cock beneath his black jockey shorts, and took a deep breath....

And then I was hooking my fingers into the waistband and dragging them down, forcing my face to remain neutral. I had to pretend I'd seen lots of erect cocks before. I was absolutely *not* going to gasp, or go wide-eyed—

I gasped, and felt my eyes widen.

It was beautiful: thick and smooth with a glossy, arrow-shaped head. It leapt upright as I freed it, and the first thing I thought was that it was bigger than my dildo—the only thing I had to compare it to. And dildos didn't throb, I realized as I gripped the shaft, or twitch in your hand. It was so *alive,* so part of him. I'd been thinking of it as almost a thing on its own...I hadn't really thought of it as being a part of Connor, that *he* would be right up inside my body.

I was glad Jasmine had told me to do it this way. I needed the time, needed the build-up. Maybe she'd known that.

"Are you sure?" asked Connor quickly, as he saw me lower my head.

I looked at him for a second and nodded. I was nervous, but I couldn't stop smiling at the idea of giving him pleasure.

I was kneeling astride his legs, one hand wrapped around the root of him to stop him springing upwards. I went to lick him, but just the touch of my breath on him was enough to make him gasp so I did it again, a little sigh of hot air that stroked his sensitive flesh. Then I was tasting him, a hint of salt and delicious male musk, but the thing I wasn't ready for was how warm he was, the incredible intimacy of that hot, pulsing flesh against my tongue.

I wanted to taste all of him, to know all of him, and I started licking down his length, slathering him until he shone. I saw his hands lift and close into fists, tight little gasps as my tongue teased his already hard cock to the straining, throbbing limit.

I took him in my mouth and sucked as Jasmine had shown me, and he arched his back and pushed with his groin, wanting more of him inside me. I worked at it with my cheeks and tongue, enveloping as much of him as I could in soft, hot wetness. I wasn't ready to try any deeper, but I suddenly *got* the idea of deep throating. I would have done, if I could. I wanted all of him.

His hand plunged into my hair, lifting me. "Stop there," he said quickly, and I climbed off him. He hitched up his jeans and then, to my delight, he scooped me up, lifting me with a hand under my legs and another under my back. As he carried me through to the bedroom, my heart boomed louder with every step he took. He kicked the door closed behind him and dropped me on the bed. I sprawled there on my back, looking up at him.

It was completely different to my dream in every conceivable way. And yet perfect.

"Take off your dress." His voice almost a growl. I could hear the blood rushing in my ears and my breath came in tight, shallow pants as I hauled the dress up around my hips...my waist...my breasts. Watching his eyes on me, seeing him drink in my body as it was revealed, sent a rush of heat straight down to my groin and I could feel it turning to slick readiness there. The dress came up and over my head and I threw it aside.

His eyes devoured me as he pulled off his shirt and kicked off his jeans and boots. Naked, he seemed even bigger; when he climbed onto the bed, one knee between my legs, I felt a sudden wave of delicious dread. I was tiny beneath him, the helpless innocent about to be ravaged. I wasn't sure if I'd be able to follow all of Jasmine's advice—suddenly, I just wanted to be *taken*.

Connor stretched out on top of me, kissing down the valley of my breasts, his hands skimming along my bare sides. Every inch of skin he touched seemed to light up in their wake, my whole body coming alive. His mouth was hot at my shoulder, my neck...God, at my ear....

I explored his back with my hands, tracing the muscles I'd wanted to touch since I'd first seen him strip his t-shirt off backstage. Again and again, I followed the hard lines of him down from his wide shoulders to that tight, trim waist...and then, at last, I let my palms slide down to his ass, the firm muscles flexing each time he moved. I wound my legs around him—

He winced, looking down behind him, and I saw I'd just dug one of the Killer Heels into his leg. I quickly unfastened them and kicked them off, figuring they'd served their purpose, and he smiled.

I was barely aware of him sliding one hand down my bare stomach until his fingers slipped under my panties. And then I gasped as he cupped me there, fingertips firm and questing against lips that were already moist. He twisted his hand, his palm grinding against my clit, and a finger slid into me. I gulped for air, hands reaching up above me to grasp at the pillows, hips arching off the bed as he plunged his finger deep and started to move it, my body clenching around him. I reached up and slid my hand around his cock, stroking his shaft in time with his thrusting finger, and as I felt him speed up I knew I'd got it right.

He put one hand under my shoulder and lifted me, and I half sat up. His fingers unclipped my bra and he let me flop back to the bed, pushing it away from my breasts. I lay there staring up at him, worried for a second about what he'd think of me.

He moved his head close, brushing a lock of hair off my cheek. "You're gorgeous," he said. "Gorgeous breasts." A hot little thrill spiraled through me. Then his mouth was on my breast, lips spread wide and tongue working at the nipple and I cried out in shock at the pleasure that arced through me. I came seconds later when he slid a second finger into me, his teeth biting lightly at my hardened nipple. He gazed down at me, our eyes locked together, as I thrashed and bucked, and for once I wasn't embarrassed at all. I could see him relishing my ecstasy; he loved the fact that he'd made me lose control and so did I.

He drew back a little and I let his cock slip from my hand. I watched as he slid my panties down my legs and off, and I pulled my bra the rest of the way off. As it fell to the floor, it seemed to mark something—I was naked, except for the hold ups, naked and ready for him, ready for—

I twisted and pulled open the drawer next to my bed. All four boxes of condoms were sitting there, cellophane removed and lids bent back. I looked at him questioningly.

He blinked a couple of times. "I'm not fussy," he said at last.

I passed him one and he ripped open the foil packet. As he rolled it on, his cock seemed even bigger. I could feel myself breathing deeper, looking up into his eyes as I let my knees loll apart....

He stopped and cocked his head to one side. "Wait...." As if sensing something.

I shook my head. "Go on."

He glanced at the condom selection in the drawer, then at the discarded Killer Heels. "Karen, is it...your first time?"

I thought of about a thousand things to say. And then I just nodded.

"You're sure you want to?" he asked quietly.

"God yes." The hunger in my voice was all he needed to hear. He slid forward on the bed, one thick forearm braced beside my head, and guided himself into me.

God...so thick and so hot, and so unlike the dildo, hard and soft in exactly the right way. The head stretched me, opening me up. I wanted him, but the size of him made me gasp...and then the head was in, my body closing around him in a way that made me catch my breath, and he was biting his lip at the feeling of me around him. He started to move, slow strokes, watching my reaction to check it was okay. But all I felt was pleasure, the liquid friction of him starting a spiraling rush of heat that twisted faster and faster. My hands found his ass, feeling the muscles there move as he thrust into me, each one taking him deeper, until he was rooted in me.

He stopped for a second, brushing the hair back from my forehead and I realized I was damp there. My whole body was trembling, a sheen coating me. He brought his other arm down beside my head, then, and settled fully on top of me, and I brought my knees up. Staring deep into my eyes, he started to fuck me, each thrust pulling him almost from me before driving in to my limits. The spiraling heat twisted faster and faster and my hands clutched at his ass, the feel of his body stroking against my stockinged thighs cementing the reality of what was happening. He sped up and his groin slapped hard against me, grinding against my clit as his cock hammered into me. I felt the heat inside build beyond any chance of control and as I felt my own body start to spasm and clutch at him, I saw his muscles bunch, his jaw tense.

"Yes," said Connor, just as he had in my dream.

My head went back against the covers, my mouth gaping wide as the climax overtook me, my thighs squeezing against his hips as I shook, black-red fireworks exploding in my brain. The orgasm rippled down through me, making me clench and grind against him, and I felt him drive into me hard and his cock throb deep inside me. He gasped, taking his weight on his forearms so that he didn't collapse onto me as I twitched and shuddered beneath him. I couldn't think, could barely breathe, my mind consumed by it. I felt my entire body go tense...and then relax into total serenity.

Connor hooked his hands under me and twisted us so we were on our sides, then lay there giving me a huge grin. It took a while for my brain to start working again. When it did, I suddenly remembered about hula-hooping, and cowgirl, and tweaking my nipples. "Was it okay?" I blurted.

He was still getting his breath back, but he laughed and stroked my cheek. "No," he said firmly. "It was great." And he kissed me.

He wrapped his arms around me, our bodies touching along every inch, lips to toe. Then he said, "Thank you."

"For what?"

"For letting me be your first."

***

I'd heard the thing about men getting sleepy after sex. I only understood it once I'd seen Connor wrap his arms around me, whisper he loved me and then doze off, all within three minutes.

I lay there awake and buzzing, fired up with an energy I'd never known before. Eventually, I slid from the bed, stripped off the hold ups and stood naked in front of the mirror.

I wasn't a virgin anymore.

Did I look different? Could you *tell?* It was weird...ever since I became self-conscious about being a virgin—at about eighteen—I'd always convinced myself that of course no one could tell. And yet now that I was on the other side, now that I'd joined the club.... I definitely felt different. Not more mature, exactly but...like I understood some things I hadn't before. I'd heard of other girls having sex for the first time and saying, "And then I wondered what the big deal was." It wasn't like that at all. I felt like I'd been introduced to food or music for the first time. I wanted *more*. I wanted to experience everything!

I checked the bed. Connor was dead to the world.

I wrapped a sheet around me and crept through to

the lounge, closing the doors behind me. I didn't really have a plan until I picked up my cello and sat down. And then I started to play...*us*. The softness of the cello, interwoven with bits that would come to life with the hardness of his guitar riffs. The ebb and flow of sex; a blend of both of us, together at last.

CHAPTER 23

THE NEXT DAY, we slept in. With Connor spooning me from behind, his strong arm around me, it took a lot of hammering at the front door before I grudgingly pulled myself out of the black syrup of sleep and into the harsh, bright daylight.

I padded to the door, wrapped in a sheet. I got there just as my father opened it from the outside.

I gave a kind of half scream, half yelp, pulling the sheet tighter around me. My father averted his eyes but, as always, found a way for it to be my fault. "I got tired of waiting," he said. "Go and put some clothes on! Do you know what time it is?" He snapped back the cuff of his tailored suit and checked his Rolex. His beard was perfectly trimmed, as always, the little glasses he wore polished to a brilliant shine. I felt my knees weaken, a hot flush of shame spreading across my face. "I'm...I'm sorry—"

My half-scream brought Connor stumbling from the bedroom in his jockey shorts. He slid to a halt in front of my father as he got the gist of the situation, then drew himself up to his full height and tried his best to be formal. "Hi," he said. "I'm Connor."

My father just stared at him—at his tattoos, in particular. "This is your recital partner?!" he asked in disbelief. "This is the violinist?"

I opened my mouth to speak, but Connor got there first. "Violinist? No. Guitar."

My father looked at him. "*Electric?*" he asked, as if the word polluted his mouth.

"Yeah," said Connor. "We're really good together."

My father glanced between the two of us, his lip curling.

"You—shouldn't have just burst in here!" I told him weakly. "I'm twenty-one." But I wasn't twenty-one. In my mind, I was six years old, being admonished for anything and everything.

"You didn't answer your phone," said my father. "You didn't answer the door. And now I find out you lied to me about your recital."

I couldn't have the conversation dressed in a sheet. "I need to put something on," I told him, and went to the bedroom. I threw Connor his jeans and then closed the door for a second while I tried to get my breathing under control. The room was spinning. All of the nerves, all of the panic I'd felt months ago, everything that Connor had helped me free myself from...it was all back. All that mattered was my father and my future.

Twenty-one years of habit grabbed hold of my soul and shook hard. I started to wonder if my father was right. If I hadn't invited Dan to Flicker that night, if I hadn't been so scared of public speaking that I flunked all my presentations in the first place—

It's all my fault.

I didn't want to face him, but I couldn't leave Connor out there alone. I pulled on some clothes and opened the door.

"Karen's amazing," was the first thing I heard Connor say.

"Mmm-hmm." My father. "And what's your plan, when you graduate from Fenbrook?"

I winced as I heard Connor hesitate. "Nothing...concrete," he said.

My father didn't help him out. He just left it hanging there, like evidence. I joined them in the hallway. "I think I need to talk to my father alone," I told Connor.

"You sure?" Connor looked between my father and me. He wasn't scared of him, I realized. I'd never met anyone before who wasn't intimidated by him.

I nodded silently. Connor disappeared into the bedroom to get the rest of his clothes and I stood there under my father's glare. When Connor returned, he kissed me tenderly on the lips, ignoring the look my father gave him.

"I'll call you later," he promised, kissed me again and was gone.

My father stood there staring at me, while I stared at the floor. There were no hugs, but then that was normal.

"Well," said my father. "This time, you've outdone yourself."

I took a deep breath, digging my nails into my palms to try to control my panic. "It's not what it looks like." Which was a mistake, because of course he called me on it.

"Oh, really? What is it, exactly? Tell me your good reason for throwing away your career and bedding an Irish dropout."

"He's not a dropout!" I said angrily.

"Straight-A student?"

I hesitated for a split second and my father gave me a look. The exact same withering look he'd given me when I was eight, and he'd come home to find me painting the side of the house purple because I thought that would turn it into a magical fairy castle that could fly.

I told him in a shaking voice about Dan and the panic to find a replacement and how Connor had saved me, carefully leaving out the part about his grades. The aching humiliation of having failed him was even worse than I'd feared it would be, but there was one small silver lining—the relief of not lying to him anymore, even if I did hold back about Connor being a hair's breadth from flunking. It was out in the open at last.

And then the relief turned to sick fear as it all went horribly wrong.

My father shook his head. "I could have spoken to Fenbrook. You know I have pull there. I could have forced them to make an exception for you—you could have performed solo. A *proper* performance, not some mismatched gimmick."

A sick dread started to spread through me, because I knew where this conversation would lead. "No," I said quickly. "I argued with Professor Harman. There's no way they'd have let me perform solo."

My father sighed. "You were probably tearful and begging. You don't know how to stand up to people—you never have. I'll threaten to sue—they can't fail you because some idiot breaks his arm."

It was exactly what I would have wanted, in the days after Dan was mugged. Now, I couldn't imagine anything worse. I shook my head, trying to head it off. "It's too late—" *No, no, no, please don't!*

"Nonsense. I'll head over there right now and have it out with Harman. I'll pick out something for you to play solo and coach you personally—I can stay here until the recital." He stood up.

And then the panic was full-blown and real inside my chest, stealing my breath. "No," I said, my voice little more than a croak. "Stop!"

He was halfway to the door. "We'll talk later, Karen, when I've cleaned up your mess."

And that was it. I had to decide, right then, between my future and Connor.

The terrible truth was that I knew my father was right. Rehearsing for a solo piece in just three weeks would be tough but, with him coaching me and no partner to worry about, we could practice night and day. As Harman had told me, the whole point of the recitals was to learn teamwork. Playing solo would give me a massive advantage. If my father pushed Harman into letting me do it, I could almost certainly get top marks and walk straight into the New York Phil. My chances would go from slim to near-certainty.

And Connor would be royally screwed. He'd be in the situation I'd been in when Dan broke his arm. *He* wouldn't be given the chance of a solo performance, and without a partner he'd be unable to perform. He'd miss out on the credits and despite all his work on the essays he'd fail to graduate.

My father opened the door. "Stop," I said again. He ignored me. "Fucking stop!" I yelled.

He slowly closed the door. "Did I just hear you curse at me?"

I held up my hand. "Just—I'm sorry, just...stop."

"Is that *him?* Is that how he affects you?" he asked, his voice tight.

"Of course not! God, I'm twenty-one!"

"You keep saying that as if it means you're automatically fit to run your own life. Clearly, you're not."

My entire life, I'd been scared of my father. I'd followed every rule he'd set, obeyed every instruction given because he was my father and therefore *right*. But for the first time, I wasn't sure.

"I need to think about it," I told him. "I don't want you to go to Harman...not yet, at least."

He shook his head. "Karen, you're not thinking clearly. I'll go and talk to Harman and—"

"If you pull me out of the performance with Connor, I'll drop out entirely." I folded my arms. "No recital at all. And that means I won't graduate."

He stared at me. "Why would you do that? Just to spite me?" He sounded genuinely hurt.

"No! I just...." I sighed. "I can't just let Connor down. Don't talk to Harman or I *will* just drop out. Okay?"

My father shook his head. "I don't know what's come over you, Karen, but if you insist on this melodrama—very well. Do your thinking. I'm staying at my usual hotel."

He walked out, closing the door quietly behind him because slamming it would have been undignified.

I leaned against the wall, letting out a long breath, and then slid down to sit against it.

When I'd met Connor, he was on a downward path—he was going to flunk. I was on my way to the New York Phil, and a stupid, random mugging had changed that. Connor had saved me, I'd saved him and maybe our plan would work...and maybe it wouldn't. But my father had just given me a chance to put everything back how it was. Was it so bad, to reset everything to before I met him?

The worst part of the decision was, I knew that if I told Connor about it, he'd say to go ahead and do it. He hadn't wanted to graduate, when I first met him. He'd seen his time at Fenbrook as a chance to party, nothing more.

And yet...I knew that it wasn't that simple. When I'd seen those lyrics in his guitar case I'd uncovered the real reason for his not trying, and by helping him I'd changed his path. I'd made him believe he was capable of more, that he could have a better future. Could I really rip all that away from him, even if he wanted me to— even if he begged me to?

But if I didn't, I'd be giving up my future—my whole career—to give someone who hadn't wanted to graduate in the first place a slim chance at success. All of my years of practice, all that time inside playing while other children enjoyed a normal life, might be wasted. If I stuck with Connor and our plan, and we didn't get the result we needed, would I blame him? Would it poison things between us? Until that morning, performing with Connor had been my only chance, a crazy, last-ditch effort—we'd try, and if we failed, we failed. But now, doing the duet with him was a *choice*...and that meant I could be wrong.

I tapped the back of my head against the wall. I didn't know what to decide. I didn't even know *how* to decide.

*****

Connor called me later that morning, and I reassured him that everything was fine. I didn't tell him about my father's offer, because I needed the decision to be mine and mine alone. I tried to tell myself that nothing had changed—we were still in love and we could stick to our plan and it would be as if my father's visit had never happened.

Except that was a lie. Everything was different, because now my father's offer sat there throbbing at the back of my mind, dark and cancerous, eating away at our happiness.

I needed a break, so I met Jasmine in Harper's for a debrief. I'd heard her, Natasha and Clarissa dissect tens of encounters between them, but I'd never before been the one with the secret, the one eager to tell her story. I put everything that was going on with my father and the recital to one side for a few moments. A girl only gets to share this particular story once. As I walked between the tables to where Jasmine was sitting, I was *gleeful.*

Jasmine already had the coffees waiting, to ensure I could launch into it as soon as I got there. "Sooo?" she asked as I sat down.

I opened my mouth and then closed it again. Suddenly, I was very aware of all the other people in the café, some of them just a few feet away at the next table.

"Go on!" Jasmine told me.

I looked sideways at the table of women next to me. Glanced at the chattering guys behind me. I'd never thought about it when it was one of the others telling their stories, but now that it was *me....*

"They're not listening," Jasmine told me. "I mean, they can *hear,* but they tune it out. You could confess to murder and they wouldn't react. It's the polite lie of the coffee shop."

I looked around again and bit my lip.

Jasmine picked up a fork. "If you don't tell me about the sex *right now,* I will do bad things to you."

I cleared my throat. "Well, we started kissing as soon as we got back to my place." That seemed safe enough. "Then we were on the sofa, with his hands all over me."

"Gropey?"

"No! Not gropey at all. Lovely."

"Go on."

"He ran his hands up under my dress." I was grinning now, remembering it. "He loved the stockings!"

Jasmine looked smug.

"And then I...I sucked his *C-O-C-K*."

Jasmine put her palm to her face. "Karen, spelling it out isn't going to stop them understanding. They're not four."

I looked around again, red-faced. No one seemed to be paying any attention—or they were doing a good job of hiding it.

"How was his cock?" asked Jasmine, quite loudly.

I ducked down in my seat. "Jasmine!"

"What?"

"I can't—do we really talk about that?"

"We always talk about it when it's one of *our* boyfriends. You must remember the Darrell vs. Neil conversation."

I did. That one had gotten quite heated. I flushed. "It just seems wrong to...you know. Discuss him."

"It's normal. Spill."

I relegated myself to it, and then smirked. "It was lovely. Gorgeous."

"Big?"

I nodded. "Yes. I mean, big compared to"—I almost said *my dildo*—"what I've...seen." Something suddenly occurred to me. "Oh my God! Is he sitting somewhere discussing *me?*"

Jasmine shook her head. "Nope. It's a girl thing. Men are too uptight."

That made me feel slightly better, although a tiny

part of me was curious as to what Connor would have said about me. "OK, so...he stopped me, because he was going to...you know. Reach his conclusion."

Jasmine winced. "Just say *come!*"

"Anyway," I said hotly, "he carried me through to the bedroom—"

"He *carried* you?"

"Yep."

"Hot."

"I know. And he dropped me on the bed, and I took my dress off. And then he took me."

Jasmine frowned. "Took you where?"

"No, *took* me."

"Oh! You didn't just lie there, did you?"

I tried to think back to it. Everything had moved so fast...now that she mentioned it, I had a horrible feeling that I *had* just lain there. But then I'd been feeling very...ravished. "I'm not sure. But he loved it. He told me."

A chattering crowd of girls were queuing next to us, and Jasmine had to raise her voice over them. "And did you?"

"Oh yes. It was fantastic."

"No, I mean *did you?* Did you come?"

"Oh!" I almost laughed. "Yes, I came twice," I said loudly.

Jasmine just stared at me. I was suddenly aware that the café was completely silent, and that everyone was trying very hard not to look at me.

Jasmine raised her hand. "Check, please."

CHAPTER 24

A S THE RECITALS APPROACHED, the other musicians went into full-blown panic mode. From behind every practice room door came strains of Mozart and Schubert, Beethoven and Brahms and—from the contemporary groups—wild rock and edgy, experimental keyboard solos. No one else was crazy enough to mix the two styles. *At least we'll sound unusual, when we fail.*

It had been a full day since my father arrived and I wasn't any closer to making a decision. Before he'd showed up, I'd been reasonably optimistic about our chances—we had four of the six sections nailed and the fifth, the one I'd composed after we'd had sex, was sounding good—but now, listening to everyone else rehearse their safe, traditional choices, a big part of me was wondering what the hell I was doing. I had an out, a chance to go back to what I knew. I could perform solo and have a much safer shot at the orchestra....

All I had to do was screw Connor over in the

process.

As if to mock my tension, Connor was happier than I'd ever seen him, beaming all over his gorgeous face and casting little glances at me across the room as we played. Every look made my heart lift...followed by a ripple of doubt and cold, dark fear, like thunder after the lightning. Was I a heartless bitch to even consider doing it...or a lovesick idiot for not having done it already? Connor would want me to do it—even beg me to—which was why I couldn't tell him.

"Penny for 'em," he said suddenly as we came to the end of the fourth section.

Since all the practice rooms were full of over-caffeinated, sleep-deprived musicians we'd bagged the main hall. A cavernous room, gloomy and cold, it nevertheless had fantastic acoustics. The notes bounced off polished wood floors and dark paneled walls, soaring towards a ceiling I could barely see. An aging but still beautiful grand piano stood in one corner, its black lacquer a mirror I'd occasionally catch a glimpse of us in. I kept seeing the dress I was wearing—nothing special, just a black and white, knee length thing—and doing a double take. The dress was sort of an experiment. It was *weird*, not being in jeans and a sweatshirt. And kind of nice.

I shrugged. "I'm thinking you need to get to work on the final section. You're behind." I meant it to sound jokey, but it came out sullen.

He stood up and closed the gap between us. I'd let my hair fall forward and cover my face, hiding behind it just like I used to before I met him. He gently brushed it back. "What's really the matter?"

I tried to think of something convincing. "I'm worried about Jasmine," I said at last. Which at least was true.

"What's wrong with Jasmine? She seems like she can handle herself."

That was exactly what I was worried about. Jasmine was so used to coping on her own I wasn't sure she knew how to ask for help, even when things got really bad. She was serious about the escorting thing and I didn't know how to talk her out of it; I sometimes wondered how far off the rails she'd already be, if she didn't have the sobering presence of the rest of us. "Money trouble," I told him. And then couldn't tell him anything else, which made me feel even worse.

He brushed back my hair from my other cheek. "You ever think you worry too much about other people and not enough about yourself?"

I gave a bitter little laugh. "Connor, all I do is worry about myself."

"I don't mean worry as in *stress about it*. I mean worry as in *look after yourself*. Like, putting yourself first sometimes."

A hard knot formed in my stomach. *Did he know?* Had my father tracked him down and talked to him, and this was Connor's way of nudging me in the right direction, without letting on that he knew?

Connor crouched down in front of me so that he was gazing right into my eyes. "Your *thing*...the New York Phil. That's what you really want? I mean, what *you* really want?"

I'd wondered the same thing since we started working together. When Dan had first broken his arm, my reaction had been almost instinctive—I *had* to graduate, I *had* to get into the orchestra, as surely as I had to breathe, or eat. Now, after the latest talk with my father, I was questioning whose dream I was trying so hard to fulfill. I wanted it...I'd wanted it for as long as I could remember. But it was starting to feel like fear of failure, not passion, was driving me.

"Yes," I told Connor eventually, and even I could hear how conflicted it sounded.

He sighed. "What you need is to relax. Put down the cello."

"We need to practice."

"Karen Montfort, put down the cello and lift your skirt."

I felt a rush of heat scald my face and instinctively turned to see if anyone had heard, but we were alone in the massive hall. "*What?!*"

He didn't give me a chance to answer, just scooped me up into his arms and lifted me with an impatient sigh, the sort you'd give when picking up an errant kitten. His strong arms pressed me to his chest and despite a yelp and a "*Connor!*" and a kicking of legs, I was carried across the room. My chin was resting on his shoulder, looking over his back, so I couldn't see where we were going. My first clue was when I heard him lift the lid of the grand piano, exposing the keys; my second was when I felt him lift the hem of my dress, exposing *me*.

I swallowed quickly. "Connor, we can't—"

He put me gently down on the keys, and I gasped as they shifted and sank beneath my ass, a discordant cacophony echoing around the hall. He'd lifted my dress up to my hips, and the panties I'd chosen—skimpy black briefs, which was my idea of daring—left a good deal of bare skin exposed to press against the chill ivory. Worse, I'd experimented by wearing hold ups again and I could feel his eyes raking over the lacy tops. I could feel the situation sliding out of control.

"The door's not locked," I said quickly.

His eyes twinkled. "I know."

His warm palms slid over the outside of my hips,

his thumbs just toying with the slender waistband of my panties. Then he dropped to his knees, his shoulders nudging my knees apart, and I gaped as I realized what he had in mind. I felt his hot breath on that sensitive crease at the top of my thigh and my hands clutched at the edge of the piano. "Connor, we *can't!*" I said tightly. He ignored me. I started to say it again, but his tongue traced that same line, drawing a burning trail just where leg meets body, and it came out as "Connor, we *caaaaaan't!*"

His fingers hooked into the waistband of my briefs. "Lift," he told me. He didn't move his face away, so the word was a hot rush of air against my tingling flesh.

I looked over his shoulder at the doors to the hall. Closed, but not locked. We'd stopped playing—how long before some curious music student—or even worse, a member of staff—opened them a crack to see if there was anyone in here?

Connor looked up at me, and in those blue-gray eyes was something I hadn't seen before. Raw lust, and *command.* He knew exactly what he wanted. "Karen," he told me, "lift your beautiful arse."

My resistance melted like snow under a spring sun. I pressed my palms against the keys, lifting myself a little, and with a whisper of fabric he slid my panties down my thighs and let them drop to my ankles. I was naked and exposed to him, soft curls of hair trembling under his breath, lips spreading as he pushed my knees farther apart. My panties were tangled on my shoes, trapping my feet together, and that made it feel even sluttier, somehow, the heat he was awakening deep inside me turning to hot slickness. My ass, naked now, pressed against ivory that was growing warm from my body.

And then he was pressing his face between my thighs and all rational thought stopped. The touch of his tongue, first, circling inwards along my thigh, slowly but inexorably, my whole body twisting in response. His lips, that perfect blend of hard and soft, laying kisses along the creases of my thighs and then along the soft, damp curls, moving towards—

I slid my fingers through his hair. My mouth was open in a silent scream of ecstasy as his tongue plunged up inside me, his lips working at my damp folds in a hungry kiss. His thumbs were stroking the soft skin of my thighs, super-sensitive places no one had ever touched before—how did he *know?!* With every brush of his hands, every thrust of his tongue, every drag of that rough, hot flesh against my silky walls, I felt myself lift higher and higher. I was actually straining upward, my head thrown back and my breasts reaching for the ceiling. I'd closed my eyes at some point and the idea that someone could silently open the door and see us, that we'd never know until it was too late, only made it hotter.

Connor started to work at me harder, faster, his upper lip rubbing at my clit until I ground myself against him. I was panting, inner thighs aching from having my knees spread wide but, as I twisted my feet and the panties finally dropped to the floor, I spread my legs even wider for him. Every time I shifted or moved on the keyboard, another few notes would echo around the room—anyone listening from the corridor would surely wonder what the hell we were doing in there, and then they might—The thought of being caught twisted together with the pleasure, building with it, both enhancing the other, until I was a helpless mass of raw nerves, twisting and bucking against him. When he drew his tongue out of me and pinned me hard against the keys, palms keeping my thighs spread wide, I knew something was coming...but I didn't know what. I opened my eyes and found myself looking right into his, staring up at me with a mixture of hunger and something that looked like victory. I just sat there panting, submissive to whatever he cared to do to me, and that was all the encouragement he needed.

His lips captured my clit, tongue licking and circling, and I let out a high shriek. I could feel the orgasm roaring towards me now, inevitable—the only question was how big it was going to be. Connor's face was pressed hard against me, his tongue insistent, working faster and faster at my throbbing bud. I instinctively tried to close my thighs, the sensations almost too much, but his shoulders were like steel between my legs, keeping me helplessly spread. I was under his control.

The energy started to spiral higher and higher inside me, unstoppable. Free now to use his hands, he pushed one underneath me, the thumb stroking at my soaking lips, the palm under my ass. My hips were swirling and thrusting now, just as Jasmine had taught me but without any conscious thought. His other hand pushed its way up under my dress, sliding up my straining body to squeeze my breast, and I felt the orgasm begin to break over me—

Just as it did, the hand under my ass moved. One finger softly pressing—

I came, crying out long and hard, the walls ringing with the sounds of my pleasure. I ground against his mouth, wanting him to touch every part of me, taste me, *eat* me. Nothing existed right then except Connor and me, all my worries forgotten.

I shuddered and cried out again, the climax rolling through my body in waves, making me alternately tense and quiver. I stared down into Connor's eyes, and I'd never felt so completely connected to anyone in my entire life.

I slumped on the keys, my hands finally loosening in his hair and falling either side of me, unleashing their own crashes of notes. I panted, unable to speak, as he stood up....

...and unbuckled his belt.

I swallowed, wanting it but not quite believing that he'd dare—that *we* would dare. "God, we can't—"

He didn't even bother arguing with me, just pushed down his jeans and shorts. His cock sprang out, rock hard.

I looked at the door one last time and then something flashed through me, white-hot and so fast I only felt its aftermath. I opened my thighs wider, feeling my moist lips throb in the cool air.

I wanted it.

He rolled on a condom and then the thick head of him was spearing into me, spreading my wet folds in a way that made me clasp my arms around his back, the hot hardness of him sliding deep along velvet walls that were already slick, my body welcoming him in. His hands lifted my legs and I let my thighs wrap around his waist as he slid deeper, my ass just barely on the keys.

He started to thrust and it was different to the first time, the thickness of him stretching me in whole new ways thanks to our position. His thighs were warm between mine and as I squeezed his body I could feel the smooth power of his muscles under the skin, bunching and flexing, driving him into me. My chin was resting on his shoulder, but as he started to thrust faster I drew back a little so that I could look into his eyes. Our faces were inches apart, both of us speechless and staring, just panting at each other as he pounded into me, long hot thrusts into my clenching tightness. My ankles pulled against the backs of his legs, pulling him in as I felt a new climax coil and tense inside me, quick and whipcord tight.

"Come for me," he said, both an order and a granting of permission. The thought exploded in my brain, that I was going to come *for him*, under his touch, my body wrapped around his cock. Connor. My boyfriend. My lover.

My fingers dug hard into the muscles of his back and I came, a different sort of climax. It didn't roll through me like the first one, leaving me weak and helpless; it was like a surge of raw energy, hot and ancient, and it left me crackling with power. I was coming for him and, seconds later, as he pushed deep, gasped, and throbbed inside me, I knew that he'd come for me, too. I'd known, on some level, that he had power over me since he'd first saved me on the steps—even if I hadn't admitted it. It was a heady rush to realize that I had the same power over him.

The silence that followed should have been heavy and awkward—we should have pulled our clothes together and blushed and been unable to meet each other's eyes. But it didn't feel like that at all—it felt like we'd connected on a new level. Like we were a team, somehow. I would have been mortified if anyone had come in and seen us but, as I slipped down off the piano and pulled my panties on, Connor's gaze didn't make me embarrassed at all. I felt...free.

"Better?" he asked, a smile in his voice.

"Better." I kissed him tenderly and lingered on it, not wanting to lose the afterglow.

"We need to do that more often," he told me. "You *especially* need it."

Now I *was* a little embarrassed. "Because I'm

uptight?" I asked, remembering what he'd said in the storeroom. That it could be fixed, and that he knew exactly how to fix it. I shivered, in an entirely nice way.

He chuckled and pulled me close. "You cling onto things very tightly. I think sex helps you let go, a little bit." He considered. "Not that I'm any better."

"You don't strike me as someone who needs help to relax." I sat down and picked up my cello.

He shook his head. "Not relaxing, but...I get frustrated. Do you have any idea how often we have to read stuff? I don't mean books. I mean blogs and TV news tickers and directions and...." He sighed, as if he was getting annoyed just thinking about it. "And every time that happens, and my brain turns it all into a jumble, I get angry."

"So how do you deal with that?" I asked.

"You've already seen. At the gym."

I thought back to him pounding the bag, the muscles in his back hard as oak, shining with sweat as he drove his fist into the canvas again and again, driven by the essay he hadn't been able to write. I remembered how angry I'd been at him that day, when I thought the problem was laziness, and winced. "Sorry," I said instinctively.

"You didn't know. And I'm glad you kept on at me, and worked it out. Knowing what the problem is makes it a fuck of a lot easier. Still makes me mad, though."

I thought of the bag swaying and creaking on its chain. It had seemed so pointless, when I'd watched him—however much he hit it, it would never break. Now I saw it in a new way—it wasn't about trying to destroy something, I realized, it was about releasing something toxic from him. The bag was just there to soak up his anger—the fact it couldn't be destroyed was the whole point.

And that gave me an idea.

"Your gym...." I said slowly. "Can anyone join?"

***

"I feel like they're all looking at me," said Natasha out of the corner of her mouth. "Are they?"

I checked behind her. Yes, a fair few of the guys were gazing at us—her, more than me—and I could see their eyes run down the length of her long, dancer's legs. It really wasn't that surprising—there probably hadn't been a woman in the gym since the last time I was there, and now there were two at once.

"Not at all," I lied. I watched as Connor spoke quietly to Darrell, showing him how to throw a jab. Darrell looked even worse than when I'd seen him in Flicker, strung out and shaky as a drug addict denied his fix. Which wasn't so far from the truth, in a way. "He hasn't worked, still?" I asked.

Natasha shook her head. "The workshop's still covered in dustsheets."

I nodded. Connor looked at home here, in his raggedy clothes; Darrell looked distinctly out of place. He had just as much muscle as the other guys here, his arms powerful from heaving chunks of metal around in the workshop. But unlike the others, he didn't want to be here. His idea of working out was hammering something into shape, not uselessly hitting a bag, and I suspected Natasha had had to drag him to meet us.

"Snap back," Connor told Darrell, his Irish accent a soft growl, "And keep your guard up."

Darrell nodded, looking unconvinced, and tapped his gloves together a few times. Then he hit the bag half-heartedly.

"I don't know," whispered Natasha. "I can see

what you were trying to do, and—seriously—thanks. But I don't think he can just let it out like Connor can. I mean, I don't know Connor, but what Darrell's dealing with is this deep-rooted thing he can't get away from...."

I nodded absently as I watched. My own fists were bunching, I wanted it to work so much. Connor's problems were pretty deep-rooted too....

"Go from the hip," Connor told Darrell, demonstrating a hook. "Try to land it in the kidneys."

Darrell thumped the bag, but he kept glancing around as if embarrassed. He was doing it, but he wasn't into it. Duty, not rage, was driving him.

I sighed and shrugged. "Sorry," I said to Natasha. "I thought—"

"Now paint a face on the fucker," Connor said.

I saw Darrell blink.

"Make it into a *him*. Or a *them*," Connor told him.

Darrell blinked another couple of times and then nodded. And his eyes narrowed.

He punched, hitting the bag dead center, and then just stopped dead, his hand still pressed hard against the bag. I could see the surprise on his face—for the first time, it had been satisfying.

He drew his fist back and hit it again. And again. And then did a hook, burying his fist into a tender kidney. His next punch was high, and it wasn't a bag he was hitting anymore—it was a face.

Natasha took a half step forward, amazed. Something was happening, right in front of us. The monster that Darrell had chained up in his head, the one that had driven him to create weapon after weapon, that kept him awake every night, was finally being released. Not into another gleaming instrument of death, but as raw energy, power that made the bag creak and swing on its chain. His punches grew harder and harder and he moved instinctively to hit the bag on all sides, to *destroy* it.

Sweat soaked his vest, his shoulders gleaming with it. There was a light in his eyes that I hadn't seen in months and even though I knew it must be scary for Natasha to see him like this—just like it had been for me, with Connor, I knew she needed to see it. This was a part of him, and always would be. His lips were drawn back over his teeth, his fists hammering at the bag with a force that must have been painful. Around us, men turned to look and then nodded with understanding.

Watching it come out of him was unsettling—it was almost as if he'd been possessed by a spirit, since he quit his job. The anger had been consuming him, and now that it was leaving him I could see the Darrell we all knew emerge from underneath. The bag swung and creaked on its chain, absorbing his rage, for a long time.

When Darrell finally dropped his hands and staggered against the bag, barely able to lift his arms, he was soaked with sweat...and he was *him* again.

"Are you okay?" Natasha asked, running over and putting her arms around him.

He was panting, barely able to speak. "I...want...to...come back tomorrow," he said at last. He looked at Connor and gave him a nod of thanks. And then he gave me one, too.

Natasha hugged him close and I could see her eyes were wet with tears. *Thank you,* she mouthed over his back. I caught Connor's eye, and he held out a hand and pulled me up against him, beaming at the other couple. He barely knew Darrell, but he was glad to have helped him—would train with him every day, if that's what he needed, just because it was the right thing to do.

And that's when I finally stopped torturing myself and accepted it. I'd known it all along, I think, from the moment my father had made his offer—I just hadn't faced up to it. I pulled Connor into a kiss and let the heat of his body soak into me, giving me the strength I needed to tell myself the truth.

I couldn't screw Connor over. No way.

And that meant I had to confront my father.

CHAPTER 25

I HAD TO WEAR A DRESS TO MEET HIM. I'd been to the hotel plenty of times before and I knew from painful experience how out of place I'd feel standing in the bar in jeans—and I needed all the confidence I could muster. But it had to be the right dress, because he'd complain if the hem was too short. Or the neckline too low. Or the fabric too gauzy.

This was why I'd spent most of the years since my mother left in jeans and a sweatshirt.

The bar was a mix of upmarket business types and old money. Everything was made of chrome or dark wood or marble—in fact, it looked a lot like my father's apartment, back in Boston. Probably why he liked it so much.

My father had a thing for punctuality but was traditional enough that he—as the man—would always be there first. Except this time my nerves made me get there stupidly early and I had to stand at the bar, sipping a mineral water and shredding a napkin while I waited. I considered getting a glass of wine to steady my nerves but I knew he'd smell the alcohol on me.

Next to me, a blonde in a tight blue dress listened with wide eyes to the stories a gray-haired man in a suit was telling her about life in the shipping business. I couldn't help but listen, because the way they interacted wasn't like anything I'd heard before. She didn't seem to know enough about him to be his wife, or daughter. Yet they couldn't be on a date, surely, because he had twenty years on her. She was far too flirty to be a secretary or colleague, so...?

And then I got it. And watched in the mirror as he ran a hand up her thigh, finished his drink and led her to the elevators. God, was that what Jasmine had to look forward to? Pretending to be awed by some forty year-old's stories, laughing at his jokes before going upstairs with him and—

And what? My mind whirled. Letting him take her, writhing under him in mock passion? Getting down on her knees and sucking him? What would he demand she let him do to her, to secure a bigger tip?

I closed my eyes. What worried me most was that, based on what I'd just seen, Jasmine was right—she'd be *good* at it. She'd be able to use all her acting talent to flirt and giggle and make the men feel like gods, and then....

I opened my eyes and saw my father standing there. "You're early," he told me, as if that was an unthinkable crime.

I wanted to go up to his room, where if I lost it we'd at least have some privacy. But he insisted on talking it out right there in the bar, in antique leather armchairs the color of dried blood.

I knitted my hands together on my lap and tried to keep my voice steady. "I've decided. I don't want you to talk to Professor Harman," I told him.

He gave a long sigh of frustration, one I knew very well. It wasn't the sound of acceptance; it was him indicating that he was speaking to an idiot, one who he'd have to spend many hours correcting. "Karen—"

"No." I said it so firmly and sharply that his eyes actually flicked up to my face in puzzlement, like an owl that's just heard a mouse answer it back. "No. I've decided. I don't want to perform solo,"—I let it hang in the air between us, giving him time to stew in it before offering him my deal—"unless you strike the same deal for Connor. He has to be allowed to play solo, too."

Once I realized I wasn't going to take my father's offer, it hadn't taken me long to come up with my ultimatum. It was simple and practical and ultimately fair, and it gave us both a much better chance of acing the recital than if we performed together. Even with just three weeks to go, we could still do it—I could pull out a cello piece I was familiar with and play that solo, Connor could play something he knew well for electric guitar and instead of fighting against our habits, we could embrace them, doing what we were really good at. We could both graduate, I could impress the New York Phil scout and everything would be *great*.

If my father accepted.

I knew he had the power to make it happen. He'd been confident that he could convince Harman to make an exception to the rules for me, so I was sure he could do the same for Connor—after all, it was only fair. It wasn't *could* he; it was *would* he?

My father looked me in the eye, long and hard. "He's changed you."

I managed—just—to look steadily back at him. "Maybe he has."

There was a long pause. Then my father said, "Okay. I'll do it."

My heart leaped. Everything was going to be okay!

"*If* you agree to stop seeing him," my father said.

And my whole world crumbled to dust. My careful plan had been swung around and turned against me. "W—What?"

"I'll do the deal with Harman, for both of you. But you give me your word you won't see Connor again."

My plan had hung on the notion of sacrifice. I knew my father hated Connor, but I'd also been sure that he'd rather see Connor succeed than both of us fail. Somehow, he'd twisted that around so that I was the one forced to choose: between our futures and our relationship.

The third option—to agree, and then go against him and see Connor anyway—wasn't an option at all. I knew what my father meant when he asked for my word. I'd never broken my word to him, nor him to me and I knew that if I did I'd be ending things between us...permanently. I tried briefly to imagine a world without him in it, and I couldn't.

I could save both our futures, or I could be with Connor. Not both.

***

At home, I ran a very deep, very hot bath. One of the advantages of being short is that you can really stretch out in the tub. I lay there submerged, my face forming a low island, my hair wafting lazily like seaweed.

I'd switched off my phone while I'd been at the hotel with my father, not wanting the sniping and arguing that a call from Connor would have triggered. A good thing, too, because the call log showed Connor had called me while I'd been there. I didn't return it. I couldn't, until I made my decision.

It should have been easy—I loved him, so I should say the hell with graduating and think about *us,* right? Except...if you really loved someone, weren't you supposed to do what was right for them, even if it meant losing them? If Connor performed by himself, he could graduate. If he graduated, he had a future, maybe here in New York, instead of a dead-end job back in Belfast. If I really cared about him, shouldn't I take the deal and sacrifice the relationship, for both our sakes? That would be the grown-up thing to do.

Or was I just kidding myself, justifying a deal that would also give me my dream back? Was I being selfish, wanting my future back? Or selfish wanting to hang on to Connor?

I closed my eyes and sighed. When I finally climbed out of the bath, I was no nearer making a decision...and Connor had called again. My thumb hovered over the icon that would call him back, wanting to hear his voice...but I couldn't. If I spoke to him, he'd know something was wrong and he'd coax it out of me. And then he'd demand that I take the deal, maybe even breaking up with me to force the issue. I couldn't let him do that. It was my father holding this over our heads, and it had to be my decision, for better or worse.

I pulled on panties and an old t-shirt and then sat on my bed, staring at my phone's screen. I knew I needed to call my father...I just didn't know what I was going to tell him.

I tapped on my father's name and held my breath while the phone rang. *Don't answer,* I prayed. *Then I can put this off until morning.*

"So?" No pleasantries; just business. The way it always was.

I opened my mouth to speak, but no words came out.

"Karen?"

I closed my eyes and took a deep breath.

"Well?" he said.

"I don't want the deal," I told him. "I'll play the duet with Connor."

There was a long silence.

"Your funeral," he said at last. "When he breaks up with you and you realize you've thrown away your future, you know where to find me."

The line went dead. I fell back on the bed, hot tears spilling down my cheeks to soak into my hair. Had I just done the right thing...or just ruined everything?

***

A half hour later, my phone rang. Connor. I took a few deep breaths and answered. *He never has to know.* "Hello?"

"Hi! I've been trying to reach you." He sounded worried, and a cold, oily dread started to rise in my belly.

"What's up?"

I heard him run a hand through his hair, and I could hear the forced nonchalance in his voice. "Probably nothing. Don't panic. But they sprang an essay on us today."

"What?! When does it have to be in?"

"Tomorrow. I had to go ahead and write it, 'cos I couldn't get hold of you."

I wanted to say *"By yourself?!"* but that would have sounded bad. "Did it...go okay?" I asked instead.

"Ruth helped me," he said, and I could hear the doubt in his voice.

I started to say something and immediately bit it back. I had to tread very carefully...Ruth was still his friend, and I couldn't flat-out question her ability...or her motives. "Okay. Well, that was good of her." I tried to sound relaxed and smiley, but I was terrified. Ruth didn't have the knowledge I had...and would she have worked as hard as I would have done, to get the essay just right? From the sound of it, they'd already finished it—if it had been me helping him, we would have been up until the early hours.... And exactly how close were they getting? I could hear her moving around his apartment in the background, humming to herself. Had she sat next to him as I had, their arms brushing as they worked?

Or was I just being a bitchy girlfriend, distrustful of his ex? Ruth had been nothing but friendly towards me, and when I'd been out of contact she'd stepped in to help. I was being suspicious when I should have been grateful.

"Say something," Connor said nervously.

"I'm sure it'll be fine," I said, trying to get a smile into my voice. It sounded good—I almost managed to convince myself.

Almost.

CHAPTER 26

THE NEXT DAY, I sat shivering on a windswept path. A particularly cold gust of wind lashed my hands and I had to flex my fingers on the bow to try to keep some feeling in them, without messing up *Bach's Cello Suite in D Minor.*

It was still too cold to play in Central Park—not that it was too cold *for us,* because when you're busking you expect to suffer, but it was too cold for there to be many passers-by. We'd only realized that after we arrived, though, and no one wanted to hump their instruments all the way home again, so we huddled under trees that dripped freezing water down our necks, put out the collection hat and played. We'd agreed we'd stop when we hit fifty bucks, or when our fingers were too numb to play—whichever came first.

Playing for charity in Central Park was a Fenbrook tradition I'd started back in freshman year—at the time people thought I was some sort of golden-hearted do-gooder, but the truth is I was just looking for a way to meet people. It's how I met Dan, who usually played violin with us. I'd managed to get Paul, a junior, to fill in and he was doing his best despite barely knowing the music. Erika (Russian and intimidatingly gorgeous) and Greg (Scottish and intimidatingly bearded) rounded out our group on viola and second violin. Dan had come along for moral support, still sporting his cast.

"We need you to dance," I told Natasha between pieces, looking at the measly collection of loose change in the hat. "Last time you danced, we doubled our take."

"Too *cooollld*," said Natasha sweetly. She didn't *look* cold. She was snuggled in between Darrell's legs as they sat on a blanket, both of them wrapped up in coats, hats and scarves and drinking steaming hot chocolates. I gave her a glower, even though they looked adorable.

"What about you?" I asked Clarissa. She was leaning against a tree, flanked by Neil and Connor and there was a very noticeable gap between her and Neil. The two hadn't exchanged a word since they'd arrived. She shook her head mutely and pointed to her four-inch leather pumps.

"*Fine.*" I launched into some Vivaldi in the hope that thoughts of summer sun would thaw us out a little. The spring weather suited my mood pretty well—the row with my father, by far the biggest I'd ever had, had left me numb and frozen. I would have felt completely lost, if not for my friends. But looking at how happy Natasha and Darrell were, looking at Clarissa and Neil—even if they weren't speaking to each other—looking at Dan and especially at Connor...I felt things starting to thaw, just a little. I'd lost contact with the only family I had, but I had my own little family right there.

Connor gave me a grin as he chatted away to Neil and I felt my heart swell to twice its size. I was cold and damp and my hands were aching, but everything was great.

And then Ruth showed up.

She sauntered down the path in her super-tight black jeans as if she'd just happened to come across us (I guessed that Connor had mentioned what we were doing). I watched as she touched Connor on the arm in greeting (I felt my hand clench on the bow) and then ruffled his hair as he made a joke (I missed two notes in a row). I saw Connor make the introductions and everyone nod pleasantly to her, although Clarissa and Natasha both gave me sympathetic looks.

"How's it going?" asked Ruth when we finished our next piece. Somehow she managed to sound friendly, concerned and incredibly patronizing at the same time.

"Not great," I told her tightly. Then, because I felt like I should, "Thanks for helping Connor with the essay. Sorry I couldn't be there."

"Don't you worry about that. I'll always take care of him." It sounded innocent enough, but in mind there were myriad undertones. *I've known him much longer than you have. I had him before you. I'm from his country. His body bears my name.*

"Great," I said, feeling sick. "Thanks." There was an awkward silence. "It's normally better than this," I said, nodding at the nearly-empty hat. For some reason, I felt I had to justify it. "But there aren't enough people. What we really need is for Natasha and Clarissa to dance. People go nuts for that."

Ruth beamed. "Oh, but I could dance. With Connor."

I opened and closed my mouth a few times.

"That's a brilliant idea, Karen," she told me, as if I was a favored daughter. "Connor, come over here!" She turned to the rest of the quartet. "Can you play something we can dance to?"

Before I could say *no*, Greg said, "Yep." I wanted to poke him in the eye with my bow.

Connor walked over and Ruth put a hand on his shoulder. "We're going to dance. To help them raise money," she told him.

Connor looked at me, worried, but Ruth put a hand on his cheek and turned him back to face her. "It was Karen's idea," she told him.

I wanted to say, *No, it wasn't!* I wanted to tell her that I didn't want her dancing with my boyfriend, but wouldn't that make me look evil and possessive? It was all for charity, after all....

Nausea churning inside me, I started to play.

It started innocently enough, Ruth and Connor doing a slow, formal dance that had them barely touching fingertips. Ruth was annoyingly good—not anywhere near the standard of the dancers at Fenbrook, but she'd obviously had lessons. What amazed me, though, was Connor—he was surprisingly adept and it hit me far too late that they must have had lessons *together*. I'd probably reawakened a whole host of memories of happy evenings spent in some dance club. I gritted my teeth.

The dance become closer, the two of them turning and twisting together, and I didn't miss the way Ruth molded her body to Connor's, her breasts—much bigger than mine—squashed against his chest. The worst part was that it worked—passers-by stopped and looked and we started to get more money in the hat. And so when the piece finally ended I had to look at the woman who'd just been writhing against my boyfriend and say, "Thank you."

"No problem," Ruth told me, still wound around Connor. She made no obvious move to disentangle herself. And then she kissed him. Just a peck on the cheek, meant in fun and certainly nothing I could sensibly yell about. But it lasted just a fraction of a second too long, and the look she gave him as she moved her head back was anything but jokey.

***

Ruth left after a while but it didn't do much to lift my mood. Was she really trying to get her claws back into him, or was I just being paranoid? The knowledge that she was still sleeping in Connor's apartment didn't make things any easier. I had complete faith in his word that he was sleeping on the floor...but in Connor's tiny apartment that put him just a few feet from her bed.

We finally hit the fifty bucks—thanks, I had to admit, mainly to Ruth and Connor's dancing—and were packing our instruments away when it happened.

"We can fly coach if it makes you feel better!" Clarissa's voice. The tail end of a conversation that had been conducted in angry murmurs, rising in volume as she got angry.

"It's not about how we fly," said Neil, his voice almost a growl. "You're not paying."

All of us suddenly found very important things to do with our instruments. Seconds later, Clarissa stomped up to us; it's difficult to stomp in four-inch heels, but she'd had a lot of practice. "Are we going, or what?" she asked.

I hefted my cello case onto my back and nodded, watching Neil stalk off in the other direction.

***

In a Starbucks, with my numb fingers wrapped around an Americano, I huddled close to the girls and

Natasha and I gave Clarissa the same questioning look. Connor had wisely withdrawn to a separate table with Darrell.

Clarissa had gone for some complex creation that seemed to be at least eighty percent cream and syrup—not a good sign. She used a wooden stirrer as a spoon, taking bites between sentences.

"I want him to come with me when I visit my folks. He *says* it's about the money—he can't afford to fly and he doesn't want me to pay for him. But I don't think that's it."

"You think he doesn't want to meet your folks?" I asked carefully.

"I think he doesn't know how to do any of that...relationship stuff. He knows *sex,*"—her eyes glazed over for a moment—"God, does he know sex...but he never wants to talk about the future. He closes down or turns away. I mean, it's stupid. He loves me." She swallowed, and her voice caught a little. "I mean, he *does* love me, right?"

Natasha and I each put a hand on her arm. "Of *course* he does," said Nat. "He's just being a biker."

"It was always going to be complicated," I said, "given the sex thing."

Clarissa hacked off a big lump of cream and syrup and sat back, holding it precariously above her doubtless several hundred dollar dress. "Sometimes I wonder if I should just accept it for what it is. Maybe it's always going to be just a sex thing." She sighed.

I'm a geek. Or a dwarf. I don't do *people*. But the weird thing is, just sometimes, I can see stuff. Maybe it's because I don't understand all the surface layers: all the lies and flirting and doubletalk. Most of the time that cripples me—it's what kept me single for so long—but occasionally, it clears my view and lets me see what's going on underneath.

I could see Neil as a machine—a big, loud, pounding machine made entirely of iron and fire, like his bike. He'd seen a delicate fairy flitting around in his headlights and had thundered after it the only way he knew how and, for a while, his simple, brutish approach had been intoxicating. But he was still going full speed and the roar of the engine was now just drowning out everything else.

Putting him in a room with Clarissa's parents was going to be like dropping a brick wall in front of him and I had a horrible feeling it would be the end of their relationship. What Neil needed was for someone to talk to him, to make him throttle back and shift gear. To pursue Clarissa in a different, gentler way.

Who, though? *Me?* Talk to *Neil?*

Just as it had with Jasmine, the fear of being wrong paralyzed me. Clarissa was one of the few friends I had. If I ruined her relationship, what then?

"Maybe you should just go ahead and buy the tickets," said Natasha. "I'm sure Neil will come round."

No! I thought. *That won't work!* But I just nodded and smiled, and felt like the lamest friend in the world.

"How's Darrell?" I asked, to cover the silence.

Natasha pressed her lips tight together and I realized she was trying not to look too happy after hearing all of Clarissa's problems. "Really good," she said at last, looking across at where he was talking animatedly with Connor. "He's actually sleeping at night. And yesterday he came home and whisked all the dustsheets off in the workshop. He hasn't actually started to build anything yet, but he's thinking about it. The gym's freed him up, you know? It's given him an outlet for the anger, so he doesn't have to funnel it into his work anymore. He can build whatever he wants."

"So is the sex back on track?" asked Clarissa.

Natasha looked shocked.

"What? Throw me a fricking bone, here! I need cheering up," said Clarissa, unabashed.

Natasha slowly smiled. "In the hot tub, last night. And then on the lawn, under the stars."

"You must have frozen your butts off," said Clarissa with a gasp.

"Didn't seem to bother us at the time," said Natasha, smirking. It was good to see her smiling again. For a second, buoyed by my success, I almost thought about intervening with Clarissa and Neil...but then held back. It wasn't just that I was scared of being wrong...it was that I knew my place in the group. I was the geeky shy one, looked after by my more experienced sisters. It was my job to take advice, not to give it.

With the private stuff over, we pushed the tables together so Darrell and Connor could join us. I snuggled in beside Connor. Darrell sat Natasha on his lap. It was perfect...apart from the absence of one person.

"Neil seems nice," Connor said to Clarissa, a little tentatively.

Clarissa sniffed, but nodded.

"We were talking about the garage the motorcycle club own. He was saying I should stop in there and work on some stuff with him, maybe make a little extra money—I know a bit about bikes."

Clarissa leaned over to me. "Don't let him get mixed up in all that," she told me with a groan.

I pulled Connor tight into me. "Don't worry. I'm keeping him close," I told her. And I meant it. I'd sacrificed my relationship with my father, maybe even both our futures to be with Connor. I wasn't going to let anything come between us.

CHAPTER 27

Two days later, Doctor Geisler dropped the bombshell.

We were all packing up to leave when he clapped his hands together and addressed the lecture theater. "So! One more thing before I let you go. There's been some concern in the department that the generous deadlines we normally give you...."—he paused for sarcastic laughter from the back—"are allowing some of you to get a little help with your papers."

My stomach knotted. Were they talking about Connor, and the sudden rise in his grades? Had my helping him been too obvious?

"My colleagues in contemporary music have already hit their students with a next-day deadline essay, just to shake things up a little," Geisler told us. It *was* about Connor. That's why they'd sprung that essay on him and the others. If only I'd been there that night, I would have been able to help him to a good grade, even with such short notice. But with only Ruth assisting him...I groaned inwardly.

"Now of course, it's only fair that since they suffered, you suffer a little too," Geisler told us. I heard a few people grumble, but I perked up. Essays were my strongest area after performances, and it would be a chance to raise my grade average a little—and maybe take the pressure off when it came to the recital.

"Don't panic, though," said Geisler. "I have no intention of burdening your already overworked brains with another essay. Instead, I want an oral presentation to the rest of the classical music department on a piece of your choice. Tomorrow."

***

"That—That—"—sometimes, I really wished I cursed—"That *idiot!* One more F and I'll flunk, even if we ace the recital!" I was pacing as much as Connor's tiny apartment allowed. When he'd answered the door, he'd taken one look at my face and sent Ruth out for the evening.

"You'll have to do the presentation, then," he told me quietly.

I let out a kind of hysterical laugh. I could feel the panic rising in me, just as it had when Harman had first told me I couldn't perform solo. Just like then, the knowledge that I was going to flunk was closing in on me from all sides, crushing the air out of me. I heard Connor say my name once, twice, but I couldn't stop pacing—

He stepped in front of me and grabbed my upper arms, lifting me off the floor. "*Karen!*"

I focused on him, though I still didn't seem to be breathing.

"It's okay," he told me. "We'll figure it out."

I was buried in the freezing ice of raw fear and his

words were nothing more than a gentle wind blowing on the outside of my tomb. But slowly, as he kept speaking to me in that soft, gentle voice, the words started to melt through to me. The ice shrank back, giving me air, and I took a long, shuddering gasp.

"It's okay," he said again, and I started to believe that maybe it could be.

Connor put me carefully down on the edge of the bed and I thought for a moment that that was his plan—to push away the fear with sex. But he crouched down in front of me, staring into my eyes, and I realized he was matching his breathing to mine, leading me to safety.

When I was calm, the embarrassment settled in. Together with a kind of tiredness, as I accepted my fate. I'd been crazy to even try to fight it. I should have given up as soon as Dan broke his arm, and I could have avoided all the stress and heartache of the last few months.

And then you'd never have gotten together with Connor, a little voice reminded me.

"Sorry," I told him.

"It's fine. But do you get them a lot—the panic attacks?"

"Only a few times before." I thought back to Boston. "Usually when...." I sighed. "Usually when I have to talk to a lot of people. That's why I don't do presentations."

He nodded. And then he said, "You have to."

"I can't."

"If you don't, you won't graduate."

"I can't," and this time I said it differently. Not belligerent or angry or hysterical, just...sad. Because the one thing I knew was that my fear was immutable.

He nodded. "Yes you can." And he kissed me. Not a kiss of passion, meant to distract me. A heartfelt, warm kiss of love that took me by surprise and filled me with strength. He believed in me, just as I'd believed in him. However scared I was, I had to try to live up to that faith, just as he'd lived up to mine.

I let out a long sigh, closing my eyes. When I opened them again, I looked into his eyes. "How?" I asked levelly.

***

He took me to a tiny bar and bought me a beer. "Now," he told me. "Close your eyes, and tell me what goes through your head when you're about to do one of these things."

I didn't understand why he'd hauled me out of the apartment. Couldn't we have done this there? "Umm...that everyone's going to laugh at me?" I tried.

"Okay. Go on."

"That they're going to heckle and shout stuff out and ask me stuff I can't answer."

"Okay."

"That I'll forget what to say and just dry up."

"Open your eyes."

I did. He was leaning back in his chair, sipping his beer. "Do you know what all those fears are called?"

"Terrifying?"

"Normal."

I looked at him doubtfully. "If everyone gets them, no one would ever do a presentation, or a speech, or anything."

"The only difference between you and everyone else is that you're a control freak."

"*Thanks.*"

He looked at me seriously. "Think of it as a play. The audience are there to play a part too. You're trying to control them and you can't. Forget about them laughing or heckling. You play *your* part and trust them to play theirs. If they're nice, you'll be fine. If they're not nice, *they'll* look like arseholes, not you." He took a long slug of beer. "That leaves forgetting your lines, for which we have a napkin." He took a napkin from the bar and pulled out a pen, then thrust both into my hand. "Choose a piece of music."

"Tchaikovsky's *Romeo and Juliet,*" I said.

"Why should someone listen to it?"

"It's incredible—it tells an entire Shakespearian tragedy without words."

"So write down the parts of the story it describes."

I did, stripping it down to the five key moments.

"It can't be that easy," I said, staring at the napkin.

"Finish your beer," he told me, "and let's find out."

***

Next door, I discovered why he'd brought me out into the city. It was an upmarket coffee shop with an open mike night. People were doing poetry, songs, and little opinion pieces about life and love and society. If a presentation about *Romeo and Juliet* would go down well anywhere outside of Fenbrook, it was there.

That didn't stop me being terrified, of course.

"*No,*" I told Connor, as soon as I figured out his plan.

"She's next," Connor told the organizer, ignoring me completely.

"*Connor!*"

He turned to me, looked deep into my eyes, and kissed me, silencing any further protest. Again, I felt that warm glow of strength seeping through me, pushing back the fear.

"What did we learn?" he asked as he pulled back.

"Play my part. Use the napkin," I recited.

And then he was pushing me to the front and leaning in front of the mike. "Karen Montfort on...Tchaikovsky's *Romeo and Juliet!*" he announced. There was some polite applause, thirty or so heads turned to gaze at me and...I was on.

Someone whacked a bass drum and I nearly yelled at them to shut up. Then I realized it was my heart.

Say something!

But I couldn't think of anything to say. The silence grew and grew.

Say anything!

There was a guy at the front with steel-rimmed glasses and an overcoat, cuddled up to a girl with frizzy hair. They looked non-threatening. "*YOU!*" I yelled into the mike, stabbing out a finger towards him. He flinched. "You...need to listen to *Romeo and Juliet.*"

There was some good-natured laughter, and it became easier to breathe. I read the first word on the napkin, and started to talk. The first few sentences were like wading through oatmeal, but as I kept speaking and the world didn't end, I started to loosen up. It was terrifying, but it was at least ninety percent less terrifying than I expected it to be. When some newcomers blundered into the coffee shop halfway through, I froze for a second. *Just play your part,* I remembered. I started speaking again, and they shuffled to their seats apologetically.

By the time I reached my fourth point, I was in full flow. By the final one, I almost didn't want it to end. As I moved away from the mike, there was a smattering of friendly applause.

I staggered over to Connor and almost fell against him in relief, burying my face in his chest. "Don't *ever* do that to me again," I told him.

"But it worked. You did well. Do the same thing tomorrow: instant A."

I didn't know about that. But it did feel like maybe I'd actually be able to speak.

"We should celebrate," Connor told me. "Do you want to go for a drink?"

I drew back and looked up at him, this man who'd cured my fear—or at least made it manageable. He was doing *that* smile again, his eyes twinkling. I felt my heart boom in my chest again, and not from fear this time.

"No," I told him. "I've got a better idea."

∗∗∗

We were kissing as we climbed the stairs to his apartment, struggling with each other's clothes even as we opened the door. My sweatshirt went over my head and I stripped off his jacket. His hands smoothed over my skin beneath my vest top, and mine traced the hard muscles of his abs under his t-shirt. We only broke the kiss to strip more clothes off, and then we were falling onto the bed, rolling over and over, my bra-clad breasts mashing against his bare pecs, denim-wrapped legs scissored together. Our mouths were wet and panting, hungry for each other.

We rolled so that I was on top, and I reached down between us and unbuckled his belt, then eased his jeans down. Maybe it was because I didn't have the virgin thing hanging over me anymore, maybe it was the adrenaline of having conquered my fear, or maybe it was just the feel of him under my hands, but I was more turned on than I'd ever been. There was a hot ache between my thighs, a need to be *filled*.

"This is new." He grinned up at me, surprised but

amused at my sudden hunger and I felt myself grinning back. All the sex in my fantasies had always been so...*serious*. Passionate, yes, but po-faced. I hadn't ever considered that it could be *fun*.

I pulled down his jockey shorts and his cock sprang out, thickly erect. I grasped it with one hand, enjoying the feel of its heat, and stroked it a few times as I leant forward and kissed him long and deep, my tongue licking his the way I planned to lick his cock. He got my meaning and growled low in his throat.

I smoothed my hands over his chest as I kissed him, sweeping them along the contours of his pecs, rubbing over his nipples. I discovered that he seemed almost as sensitive there as I was, and leaned down to enclose one with my mouth. I tried giving it an experimental nibble with the edges of my teeth and his back arched off the bed in response. I was on my hands and knees above him, my ass in the air, and he gave it a slap. It was just a playful swat, really, especially through my jeans, and I giggled. But there was something deep inside me that did a little flip-flop at the sensation. Something that awoke and sent a whole new current surging straight to my groin, one I'd never felt before. I thought of Clarissa and her games with Neil. *Something to explore later,* I decided with a little thrill of excitement. We had all the time in the world and there were a *lot* of things I wanted to try.

I left his nipple gleaming wetly and moved down to his cock. Sliding my mouth down over the head, I closed my eyes, my mind going dreamy as I started to suck, my hand starting a slow rhythm on his shaft. I had more time, now, to concentrate on the sensations. The taste of him, salty and male on my tongue. The heat of him, throbbing against my palm. I felt his hands unbuttoning my own jeans, and between us we managed to strip them down off my legs while I sucked him, my panties sliding down along with them.

I hollowed my cheeks, my tongue sliding around and around the straining, swollen head of him, relishing every moan of pleasure I drew from him. As I stroked him with one hand, the other slipped down between his legs, cupping his balls. I let them roll over my fingers, marveling at them. Something connected in my brain, the thought of all that male seed locked up inside him, waiting to gush out. Waiting to...I gulped, words like *fertile* suddenly filling my head. The thought of that part of it, of the primal nature of it, hadn't really sunk in until then, and when it did a ripple of something between fear and arousal went through me. Not that I wanted to get pregnant—*obviously*. But the idea of it....

I felt his hand between my legs, then, nudging my thighs apart a little and then cupping my sex, fingertips parting me and finding me already wet. His thumb circled my clit while two broad fingers slid over me and then—*God!*—into me. He started to move them and his speed guided me as I sucked and stroked him, both of us building to a frenzy. I knew I had to stop before he came, but part of me almost didn't want to.

He gently lifted my head with his free hand, his chest rising and falling beautifully as he panted, and started to roll us over.

"No," I told him. "I want to go on top."

He blinked and then grinned again. "You really are different tonight."

I flushed. "I have a lot of catching up to do." I reached back behind me and unclipped my bra, ready to shed the last bit of my clothing but feeling that flutter of nerves again. He'd already seen my breasts, but—

I took it off, looking into his eyes the whole time, and saw that delighted gleam in them when my breasts were freed. He put both hands on them, his warm palms just grazing my nipples, and I closed my eyes and shuddered, a wave of heat rippling down between my legs. He started to circle his hands, lifting each breast just a little each time, and I felt my nipples stiffen at his touch.

He pulled out a condom and rolled it on, and I swung a knee over him. We gazed at each other for a second, and I must have looked nervous because he nodded at me minutely.

I lowered myself down onto him. God...it was so different, being in control. I could let his straining cock just tease my folds, brushing the heat of him against me again and again before letting it slowly part me. My thighs tensed as I settled lower, the head spreading me wide, my breath coming in tight little pants. Every millimeter brought new ripples of electricity as his cock slid deeper, stretched me wider. I sank down and down...until at last he was completely buried in me. I knelt there for a moment, just staring down into his eyes, enjoying the feel of him there.

And then, planting my hands on those deliciously full, hard pecs, I started to fuck him. Slowly at first, drawing him from me inch by exquisite inch, and then faster, until I was almost falling onto him with each downward stroke. His hands slid under my ass, lifting me higher, until I was riding him fast and hard, gasping for breath, tight and silken around that plunging hardness. He pressed against my breasts, encouraging me to lean back—I tried it and *OhMyGod!* Suddenly he was stroking against a whole new spot, and I put my hands behind me, supporting myself there, my breasts straining up towards the ceiling as I felt the orgasm rise inside me. I came like that, quick and almost violent, left breathless from the suddenness of it. Then he coaxed me forward, so that I was leaning over him, and we kissed, gasping into each other's mouths as our groins slapped and thrust. He pushed my hair back from my ear and whispered:

"I love fucking you, Karen Montfort."

And a different kind of orgasm thundered up inside me, one without any notion of romance or delicacy, one formed from raw heat and filth, and I found myself gasping.

"I love fucking you, Connor Locke."

And the climax overtook me, my whole body shuddering as he shot and shot inside me.

CHAPTER 28

The next morning, I woke to find myself alone in the bed. I panicked for a moment...until I heard the sound of his guitar.

When I'd pulled on my clothes and rubbed the dreams from my eyes, I stumbled up the stairs and emerged blinking onto the roof. He was staring off into the distance, hands sure and quick on the strings. He saw me, but didn't speak and I didn't interrupt him. I just stood there and listened. He'd written his final section and it was *us*, together, but from his point of view. I'd written something based on that first night, all slow and intimate. He'd based his on the sex we'd just had: urgent and powerful and...God, I could almost relive it, just listening to it. I knew I was going to go red every time we got to the...*ahem*...crescendo.

***

I have a tendency to trudge, rather than walk.

Some of that I blame on carrying the cello case, but I know that some of it's me. That morning, though, leaving Connor's apartment, I *bounced,* the goodbye kiss he'd given me making me feel lighter than air. If I'd had a little more coordination, I might have skipped.

I bounced down the stairs and ran straight into Ruth coming the other way.

"Oh," she said, with an air of great disappointment. "I was going to see Connor. But if he's just spent a night with *you* I suppose he'll be going straight back to bed for a lie-in."

There was no reason at all I should have been embarrassed, but I could feel my face flushing anyway.

"Let's have coffee instead," Ruth told me, slipping an arm around me and leading me down the stairs. "You can tell me all about it."

I wanted to tell her that I had to get to Fenbrook to get some cello practice in before classes. I wanted to tell her that I had my presentation that morning, and that I was nervous enough without talking to her. I wanted to tell her that this whole thing was getting to be invasive and creepy, and that she should have the decency to go back to Ireland and leave us the hell alone.

But she was his friend, so I bit my tongue so hard I almost drew blood, and smiled.

***

We went to a diner because, in Ruth's words, "Starbucks can't make a decent cup of tea to save their lives." She left the teabag in until the tea was the color of tar, dumped in half a cup of milk and then sat there stirring it as she talked. "I'm *so* glad Connor met someone like you. I mean, I was surprised, but don't take that in a bad way."

"Surprised?"

"Well...you're very different. I mean, you're posh and you've got money oozing out of you—don't argue, luv, you have—and you're *clever*—"

"Connor's clever."

She made an *Oh! Isn't that cute* face, as if I were a child who'd just said my teddy bear was an astronaut. Her spoon tinkled in her cup as she stirred endlessly, making me grit my teeth. "You're very different, anyway. Oh, don't get me wrong, though, luv. I can see what he sees in you, clear as day."

She made it sound like a compliment, but I found myself asking, "What?"

Ruth smirked. She was *still* stirring her tea—what could there possibly be left to mix? "You know...you're the lady of the manor. The princess. He's your bit of rough."

I flushed. That was uncomfortably close to my dream. "That's ridiculous," I told her. "Connor doesn't see me like that."

"Nothing wrong with it, luv. We've all got to have our roles to play."

I wondered what her role was. And I thought of Clarissa and Neil, trapped in a shallow relationship by their sex games. "It's not like that. I mean, I know we're different, but it's not...I mean, there's more to it than that."

"Is there, luv? You sure?"

I went to speak, but couldn't think of what to say.

"Because if there isn't...." Ruth left it hanging there. "Well. I've said my piece." She tapped her spoon twice on the edge and then drained the cup in one long swallow. "I just want what's best for him. For both of you. You know that, don't you?" And then she kissed me once, on the top of the head. "Ta ta." And she was gone, leaving me in stunned silence.

***

Three hours later, I sat in the lecture theater waiting for my turn, trying to stop my foot tapping nervously on the floor. *Just play the role. Use the napkin.* The napkin that was rapidly going damp from my sweating hands.

Ruth was wrong. We were in love, and there was a lot more to us than some roles of rich girl, poor boy. What did she know? I tried to push it from my mind and focus on the presentation. *Play the role. Use the napkin. Play the role. Use the napkin. Play the napkin. Use the role. Wait, what?*

"Karen, your turn," said Doctor Geisler.

I stood up.

***

When I emerged from my class I wasn't quite back to bouncing but I did feel like a huge weight had been lifted. The presentation had gone just fine—maybe not an A, but a solid B, at a guess. I wanted to tell Connor. I wanted to thank Connor. I wanted to celebrate with Connor. I wanted to fu—

"Did you remember?" asked Jasmine, grabbing my arm.

"Of course," I lied.

"Liar. Come on, we have to get across town." She leaned in close. "It's my interview."

My mind went blank for a second. She was wearing a suit I'd never seen her in before—actually, I'd *never* seen Jasmine in a suit. Was she going for a job?

And then I remembered and the world turned cold and gray. Oh yeah. *That* interview.

CHAPTER 29

In the back of the cab, I looked again at Jasmine's suit.

"I borrowed it from Natasha," she told me. "That's why the jacket doesn't close." She wriggled in her seat. "And I keep worrying the skirt's going to rip."

"Good thing you didn't borrow it from Clarissa— you'd never have got it on."

"Are you saying I have a big ass?"

"Jasmine, *I* have a big ass compared to Clarissa. She's a stick. Your ass is...."

"Perfect for the job I'm interviewing for?" Jasmine asked, a little tightly.

Shamefully, that was exactly what I'd been thinking. I had no doubt at all that Jasmine's curves would go down very well with men. Or that they'd be willing to pay to—

"Are you sure about this?" I asked for the fifteenth time. "I mean, *really?*"

Jasmine's lip quavered. "You said you'd support

me."

"I will! I am! I'm just...are you *sure?*"
She nodded. And then we were there.

***

I'd expected the interview to be in a brothel, with some fifty-something madam who was all heavy makeup and perfume. In fact, it was held in a quiet corner of an upmarket hotel bar, and the head of the agency—who introduced herself as Tabitha—looked to be no older than forty, her dark hair pinned up in a sexy bun. We could have been sales executives or pharmaceutical reps. Well, the other two could. I was in my usual jeans and a sweatshirt.

"Umm. Is it okay if my friend sits in?" Jasmine asked.

Tabitha gave me a quick glance. "Absolutely." She took a photo of Jasmine's driver's license, ticked a couple of boxes on an official-looking form and then got started. "I already have your answers from the phone interview, so this is really more about *you*," she said. "Let's talk."

They chatted for a few minutes, with Tabitha abruptly changing the subject every so often. Politics, wine, sports, movies...she was being a client, I realized. Seeing how good Jasmine was at small talk, at putting people at ease. And the truth was, between Jasmine's natural charisma and her acting training, she was superb...which only made me worry more.

"Good," said Tabitha. "When would you be available to work?"

Jasmine swallowed, and I sensed she was getting nervous. "Any evening."

"Excellent. In-call or out-call?"

Jasmine looked blank.

"Can you entertain clients in your apartment, or meet them in their hotel rooms, or both?"

"Hotel rooms," said Jasmine. The two words hung there, seedy and incriminating.

"Isn't that dangerous?" I asked suddenly. They both turned to look at me. "I mean...isn't it?"

Tabitha smiled. "Nearly all our men are repeat customers and we only take new clients with personal recommendations. We need a valid credit card to accept a booking, and we only send girls to hotels that also require ID at check-in. The men are never anonymous."

That doesn't make it safe, I thought. *It just means the cops can catch them, afterwards.*

"There are safety procedures, which I'll explain closer to your first booking," Tabitha told Jasmine, although it felt like it was as much for my benefit. "You'll call us a little way into each appointment, to let us know that everything's okay."

Jasmine nodded. I nodded too, but less eagerly.

"Name?" asked Tabitha.

"Jasmine."

Tabitha smiled patiently. "The name you'll use when escorting."

"Oh!" Jasmine looked at me, panicked. "I didn't think of that. How did I not think of that?"

We both stared at each other.

"Vanessa," I said. I don't even know where it came from.

"Ooh, I like that," said Jasmine. "Classy."

"Vanessa will do fine," said Tabitha. "That about wraps it up. We'll need to take some pictures of you—I'll send you along to a photographer we know, and he'll do you some shots. Don't worry: no faces."

"Wait, I'm...I'm *in?*" asked Jasmine. "That's *it?*"

"Oh yes," said Tabitha, sounding a little surprised.

"I even have someone I can set you up with—he likes to meet the new girls and he's in town at the moment. Could you manage tomorrow evening?"

Jasmine nodded dumbly.

"Excellent." Tabitha made a final mark on her form. "Now, what about you?"

I realized she was talking to me. "*Me?!*"

"Yes. You could do very well, you know. Men really go for the wholesome look."

***

When I'd politely but firmly assured Tabitha that I didn't want to become an escort, we left and immediately found the nearest Starbucks for a post-escort-interview-debrief.

"Wow..." said Jasmine, stirring her hot chocolate. "I mean...just *wow*. I can't believe that I'm...you know."

I couldn't, either. Somewhere, someone was entering the information Tabitha had collected into a computer. Jasmine's driving license was going on file somewhere, to prove she wasn't underage. A page was being created for her on the agency website, with all the things she would and wouldn't do for money there in black and white for everyone to see.

"I couldn't believe she asked *me*," I said, because I didn't know what else to say.

"You totally should have gone for it," Jasmine told me.

I gave her a look.

"I'm serious! We could have gone to guys' rooms together. We could have done threesomes. Or a twosome, and they just watch."

I spluttered about half my coffee over my sweatshirt. "*JASMINE!*"

In Harmony

"What? I don't mean...you know. But if they were paying us, I'd do you. I'd totally do you."

I just stared at her, open-mouthed. Sometimes, it was impossible to know if she was joking.

"There's still time to rethink this before tomorrow night," I told her.

She shook her head. "Rent's due at the end of the week. I'm already behind—I'm straight out on the street if I don't pay." She sighed. "Or do you think I'm better off sleeping with my creep of a landlord, in a building *he* controls, instead of a nice, rich guy in a suit who's known to the agency?"

"You could call your brother," I said in a small voice. "Ask to move in with him."

She rolled her eyes. "Karen, we've been over this and over this. I am *not* getting mixed up with my brother."

I had an awful thought, and started to mop up some of the coffee I'd spilled while I processed it. Very, very carefully, I asked "Jasmine...your brother...is there something you're not telling me? Some reason...?"

She gaped at me for a moment. "Do you mean— Jesus, *no*, Karen, he didn't rape me or abuse me or anything!"

"Sorry," I said quickly. "I just—"

She shook her head. "No, it's my fault. I've been all mysterious about it and I should have just told you." She sighed. "He's not a bad guy, but he did time a few years ago—drugs. Then he got mixed up with more drugs when he was inside, and as soon as he got out he got caught again. That time the charges didn't stick, but I just know he's bouncing from one deal to another." She put her head in her hands. "And it's not just him. My family...." She closed her eyes. "Please let's not get into my family. They're just...not people you want in your life, okay?"

335

I realized in that moment that I knew almost nothing about Jasmine's family. I didn't even know where she came from. She was so bouncy and easy to talk to, and had such a rich and chaotic life *now,* that asking about her past had never occurred to me. I'd had a vague image in my head of arty parents somewhere in New York or maybe Chicago—actors, maybe, and she'd followed in their footsteps. Not much money—that much was obvious—but *nice.* And yet, if you'd asked me, I couldn't recall a single conversation over the years when she'd said any of that. I'd just presumed. All of us had just presumed.

"Karen," she said softly, "you didn't think Jasmine was my real name, did you? Who's called *Jasmine?*" And I saw there were tears in her eyes.

I leaned across the table and pulled her into a hug, knocking the remains of my coffee to the floor in the process. "Come here, you idiot," I gasped, holding her tight. I was crying myself, now.

"Will you still be my friend? Even now I'm a hooker?" Jasmine whispered in my ear.

"Of course I will," I said between sobs. "And you're not a hooker. You're an escort."

***

A few days later, we got our presentation scores back. Doctor Geisler read them out in a list, which was how he always did it. Except normally, my name was missing because I hadn't shown up to do the presentation. This time, my name was there, buried with all the other Ms.

"Karen Montfort...B."

I closed my eyes and sank back in my chair. My grade average was safe. It had actually improved a little.

Now, with a good score in the recital, I could not just graduate but graduate *well*.

God...all those presentations that I'd missed through my stupid, stupid fear! All those Fs that could have been Bs or even As! If I'd met Connor a year earlier, the recital wouldn't have even been important. And, ironically, if the recital hadn't been so important, I never would have met Connor.

The second I was out of class, I went to call him...but found a text message already waiting for me. He needed to talk, *now,* at my apartment. And I had a horrible feeling I knew what he was going to say.

***

Connor was waiting for me outside my apartment block, and held out the essay so I could see the red, circled D in the top corner.

We trudged inside and he waited until the door was closed before he spoke.

"Harman called me in to see him this morning. *That,*"—he nodded at the essay—"dropped me too low to graduate. Even if we got a perfect score on the recital. I'm out."

I shook my head. "They can't," I said softly. "Not when you were so close. It's not fair."

He came up behind me and put his hands on my shoulders. "I know."

"There must be something we can do. There's got to be some way that—it's just an essay! It's just one essay!"

He shook his head. "It's not." And I knew exactly what he was thinking—the same thing I'd been thinking when I got my presentation score back. If only we'd met each other sooner, if only he'd gotten help with the dyslexia before.

If only I'd answered the phone that night, instead of arguing with my father.

"I'm sorry," I told him. "I'm sorry, I'm sorry—"

"Karen, you did everything you could." He sighed. Then, his voice gentle, "Karen...you know what this means?"

And then it clicked. He wasn't at Fenbrook anymore, and that meant he couldn't do the recital with me. And that meant I wasn't going to graduate, either.

I wasn't going to graduate. Just a few months ago, I'd been worried about whether I'd get into the New York Phil. Now I was going to be a college dropout.

He watched me slowly slump to the floor. We were in the kitchen and my back slid down the cabinets until I sat on the tiles, looking dazedly at his legs. It wasn't a panic attack—it was more like all the energy had just been drained out of my body.

He crouched so that he could look me in the eye. "I am so, so sorry," he told me. "This is exactly what I was afraid of happening. That I'd let you down."

I shook my head. He hadn't let me down—

"Look. There's something else."

That was weird. It was like he was prepping me for bad news. What more bad news could there possibly be?

"Karen, it wasn't like I could ever offer you much of a future, even with a degree. Without one...what am I going to do, really? Neil's found me some work fixing bikes, down at the MC. Maybe I keep playing in bars, and maybe we scrape together just enough to rent a two-bit apartment with walls so thin you can hear the neighbors fucking. But—"

Oh God—

"Without me...you could go back to Boston. Patch things up with your dad. Maybe go back to college there, if you wanted to."

Oh God no—

He sighed. "Maybe we jumped into this thing too fast. I don't know...I thought we had something, but now it's been brought home to me, clear as day."

No please please no—

"We're different. We're always going to be different. You're better off without me."

He stood up just as I saw something I thought I'd never see—those big, beautiful blue-gray eyes fill with tears. Then he was backing away towards the door and the realization that *I'm never going to see him again* reached up and grabbed my heart and started crushing it like a vice. I tried to scramble to my feet, but my legs wouldn't work. I managed to stumble to the apartment door in time to see it close, and as tears flooded my eyes I slumped against it and howled.

CHAPTER 30

ORNING TURNED TO NOON turned to afternoon turned to evening. I didn't bother switching on the apartment lights, just sat there and stared out at the city as it lit up.

Somewhere out there, Clarissa and Neil were probably arguing again, their relationship hanging by a thread, and I didn't have the confidence to talk to Neil to try to fix it.

Jasmine was no doubt preparing for her client, shaving and perfuming herself for his delectation. And in another few hours she'd accept his money and allow him to.... And I didn't have the guts to stop her.

And even if I was able to help my friends with their current crises, I wasn't going to be around for the next ones. I wouldn't even get to see Darrell and Natasha finally happy, the one thing I'd managed to do right, because in another week, unable to play the recital without Connor, I'd flunk out, too.

I wasn't going to perform in an orchestra. I wasn't

even going to get a degree. I was going to crawl back to Boston, admit that my father had been right and then...I had no idea. I knew it was going to be a life without music but, for the first time, that didn't matter. What mattered was that it would be a life without Connor.

My legs started to grow numb—my head, too, where it rested against the hard wood of the door. The one solid thing in my life, my apartment, and it was provided by my father. My father, who'd been right all along. My father, who'd never wanted anything except the best for me—and I'd thrown it back in his face to pursue some stupid, teenage dream of love. So what if he'd been cold and controlling? He'd been right: I shouldn't have gotten mixed up with Connor, or moved away from the nice, safe world of the cello. I was a mouse, a dwarf, and I should have stayed wrapped up in my cave practicing instead of trying to have an *adventure*.

The worst part was that everyone had seen it apart from me. Oh, my friends had thought Connor was hot, but they'd warned me about how different we were. Professor Harman had told me it was a bad plan. And eventually, even Connor had seen it, *"clear as day."* The only one too stupid to see it had been me.

...

Clear as day. A weird expression. Very British, or maybe very Irish. It wasn't something I recalled Connor ever saying before.

...

Ruth had said it, when she'd met me for coffee just before my presentation. What else had Connor said? The conversation was burned into my mind. *"It's been brought home to me, clear as day."*

It's been brought home to me.
Ruth.

Connor's essay was lying on the hallway table, bearing its red circled D. I reached over and grabbed it with hands that were suddenly shaking.

They didn't have a computer at his apartment, so she'd hand-written it for him in her scratchy, angular script. He wouldn't have read it back, of course. He'd just have trusted her. That was his one weakness.

The sentences barely made sense. They weren't what Connor would have dictated—they were like a cruel parody of a dyslexic's writing. She'd screwed him over.

I didn't really have a plan when I picked up my phone. I suppose I wanted to check to see if I was right, although I didn't know, then, what I'd take as evidence.

Connor's phone rang three times and then, "Hello?"

Not Connor's voice. Ruth's. I could hear noise in the background—tools, and two-stroke engines. The motorcycle club.

"I need to speak to him," I said. Barely a whisper. It felt like an elephant was sitting on my chest, crushing the life out of me.

I heard Ruth put her mouth very close to the phone, so that only I could hear her. "Fuck off, you Yank bitch," she said, her voice like a weapon.

"Who is it?" Connor's voice, in the background.

"Wrong number," Ruth told him. And she hung up on me.

As I sat there staring at my phone, I felt something start inside me. It was as unexpected and *real* as when I'd first felt that stab of desire for Connor. Except that hadn't been completely alien—I might never have felt that way about a particular man before, but I'd known what it was like to be turned on. This, though...this was utterly new. It was like a trickle of red-hot lava, gradually breaking through the rocks to reach the surface. Growing hotter and stronger until it erupted into a volcano.

It was *rage*. My entire life, I'd never really gotten angry—not *really* angry. My father had crushed that emotion from me, teaching me how to be cool and calm and professional—just like him.

But I was angry now.

I was such a scared little mouse. I hadn't spoken up all those years when my father sculpted my future in his own image. I hadn't spoken up when Neil needed someone to talk sense to him, or when Jasmine became an escort. I'd let Ruth convince me that Connor and I wouldn't work and, worst of all, when Connor broke up with me I hadn't even fought for him.

I got to my feet.

I was damn well going to fight now.

CHAPTER 31

THE BIKER GUARDING THE GATE at the motorcycle club was in his forties, thick layers of muscle straining his jacket. He was a full foot taller than me and three times my weight. He looked like he'd stood his ground in the face of every sort of would-be intruder—cops, lawyers, rival biker gangs....

But never a 5'4" and very determined cellist. I gave him a *look,* and he swung back the gate for me.

Once inside the compound, the garage wasn't hard to find. The door was rolled up and I could see Connor stripped to the waist, working on a bike. Ruth was still there, too, leaning against the wall with a can of Coke. With the lights blazing inside and the darkness outside, they didn't see me until I was standing on the threshold.

Connor looked up and his mouth dropped open. Ruth lounged nonchalantly, her mouth twisting into a cruel smirk. "Don't think this is the place for you, luv," she told me. "Why don't—"

"Get away from my man, you *bitch!*" I said, the

rage boiling out at her like a flamethrower. She lost her smirk instantly and took a step back.

"Karen?!" Connor sounded as surprised by my words as he was by my being there. "Karen, you know we can't—"

"I don't care!" I told him. "I don't *care* that we can't graduate, I don't *care* if we have no money. I want to live in a two-bit apartment with you, with walls so thin—"

"We can hear the neighbors fucking?" said Connor.

"Hell no. They can listen to *us!*" And I ran to him and leapt into his arms, kissing him savagely, and he returned the kiss just as hard, wrapping one arm around my waist to hold me while he buried the other hand in my hair, and as he gave a delighted, relieved chuckle I knew I'd got him back.

"Connor?" Ruth's voice had always been like granite. Now it sounded like it was splintering, cracking open to reveal the rot beneath. "Connor?"

Connor stopped kissing me for a second. "No," he told her simply. And as we went back to kissing, I heard her slink away.

I ran my hands over Connor's bare shoulders. He was in grease-stained workpants and heavy boots, his hands and torso smudged with oil. I pushed up against him even closer.

I heard the creak of leather as a biker walked over to the open garage door. "I was gonna ask if everything's okay in here," rumbled a familiar voice. "But I guess it is."

Neither of us replied and I had my eyes tight closed as I kissed Connor, but I felt his arm shift and extend, and guessed that he was giving Neil a thumbs-up. I heard Neil chuckle, and then his footsteps faded away.

There was an old tarpaulin on the floor and Connor laid me gently down on it. He pushed my sweatshirt, top and bra up, baring my stomach and breasts, and then his hands were smoothing over my skin, leaving dark, oily marks behind.

"I'm getting you filthy," he said warningly.

"I want to be filthy," I told him.

That was all the encouragement he needed. We started rolling over and over on the tarpaulin, first me on top and then him, his hands rough at my breasts, mine sliding down over his back and ass. His jeans came off, and then mine. We didn't even stop to take them all the way off, just left them bunched around our knees. Both of us were panting with desire, filled with the need to restore what we'd broken.

Connor abruptly stood up and left me, half-naked and sprawled on the garage floor. It occurred to me that the main door was still open. Down on the floor, we were a little more hidden than we had been, but any bikers in the compound who strolled past the garage door would be able to see us just fine....

Connor returned seconds later with a box of condoms. Not our usual, high-tech, glossily-packaged brand. Some basic, generic type, purely functional, for when it's just about the sex. The same box shared by everyone at the club, dipped into when a girlfriend or a hooker or an *old lady* stopped by. Biker condoms.

It seemed appropriate.

He rolled one on as I lay there panting up at him, and for a second I was back in my apartment, all those months before, pleasuring myself with my dildo. *How would Connor Locke take me?*

"Turn over," he told me in a voice thick with lust. "Hands and knees."

I assumed the position, palms flat on the greasy fabric, feeling the chill of the concrete soaking through to my knees. With my back to the open doorway, I had no idea if anyone was watching us or not, and not knowing sent a dark thrill through me.

I felt Connor come up behind me, his dirty hands tracing up my bare thighs...my ass. And then his face was between my legs, his tongue flicking out to caress folds that were already moist. I shuddered and pushed back against him, my upper body sinking towards the floor. Again and again, his tongue traced the shape of me, until I was a helpless, writhing mass, drunk on pleasure.

And then I felt his hard length slide into me and I arched my back as I took him deep, his hands clasping my hips. Three long, slow thrusts into my tightness and he was completely within me. As he started to move, I let my shoulders sink the rest of the way to the floor, my cheek pressing against the tarpaulin. Hot red lust was throbbing through me, getting stronger with each thrust, my whole body jerking to the rhythm. I had my eyes squeezed tight shut, the world narrowing down to the feeling of him inside me, his thighs slapping against my ass. His hands came forward to squeeze my breasts, my nipples caught between his fingers, rubbing and—*God*—pinching me just right, and I knew he was leaving black smears on my pale skin and didn't care. Every silken movement of him inside me added a new layer to the rhythm, the climax reaching up inside me to steal my voice, steal my breath—

"Connor!" I managed as the orgasm overtook me, and I pushed back with my hips, wanting him as deep as he could be. He thrust into me hard and my pleasure blossomed and spread, and then I felt him jerk and pulse inside me.

He slumped over me, his chest against my back, so

close I could feel his heartbeat. His huge, calloused hands came down to cover my much smaller ones, rubbing over the backs of them again and again. Comforting and protecting me, forever.

***

As he pulled on a t-shirt, Connor asked me, "So, how do you want to spend your first night of poverty? I can stretch to a takeout pizza. Maybe."

I kissed him while fastening my jeans. "Later. First, there's something I need to do."

CHAPTER 32

JASMINE HAD TOLD ME the hotel she was meeting her client at. I just prayed that she'd be early...or that he'd be late. Neil gave me a lift on his bike, grinning and muttering something about how Darrell was the one who'd got to do this, last time. We roared through the streets with me clinging onto his back and his long hair whipping me in the face. A few times I wondered if we were going to survive, but he got me there faster than any cab could have.

"Wait there," I told him as I handed him back his helmet. My hair, already tousled from the sex, was now a complete mess. "I need to talk to you, too."

He looked a little unsettled at that, but I ignored him. I also ignored the hotel doorman, who looked aghast at my appearance.

I found Jasmine at the bar, in a long green dress. When she saw me, she turned on her stool to gape.

"What the hell are you doing here?" she asked. "He'll be here any minute!" She looked closer. "Is that oil on your face? Why's your hair all scrunched up?"

I didn't have time for long explanations. "I had filthy sex on the floor of a biker garage," I told her. "Neil brought me here on his bike."

Her eyes went huge as she made the wrong connection.

"The sex was with Connor, you idiot! Grab your purse. You're coming with me."

She shook her head. "You know I can't. He'll be here—"

"Call him and cancel. Tell him you're pulling out. You're not going to be an escort."

Her face darkened. "I thought you were supporting me!"

"I am supporting you. I'm doing what I should have done from the start and slapping some sense into you. You are an *amazing* actress, you *are* going to be a success and you do *not* need to do this."

She froze, as if I'd broken some spell by saying the magic words. "But—I don't have any other place to go," she said. "Karen, I can't move in with my brother...."

"I know. You're moving in with me. You can sleep on the couch."

She shook her head. "No. God, I couldn't—"

I grabbed her by the shoulders. "Yes you can and yes you will." My voice softened slightly. "Part of being a good friend is letting your friends know when they're being fucking stupid, and saving them even when they don't want to be saved. I'm...sorry I didn't see that before."

We clutched each other tight, and suddenly we were both blinking back tears.

"Wait. Did you just *curse?*" Jasmine asked.

I giggled through my tears.

A man in his forties tentatively approached us.

"Vanessa?" he asked uncertainly.

Jasmine turned to him. "Nope," she said, wiping her eyes. "Never heard of her."

***

I filled Jasmine in on what she'd missed, put her in a cab and told the driver to keep the meter running. Then I walked over to Neil.

He was still sitting on his bike, parked right in front of the hotel's main doors. The doorman looked like he wanted to say something, but clearly wasn't going to mess with Neil. I wasn't surprised. I'd found Neil pretty intimidating, too.

Until I got angry.

"You need to tell Clarissa that you love her," I told him.

"I—*What?!*"

"She's unhappy and worried and you need to fix it. She and Natasha have been trying to figure out a way that she can fix it, but *she's* not the problem. *You're* the problem."

"Now hold on just one second—"

"You're tough and moody and you can growl in her ear and make her drop her panties in three seconds flat, *okay—we get it!* But I know there's more to you than that. Natasha said you helped Darrell, back when they nearly split. You helped me tonight. Open up and talk to Clarissa or you're going to lose her, you big...lunk!"

He went quiet. Then he swung one leg off his bike so he could turn all of his powerful body to face me. "'Lunk'?"

"It was all I could think of," I said, flushing.

He gave me a long look. "Open up, huh?"

"Open up. If you really love her."

He didn't answer at first. He swung his leg back over his bike and started it up, and a terrible fear clutched at my chest, that I'd just tipped some awful balance and driven them apart.

Staring at the road ahead, Neil said, "I love that girl more than words can say."

And he was gone, powering off into the traffic.

***

We swung by the motorcycle club to pick up Connor. It was a weird cab ride back to my apartment, with Jasmine sitting between us. It should have been awkward, but somehow it wasn't—we held hands across Jasmine's lap and she slipped an arm around each of us and we all just sat there in silence, letting everything that had happened sink in. I'd glance at one or the other of them and we'd exchange smiles in the brief flashes of light from the streetlights. I had my man back, I had my friend back, and that was all that mattered.

***

In my apartment, Jasmine declared that her first day of work had exhausted her and that she was going to crash out. Connor and I moved into my room.

"What was she doing, anyway?" Connor asked. "She said she was working, but she's dressed for a date."

"Long story," I told him. "And one I'm not going to tell you." Jasmine's brief career as an escort would stay between her and me.

"Can I take a shower, before we do anything else?" he asked. "I'm covered in oil."

"I'm covered in oil too." I looked at the bed. "So it

doesn't much matter."

Connor considered. "Or...we could take a shower together."

The bed sounded good, but that sounded even better.

Jasmine must have been able to hear us. The lounge was just down the hall from the bathroom, and even though we started out quiet, with Connor soaping my back and sliding his hands down my flanks, it soon got a lot noisier. Kneeling in front of me, the water thundering down onto his head like a warm waterfall, he had me groaning and thumping on the wall with my fist. When he fucked me, my back braced against the wet tiles and my legs wrapped around his waist, my cries must have reached the next apartment, never mind the lounge. But when we emerged, wrapped in towels, and crept back to my room, all we could hear from the lounge was gentle snoring.

Of course, she *was* a very good actress.

CHAPTER 33

THE NEXT MORNING, I took Connor with me to Fenbrook to collect a few things and say my goodbyes. Technically, I could have kept going to lectures right up until the recital, but I knew I couldn't perform without Connor, and Connor had flunked out—so what was the point?

The place was quiet, everyone either in classes or huddled in practice rooms working away at their recital pieces. Exactly where we would have been, if Ruth hadn't screwed Connor over on the essay. I trailed my hand along the wall as we trudged down the corridor. The place had been my home for almost four years, and now—

I realized Connor wasn't with me. He'd stopped a few paces back, staring at something on the wall. I backed up to see what it was.

It was the poster I'd pretended to read when I'd been stressing about being a virgin the day of our first real date, what seemed like a lifetime ago. *The Fenbrook*

Improvisation Challenge! A Timed Composition for Extra Credit. "What?" I asked Connor.

He looked at me, and then looked at the poster.

Extra credit.

"Connor, they just run that for snob value. It's for the *super-elite.* No one actually enters it. Certainly no one manages to do well in it!"

"Technically," he said slowly, "we don't have to do well in it. We just have to enter."

I blinked. The improv challenge was held *after* the recitals. If Connor and I entered it, *theoretically* he still had a shot—however unlikely—at getting the grades he needed to graduate. And therefore they'd have to let him do the recital. And if we aced the recital, I could still graduate. Connor had come up with a sneaky, backdoor way to give me my dream back.

"We don't even have to show up for the challenge," he told me excitedly. "Entering just gets us back into the recital."

I thought about it. We'd have to rehearse like hell for the recital, with Connor knowing that however well we did in it, he still wouldn't graduate. It melted my heart that he was willing to go through all that just to give me a chance, but it would break my heart to do it.

I shook my head. "No," I said firmly. "It's not enough."

"You could graduate!"

"I'm not putting you through all that if you don't have a chance too. If we do this, we do it for real. We get you back into Fenbrook, we ace the recital and *I* graduate, then we ace the improv and *you* graduate, too."

Connor gaped at me. "You just said it was for the 'super-elite'. You said before it was *hardcore,* remember?"

I squared my shoulders. "Then we'll just have to be hardcore. We're in this together, or not at all."

He stared at me for a long time. "You can be a stubborn bloody mare at times, you know." He pulled me into a hug, my head against his chest. "Thank you."

We went to see Harman.

***

"No," said Harman. "Definitely not. You shouldn't even be on Fenbrook property, Connor."

"If he enters the improvisation challenge, he could still get the grades he needs to graduate," I told Harman.

"*Barely!*" said Harman. "And he can't enter. He's already been kicked out."

"*Technically,*" I told him, a warning note in my voice, "you shouldn't have kicked him out. It was still possible for him to graduate—how did you know he wasn't going to enter?"

That threw him, and he gave me a long look before finally sighing in defeat. I'd trapped him in his own rules again. "Okay," he admitted. "We missed that one."

"So if we sign up for the improv challenge, Connor's back in?" I asked. "He can do the recital with me? He could still graduate?"

"*If* you were to ace the recital, *you* could still graduate," Harman said tiredly. "I suppose in theory, *if* you scored top marks on the improvisation...yes, Connor could too. But—no offense—that's a big 'if'. No-one's ever scored *that* highly in the improvisation. Certainly not with your...unusual choice of instruments. With all due respect, Karen, I admire your determination, but I'd advise you—"

I leaned over his desk, all five foot four inches of me. "With all due respect, Professor Harman...I think it's time I started making my own decisions."

***

We had one week to not only nail the recital, but learn how to improvise together. We needed more than just rehearsals; we were going to war.

We chose Connor's apartment as our bunker. Ruth had packed her bags and left, destination unknown. With Jasmine crashing at my place, it made more sense to work at Connor's—besides, his neighbors were more forgiving than mine and we weren't going to have time to be considerate about when we practiced.

When we arrived, I eyed the space. I'd forgotten just how small it was. Rehearsing there as we had in the past was one thing, but with two of us living there we were going to be crawling over each other. And yet somehow, because it was Connor...that didn't sound so bad.

I drew up a planner. I couldn't find a piece of paper big enough, so I drew straight on the wall, constructing a massive grid eight feet wide and as tall as I could reach, and then filling it in. "Rehearsals are light green through dark green," I told him. "Lightest green for the first piece, darkest green for the final piece. Improv practice is yellow."

"You think this'll get us there in time?" he asked.

I gave him a look. "This is what I *do.*"

"What's red?"

"Mealtimes."

"What's blue?"

"Showers."

"What's pink—Oh. *Really?!* You even scheduled—"

"I could take it off the grid if you want," I deadpanned. "More time for rehearsing."

He put his hands together in prayer. "Please don't."

***

In the improvisation challenge, we'd be given a basic melody and would have to compose around it—in thirty minutes—and then perform what we'd composed. There'd be no time for back-and-forth and second-guessing each other. We had to function as one, despite our very different instruments.

The first time we tried it, we'd barely strung together ten bars when we ran out of time and the cello and guitar never blended. Connor was better at it than I was—he'd had years of jamming in bars. I'd spent my entire life with organization and structure.

"I can't do it," I told him. "I can't not know in advance what I'm going to do. I can't walk in there without any idea of what the music's going to be."

He put his hands on my shoulders and made me look at him. "If there's one thing you've taught me, it's that we can change," he said.

And so we practiced. We found an old kitchen timer and set it at random, behind our backs. When it went off, we had to stop whatever we were doing, turn on an old, thrift-store radio and listen to the music that was playing—whether it was rap or classical or a commercial for toothpaste. And then we had thirty minutes to come up with something based on that melody that didn't suck.

We clashed at first, wasting time by arguing. Even after all our time rehearsing together, it was difficult to get past that, to stop thinking on our own and start trusting each other to do our parts. But we ran the exercise five or six times a day and, gradually, we got slicker. After a few days, we could use every second of the thirty minutes productively, him focusing on the flowing parts that could be winged and me focusing on the ones with heavy structure that needed precision. I was the tent poles; he was the canvas.

Meanwhile, we had to get the recital nailed. Playing through it again and again was like reliving the course of our relationship: the first pair of sections, written when we hardly knew each other, both of us separate and aloof. The second pair, when I'd written him into the music and he'd written me. And then the final pair, the ones written after we'd had sex. Mine a delicate blending of our two styles, intimate but romantic; his urgent and powerful, the guitar parts hard and almost brutal as the cello wrapped itself around them—

We were usually tearing each other's clothes off within seconds of finishing that part.

We rehearsed on the roof whenever the weather allowed it, the music floating out across the neighborhood. We'd refuel on coffee and work late into the night, and then be too wired to sleep, talking or fucking until the early hours.

Fucking. I remembered the days when I would have thought of it as *him taking me*. A lot of things about me had changed.

***

Midway through the week, Clarissa and Neil stopped by. I didn't even have to ask how it was going—I could see by the way Neil stood next to her in the corridor. There was a new ease about them, a new level of intimacy beyond the sexual.

"We figured you could use these," said Clarissa,

handing me a stack of Tupperware containers. "Home cooked food. No doubt you've been living on pizza while you've been hunkered down in there."

"Of course not," I told her, pushing the stack of pizza boxes behind the door with my foot. I opened the top box and the lemon chicken inside didn't just look edible—it looked amazing. "I didn't know you cooked."

Clarissa glanced over her shoulder at Neil. "I don't," she said. She leaned in and hugged me. "I don't know what you did," she whispered, "But thank you."

"Are you two...okay?" I asked.

She smiled. "Early days. But I think we're going to be."

***

Lying in bed one night, we got to talking about our dreams. A million miles from the money of Boston and the lofty academia of Fenbrook, I finally had room to ask myself what I wanted.

The answer, when I figured it out, surprised me. What I wanted was to join the New York Phil. Not for my father. Not because it was what was expected of me. Because they were the best, and I wanted to be the best, too. That chubby-fingered six year-old who'd first fallen in love with the cello was still inside me, and it had taken losing my dream to remember what had started it. I'd come full circle, wanting the same thing I'd wanted that day I'd nearly fallen down the steps of Fenbrook, but for completely different reasons. I wasn't driven by fear any more—fear that if I failed to get into the orchestra, I'd be nothing. I knew now what it was like to lose the dream, and it didn't scare me anymore because I'd discovered something better. I'd found that as long as you have someone who loves you, who'd do anything in the world to save you...well, the rest of the world can go hang.

I called my father the next morning and told him when the recital was, that I'd be performing with Connor and that he could come if he wanted to. But that, no matter what, I was living my own life from now on.

Connor listened in. When I hung up, he hugged me. "I'm proud of you," he told me. "That took guts."

I looked at the floor. "That was his voicemail," I said. "That's still sort of brave, right?"

He hugged me again.

***

Between rehearsals and practicing improv, the days passed in a blur. If we weren't showering or grabbing a bite to eat, we were working...and when we couldn't work any more, we slept. We didn't leave the apartment, except to go up onto the roof, the entire week, sending out for groceries when Clarissa's food ran out. We were holed up in a room not much bigger than a prison cell, and yet the proximity didn't grate...it made us closer.

And hornier.

After months of lusting after each other and not being able to do anything about it, having the freedom to just lunge for each other was intoxicating. The apartment was tiny, but we got creative. On the roof, under the stars, an old blanket thrown down on the concrete. In what we laughably called the kitchen, the hard back of a wooden kitchen chair pressed against my thighs as he bent me over it. And in his bed, my arms stretched out over my head and clutching at the pillows as I moaned and kicked and gasped, his head between my thighs.

***

The night before the recital, the nerves started to hit me. We were as ready as we could be—the recital was slick and polished and when we improvised we were doing the musical equivalent of finishing each other's sentences. But I was still scared as hell. When Connor was asleep, I slid out of bed and stood by the window with a sheet wrapped around me, gazing out at the city.

A few months before, my biggest worry had been whether I'd make it into the New York Phil. Now, even after all our efforts, my entire college career hung on one ten minute performance and one half hour test. If we messed up tomorrow—or if the panel decided our crazy mash-up between classical and rock was garbage—

Just as I felt my shoulders start to tense up, large warm hands stroked down them. His body pressed up against me from behind, the heat of him soaking through the thin sheet to soothe me.

"You're scared." Not a question.

"How can it be fair that everything comes down to one morning. *Less* than a morning. Less than an hour! Four years at Fenbrook and if we're ill tomorrow or we have an off day or we just mess up or—"

He kissed the back of my neck. "Or if you don't get enough sleep...."

"You're not helping."

He kissed me again, right in my secret spot just behind my collarbone, and I went weak.

"Come to bed," he told me.

"You go. I'll just toss and turn and keep you awake."

"Karen Montfort, get that sweet arse of yours in my bed this instant!"

I felt a sudden rush of heat push away my nerves...and just a hint of what Clarissa must feel, when

Neil spoke to her like that.

"I don't think I can sleep," I told him.

His lips twisted into one of those filthy smiles. "I know a way to tire you out."

CHAPTER 34

BACKSTAGE, with five minutes to go. I was perched on the edge of the same chaise-longue I'd been put on after I fainted, listening to the quartet who were on before us while I waited for Connor to change.

He'd gone out early that morning to pick up his outfit and had been very mysterious about it, hiding it in a suit carrier and insisting on only changing into it at the very last second. I'd gone for my normal, reliable black dress, the same thing I'd worn for every recital since I'd started at Fenbrook. Except this time I'd added the Killer Heels, and hold ups. It wasn't a big change—I doubted anyone else would even notice. But it was important to *me*.

I stood there nervously fingering my cello, slowly turning it around and around in my hands. Then I almost dropped it and a hot flash of panic surged through me as I grabbed it to stop it crashing to the floor. *Okay. No more playing with it.*

Then Connor emerged from the toilets.

I'd had a vague idea in my head that he might have traded his usual jeans and t-shirt for a shirt and pants, but he was in a *suit!* A charcoal gray suit, just one shade off black, with a crisp white shirt left open at the collar to reveal tantalizing glimpses of his chest. I gaped. I mean, my mouth actually dropped open. Some men don't clean up well—put them in a suit and they look imprisoned and uncomfortable. Connor looked like an Irish billionaire.

"Where on earth did you get *that?*" I asked, fingering the fabric.

"I stole it."

My eyes went wide.

"No, not *really*—Jesus, woman! I left the tags in. I'll take it back this afternoon."

I relaxed—a little. "But you still had to buy it! How did you afford it?"

He looked nonchalant.

"Connor, did you spend *every penny we had* on that suit? Do we, in fact, have *no money* until you take it back?"

"Put it this way," he said. "Don't spill anything on the suit."

And I couldn't help but laugh, because it was so *him.* This is what life would be like with him, I knew—living on a wing and a prayer, one paycheck from disaster. And as long as we were together, that suited me just fine.

A nervous sophomore, who'd been landed with the job of floor-managing the event, put his head around the curtain. "Karen Montfort and Connor Locke?" he asked.

I liked the way that sounded. We nodded.

"You're on."

Just as we walked through the curtain, I grabbed

Connor's hand and we walked out like that, hand in hand. Maybe I wanted to make a statement; maybe I was just terrified. But either way, it felt good.

The hall was packed. Seniors who'd be performing later in the day, sitting there nervously fingering their instruments. Juniors who wanted to get a feel for the horror they'd be facing next year. Freshman and sophomores watching boredly, there only because they got the day off class to attend.

And parents. Row after row of proud moms and dads, watching and taking photos and applauding politely for everyone else and in a frenzy of hands for their darlings. And somewhere amongst them, my father, sitting silent and watchful, waiting to see whether his dreams for me would soar to the heavens, stand proudly or be crushed into the mud. Orchestra, graduate or fail.

Or more likely, he wasn't there at all. He'd never returned my message.

As we approached, a couple of freshmen removed two of the chairs the quartet had used, leaving just the two we'd use in the spotlight. Everything was slick and professional...but then Fenbrook had been doing these recitals for fifty years.

The judging panel sat behind a desk at one end of the stage, out of the glare of the spotlight so that they didn't distract the audience. It made them look like waiting monsters, ready to devour us.

Professor Harman was there, as he always was. They rotated the other music department representatives, and this year they were Doctor Geisler, who I knew well and Doctor Parks, a woman with frizzy blonde hair who taught some of the contemporary music classes and who couldn't have been over 35—young, for Fenbrook's staff.

Next to her was the person I'd been thinking about

for four years, though I'd only glimpsed him three times. The scout from the New York Phil. Tall and almost gaunt looking, he had a tendency not to blink. He'd unnerved me even when I'd watched each year from the audience, but standing six feet from him on stage was absolutely terrifying. This was the man I'd needed to impress ever since I was a kid. To him, I was just one student among hundreds, barely a blip on his radar, but to me he was the final gatekeeper on a journey I'd begun when I was six years old. My destiny ended with him, either in an ascent to the clouds or in a plunge off a cliff.

There was one more person sitting behind the desk, someone I'd almost forgotten about. A fragile-looking woman with pale skin and straight brown hair, twirling a pencil around and around her fingers. She seemed a lot more interested in Connor than in me, and I realized she must be this year's scout from the record label.

I cleared my throat, immediately horrified at how loud the sound was in the silent hall. I'd pleaded with Connor to do this part, but he'd convinced me that I needed to keep building on the success of my presentation, or I'd slip straight back into being scared.

Just play the part. Use the napkin.

Wait: there is no napkin.

I don't need a napkin.

"Karen Montfort and Connor Locke," I said, and I liked it even more, saying it myself. "We'll be playing an original composition for cello and electric guitar."

Harman glanced at Geisler and I saw the twitch of his eyebrows. He didn't actually say *"This should be interesting,"* but I could tell he was thinking it and a hot stab of anger flashed down my spine. How dare he?!

We sat down. Every squeak of the chair, every bump of a foot echoed around the huge room. The smell of fresh floor polish hit my nostrils and I felt sick, panic closing in around me. I was going to run off stage and throw up, I was going to run and hide, I was going to—

And then Connor brushed my hand with his, and when I glanced up at him he was giving me a steady, tender gaze that said *you can do this.*

I glanced at the audience and immediately wished I hadn't. I didn't normally get nervous when performing, only speaking, but this was anything but a normal performance. There were so many faces, so many strangers...and then, on the front row, I saw them. Natasha and Darrell. Clarissa and Neil. Jasmine. Dan. Paul, Erika and Greg from the quartet.

I didn't know if my father was out there somewhere. But my real family was.

I started to play.

I'd composed the first section when I barely knew Connor, in those awkward first rehearsals when I thought I hated him. The guitar didn't even come in until one third of the way through and, for a while, as the cello's velvet tones filled the room, it was just like performing solo. I could have been back in my safe little world, before any of it started.

And then Connor's guitar joined me, and my whole perception of the way the cello sounded shifted. When its smoothness combined with the guitar's rough, brutal tones, it became something new...something better. Suddenly, it didn't sound right *without* the guitar. Every time the guitar broke off, the cello wasn't solo. It was *alone.*

We moved into the second section, the one Connor had written when we'd first started, sad but with a thread of hope running through it. I hadn't had any idea, back then, of what he'd been thinking about when he composed it. Now I had a pretty good idea—his own life, his lack of a future, the dyslexia...the only thing I didn't understand was what the thread of hope represented.

Back then, we hadn't made any attempt to change how our instruments sounded. We were combining what we knew, trying to join two things that didn't quite fit. The cello was just a little too timid, too flighty, edgy and nervous as it climbed through the notes, chased by the guitar. The guitar was too confident, too loud, drowning out protest, chasing that slender thread of happiness but always breaking off at the last moment—

Just as we played the final note, it hit me. A sharp, arcing current that started in my brain and slammed straight into my heart.

The thread of hope was *me*.

I turned to look at him, open-mouthed, and he seemed to know what I was thinking. He gave me a slow nod.

Someone in the audience started clapping, even though it was only the end of the first pair of sections, and then stopped when they realized they were the only one. I looked round in time to catch Jasmine red-faced, being poked in the ribs by Clarissa and Natasha.

I risked a look at the judges. Harman was dour-faced, while Geisler looked uncertain. Parks was leaning forward as if interested. I didn't have time to check the scouts because we were launching into the next section.

This was the one I'd written as I got to know Connor, the one that described *him,* or at least the Connor I knew at the time: angry and stubborn, intimidating...and deeply hot. As he played the harmonies with me, it hit me how much he'd changed. Not just the obvious stuff—rehearsing instead of goofing off, writing essays instead of getting drunk. But opening up to me, sharing how scared he was inside, how he doubted his own skill. The Connor I'd unwittingly described in the music, all swagger and attitude, had only ever existed as a shell—but it was the shell that everyone had seen the whole time he'd been at Fenbrook. Every girl he'd slept with, every guy he'd got drunk with...they'd never known the real Connor. Only I did.

We flowed smoothly into the fourth section, the one Connor had written—the one I'd eventually realized was about me. Just as I had, he'd based it on the person he thought he knew. Only he'd got a lot closer than I had, capturing not just my nerves and my shyness but what lay underneath...he'd portrayed it with a slow rhythm that built and built—the mousy librarian with powerful, hidden passions—and I flushed at the idea that he'd thought of me like that, even back then.

We stopped again, a brief pause before the final pair. When I glanced at the judges, Harman had sat back in his chair and Geisler was tapping his pencil on his teeth. I had no idea whether that was good or bad.

This was it, then. A handful of minutes that would decide our future. I looked down at the front row to see Natasha give me a reassuring nod.

I took a deep breath and touched my bow to my strings. There was absolute silence.

It was the section I'd composed after we'd first had sex, the one that was *about* sex, and I knew that I should be embarrassed to be sharing it with everyone...to be sharing *us*. The old Karen would have been, but sitting there on stage with Connor just a few feet from me, our music blending together...all I felt was proud. *Do they know?* I wondered, *do they know I can feel his hands on me, every time I play this part? Do they know this is him licking my breasts? That this, right here, is where he thrust into me for the very first time?* We'd played it so many times that we didn't need to look at the music. We could gaze into each other's eyes as my hand moved, as his fingers worked the strings. *Never let this end,* I prayed. *Even if we don't graduate, I want to always be able to play like this with him.*

We moved straight into the final section, the one he'd written. His version of sex, written up on the roof after our second time. Urgent and hard and building and building, those blue-gray eyes sparkling as he stared at me, coaxing me, dragging me with him, higher and higher until our rhythms locked together perfectly, the cello and the guitar becoming one, until there was no melody and no harmony, until we were two equals, playing together.

Forever.

The final flurry of notes came in a rush, the last few bars leaving me breathless. In the seconds of silence that followed, I could hear my own heartbeat very loudly, and then I couldn't hear anything at all. I'd gone deaf.

I looked across at the judges and Harman was smiling. And then he stood up. Why was he standing up?

I looked around at the audience, and they were all rising to their feet, too. What the—

And then my brain got around to processing the sound, and I realized I hadn't gone deaf. They were applauding.

A hand clasped mine, our fingers entwining, and Connor drew me to my feet. The applause was like a physical force, pressing in around us as my panic attacks used to. Only this felt nothing but good, like a warm wave you could bathe in. We bowed, and the applause got louder. And then, halfway back on the left-hand side, someone stepped out of their aisle seat so that I could see him better, his hands pounding together so hard they must have hurt.

My father.

Harman spoke briefly to the other judges and they all nodded. Then he said something to us and Connor pulled me close.

"What?" I said stupidly.

Harman grinned. "I said that's an A for both of you. Well done."

In my mind, the scales that represented my future suddenly lurched from one side to the other as Harman heaved a breezeblock-sized weight onto the positive side. I'd just graduated. I'd just graduated *well.*

The applause finally started to die away. Connor squeezed my hand and I smiled at him, blinking back tears. And then, after a second, I squeezed back, harder.

It wasn't over. We'd saved me, but now we needed to save him.

Helena Newbury

CHAPTER 35

There was only one other group crazy enough to enter the improvisation challenge—a harpist named Lucita, who was as placid and spiritual as her instrument suggested, and her partner on the violin, a very serious guy named Cho. Both of them already had more than enough credit to graduate, and I suspected the challenge meant different things to them. Pure fun, for Lucita, and a chance to impress his parents, for Cho. From the few times I'd spoken to him, I got the impression that his folks were even pushier than my father.

We watched them listen to the melody they'd have to work with—we'd be given a different one, so we couldn't gain any advantage. Then the two of them hurried off to a practice room and the clock started. The audience milled about and drank free wine. For us, the thirty minutes seemed to drag on forever. For the two musicians, it was no doubt gone in a flash.

Lucita and Cho hurried back in. Lucita looked vaguely unsettled, but Cho looked downright terrified.

They took their seats on the stage, glanced at one another and started to play.

At first, I couldn't see what they were worried about. They'd come up with an inventive, elaborate piece that wound around the melody, approaching it from a few different angles. But then the harp separated from the violin for a solo and, as it handed back to the violin, I could see Cho panic as he came in too early. His own solo didn't match—it was note-perfect, but the style didn't gel with Lucita's at all.

I knew exactly what had happened, because we'd done the same thing in our early trials. They'd worked out the first part together and then, running out of time, agreed to compose separate solos, with no idea of what the other one would do. We'd found out the hard way that that didn't work.

When they joined again for the rest of the piece, they were both shaken and clumsy. Lucita would make a mistake and Cho would amplify it, and that in turn would make Lucita more nervous. They were both incredibly skilled, but there was no trust.

When they finished, we applauded harder than anyone else because I knew exactly what they'd just gone through. When Harman announced their grade—a D— they took it well, but I felt my stomach sink through the floor. Lucita and Cho were two of the best in the department and if they couldn't pull it off, what chance did we have? After the D Connor got for the essay Ruth "helped" him with, he needed a B to graduate.

We took our places on stage. I closed my eyes as the melody we'd have to work with came over the speakers. It was simple and almost featureless— frustratingly so, like a minimalist house with a white couch on a white rug in a white room. It gave us no help with tone or style and part of me swore that it was a tougher piece than Lucita and Cho had been given...although deep down, I knew it was probably no worse.

We stood, and I saw Harman look at the clock on the wall. I half expected him to say, game-show-host style, *"And your time starts...now!"* But he just nodded to us and smiled—after all, the recital was done. This was just a friendly challenge—a bit of fun. And for him and everyone else—even me—that was true. For Connor—a band clenched tight around my heart—for Connor, this was make or break time.

The same sophomore who'd showed us onto the stage led us up to a practice room—the same one we'd used for our very first rehearsal. I wished we were allowed to do it on Connor's roof, or even in my apartment. The tiny space only added to my rising panic.

"Do you have any idea what to do?" I asked as soon as the door was closed. "I have no idea what to do."

"Karen," Connor said firmly. "Chill. You've graduated."

"But *you* haven't." My breathing was getting faster now. They'd given us a room with a clock, of course, a *ticking* clock and with every tick it seemed to be speeding up, eating away our precious time and all the oxygen in the room. "It's all on this—it's totally unfair, that melody is ridiculous and if we screw this up you're not going to graduate and I don't even know where to start and we only have twenty-eight minutes left and—"

"Karen." His warm palms settled gently on my shoulders.

I stopped.

"We can do this. But I can't do it without you. I need you with me. Take a deep breath."

He was right. Connor was great at turning ideas into music, but in our improvisation practice we'd found that the initial spark of inspiration, the angle we took, usually came from me. I took a long, shuddering breath and managed to suck in some air.

"Now help me," he said. "What comes to mind when you hear the melody?"

"*Nothing!*" I looked at the clock. Twenty-seven minutes left.

"Close your eyes. Stop looking at the clock. Come on, Karen. There has to be something."

I sighed and shook my head. "It's just neutral. Soulless. Mechanical."

"Mechanical?"

I considered. "Like machines in a factory. Industrial." Without opening my eyes, I grabbed my bow and tried something. It sounded awful, but the glow of the idea held back the freezing fear. "Not that. More like...." I tried again, and this time inspiration came—a short, jerky riff, repeated over and over. "There. Like that."

"What if I...." Connor adjusted the distortion on his pedal and played a couple of chords, adding another layer to my driving backbeat. "And then...." He continued and I joined him. Within seconds, anyone watching would have been unable to follow our conversation. It was all nods and signals and half-finished sentences that made perfect sense to us. We hadn't just connected—we'd blended, the best parts of both of us fusing together and becoming something more. It was the exact opposite of what I'd used to feel each morning, trudging through the snow to Fenbrook. I wasn't alone anymore.

We lost ourselves to it, playing and stopping and scratching down hurried notes and then playing again. There was a knock on the door and I let out a huge sigh of exasperation at being interrupted after just a few minutes.

"It's time," said the sophomore, putting his head round the door.

I looked at the clock. Our thirty minutes were up. *What?!*

"It's good," said Connor. "We're ready."

"Ready? We're not *ready!*" I could feel the panic surging up in me again. "We've barely begun, we've just—"

He kissed me. Deep and hard, sweeping me up in his arms and devouring me, my body crushed to his. The panic stalled, right in my chest. Then Connor's hand was on my breast, stroking the nipple through my dress, and the panic was pushed back down by something much stronger.

"Er—" said the sophomore, who was still standing in the doorway.

Connor released me. "Better?"

I panted and nodded. When I looked at the sophomore, for once I didn't blush. I was *proud.*

"Um...this way," the sophomore told us, rapidly turning red.

I took Connor's hand and we walked down the stairs together.

***

Sitting there on the stage, I felt like we were gazing at two possible futures. In one of them, Connor graduated and found work, stayed in New York and by my side. In the other....

My fingers tightened on the bow. In the other, if I graduated and he didn't, I'd damn well go to Ireland with him, or help him find some way to stay in America. I'd fought for him. I wasn't going to lose him now.

Helena Newbury

"You may begin," Harman told us, leaning forward.

We hadn't rehearsed—most of what we'd worked out, we'd only played once, while the other one listened. There was only a single sketchy lead sheet to jog our memories. The whole point of the exercise was for us to improvise, piecing together the ideas we'd come up with, combining our sounds. My cello began the piece with a dry, jerky riff, like a machine warming up, gradually building in intensity until it became a driving beat rebounding back to us from the walls and filling the space. Then the guitar, harsh and powerful as a jackhammer, carving up the cello's melody and shaping it into something new.

With no conductor to meld us together, we had to rely on signals from each other to keep time, to know when to shift to the next section. Our eyes were locked on each other's, quick little nods as we shifted the pace, the bow rising and plunging on the strings, Connor's hands quick and savage as he made the guitar howl. Adrenaline coursed through my veins, the whole world narrowing down to just Connor's face as I focused like I'd never focused before.

Two bars of the driving mechanical riff, like a question. A flurry of chromatic scales from Connor—his response. Back in with the riff, this time extended and truly improvised. I kept holding my breath and had to force myself to breathe, my bow just a blur as we went into the final section.

Connor broke off with a flourish and slapped the guitar's wood, and I filled with a flurry of notes. Seconds later, he did it again, faster and more violent than before, and I filled again, the bow an extension of me. He did it one final time, a hard slap that reverberated around the hall, and I gave it everything I had, coaxing notes from the cello faster than I could think about them, operating on instinct alone. Connor came back in for the final bar, cello and guitar winding around each other like lovers, hard and soft embracing, and we were done.

We sat there in complete silence and stared at each other. He was giving me one of those grins, and panting as hard as I was, and I knew that whatever happened I was going to be with this man for the rest of my life.

The room erupted into applause. I grudgingly wrenched my eyes away from Connor to see the first few people stand up, and the rest of the room follow their lead.

Connor twisted around to look at Harman and the other judges. Just months ago, graduation hadn't been part of his plan—he'd done the bare minimum necessary to stay at Fenbrook and keep partying. But now I could see the concern on his face, the breathlessness as he dared to hope....

Harman gave him a long look...and then nodded and announced our improvisation grade: an A. As Connor beamed, Harman gave me a different sort of nod. One of respect, and admission that he'd been wrong.

***

It was only when we climbed down off the stage and my body finally started to release some of its tension that I became aware of things. The ache in my shoulders from the relentless playing; the pain in my jaw from grinding my teeth. My legs felt like they might buckle under me at any moment. Connor seemed to sense it and slid an arm around my waist, holding me up even as he blinked and stumbled himself, walking half his usual speed. We were both in shock, unable to grasp that somehow, against all odds, we'd *won.*

Natasha hurled herself into me from one side in a body hug, and I would have gone sprawling if it wasn't for Clarissa doing the same thing from the other side. Then Jasmine jumped on my front and only Connor's arm let me maintain balance.

"That was *incredible!*" said Natasha. "You didn't see Harman's face when you did that fast bit at the end. His jaw was on the table."

Neil and Darrell joined the crush. They also slapped Connor on the back, which would have knocked over a smaller man. And then my friends all moved back a little to make way for someone. I couldn't see who it was at first, and then, as Jasmine's auburn curls moved out of the way—

"Karen," said my father. "That was...extraordinary." He stopped and stared at Connor. "Both of you."

And then he stepped closer to me, which almost made me laugh because if I hadn't known him better I would have thought he was going to hug me. Then his arms were sliding around my back and—*wait, what was he—*

He hugged me, his head on my shoulder, my body enveloped in his warmth, and I felt hot tears flood my eyes.

When he eventually stepped back, something was different. Staring at him, I finally figured out what it was—it was the expression on his face as he looked at me. He was seeing me as an adult for the first time.

A tall man was standing beside him, and as I blinked my tears away it took a second for me to register who he was.

"Karen?" he said gently, his voice deep and melodious and not matching his gaunt appearance at all,

"I'm Walter Koss, with the New York Philharmonic."

So much had happened in my life that I swear part of my brain asked "*The who?*"

"That was some of the finest, tightest ensemble playing I've seen in a long time. How would you feel about a trial with us?"

I must have looked weirdly calm and collected for a few seconds, until my brain finally caught up. And then a decade and a half of preparation: every rehearsal, every performance, every hour of solo practice, slammed into me, reducing me to the gaping, spluttering mess he was expecting. "That...would be great," I managed, before I lost the ability to speak altogether.

Connor pulled me to him and drew me into a long kiss—about the only thing that had the capability to unfreeze my brain. I let the room fade out and lost myself in the feeling of his lips, of his body under my hands. When we finally broke the kiss, there was a woman waiting patiently beside us, an amused expression on her face. The record label rep who'd sat with the judging panel.

"Rachel Liebermann," she told us. "From TTX Records. That was quite something—not like anything I've heard before."

"You want Connor to record a track?" I asked breathlessly.

She looked at the two of us closely. "Actually, I was hoping the two of you might want to do one together."

Connor pulled me to him again, laughing, and suddenly I was laughing, too. I felt something settle into place, deep in my mind, warm and comforting and utterly *right,* and I knew that it wasn't graduating, or the New York Phil, or a record deal. It was him, making me complete.

CHAPTER 36

ONE MONTH LATER

"This is ridiculous," said Jasmine. "This is meant to be the part where you have to move your stuff aside to make closet space for him. It's symbolic. But you don't *have* any stuff. You could move, like, five guys in here and they could have a drawer each."

"Good to know, if I ever find myself in that kind of a relationship," I told her. I moved a few more of my things aside. There. Connor now had a complete closet to himself, and a couple of drawers. I stared at the empty space. "You going to be okay on your own, at Connor's place? It's not a great neighborhood."

"Better than my old one, though," said Jasmine. "And rent free, up until the end of the month." Connor had had to give a month's notice when I'd asked him to move in with me a few days before, and we'd all agreed there was no point in an apartment going empty. "Seriously, Karen, with the money I've saved crashing on your couch and another month without rent, I'll have enough for a deposit on a new place. I'll be fine. Besides, no way am I sleeping on the couch of a newly-moved-in couple. I need *some* sleep."

I punched her on the arm. She was right. She'd be fine.

Natasha came in with a box of sheet music from the lounge. "Where do you want this?"

"Slide it under the bed for now," I told her. Then, "Wait!"

But it was too late. She'd already knocked it against the other box under my bed, the one packed full of bodice-rippers. "What's *this?!*" she asked, part shocked and part delighted. "'*The Countess's Dark Temptation*'?"

I snatched the book out of her hand. "Nothing!"

Jasmine was already digging through the box, perilously close to where I kept the dildo. "Oh, wait, getting better: '*Bound by the Pirate King*'?"

I flushed and crammed the box back under the bed before she could dig any deeper. "Yes. Well. Anyway."

Natasha shook her head. "You need to get with the program and get yourself a Kindle. Easier to read with the lights out."

Jasmine frowned at her. "You turn the lights out when you—"

"*Enough!*" I pleaded.

"Come on," said Natasha, dragging Jasmine away. "I hear Clarissa."

I heard it too: the thump of a two-stroke engine. Clarissa had volunteered to go out and get groceries for the party we were throwing that night—a combined boyfriend-moving-in and housewarming party. I'd been in the apartment for three years, but this was the first time it was in my name. I'd be paying the rent and bills, now—another, slightly less romantic reason to ask Connor to move in with me.

In the week after the recital, when I'd had a long, serious talk with my father and he'd agreed that it was time for him to back off, I'd spent a lot of sleepless nights worrying about operating without a safety net. Then I'd convinced myself that Nat, Clarissa and Jasmine had all managed jobs, bills and rent just fine their entire time at Fenbrook. Well, maybe not Jasmine. I'd leapfrogged them, going from having my life run for me straight to being out there on my own in the workplace, but it helped that it was the tight-knit and reassuringly kooky workplace of an orchestra. Musicians, it turned out, were musicians wherever you found them, and I was settling in with the rest of the dwarves already. And I realized that I *did* have a safety net; I'd always had one—I'd just never relied on it until these last few months. People don't have to be related to you to be family.

As we stood there waiting for Clarissa and Neil to arrive, I pulled Natasha close. "Thanks," I told her.

"I should be thanking *you*. You and Connor. Darrell's like a different person—the happiest I've ever seen him. He's had maybe one nightmare in a month and when he works it's like...*regular work,* you know? I mean, I still have to drag him out of the workshop at 3am sometimes, but he's doing it because he loves it, not because he feels he has to."

"How do you drag him away from it?" I asked, puzzled.

She gave me a wicked smile.

Oh. "And you? How are you doing?" I asked.

Natasha gave me a slow, solemn nod. "Okay. I think. Better, at least. The pen helps, when I feel like I have to cut."

A few days after the recital, confident in my ability

to help my friends—or, at least, not screw up any more than anyone else—I'd gone online and spent a full day reading everything I could about self-harming and coping strategies. I'd eventually presented Nat with a gift-wrapped box containing a non-toxic red marker pen, and told her to use it instead of the razor blades, if she felt like she was going to cut. She'd looked at me as if I was crazy at first, but a week later had reported that it worked. She'd only needed it twice that I knew of and the slips seemed to be getting farther apart.

Jasmine opened the front door and Clarissa walked in, her arms full of grocery bags. Neil was right behind her, with two cases of beer. They walked straight through to the kitchen to unload and, even though I knew it was wrong, I couldn't help but follow after them, staying in the hallway but pressing up against the doorway so that I could hear what they were saying. Things seemed to be better since my rant at Neil, but I wanted to check.

"—could at least help me, now you've put the beers down, instead of just standing there," Clarissa was saying. "Why do you need that many beers, anyway? You and Darrell and Connor are going to get steaming drunk again, aren't you? And then you're going to start pawing me in front of them—"

Neil's low rumble: "You like it when I paw you."

"I—No! I mean, not in front of—"

"Like this...."

"Ah! That's not fair! I've got my hands full!"

I could hear the smirk in Neil's voice. "So have I."

"Bastard! Ah! God, don't,"—her voice went high, and I imagined his hand sliding up her thigh. "*Ah!* Neil, you can't just—"

The sound of lips meeting, hungry and urgent. Yep. They were back to normal.

Just as I was about to draw back and stop eavesdropping, I heard Clarissa say, "God, what if Karen walks in?"

"She's already seen us fucking, and from what you said she liked it enough to keep watching," said Neil.

I flushed. *She'd told him!*

"Think she'd be up for watching the real thing?" Neil asked, and his dark, smoky voice sent the words straight down my spine to throb in my groin. "Or maybe joining in? Would you like that?"

I never heard Clarissa's answer, because I was running to my bedroom to get out of earshot. *Oh, great—how was I ever going to be able to look Neil in the eye now?!*

I ran straight into Jasmine, who was stringing fairy lights around the lounge. And the hallway. And the bathroom. "It's going to be like a fairy grotto," she told me. "Only sexier. A fairy boudoir."

I wasn't sure what Dan—whose cast was finally off—or the rest of the quartet would make of that. Not to mention the friends I'd made in the orchestra, or the few biker friends that Clarissa had allowed Neil to bring. It was going to be an interesting party.

"All I need now is a date," said Jasmine, without turning round from trying to string fairy lights around the shower—an electrocution waiting to happen. "It's no fun being the sole singleton."

That, I decided, was a challenge for another day.

Strong arms suddenly encircled me from behind and I was lifted off my feet. I knew who it was, but I gave a little scream anyway, just *because.*

Connor kissed my neck and I squirmed in delight, electricity arcing straight down my body to the tips of my toes and bouncing back to turn to heat in my groin. Jasmine watched patiently as I was turned around to face him and then slowly lowered to the ground. He gave just a trace of a wince as his jacket rubbed against the sore patch where the tattoo used to be.

"Hi, beautiful," he told me. That accent still did it to me, the words caressing my brain like silver wrapped in silk.

"Hi yourself." I tilted my face up as he kissed me. First quickly and then slow and deep, his fingers entwining with mine as his tongue explored my mouth and all sense of time slipped away, a deep warmth blossoming in my heart and radiating to every corner of me. I noticed that Jasmine had made herself scarce, leaving us alone for a moment.

"Don't drink *too* much tonight," I told him. "We have to rehearse tomorrow. It's our last chance before the studio."

Rachel, the record label rep, had turned out to be serious about us recording a track and we'd put something together based on our recital and the improvised piece. Cleaned up and smoothed out, it was sounding good—but there was always room for improvement.

Connor kissed me again. "That's not very rock n' roll."

"You could use a little taming, Connor Locke."

"Oh." He leaned even closer. "You going to be the one to tame me?"

I could whisper, he was so close. "I was under the impression I already had." And then I kissed him.

<<<< >>>>

Clarissa and Neil will return in the free story I'm releasing in late 2013, exclusive to my mailing list. To ensure you get your copy, sign up at:

http://list.helenanewbury.com

FROM THE AUTHOR

I hope you enjoyed *In Harmony*. If you did, please consider leaving a review so that other readers can find it.

If you have a question, want to know when future books are released or just want to chat, you can find me at:

Blog: http://helenanewbury.com

Twitter: http://twitter.com/HelenaAuthor

Facebook:
http://www.facebook.com/HelenaNewburyAuthor

Goodreads:
http://www.goodreads.com/helenanewburyauthor

Google+: http://gplus.to/HelenaNewbury

Pinterest: http://pinterest.com/helenanewbury/

Amazon Author Page:
https://www.amazon.com/author/helenanewbury

Mailing list sign-up:
http://list.helenanewbury.com

Remember, the mailing list is the ONLY way to get the free Clarissa and Neil story I'm releasing in late 2013. Subscribers are also notified when I release a new book and have the chance to buy the ebook version for an earlybird price of 99c. Your email address is safe with me and I promise not to spam you!

THE MUSIC

For anyone who'd like to listen to the pieces Karen plays....

When she's a child: *Bach Cello Suites* (she also uses one specifically when she's busking—see below).

The piece she plays solo when she's twelve: *Haydn's Cello Concerto*

The piece she would have played with Dan for the recital, had he not broken his arm: *Brahms Double Concerto*

Busking in Central Park - *Bach's Cello Suite in D Minor*

...and then *Summer* from *The Four Seasons* by Vivaldi

The piece she gives the presentation on: *Romeo and Juliet* by Tchaikovsky

ACKNOWLEDGMENTS

Thank you Jane, for helping me to understand what it's like to play—and carry—a cello. Elizabeth, you taught me many, many things about composing, improvisation and the culture of music departments. Simone, thank you for the help with Connor's dyslexia.

Thank you to Julianne and Aubrey, my beta readers and, as always, to my editor Liz.

Thank you most of all to my readers, who made Dance For Me a success and so allowed me to write this book.

Made in United States
North Haven, CT
11 June 2024

53454969R00243